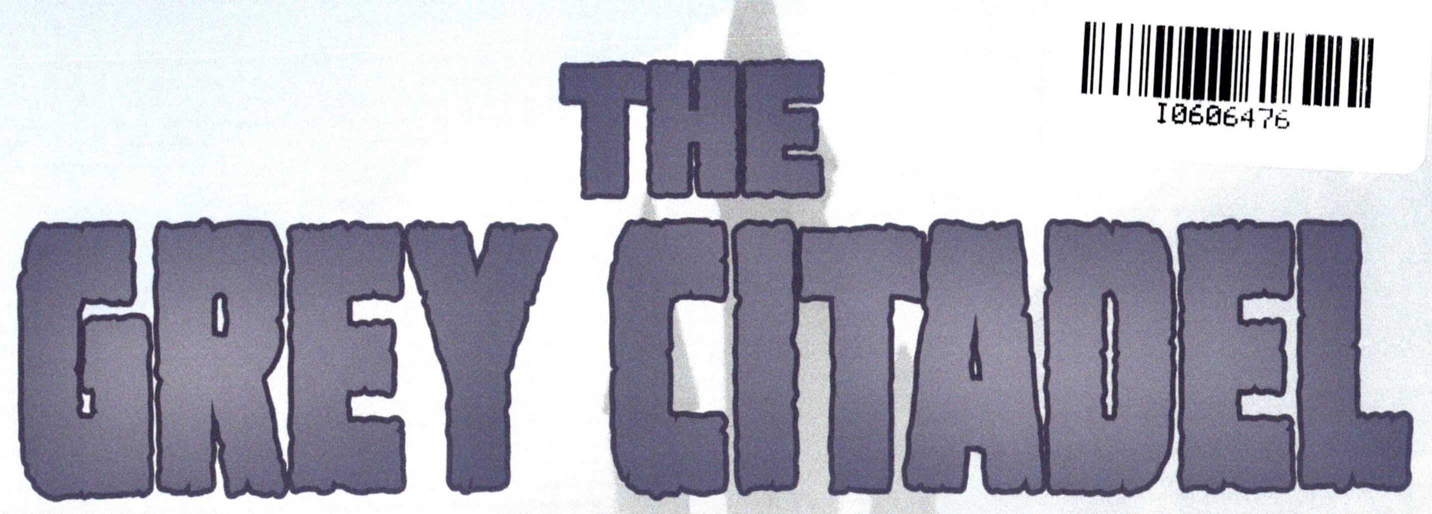

THE GREY CITADEL

Author: Nathan Douglas Paul
Project Manager: Edwin Nagy
Editor: Jeff Harkness, Andrew Bates, and Mike Johnstone
Pathfinder Conversion: Micahel "Mars" Russell
Art Direction: Casey Christofferson
Layout and Graphic Design: Charles A. Wright
Cover Design: Charle A. Wright
Cover Art: Michael Syrigos
Interior Art: Michael Syrigos, Brian LeBlanc, and Tyler Walpole
Cartography: Robert Altbauer

ADVENTURES WORTH WINNING

FROG GOD GAMES

ISBN: 978-1-62283-856-1

FROG GOD GAMES IS:

Bill Webb, Matthew J. Finch, Zach Glazar, Charles A. Wright, Edwin Nagy, Mike Badolato, John Barnhouse

TABLE OF CONTENTS

Introduction 3

Chapter One: The City of Dun Eamon — An Overview 6

Chapter Two: Timed Encounters, Rumors, and Myster Elements 9

Chapter Three: The Grey Citadal Encounter Areas 23

Chapter Four: Level 1 — Tales from the Crypt 47

Chapter Five: Level 2 — Fungus Among Us 55

Chapter Six: Level 3 — A River Runs Through It 64

Chapter Seven: Level 4 — Mamuthek's Managerie 76

Chapter Eight: Resolution, Rewards, and Development 83

Appendix A: New Creatures 84

Appendix B: New Magic Items 85

Appendix C: NPC Descriptions 86

Appendix D: Wilderness Encounters 95

Legal Appendix 106

INTRODUCTION

The Grey Citadel is an adventure designed for a party of four or more characters of at least 5th level. It combines wilderness adventuring, urban detective work, and underground exploration.

The Grey Citadel of Dun Eamon is a vibrant and busy city, full of adventure and opportunity, but its prosperity is threatened by the actions of a series of factions working together and separately to destabilize the community. Demons roam the streets, criminals rule the night, and an important local power figure is missing... with no apparent connection. The heroes become involved in a chain of events that leads them through every social element of the city, into the hearts of its inhabitants, and far below its streets in search of answers.

ADVENTURE BACKGROUND

Before the first patriarch of the Angus clan founded his trading post on the River Eamon, the greatest threat to his descendants was already brewing in distant lands. An ambitious conjurer named Mamuthek conspired to build a device that he could use to dominate the kingdom in which he dwelled. His completed project — which created an aperture in the planar barrier through which outsiders could be called — was powerful, but not without flaws. The most dangerous of these flaws was that it lacked the ability to grant control over the creature to the summoner. Mamuthek found this out when the creature he had called ended his coup and his life. *Mamuthek's Aperture* has since drifted across the known world, bringing death everywhere it is used, and none have managed to unlock its secrets. Very recently, one wizard came close, but she did not learn enough to prevent the carnage that goes hand-in-hand with *Mamuthek's Aperture*.

Elinda Bannon is an artificer (a wizard who specializes in artifacts and magical devices) who dwells in the Grey Citadel. She was the most recent owner of Mamuthek's creation. She had great success in her research, with one exception: she believed the device was used for communication across the planes, not for summoning. She acquired the artifact and activated it. The unforeseen result of her experimentation was that the device recognized and retrieved the previous being called, a powerful succubus demon named Lilith. Imprisoned in the Abyss for transgressions against a demon prince, Lilith did not hesitate when the shimmering portal opened in her cell. Two hundred years had passed since *Mamuthek's Aperture* last offered her passage into mortal realms, and she was glad to return. She defeated the wizard, took the device, and fled into the water-carved caverns beneath the city.

When she arrived, she found that a gang of thieves was already ensconced in her chosen lair. Their master, a wily rogue named Devlin, had led them there after their guild was expelled from a neighboring city. Lilith quickly seduced Devlin, giving her effective control of a skilled group of evil agents with a competent understanding of the city. They immediately began securing the components she needed to activate the artifact and reinforce her position with an army of outsiders. She also allied herself with Gethrax, a displaced antipaladin who found her a new patron. Many elements of the city, both above ground and below, that had once lived in relative harmony are now being drawn together in a deceptive and violent plot that will impact each and every life in the Dun Eamon. The heroes' arrival coincides with the disappearance of Elinda Bannon and the emergence on and below the streets of the minions (both summoned and seduced) of the new owner of *Mamuthek's Aperture*.

HOW TO USE THIS MODULE

This adventure involves a city-based investigation and a difficult dungeon that are intricately intertwined, with actions above ground being reflected in the events below. That is not to say that simply kicking in doors and spilling a great deal of blood won't complete the adventure; there is plenty of mayhem for those who crave it (and maybe more than some would choose!). Hopefully, though, the players will realize that clever, attentive role-playing in the city will give them several advantages when they descend into the underground, allowing them to reap great rewards without undue risk.

You may either bring the party directly to the Grey Citadel and begin the adventure proper, or, if you wish, you may begin by having the party travel to the city itself. If you chose the latter, feel free to either use encounters appropriate to your campaign world or include one or more of the encounters or areas detailed in the Wilderness Encounters Appendix found at the back of this book.

READ-ALOUD TEXT

Text blocks are provided for some locations and encounters, but not all. Usually, these text blocks involve important role-playing encounters with NPCs or dungeon locations that might be difficult to visualize. Other times, they are included to reinforce the character and feeling of the adventure. Use as much or as little as you wish. When read-aloud text is absent, the description has been written with paraphrasing in mind.

ENCOUNTER TYPES: KEYED, TIMED, AND RANDOM

Encounters are handled in three different ways in this adventure:

Random Encounters can be selected or randomized from the City Random Encounters Table (see Chapter One) whenever you think it appropriate.

Timed Encounters happen at specific times in the storyline, although they can be modified, rescheduled, or cancelled without disrupting the plot.

Keyed Encounters take place at a specific location (such as a room in a dungeon) whenever the characters choose to go there (locations important to the plot are fully developed; others are structured, but left for the DM to detail in the future).

NOTATION

All of the descriptions in this adventure are titled with a letter and number combination that indicates where or when the encounter is to be used. Keyed Encounters include a letter referring to the map key, and a number referring to the area or room within that location (for example, D-1 is location D, the Market Tavern, and Area **1**, The Coat Hall). Dungeon levels are similarly titled with the number of the dungeon level and the number of the area (for example, Area **2-9** is the 9th room on the 2nd level). Timed Encounters are titled with a number for the day, a number for the encounter, and a short phrase (for example, Timed Encounter 1.2 is the 2nd event on the 1st day).

BACKGROUND

The real facts behind the mystery are best understood by reading the entire adventure carefully and possibly by re-reading the Mystery Elements section (see **Chapter Two**). Here are a few facts to keep in mind as you do so:

• The succubus Lilith is building an army of outsiders and plotting to take control of the Dun Eamon.

• The wizard Elinda Bannon took it upon herself to undo the damage she did with her experiments and pursued the fleeing demon. She was defeated and is now held captive in Lilith's lair.

• Devlin and the Ebon Union thieves' guild are hard at work providing materials for the artifact's operation, but they may take time out to make an attempt on the party.

• An antipaladin named Gethrax has loosely allied himself with Lilith and the Ebon Union.

• An NPC adventuring party called the Band of the Crimson Mantle is competing with the heroes, leading to some potentially interesting side effects.

Good detective work in the city will be rewarded with information about the dungeon, including the identities of its occupants, their weaknesses, and the weapons to use against them.

The Rule of Three

The adventure elements are arranged in groups of three to make tracking the heroes' progress easier. The mystery is comprised of three elements: wizard, thieves, and demons. Each element offers three ways that the heroes can approach the mystery: they can collect three clues left by the wizard; they can analyze three major burglaries of the thieves; and they can investigate three citizens seduced by the succubus. Each of these approaches reveals secrets that serve the heroes well when they venture underground. Not all (or even any) of the leads must be pursued, but each one increases the heroes' chances of success. These clues are described fully in the Mystery Elements section (see Chapter Two) and referenced in the appropriate Keyed Encounter.

Elinda's Clues: These are located in the Tower Library (Area **L-8**) and lead to The Secret Workshop (Area **L-9**), The Temple Courtyard (Area **I-9**), and Stump's Hovel (Area **S**). These clues reveal a potent weapon against the demon and the artifact's functions.

Lilith's Thralls: The men who have been *charmed* by Lilith include Ulf Ironfist, the master smith (Area **Q-4**); Herrick Mendon, a merchant (Area **H-4**); and Danver, the miller (Area **R**). Each of these men guards an entrance to the caverns.

The Crime Scenes: Burglaries have been committed at several locations: The Root-Cutter's Shop (Area **T**), The Seer's Parlor (Area **N**), and The Finesmith's Shop (Area **H-9**). The stolen items suggest the nature and origins of the dungeon creatures.

Also in groups of three are the Timed Encounters. These are events scheduled to take place during the first three days the heroes are in the city, with three events to occur on each day. Some of them involve combat, others focus on role-playing, and some could go either way. They do not represent a rigid timeline, nor do the heroes need to participate in all of the encounters; feel free to change, reschedule, or cancel them to suit your style of play. Letting the plot lead the players through them in order without "railroading" them, however, should be possible.

Day One: 1.1 — An NPC adventuring party celebrates a victory over the demons; 1.2 — Arb Angus enlists the heroes' help; 1.3 — The party encounters demons in the streets (night).

Day Two: 2.1 — A local shares his suspicions (morning); 2.2 — The NPC adventurers challenge the party; 2.3 — Demons actively hunt the heroes (night).

Day Three: 3.1 — Thieves storm the inn and attack the party (early morning); 3.2 — The rival adventurers enter the sewers; 3.3 — The heroes interrupt a burglary (evening).

TIMELINE

In the course of the investigation, the players will likely ask many "when" questions. Nothing in the adventure hinges directly on timing, but a brief timeline of past and future events is provided below for the sake of consistency. Day 1 marks the party's arrival in the city; negative numbers indicate the amount of time prior to the party's arrival (for instance, "–2 days" is two days before the heroes arrive, and so forth).

Completion of the adventure may require several trips into the underground tunnels over several days. Parties may find it difficult to complete the dungeon portion without visiting the surface at least once. The days that the party spends completing its investigation and adventuring underground have no specific events in the city; assume that Lilith's demons continue to terrorize the population as the Mist Watch struggles to maintain order. Emphasize the deteriorating conditions each time the party returns to the city.

Time	Event
–1 month	Elinda leaves to retrieve *Mamuthek's Aperture*.
–2 weeks	Elinda returns to Dun Eamon with the artifact.
–13 days	Elinda buys silver from Crenshaw the Finesmith.
–12 days	Elinda activates the artifact, summons Lilith, and is defeated.
–11 days	Lilith arrives in her new home on **Level 4**.
–10 days	Elinda places her clues and pursues Lilith.
–8 days	Lilith steals charms from Amarathea the Seer.
–7 days	Dretches appear in the streets (thanks to the Abyssal iron ore).
–6 days	Lilith seduces Devlin; thieves steal silver from Crenshaw.
–5 days	Lilith seduces Ulf Ironfist.
–4 days	Lilith seduces Herrick Mendon; the Band arrives.
–3 days	Lilith seduces Danver; thieves steal items from Caledon.
–2 days	Large groups of dretches panic the citizens; Elinda is captured.
–1 day	Tunnels are now full of Lilith's summoned creatures.
Day 1	The party arrives in the city; Timed Encounter 1.1, 1.2, and 1.3.
Day 2	Investigation begins; Timed Encounters 2.1, 2.2, and 2.3.
Day 3	Timed Encounters 3.1, 3.2, and 3.3.
Day 4+	Investigation and demon attacks continue, if necessary.

REPLACEMENT CHARACTERS

Many adventures include pre-generated characters, either for player use or to give an idea of what types of heroes best suit the adventure. In this module potential characters have been written into the story as NPCs. They are not intended to be the starting party. They can provide additional characters for a party whose numbers are dropping or perhaps extra support for a small or underpowered party — but they are not high-powered heroes. Rasputin, Fitch, Brother Melph, Stump, or even Yelm have skills and abilities that can benefit the party over the course of the adventure. Some of them, notably Rasputin, Stump, and Yelm, also have small roles to play as NPCs, so handing them over too early might require some adjustment. Once the party has wrapped up the city investigation and is ready to proceed underground, most of these NPCs will have served their purpose and likely have a motivation to join the party as well. See **Appendix C** for descriptions.

ADAPTING THE ADVENTURE

The Grey Citadel is written for a party of four characters of 5th level. The mysteries in the city should present adequate role-playing and problem-solving challenges for a group of any level. City encounters consist mostly of groups of creatures and so are adaptable by varying the number of creatures encountered (dretches, guild thieves, howlers, and so forth). The dungeon encounters will need more adjustment, possibly including adjustment of trap damage and DCs and replacement of powerful creatures.

Lower-level parties will need to take their time and rest frequently, but a large 3rd- or 4th-level party can gain enough experience during the city portion to survive an upper dungeon level, which earns them enough experience to survive the next level, and so on. A 5th-level party is presumed to have done a thorough investigation in the city and thus gained an advantage against the underground foes (such as taking acid to deal with the troll). More powerful parties (6th-level characters or parties numbering six or more) will find that they can survive the encounters without needing those advantages and go longer without rest. Parties of 7th-level and higher will need most of the encounters upgraded (extra trolls, gricks, and so forth) to provide a significant challenge. Devlin, Gethrax, and Lilith should have approximately twice the hit points of the party average. Kubris, Thurf, and the Band of the Crimson Mantle, and other minor opponents should be approximately equal to or one level lower than the party.

An alternative would be to run the module as a high-level solo adventure. The profiles for the Angus brothers fit the range for this option, providing that some henchmen are included to give spellcasting support. For example, either Bron or Cael Angus has the ability and the motivation to undertake the adventure himself, perhaps with Stump and Rasputin for arcane spells.

SETTING

The setting should be easily inserted into any fantasy campaign: all you need is a city and an underground cavern complex. The city could easily be relocated to any location — desert, arctic, or anything in between. The special conditions are present for effect, but are not necessary. Similarly, the river, the trade road, the frontier location, and the economic politics are not necessary to the plot, although many of the hooks for future development relate to them.

The surrounding wilderness areas are not of great importance to the city and the adventures to be had there, allowing easy integration of the adventure into your specific campaign world. If, however, you desire more information on the surrounding wilderness and perhaps a few more adventure hooks and NPCs, that material is presented in the **Appendix D** detailed in the back of this module. If you desire, you may use some of those encounters as the characters travel to the Grey Citadel before running the primary adventure.

Chapter One: The City of Dun Eamon – An Overview

This adventure takes place in the city of Dun Eamon, the center of government for Eamonvale. Located high in the mist-shrouded mountain crags of the Stoneheart Mountains, it is a city like no other. Locally known as the Grey Citadel, Dun Eamon is an important trading city and a key crossing point on the turbulent river. Thanks to its economy, Dun Eamon is highly successful, but its remote location also ensures that it will never be terribly sophisticated.

The River Eamon has only viable crossing in the Stoneheart Mountains — a broad ford at the base of a plunging waterfall. Just below the ford, the river tumbles several hundred feet over a second waterfall before continuing down the rocky gorge. Midway across the ford, a huge slab of bedrock divides the river into two channels. On this island, many generations ago, Eamon Angus staked a claim and founded a tiny trading post. Now, centuries later, expansion of the duchies and kingdoms on either side of the Stoneheart Mountains and the development of trade between them have caused the tiny trading center and way station to grow into a heavily fortified citadel, with the charter and lordship still in the hands of the Angus family.

Three brothers rule the city. Arb Angus is the eldest; he inherited the land and title from his father. Bron is the middle brother and the Captain of the Mist Watch. Cael is the youngest brother and Master of the Temple of Fortitude. More than 5,000 citizens dwell within the city walls and pay homage to the brothers.

The Grey Citadel is renowned as the location of the finest forges in the land. Nearly any tool, weapon, or other metal item can be crafted here, and the quality of their alloys and the strength of their castings are unsurpassed. The quality and availability of tools and the location on the trade road have resulted in Dun Eamon becoming a city of artisans and craftsmen. The attention of foreign guilds wishing to expand their influence and tap the region's unique market has also been attracted, but the Angus family has always enforced strict regulations that limit guild activity and encourage free trade. Today's rulers are no exception, and their policies have not made them popular among the powerful merchant houses.

In addition to its mercantile presence, the Grey Citadel is a well-known frontier fortress. In times of war, its walls are the outer line of defense for the lowland below the Stoneheart Mountains. Many hunters and trappers pass through the gates every season to sell their pelts and to re-supply for another trip into the wild mountains. It is a hiring point for caravan laborers and guards for the dangerous journey over the mountains to the distant kingdoms beyond. Traveling minstrels, adventurers, and highwaymen all call the city home from time to time.

The Grey Citadel

The Grey Citadel of Dun Eamon
LG Small City
Corruption 2; **Crime** 4; **Economy** 4; **Law** 3; **Lore** 2; **Society** 2
Qualities Government Capital, Massive Underground, Prosperous, Strategic Location
Danger 15

Demographics

Government Autocracy
Population 5,722 (79% human, 7% dwarf, 4% gnome, 4% half-elf, 3% halfling, 2% elf, 1% half-orc)
Noteable NPCs
Lord Arb Angus (Lord of Eamonvale)
Captain Bron Angus (Captain of the Mist Watch)
Master Cael Angus (Master of the Temple of Fortitude)
Elinda Bannon (female human loremaster)
Rasputin (male half-elf bard)
Stump (male gnome arcane trickster)
Brother Melph (male human cleric of the god of roads)
Ulf Ironfist (male dwarf expert [master smith])
Herrick Mendon (male human expert [merchant])
Danver the Miller (male human expert [miller])
Crenshaw (male human expert [finesmith])
Amarathea (female halfling adept [seer])
Caledon the Root-Cutter (male human druid [herbalist])
The Band of the Crimson Mantle (Pratchet [male half-elf rogue]; Isidra [female human cleric of the god of death, Orcus]; Dresden "the Mad" [male gnome sorcerer]; Yelm [male human barbarian])
Devlin (male half-elf rogue [Guildmaster of the Ebon Guard])
Gethrax (male human antipaladin [demonic agent])
Lilith (succubus demon)

Marketplace

Base Value 6,000gp ; **Purchase Limit** 40,000gp ;
Spellcasting 6th
Minor Items 4d4; **Medium Items** 3d4; **Major Items** 1d6

City Random Encounters Table

These encounters should be used to provide action, inspire role-playing, and develop the unique character of Dun Eamon. They can also be used to develop the plot with the delivery of an important rumor at the right moment.

1d8	Encounter
1	Mist Watch City Patrol (9 **guards**, 1 **guard officer**): With the developing events in the city, patrols are larger, more frequent, and increasingly reactive. They have standing orders to question anyone out after dark or who appears to be engaged in questionable behavior. Reactions depend on the party's activities, reputation, and level of cooperation.
2	**Cutpurse:** Equally at home working a crowded market or dark side street, these thieves of the Ebon Union always try to flee a confrontation, attempting to lose pursuers before going underground through one of the drains in the Market. They fight only as a last resort.
3	**Dretches** (1d2): When encountered in numbers this small, these creatures are usually wandering erratically instead of serving their demonic mistress. They create a panic whenever they appear in public view. They are most often found scavenging scraps in an alley refuse pile.

1d8	Encounter
4	**Confrontational Drunk:** An inebriated caravan guard stumbles into the party and belligerently challenges a random character. If diplomacy fails, the heroes should make an effort to end the fight without loss of life to avoid repercussions.
5	**Perfumed Harlot:** These women roam the city in revealing gowns and heavy makeup, attempting to attract wealthy (or at least employed) men to various dances and festivals at the inns or to rendezvous at the bathhouse. They know 1d3 items from the City Rumors Table in Chapter Two if questioned.
6	**Raving Prophet:** These wild-eyed fanatics pester anyone who shows an interest in their rants, which will always pertain to a deity/faction/cult of which the party has never heard, unless it benefits an outside story connection. They know a single rumor from the City Rumors Table in **Chapter Two** if asked, but always twist it to favor their cause.
7	**Ragged Beggar:** There are very few independent beggars in the citadel; 90% have been bullied into loyalty to the guild, but 30% of those report secretly to Rasputin as well. Any beggar will know 1d4 rumors from the City Rumors Table in Chapter Two (re-roll those that pertain to the thieves' guild unless the beggar is one of the truly independent 10%).
8	The Elite: One of the three Angus brothers (see **Appendix C**) is out on business in the city (chosen or determined randomly). Arb may be responding to a simple legal or economic matter; Bron might be investigating a crime or reviewing Watch stations; Cael will most likely be ministering to his congregation's needs. All are on business unrelated to the demon crisis and, depending on the heroes' level of involvement, may approach the characters for an update. Day or night, two trusted **guards** accompany them from the Mist Watch or the acolytes of the Temple, as appropriate.

Guard (9)   CR 1
XP 400
hp 19 (Pathfinder Roleplaying Game GameMastery Guide, "Guard")

Guard Officer   CR 3
XP 800
hp 34 (Pathfinder Roleplaying Game GameMastery Guide, "Guard Officer")

Cutpurse   CR 1/2
XP 200
hp 10 (Pathfinder Roleplaying Game NPC Codex, "Cutpurse")

Dretch (1d2)   CR 2
XP 600
hp 18 (Pathfinder Roleplaying Game Bestiary, "Demon, Dretch")

Confrontational Drunk   CR 1
XP 400
hp 23 (Pathfinder Roleplaying Game GameMastery Guide, "Drunkard")

Perfumed Harlot   CR 1
XP 400
hp 11 (Pathfinder Roleplaying Game GameMastery Guide, "Prostitute")

Raving Prophet   CR 1
XP 400
hp 10 (Pathfinder Roleplaying Game GameMastery Guide, "Doomsayer")

Ragged Beggar   CR 1
XP 400
hp 13 (Pathfinder Roleplaying Game GameMastery Guide, "Beggar")

The people of Dun Eamon are hardy and self-sufficient; hardships are taken in stride, and respect is reserved for those who have earned it. Two dominant social groups exist in the city, and they are usually at odds with each other. The woodsmen who occupy the forested slopes around the citadel regard the merchant class as arrogant foreigners from pampered lowland cities; the merchants regard the woodsmen as savages whose uncouth lifestyle they tolerate only in the interests of profit. Rangers, druids, and barbarians are welcomed into the community, as are fighters and bards to a slightly lesser degree. Paladins are not unwelcome, but the citizens are intolerant of judgment by outsiders. Dun Eamon attracts plenty of rogues, mostly bandits and highwaymen rather than burglars. Wizards and monks are uncommon, mostly due to the lack of social refinement. Clerics and sorcerers are not treated any differently than anywhere else. Adventuring parties are generally regarded as a natural part of the traffic through the gates.

In appearance, the Grey Citadel of Dun Eamon is imposing yet dreary. Its stone buildings are quarried from the same grey basalt as the bedrock on which they sit, as are the city walls and the keep. The rest of the buildings are half-timbered two- and three-story structures, with roofs of thatch or shingle. The cobblestone streets and alleys are always shiny and damp, and everything in the city hosts at least a thin sheen of green moss; many buildings even have thick clumps of ferns growing on the roof. Amid the green-fostered slopes and drifting grey rain clouds, the grey-green edifices of the city blend right in.

City Random Encounters After Nightfall Table

After nightfall, use the following table:

1d8	Encounter
1–2	**Mist Watch Night Patrol (9 guards, 1 guard officer)**
3–4	1d2 **Ebon Union Burglars**
5–6	1d4 **Dretches**
7	1d4 **Confrontational Drunks**
8	**Ragged Beggar**

Guard (9)   CR 1
XP 400
hp 19 (Pathfinder Roleplaying Game GameMastery Guide, "Guard")

Guard Officer   CR 3
XP 800
hp 34 (Pathfinder Roleplaying Game GameMastery Guide, "Guard Officer")

Ebon Union Burglar (1d2)   CR 2
XP 600

hp 16 (Pathfinder Roleplaying Game GameMastery Guide,
"Burglar")

Dretch (1d4)   CR 2
XP 600

hp 18 (Pathfinder Roleplaying Game Bestiary, "Demon,
Dretch")

Confrontational Drunk (1d4)   CR 1
XP 400

hp 23 (Pathfinder Roleplaying Game GameMastery Guide,
"Drunkard")

Ragged Beggar   CR 1
XP 400

hp 13 (Pathfinder Roleplaying Game GameMastery Guide,
"Beggar")

The trade road bisects Dun Eamon through the lower city, and a
massive gatehouse guards each entrance where the road rises up from
the ford. A rampart wall surrounds the entire island, with watchtowers
evenly distributed along it. Where the second falls spill over the edge,
the island rises steeply to a flat-topped promontory. On this slab of
rock sits the upper city, consisting of the craftsman's district, the vast
market, and the largest taverns. Rising from the very tip of the island
and towering over the dizzying waterfall is the Angus castle and keep,
the central point of defense for the entire region.

CONDITIONS IN THE CITY

The Grey Citadel has some special characteristics that will make
role-playing within its walls both dangerous and unforgettable. Two
special rules apply whenever the heroes are outdoors in the city.

Visibility: The city's position on a ford between two waterfalls and
the combination of rain and fog that drift down the slopes constantly
shroud the city in thick mists and drizzle. The result of this constant
precipitation is badly restricted visibility. Treat any encounter that
is not inside or underground as taking place in an area of partial
concealment; any existing concealment factor is increased to the next
category. Note that this situation is not as extreme as fog, although
heavy fog does occur and can make adventuring even more difficult.

Footing: Eamonvale's moist climate ensures heavy growth of
mosses and lichens in the city, and nearly every surface has a thin
green coat of slick vegetation. As a result, footing is treacherous,
especially for visitors who are unused to the conditions (those who
have been in the city for less than 1 month). Walking under normal
circumstances does not present a problem, but once another activity
(such as combat or attempting a skill) distracts a character, faces a
chance of slipping on the slimy surface. Following a result of a natural
"1" on an attack roll, skill check, or ability check, the character must
make a DC 15 Reflex saving throw. If this save is failed, the character
is flat-footed until the beginning of their next turn; the character has
slipped and recovered but cannot effectively dodge incoming blows.
A character that fails the saving throw by more than 10 falls prone
and suffers 1d6 non-lethal damage. The use of this check is more
applicable to Acrobatics and Climb checks than Perception checks.
Use your judgment on when and how to apply the footing conditions.

THE UNDERGROUND CAVERNS

Beneath the city, thousands of years of erosion have carved a
complex network of tunnels and chambers. In addition to the natural
caverns, a burial crypt and a gnome stronghold add variety to the
dungeon levels.

The descriptions of the underground caverns beneath Dun Eamon
are divided into four levels, although several passageways connect
them and the party need not visit every level to be successful. The
encounters in these levels are based on a party of four characters of 5th
level as the minimum requirements for survival: such a party will find
the dungeon challenging and should expect to need regular rest, well-
refined tactics, and a broad range of abilities to succeed. Hirelings or
NPC allies from the city are other options that can reduce the overall
wear and tear on the party.

Parties entering through the drains in the market will have a good
chance of exploring the levels chronologically. The first three levels
are connected by side tunnels that allow them to be explored in any
order. The final (and most challenging) level can only be reached after
completing at least one of the upper levels.

The Band of the Crimson Mantle has likely been in the dungeon
longer than the party, and the heroes have several opportunities to
interact with them. Dresden has been killed and his body remains on
Level 2. The bulk of the Band waits to share an encounter with the
party on Level 3, and the survivors of that encounter may be involved
in the final confrontation on Level 4.

Lilith's use of *Mamuthek's Aperture* with the items she stole from
various citizens has resulted in several creatures summoned directly
from the Abyss.

Chapter Two: Timed Encounters, Rumors, and Mystery Elements

This adventure is driven by three components: **Timed Encounters** are events that happen to the heroes, essentially bringing the story to them. **Rumors** are the results of their investigation and can be gained at every turn, from anyone in the city. **Mystery Elements** are the "hot" leads that bring the heroes closer to the answers they seek.

Timed Encounters

These encounters are milestone events in the timeline that serve to draw the heroes into the plot — for they are victims as much as anyone in the city. Not all of the encounters are combat encounters; some of them are strictly role-playing oriented and should help enforce the notion that city life goes on around the characters.

Timed Encounter 1.1: Arrival Amid Revelry

Use this encounter soon after the heroes enter the Grey Citadel, perhaps after they have stabled their mounts and are looking for lodgings. The Band of the Crimson Mantle has defeated and crucified a dretch, and it is parading the demon through the streets as a trophy. A crowd of relieved citizens follows the adventurers, who are on their way to the keep to claim their bounty.

> As you move down the cobbled streets, a commotion catches your attention a few blocks away. From where you stand, a group of hardy-looking adventures dressed in red are apparently bearing a corpse up the street on a crucifix. A crowd of people surrounds them, laughing and cheering. They seem to be going up the hill toward the city center and the castle on the bluff.

Be prepared to elaborate further on the grisly, bloated, and obviously non-human nature of the corpse or to describe the Band of the Crimson Mantle (see **Appendix C**). If the heroes join the procession, they witness Lord Angus presenting a sack of coin to Pratchett, the Band's leader. Pratchett will pander to the crowd, playing the hero, while the others stand back; Isidra looks disgusted with the bravado, Dresden looks typically on edge, and Yelm just looks uncomfortable, like he would rather be someplace else. The corpse is hung on the wall next to the gatehouse.

The heroes can gather quite a bit of information from the citizens. General "What's going on?" questions produce responses that tell of the demon infestation and are full of praise for the Band of the Crimson Mantle, derogatory toward Elinda Bannon, and apprehensive about the city's future. Refer to the City Rumors Table later in this chapter for specific rumors and responses.

Timed Encounter 1.2: The Lord's Offer

This encounter begins after the heroes have been in the city for a short time, perhaps moving about the market or leaving their lodgings to explore. It can also be inserted directly following Timed Encounter 1.1. If the party does not seek out the local authorities on their own, a young herald approaches them with a summons to the gate of the keep from Lord Arb Angus of Eamonvale (see **Appendix C**).

Arb Angus, Lord of Eamonvale   **CR 13**
XP 25,600
hp 73 (Appendix C: NPC Descriptions, "Arb Angus, Lord of Eamonvale")

When the heroes attend or approach on their own, Arb voices his concerns over the events in the city and offers a proposal to the party. Allow the heroes' reputation to precede them if they have one in the region. Arb stands at the gatehouse of the castle, flanked by a Mist Watch unit. He is gregariously greeting citizens and visitors, but breaks away to attend to the heroes.

> "Well met, travelers. Allow me to extend a welcome on behalf of the citizens of Dun Eamon. I am Arb Angus, Lord of Eamonvale, and I have a proposition for you.
>
> "Your arrival is ill-timed, yet fortuitous, for while you have come during trying times, I believe you may be able to assist us. Dun Eamon has been troubled by a plague unlike we have known before, a plague of evil creatures who walk like men but kill and plunder without remorse — demons, I am quite certain, from a world beyond our own. While I have known them to exist, I never dreamed that they would appear in the streets of the Grey Citadel.
>
> "The Mist Watch is able to safeguard the citizens and their property for the most part, but the origins of the problem are a mystery. I have offered a bounty on slain demons, and a few adventurers, such as the group you may have seen earlier, have been able to collect. Yet I fear that killing a few demons will not bring an end to our troubles. While my people need victories like this afternoon, I need someone who can finish the job.
>
> "A separate circumstance has arisen as well. A wizard who lives here in the Citadel has disappeared. The timing may or may not be coincidental; she vanished just prior to the first appearance of the creatures. Knowledge of this may aid you in your investigation; I pray that your success may return her to us unharmed.
>
> "I am prepared to offer a reward to anyone who can successfully identify and eradicate the source of the infestation. Of course, the original bounty still stands: 50 gold ducats for every demon slain. Find and eliminate the source of the threat, and another 2,000 ducats will be yours, as well as my gratitude.
>
> "What say you?"

If the party asks, Arb is willing to advance 50 gp to the party to begin the investigation. He answers any questions truthfully, according to his knowledge. He knows that Elinda Bannon was last seen three nights before the demon's appearance, and he knows about the three burglaries, but does not speculate as to their significance. He also has heard most of the rumors from the City Rumors Table (see later in this chapter), but does not reveal them unless questioned directly — they are just rumors, after all.

TIMED ENCOUNTER 1.3: THE DEMON ATTACK

This encounter brings the heroes face-to-face with the demons that are terrorizing the city. Introduce it when the heroes are settled at the inn on the evening of their arrival. You may need to modify the text for characters that are not in the common room (sleeping, tending horses, returning from business, and so on).

The cheerful, noisy atmosphere of the common room is abruptly shattered by a scream of unmistakable horror, coming from beyond the side door of the inn. The sudden hush in the room is broken only by the sound of weapons being readied, but nobody seems eager to leave the safety of the inn to investigate. They know all too well what most likely waits outside. The scream comes from a boy, **Mert**, who is returning home late with his merchant father **Kelvin**. A roaming group of 6 **dretches** has cornered them behind the inn, and unless the heroes intervene, Mert and Kelvin are overpowered in a few rounds. Read the following when the party exists the inn:

> In the dim light of the alley below is a terrified-looking man brandishing a club in one hand and a dim lantern in the other. He shields a small boy behind him as several bulky shapes emerge from the thick fog. They stand as tall as a man, but are proportioned like grotesque, misshapen children. One of them steps into the lantern light, grinning maliciously as the boy screams again.

Dretch (6)   CR 2
XP 600
hp 18 (Pathfinder Roleplaying Game Bestiary, "Demon, Dretch")

Mert   CR 1/3
XP 135
hp 4 (Pathfinder Roleplaying Game NPC Codex, "Apprentice Jeweler")

Kelvin   CR 1
XP 400
hp 13 (Pathfinder Roleplaying Game GameMastery Guide, "Shopkeep")

The two citizens are cornered at the bottom of the ramp between the upper and lower city, right below the woodlot. They are surrounded by four of the dretches, which are closing in; two more wait in the mist. If they run for the inn, characters must make a DC 20 Perception check to catch sight of them. If the heroes position themselves between the dretches and their intended prey, the father grabs his son and rushes for the inn's side door. Unless the party has a favorable reputation at the inn (a *helpful* attitude, having bought several rounds, and so on), the patrons do not join in the fight, but they stand guard at the open door to admit retreating characters. The exception is **Rasputin**, who intervenes (with thrown daggers and song) if one or more of the heroes loses consciousness. After 10 rounds, a Watch Patrol arrives on the run. This patrol is made up of 9 **guards** and 1 **guard officer**. This patrol also has a 25% chance of a **constable** and a 10% chance of a **mist mage** being present. Remember that the special circumstances for restricted visibility and poor footing apply in this encounter, in addition to the low light that is the base condition.

Rasputin   CR 5
XP 1,600
hp 27 (Appendix C: NPC Descriptions, "Rasputin")

Guard (9)   CR 1
XP 400
hp 19 (Pathfinder Roleplaying Game GameMastery Guide, "Guard")

Guard Officer   CR 3
XP 800
hp 34 (Pathfinder Roleplaying Game GameMastery Guide, "Guard Officer")

Constable   CR 7
XP 3,200
hp 49 (Pathfinder Roleplaying Game NPC Codex, "Constable")

Mist Mage   CR 5
XP 1,600
hp 33 (Pathfinder Roleplaying Game GameMastery Guide, "Battle Mage")

Tactics: When the heroes approach the scene, the dretches have already scared the merchant and his son. They attempt to frighten the party before moving in to attack. Their strength is in their numbers, so they use simple mob tactics to maximize their advantage, attempting to surround and flank individuals. They fight until four of them are slain, then attempt to retreat into the darkness, using their *stinking cloud* to cover their escape. Once broken, they do not attempt to stay together but flee randomly into different parts of the city to continue their mischief. Tracking them does not lead the heroes to any place of importance. The dretches have already used their *summon dretch* ability today.

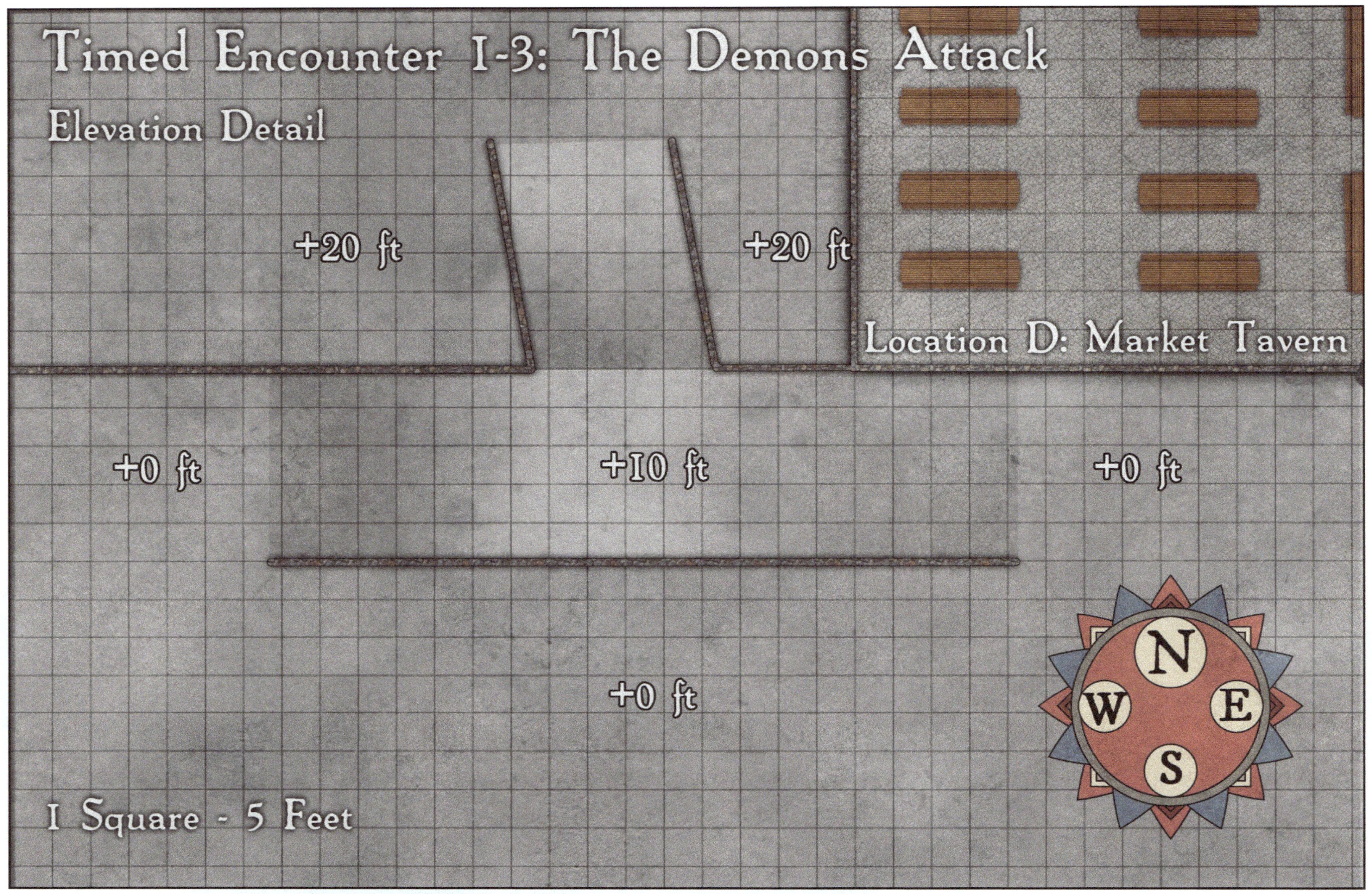

Timed Encounter 1-3: The Demons Attack
Elevation Detail
+20 ft
+20 ft
Location D: Market Tavern
+0 ft
+10 ft
+0 ft
+0 ft
1 Square - 5 Feet
N
W
E
S

Development: The dretches carry no treasure, but a reward of another kind awaits the heroes if they succeed. Word travels quickly in the Grey Citadel, and by morning the heroes find that their notoriety has opened many doors. Citizens are more inclined to cooperate with the investigation, the ruling family is impressed, and every innkeeper and merchant in the city is competing for their business. If the party performed admirably with no losses, grant a +2 circumstance bonus on Charisma based checks while the heroes are in the city (the party makes these rolls at a -2 penalty if they lose the encounter).

The Band of the Crimson Mantle is not happy at being outdone, however, which sets the stage for Timed Encounter 2.2: Unfriendly Competition. Thanks to the eyes and ears of the thieves' guild, Lilith needs very little time to order the assassination attempt described in Timed Encounter 3.1: The Guild Strikes.

Whether Rasputin participates or not, he invites the party to join him for a late breakfast, described in Timed Encounter 2.1: Rasputin Speaks Out. If Kelvin and Mert survive, they give each hero a waterproof cape or hooded cloak.

Timed Encounter 2.1: Rasputin Speaks Out

The heroes may find their way to the local bard in their search for information, following other people's recommendations or their own instincts. Unless the party approaches Rasputin, use this encounter on the morning of the second day in the city.

As the heroes descend the stairs in the morning, a small monkey wearing a red vest and fez approaches them. The monkey seems quite insistent that they accompany him to a table at the rear of the common area, where **Rasputin** waits for them. He has an important piece of information for their investigation and wishes to enter into an agreement with them. Whenever the heroes approach Rasputin, introduce him and read the following in your best eastern European accent:

> "I know a great deal about what goes on in this city. I know, for example, that Arb Angus wants your help in eliminating the demons and finding the missing wizard. I know from watching you last evening that you are capable, but I also know a few things that may help you in your quest. I suggest we exchange information in hopes that we can work together to mutual benefit.
>
> Many of my sources have ceased to provide me with information; others are nowhere to be found. The thieves of the city are no longer independent; they have formed some sort of organization and, frankly, they are making my life very difficult. I will find out what I can to assist your investigation, and you will tell me if you discover who is marshalling the thieves. Like many people in the city, I am a merchant, not of goods, but of words. Most people hear my words as pretty songs, but you may hear far more, if you know how to listen. Come and watch one of my nightly performances here, put a few coins in Vlado's cup, and you shall hear what I know.
>
> Now be careful, and let me give you some advice: listen to everyone, but trust no one."

You may need to modify the text slightly to accommodate the heroes' reactions or other major deviations from the plot. They may wish to question Rasputin further, but he is very reserved with his information; he insists that they come see his next performance before he gives them anything more. Remember, Rasputin may be used to feed important rumors to stumped parties, he can support them in a fight, and he could even replace a deceased character. He is a valuable tool, so consider how best to play him.

For example, his next performance can yield information about the three burglaries. If the party watches (and tips) any of his performances that day, he sings of the "cutter of roots," the "seer of stones," and the "winder of golden wire." These are the three citizens whose shops were burgled to provide for the operation of the summoning device, though Rasputin does not know this. Chatting with nearby patrons (Diplomacy DC 15) reveals the theme of his song and the location of the shops; otherwise, the party may just need to figure it out through trial and error (i.e., "If I wanted a root cut, who would I see?"). Use the same format to deliver any other information the party might be missing, over several performances if necessary.

Rasputin   CR 5
XP 1,600
hp 27 (Appendix C: NPC Descriptions, "Rasputin")

Timed Encounter 2.2: Unfriendly Competition

Use this encounter on the second afternoon or any time after the heroes have distinguished themselves in the city (after successfully completing Timed Encounter 1.3, for example). **The Band of the Crimson Mantle** confronts the heroes and warns them to stand down. Consider adding some hired hooligans (as **street thugs**) if the party greatly outnumbers the Band. This encounter is appropriate whenever the party is in a relatively peaceful setting or at least during a quiet moment. Potential opportunities are at the Market Tavern, in the Market, or in the Crafthall. If it develops into a combat encounter, be prepared to improvise the location. A bystander summons the Mist Watch, which arrives seven rounds after the Band enters. Read or paraphrase the following:

> You are interrupted by crash of an opening door, and all eyes turn to stare at the newcomers. The party of adventurers you saw in the city parading the crucified demon is walking toward you, wearing their distinctive red garb. The dark half-elf is in front and looks to be in charge. The pale, gaunt woman, the wild-eyed gnome, and the tattooed warrior are right behind him, all looking fierce and determined.
>
> "You think there's enough room in this town for all of us?" the dark half-elf says. "I think not! This demon plague is our business, you lot need to stand down. We'll wrap this mystery up before you get yourselves killed — you'd better leave the glory work to the real heroes!"

The heroes have a great deal of control over where this encounter goes. If they respond non-violently, play out the exchange of venomous remarks as far as the heroes wish. If this is the case, Pratchett eventually spits at someone's feet, makes one last colorful remark, and retreats with his group in tow. The Band did not come here looking for a fight, but they are ready for one. If the party rises to the occasion, returns their taunts, or otherwise escalates the threat of violence, the situation may deteriorate into a brawl.

The Band of the Crimson Mantle: The entire Band is present for this encounter. See **Appendix C** for complete stats.

Pratchett   CR 4
XP 1,200
hp 28 (Appendix C: NPC Descriptions, "Pratchett")

Isidra   CR 4
XP 1,200
hp 24 (Appendix C: NPC Descriptions, "Isidra")

Yelm   CR 4
XP 1,200
hp 48 (Appendix C: NPC Descriptions, "Yelm")

Dresden "the Mad"   CR 4
XP 1,200
hp 43 (Appendix C: NPC Descriptions, "Dresden 'the Mad'")

Street Thug   CR 1
XP 400
hp 16 (Pathfinder Roleplaying Game GameMastery Guide, "Street Thug")

Tactics: The Band does not use lethal force unless their lives are in danger, as they have no desire to wind up in jail. Pratchett produces a leather sap, and Yelm wades in enthusiastically with his fists, so both of them deal nonlethal damage. Isidra uses spells such as *bane*, *bull's strength* (probably on Yelm or Pratchett), *cause fear* and *hold person*. Dresden uses *grease* (against a hero with a lethal weapon, or to cover the Band's escape), *color spray*, and his sling. If the fight goes badly against them, or when the Watch is summoned, the Band makes a withdrawal to escape the fight (spiced by lots of threats and oaths).

Development: At a minimum, the heroes may need to explain what happened to the Watch when it arrives. They may also be responsible for damages, depending on where the incident takes place. At worst, they may be responsible for someone's death. Keep these issues in mind as you develop the encounter. On the positive side, the Band has shown its true colors. As a result, a sympathetic bystander might approach the heroes with some basic information about their skills and hierarchy; paraphrase a few select items from their background in **Appendix C**.

Timed Encounter 2.3: Howlers in the Night

Use this encounter any time on the day following the dretch attack, probably the second day in the city. The later in the day it occurs, the less time heroes will have to recover before Timed Encounter 3.1: The Guild Strikes. It can occur anywhere in the city.

> As you move down the street, a long, mournful howl rises through the misty air, chilling your spine. Immediately following it are the cries of panicking citizens, and they sound like they are coming right toward you.

In addition to fighting the 3 **howlers**, the heroes may try to deal with the tide of panicked citizens. With the fleeing **citizens** are 4 Mist Watch **guards** whose unit has been decimated. The party may be able to reinforce its numbers with the soldiers or a mob armed with improvised weapons. Paladins, bards, and any charismatic hero can really shine here; reward good role-playing — especially good "stand together" speeches — with a small knot of temporary followers. This development can complicate the combat but it also helps the heroes preserve their spells and hit points and makes for a cinematic fight scene.

The 10 citizens have no weapons, though they fight with anything they are given.

Howler (3)   CR 3
XP 800
hp 30 (Pathfinder Roleplaying Game Bestiary 2, "Howler")

Citizen (10)	CR 1/2

XP 200

hp 10 (Pathfinder Roleplaying Game GameMastery Guide, "Farmer")

Guard (4)	CR 1

XP 400

hp 19 (Pathfinder Roleplaying Game GameMastery Guide, "Guard")

TACTICS

Give the party at least 5 rounds between the citizens and the howlers to rally, plan a defense, or take up positions. The howlers were sent into the city to hunt the heroes, and they only attack citizens for fun or if they try to stand their ground. Howlers are instinctive pack hunters, and when they encounter the party, they attempt to encircle it. They attack by charging in and then racing away. Each howler continues this action as long as the party remains in a defensive posture. As soon as a howler is charged or followed, it turns and focuses on that opponent. The heroes must decide when they shift from defense to offense.

The commoners have no combat skills and need the party's leadership to survive. They fight defensively unless a character passes a DC 15 Diplomacy check to inspire and encourage them.

DEVELOPMENT

Even after these howlers are defeated, there is a 60% chance per hour that one or more howlers in or around the city will use their howl ability. Chances are that the heroes will not be affected unless they pursue the creature (which is up to you to administrate). The effects on the population are profound; however, people tend to stay inside or hurry from place to place, sleepless and haunted. Reinforce this "city under siege" atmosphere to the heroes when they next venture into the city.

TIMED ENCOUNTER 3.1:
THE GUILD STRIKES

Use this encounter early in the morning following the encounter with the howlers. Lilith has ordered Devlin to eliminate the party, and he sends two guild agents, **Kubris** and **Thurf** to lead a gang (6 **thugs**, 4 **knives**, and 2 **nets**) to do the job. The guild intends to strike while the party is weakened from the previous night's battle, and unless the heroes were highly successful at rallying citizens to fight with them, they may not be fully recovered. During the fighting, Fitch is wounded and struck unconscious and Molly is killed to prevent her from identifying the assassins (she had been informing for the Ebon Union; see **Area D-2**).

In this battle, remember that most of the party was likely sound asleep. Also, note the rules for donning armor, as the heroes may find themselves fighting without it. Until the heroes provide a light source, the encounter takes place in near total. This encounter is probably very different from the party's usual methods, with unarmored fighters and spell-less casters swinging fists in the dark.

Have the characters make a DC 15 Perception check (remember to include the penalties for being asleep) and read the following to those who succeed:

Knife (4)	CR 1/2

XP 200

hp 5 (Pathfinder Roleplaying Game GameMastery Guide, "Pickpocket")

Net (2)	CR 3

XP 800

hp 30 (Pathfinder Roleplaying Game GameMastery Guide, "Slaver")

Thug (6)	CR 1

XP 400

hp 16 (Pathfinder Roleplaying Game GameMastery Guide, "Street Thug")

Tactics: If the heroes only took one room, the attack takes place as written. If they occupy two rooms, divide the attackers evenly (ignore any further rooms, as the attackers prefer to focus their strength). If eight thieves are killed (or four, if either Kubris or Thurf is among them, or if both of them are killed), the survivors attempt to withdraw using their caltrops. If the ram fails to break down the door, the heroes barricade themselves in, or the heroes meet the thieves in the gallery, the rounds may need to be adjusted, but the plan is the same. The thieves have carefully timed their attack on the party and act in a specific order:

Round 0: The thieves enter the inn and surprise the barman dozing by the fire; make DC 15 Perception checks for the party.

Round 1: The thieves ascend the stairs and prepare their rams; the heroes take their 1st actions (rising, arming themselves, and so on).

Round 2: The thieves smash in the door(s) (+4 to Strength check with ram); 2 **Thugs** enter the room and fight defensively; heroes take 2nd action.

Kubris & Thurf

Kubris

Kubris is a mean and spiteful man, detested by everyone except Thurf, who idolizes him, and Devlin, who needs a man willing to do the unspeaking with only financial conditions to be met. He has greasy black hair and stained armor, but despite his slovenly appearance, he is a quick and capable swordsman. He aspired to be a great mercenary captain, but his greed and maliciousness have led him down the dark path too many times to turn back.

Kubris   CR 3
XP 800
Human unchained rogue 4
NE Medium humanoid (human)
Init +8; **Senses** Perception +7

___

AC 16, touch 14, flat-footed 12 (+2 armor, +4 Dex)
hp 26 (4d8+8)
Fort +2, **Ref** +8, **Will** +1
Defensive Abilities danger sense +1, evasion, uncanny dodge
Speed 30 ft.

___

Melee mwk rapier +9 (1d6+4/18-20)
Special Attacks sneak attack +2d6

___

Str 13, **Dex** 18, **Con** 12, **Int** 14, **Wis** 10, **Cha** 8
Base Atk +3; **CMB** +4 (+6 disarm); **CMD** 18 (20 vs. disarm)
Feats Combat Expertise, Improved Disarm, Improved Initiative, Weapon Finesse, Weapon Focus (rapier)
Skills Acrobatics +11, Bluff +6, Climb +8, Diplomacy +6, Disable Device +13, Intimidate +6, Knowledge (local) +9, Perception +7, Sense Motive +7, Sleight of Hand +11, Stealth +11
Languages Common, Dwarven, Elven
SQ debilitating injury: bewildered, debilitating injury: disoriented, debilitating injury: hampered, rogue talents (silencing strike, weapon training), trapfinding +2
Combat Gear weapon blanch (silver); **Other Gear** leather armor, mwk rapier, 13 gp, 19 sp

Special Abilities

Debilitating Injury: Bewildered -2/-4 (Ex) Foe who takes sneak attack damage takes AC pen (more vs. striker) for 1 rd.

Debilitating Injury: Disoriented -2/-4 (Ex) Foe who takes sneak attack damage takes attack pen (more vs. striker) for 1 rd.

Debilitating Injury: Hampered (Ex) Foe who takes sneak attack damage has speed halved (and can't 5 ft step) for 1 rd.

Silencing Strike (2/day, DC 11) (Su) Your sneak attacks silence foes for 1 rd. (Will neg).

Thurf

Thurf is as large and powerful as he is slow and thick-witted, with broad shoulders and fierce black eyes. His career as a mason was cut short by a lethal outburst of rage. Kubris tool him on as a friend and as a bit of reinforcing muscle, and the pair was notorious as thugs, enforcers, and extortionists in the city by the time Devlin's gang arrived.

Thurf   CR 3
XP 800
Half-orc slayer 4
CE Medium humanoid (human, orc)
Init +1; **Senses** darkvision 60 ft.; Perception +7

___

AC 14, touch 11, flat-footed 13 (+3 armor, +1 Dex)
hp 42 (4d10+20)
Fort +7, **Ref** +5, **Will** +1
Defensive Abilities orc ferocity
Speed 30 ft.

___

Melee heavy flail +8 (1d10+4/19-20)
Special Attacks sneak attack +1d6, studied target +1 (1, move action)

___

Str 16, **Dex** 13, **Con** 16, **Int** 8, **Wis** 10, **Cha** 12
Base Atk +4; **CMB** +7; **CMD** 18
Feats Power Attack, Skill Focus (Intimidate), Toughness, Weapon Focus (heavy flail)
Skills Acrobatics +7, Craft (stonemasonry) +6, Intimidate +13, Knowledge (local) +6, Perception +7; **Racial Modifiers** +2 Intimidate
Languages Common, Orc
SQ combat style (two-handed weapon), orc blood, slayer talents (ranger combat style, weapon training), track +2
Other Gear studded leather, heavy flail

Round 3: 4 **Thugs** enter the room and charge; heroes take 3rd action.

Round 4: 4 **Knives** enter the room and move to flank the heroes, trying not to provoke attacks of opportunity. Two **Nets** burst through the shutters and swing in on ropes; heroes take 4th action.

Round 5: The Thugs and Knives pair off and try to flank individuals to enable sneak attacks; the Nets seek out spellcasters from behind the party and try to entangle them; heroes take 5th action.

Round 6: Kubris and Thurf arrive from downstairs to join in the fight (Kubris is Molly's murderer); Kubris tries to disarm the most threatening characters, and Thurf tries to crush the largest ones; heroes take 6th action.

Round 10: A **Watch Patrol** arrives downstairs (see **Appendix C** for full stats).

Development

At this point, the party may be badly weakened or even dwindling in number, depending on the battles with demons and assassination attempts. The death of Molly, the serving girl, is a good pretense on which to integrate new party members. Depending on what the party lacks (magic, muscle, and so on), Rasputin and Fitch now have enough personal stake in the matter to want to join in the quest. At this point in the adventure, either NPC could become a permanent player character without derailing the plot.

Timed Encounter 3.2:
The Rivals Depart

Wherever the party is on the afternoon of the third day, allow them to hear of the Band of the Crimson Mantle and their mission below ground. A friendly NPC (Fitch or Rasputin) or an excited child on the run tells them that the "heroes" are going underground in search of the source of the demons. If the party chooses to attend, use the following:

> As you reach the Market, you can see that the words of the citizens were true...half the city has turned out to see the adventurers off. A drain has been opened in the middle of the Market, and a huge knot of people crowd around it. An escort of Mist Watch soldiers looks on as the four adventurers in their red capes light torches and sling on their packs.
>
> The half-elf cries out to the gathered crowd: "Friends, citizens, take heart, for the Band of the Crimson Mantle goes now to seek the source of your troubles. Do not fear for our safety; instead, prepare the feast for our return, for we will be victorious! Farewell!"
>
> A huge cheer goes up from the crowd; the members of the Band raise their torches in salute and descend through the drain.

If the heroes scan the crowd, they may find the Angus brothers with a DC 18 Perception check. If the heroes succeed, they find the brothers watching the display with interest. Their sentiments toward the Band are unchanged: they believe the adventurers are good for the morale of the city, but doubt that they will meet with success. Stump is with them, but he is certain the Band will fail based on his assessment of them and his knowledge of dungeoneering.

The heroes may find themselves being looked at questioningly by those who know of their investigation. If the party had no idea that the underground caverns were involved, this event hands that information to them. More likely, they have found one or more of the secret entrances to the tunnels — something the Band did not find — and using the hidden entrances can save them time and energy. They may choose to abandon whatever leads they were following and pursue the Band, or they may continue with their detective work and discover advantages to aid them in their quest. The party may even disagree on the proper course of action — possibly leading them to an interesting discussion over a few pints!

Timed Encounter 3.3:
Caught in the Act

This incident provides an opportunity to learn more about the activities of the Ebon Union and their connections to the demons. The party also gets another chance to learn about one of the secret entrances to the tunnels. Use this encounter any time late on the third day while the party is in or near the Market. Initiate it with DC 15 Perception checks for the heroes to see if they notice cloaked figures descending a drainpipe from the roof of a house at the end of Grocer's Lane.

> As you pass near Dun Eamon's market, an out-of-place movement catches your eye. Several black-garbed figures swiftly descend a drainpipe, one of them dropping a gunnysack to another as they go. Quickly, they scatter and disappear into the grey evening mist in the market.

A team of thieves from the Ebon Union has robbed the home of a wealthy merchant in the city; the party notices them as they leave the scene. Out of laziness and to avoid getting soaked, the burglars choose to disobey orders and return via the secret entrance in the basement of the now-empty Ironworks (Area **Q**). The gang consists of 2 **burglars**, 2 **bolts**, and 4 **knives** and **Gulik**, a wizard who usually accompanies housebreaker heists.

Bolt (2)   CR 3
XP 800
hp 22 (Pathfinder Roleplaying Game GameMastery Guide, "Dealer")

Burglar (2)   CR 2
XP 600
hp 16 (Pathfinder Roleplaying Game GameMastery Guide, "Burglar")

Knife (4)   CR 1/2
XP 200
hp 5 (Pathfinder Roleplaying Game GameMastery Guide, "Pickpocket")

Tactics: The activities and reactions of the Ebon Union thieves and the actual location for this encounter depend on the heroes. The encounter begins when the party spots the thieves leaving the scene of the burglary. The heroes may decide to confront the thieves on the spot, or they might try to follow them back to their destination. Use opposed Perception and Stealth checks to manage the shadowing pursuit through the market. The thieves' initial reaction is the same regardless of location.

When they are accosted, either by force, by ambush, or by shouts, the thieves assume they have been spotted either by the Watch or by some private security faction. Their reaction is an attempt to escape with the booty. The Knives turn and stand to allow the Burglars to make a run for the nearest access point with the loot. The Bolts move past the Knives and take up firing positions to cover the retreat. Gulik follows the Bolts, stopping to use spells such as *grease* and *web* to discourage pursuit. If this encounter happens in the Market or at the scene of the crime (at the end of Grocer's Lane), citizens scatter and cry for the Watch, and the thieves head for the drains in the Market (**Areas F** and **G**).

If the thieves are allowed to enter the Ironworks unmolested, they take up positions in the shadows of the shop to ensure they have not attracted any attention. If they are out of the Market and near the Ironworks when confronted, they attempt to draw their pursuers inside and dispatch them.

If the thieves have any time along in the Ironworks, establish surprise using their Stealth checks and the party's Perception checks, but if the heroes are right behind them, begin the combat immediately. From just inside the foundry (**Area Q-4**), Gulik casts *web* at the party so the Bolts can target them. The Knives work their way around the outside of the web to flank heroes who avoid or escape the area of effect, readying their actions if the entire party is restrained. Remember the special factors for fighting in and around hot forges (**Area Q-2** and **Q-4**).

Gulik and the others are determined not to reveal the secret entrance and do not enter the Storeroom (**Area Q-7**). If they are discovered, they fight to the death or attempt to flee into the city to hide. If the heroes dispatch them, they must draw conclusions about the significance of the Ironworks on their own.

GULIK

Gulik | CR 4
XP 1,200
Elf conjurer 5
NE Medium humanoid (elf)
Init +3; **Senses** low-light vision; Perception +6

AC 14, touch 14, flat-footed 11 (+1 deflection, +3 Dex)
hp 23 (5d6+5)
Fort +1, **Ref** +4, **Will** +3; +2 vs. enchantments
Immune sleep
Speed 30 ft.

Melee dagger +2 (1d4/19-20)
Ranged shortbow +5 (1d6/×3)
Arcane School Spell-Like Abilities (CL 5th; concentration +9)
   7/day—acid dart (1d6+2 acid)
Conjurer Spells Prepared (CL 5th; concentration +9)
   3rd—*flame arrow, sleet storm, sleet storm*
   2nd—*acid arrow, knock, summon swarm, web* (DC 17)
   1st—*burning hands* (DC 15), *grease, mage armor, magic missile, obscuring mist*
   0 (at will)—*detect magic, mage hand, ray of frost, read magic*
Opposition Schools Illusion, Necromancy

Str 10, **Dex** 16, **Con** 11, **Int** 18, **Wis** 8, **Cha** 12
Base Atk +2; **CMB** +2; **CMD** 16
Feats Augment Summoning, Combat Casting, Scribe Scroll, Spell Focus (conjuration), Spell Mastery
Skills Acrobatics +8, Craft (alchemy) +12, Knowledge (arcana) +12, Perception +6, Spellcraft +12 (+14 to identify magic item properties), Stealth +8; **Racial Modifiers** +2 Perception, +2 Spellcraft to identify magic item properties
Languages Celestial, Common, Draconic, Elven, Gnome, Sylvan
SQ arcane bond (Jak the cat), elven magic, summoner's charm (2 rounds)
Combat Gear potion of *gaseous form*, scroll of *confusion*, scroll of *haste*; **Other Gear** arrows (30), dagger, shortbow, ring of protection +1, flask, scroll case, spellbook

Special Abilities

Acid Dart (1d6+2 acid, 7/day) (Sp) As a standard action, ranged touch deals acid dam vs. foe in 30 ft.
Augment Summoning Summoned creatures have +4 to Strength and Constitution.
Summoner's Charm (+2 rds) (Su) Increase duration of summoning spells by 1/2 level (permanent at 20).

Jak | CR —
XP —
Cat
N Tiny magical beast (animal)
Init +2; **Senses** low-light vision, scent; Perception +9

AC 17, touch 14, flat-footed 15 (+2 Dex, +3 natural, +2 size)
hp 11 (1d8-1)
Fort +1, **Ref** +4, **Will** +5
Defensive Abilities improved evasion
Speed 30 ft.

Melee bite +6 (1d3-4), 2 claws +6 (1d2-4)
Space 2 ft.; **Reach** 0 ft.
Special Attacks deliver touch spells

Str 3, **Dex** 15, **Con** 8, **Int** 8, **Wis** 12, **Cha** 7
Base Atk +2; **CMB** +2; **CMD** 8 (12 vs. trip)
Feats Weapon Finesse
Skills Acrobatics +10, Climb +6, Perception +9, Spellcraft +4, Stealth +22; **Racial Modifiers** +4 Climb, +4 Stealth
Languages speak with master
SQ empathic link
Other Gear jeweled collar (worth 65 gp)

Spellbook (includes prepared spells noted above, and the following): 0 — all; 1st — *charm person, color spray, detect secret doors, sleep, summon monster I.*

RUMORS IN THE CITY

In this mystery, the success of the heroes — and even the difficulty of achieving it — is directly related to the depth of their investigation. The heroes should be prepared to ask lots of questions, follow up on answers, and constantly weight the worth of the information they receive. The DM must likewise be prepared to adapt to unforeseen questions, make up answers, and humor the players as they pursue fruitless dead-ends. The rumors described rumors; more specific facts can be found in the Mystery Elements section.

These rumors are categorized by subject for when the heroes are pursuing a particular topic, and the Diplomacy DCs reflect the degree to which a particular rumor is common or rare. Be prepared to recycle and paraphrase the DC 5 and DC 10 rumors, because they represent the majority viewpoints of the community. Do not underestimate the significance of the rumor information, and be careful not to distribute too much at one time — limit one rumor per NPC unless otherwise indicated.

RUMOR SUBJECT

Unless the heroes are asking about one of the specific topics, randomize the subject.

1d6	Rumor Subject
1	The Demons
2	The Underground
3	The Brothers
4	The Wizard
5	The Thieves
6	Other Rumors

DC	Rumor
5	"The foreign merchants have always plotted to overthrow the brothers' rule. I fear that this is their insidious doing." (*False*. The Angus family has never been popular with foreign guilds, but they have no hand in the demonic infestation.)
5	"There's a fine reward from Lord Angus for the body of a demon. You look like the kind of bunch to collect it." (*True*. Angus is offering 50 gp for the body of what he defines as a demon, currently a dretch.)
10	"I saw a dark, powerful figure skulking around town the other night… it seems to me it was over by the mill. With all the talk of demons abroad, I'd rather stay in at night, if you know what I mean." (*Mostly True*. This man actually saw Gethrax leaving the mill on some nightly errand.)
10	"Someone says that one of the market drains was open this morning, with horrid claw marks all around. Whatever it is that plagues us, it dwells beneath the streets." (*Mostly true*. The claw marks are an embellishment, but an emerging dretch did leave the grate open.)
10	"An old legend tells of a demon prince who was imprisoned at the bottom of the pool below the falls. I fear he has broken free and dwells deep beneath the city." (*False*. The legend is a wives' tale, although a powerful demon does dwell below the city.)
15	"I saw one of the beasts in the market one night, with my own eyes. Horrible and hunched it was, with a blubbery face and dripping lips. If I never see such a thing again, it will be too soon." (*True*. This man saw a dretch.)
20	Í reckon it's got something to do with that damned witch in the tower [i.e., Bannon]. Always with the flashing lights and smoke; she's in league with them demons, and now she's gone off to join 'em." (*Partly True*. Bannon is responsible for the demons, but she has gone to eliminate them, not to join them.)

RUMORS ABOUT THE UNDERGROUND

DC	Rumor
10	"I don't believe all the talk of demons underground. They say there's an underground river beneath the city, runs right down the middle. Nothing could live in those sewers." (*Partly True*. The underground river is there, but so are many nasty creatures.)
10	"There's a cesspit under the mill, where all the sawdust and grain hulls are thrown. They say it's spawned its own life force." (*True*. The caves below the mill are infested with sentient plants and fungi.)
15	"This city came under siege many years ago, and the heroes that saved it were buried in lavish tombs near the gates of the Keep. Those burial chambers are still under there…" (*True*. The catacombs are beneath the Market.)
15	"Every so often, somebody disappears without a trace, no bodies, no remnants. They say a tribe of evil, flesh-eating gnomes live below the city." (*False*. The gnomes are long gone, but their halls are now occupied by the Ebon Union. The body snatcher is more likely Gethrax, the antipaladin.)

DC	Rumor
20	"It's rumored that an ancient, forgotten race had a great city right under our feet, abandoned now, but still rich with treasures and fearsome traps." (*True*. The Ebon Union occupies the gatehouse of an old gnome city.)

RUMORS ABOUT THE BROTHERS

DC	Rumor
5	"Them boys are the best thing that's ever happened to the city, an' I been here for three generations of Angus law. Tough an' fair, they are, bless 'em." (*True*. This is the general sentiment toward the brothers.)
5	"There's talk that Lord Arb and Captain Bron are feuding over Elinda Bannon. Now of all times, when we need them the most." (*False*. Arb and Bron both figure in the affections of Bannon, but neither let anything come before their responsibilities.)
10	"We've had some tough winters, an' bad crops, but nuthin' like this has ever happened. I can't say I'm sure Lord Angus'll see us through it." (*True*. Some citizens are losing faith in their leaders in this time of troubles.)
20	"The Angus bloodline is corrupt! Old Colm Angus was in league with dark gods, and now we all must pay the price!" (*False*. This man feels the Angus clan wronged his family in a previous generation.)

RUMORS ABOUT THE WIZARD

DC	Rumor
5	"That crazy woman! Just look at what she's brought down upon us this time! Left just in time to save her own hide, too." (*Partly True*. Elinda Bannon is responsible for the demon problem, but she has left to solve it. This is becoming the majority view toward Bannon.)
10	"I don't care what the others say, she's always been a sweet girl. She lost her father so young and was raised the best that old gnome knew how, so it's no surprise she's a bit… eccentric." (*True*. This may lead the heroes to Stump, who can provide more insight about Elinda Bannon.)
10	"She used to work with Ulf Nine-Fingers, over at the Ironworks. They say he ain't been quite right since she left." (*True*. Elinda and Ulf collaborated on magic items, but now Lilith has seduced him.)
20	"I hear she has a secret laboratory, where she performs all sorts of strange experiments. Some folks say it's guarded by a dragon!" (*Mostly True*. Except for the dragon.)
20	"A couple of weeks ago, she came home from a long journey with something in a big strongbox. Things just ain't been right 'round here since then." (*True*. Elinda traveled far to acquire *Mamuthek's Aperture*, which began causing problems almost as soon as it arrived.)

DC	Rumor
5	"It's the damned trade guilds. They've always envied our market, and I believe this is their effort to upset our economy." (*False.* The foreign merchants will exploit the circumstances, but they are not the cause.)
10	"They got old Herrick Mendon shook up real bad. I've heard he ain't been himself since all this started." (*Mostly False.* Mendon the Merchant has not been himself since Lilith seduced him.)
10	"Ha! Some thieves — they robbed the old halfling hag of her magic rock collection! Bet they were disappointed when they didn't turn out to be diamonds or something!" (*True.* The thieves did steal the seer's "magic rocks," which are not diamonds but mineral samples from other planes.)
10	"They hit Crenshaw's shop over at the Crafthall... if the Crafthall ain't safe, then nothin' is." (*True.* Crenshaw was not the only victim, however.)
25	"I heard they ran a buncha theives outta Reme [*or any large city in your campaign world.*] Betcha them scoundrels set up shop here." (*True.*)
25	"The merchants say there's a gang of highwaymen robbing travelers on the road outside the city — perhaps they are moving into the city." (*Mostly True.* The Ebon Union has an allied wilderness counterpart.)

DC	Rumor
10	"Buncha kids wuz throwin' rocks at some sorta big lizard down on the rocks yesterday. Ain't never seen nuthin' like it. Mighty strange stuff afoot these days, mighty strange." (*True.* The children attacked a lizardfolk infant who had made its way out of the forest. Returning it unharmed to the tribe can win favor with the leaders; see the Wilderness Encounters Appendix and Area **U** in Chapter Three for details.)
10	"The girls who work at the baths are real disappointed. I guess Herrick Mendon quit bringin' his business in; he used to be good for a nightly massage." (*True.* Mendon has not engaged the services of the ladies since his first visit from Lilith.)
10	"They say a bunch of drunks broke into the herbalist's shop lookin' for wormwood juice. Oughta' crack down on 'em if ye ask me! (*Partly True.* Caledon's shop was robbed, but it was theives, not drunks.)
15	"Danver finally got hisself a woman! Somebody seen her comin' outta the millworks the other evening." (*True.* It was Lilith leaving the building on business in the city.)

MYSTERY ELEMENTS

In this adventure, a great deal of information (and advantage) can be gained by thoroughly investigating a series of recent events. The guidelines for revealing information to the players are presented below using the "rule of three" as described in Chapter One. All pertinent NPCs are fully described and profiled in the appropriate Keyed Encounter locations, which are referenced below.

These clues, especially those regarding the thefts and the seduced citizens, can be introduced in several ways. The best way is to have the heroes draw their own conclusions from rumors and interviews (as in, "Hmmm. It sounds like a lot of people are 'acting strangely,' doesn't it?" or "Burglaries, huh? So who was robbed?"). If they gather too few rumors or ignore obvious leads, Rasputin, Arb Angus, and other NPCs can help fill in the gaps (i.e., "There has been a rash of burglaries lately. You should look into it.").

Force-feeding your players all the clues should not be necessary; just drop the first one in their laps (such as the wizard reference in Timed Encounter 1.2; The Lord's Offer or the thieves' guild reference in Timed Encounter 2.1: Rasputin Speaks Out) and see how far they can follow it.

THE CRIME SCENES

Three unusual crimes have occurred in the city since the disappearance of Elinda Bannon and the beginning of the demon attacks. All have certain elements in common: the thieves were efficient, seemed to know what they were looking for, and took uncommon items of questionable value. If the heroes investigate the three crime scenes carefully and interview the victims, they should be able to establish connections with some of the other components of the mystery, such as Bannon's activities and the corrupted citizens. The party may find out about these crimes from listening to rumors or receiving tips from Lord Angus, Rasputin, or other citizens.

VISITING THE SEER

In a cramped shop in the lower city, the heroes can find **Amarathea the Seer**, one of the burglary victims. Lilith herself entered the shop soon after her arrival, looking planar material to fuel her summoning device. When Amarathea is asked about the robberies, she responds as follows in her "little old lady" voice:

> "I don't know why anyone would want to rob a harmless old woman. There are those who mistrust my gift, but I've never done anyone any harm. They stole simple things, but things that were important to me. Money I can do without or get more of. But they left that and took some of my charms, my precious charms."

If asked to describe her "charms," Amarathea says they were all "trinkets from the far corners of this world... and other worlds as well" — meaning other planes. Some of the items were planar in origin:

- A chunk of iron ore from the Abyss
- A moonstone from a fortress on the Astral Plane
- A vial of soil from the fields of Elysium
- A piece of obsidian from the Elemental Plane of Fire

The other items were all mundane common minerals from exotic locations (volcanoes, great canyons, other unique landforms) of the Material Plane. She wore them all on a cord around her neck, the chunks of stone, pendants, and little glass vials all rattling together. She believed that having them would help gain the favor of natives of those regions if she encountered them while "seeing."

The collection included what Lilith hoped to find: the Abyssal core, which she uses to establish the source plane for the creatures summoned with *Mamuthek's Aperture*. The other items are still in Lilith's possession and could also be used with the device. If the heroes deduce the nature of the artifact, knowledge of the Elysian soil can give them a powerful weapon.

While the heroes are visiting, Amarathea insists on performing a "seeing" for them; see Area **N** for details.

Amarathea the Seer   CR 6
XP 2,400
hp 28 (Area N: The Seer's Parlor, "Amarathea the Seer")

VISITING THE ROOT-CUTTER

Caledon is a druid who runs a small herbalist shop in the city. The thieves came here a few nights who and made off with several organic components to use with *Mamuthek's Aperture* (see **Appendix B**). Caledon is not terribly perturbed at the incident, although the components were quite rare. When he is questioned, read or paraphrase the following:

"I always fancied myself the least likely to be burgled. People know that I take most of my work in trade and keep very little of value. It was the oddest burglary I could imagine; the items stolen were all body parts from exotic creatures that I experiment with in some of my preparations. I cannot imagine them being of any use to anyone else.

"The one oddity that strikes me, though, is that Herrick Mendon was in here just the day before the robbery. He was asking me about flowers, of all things — and he is not by any accounts a romantic man. Before he left, he asked about my use of organic material in my concoctions, and I showed him a few of the things that were later stolen. Still, I don't imagine that he has anything to do with it. He seemed a bit out of sorts, and I sent him home with some herbal tea to ease his mind."

Caledon wondered about the crime coinciding with Elinda's disappearance, but does not suspect her; he says she had never expressed any interest in anything with which she could not tinker. He actually believes that the burglars were drunks looking for his distilled essence of wormwood (absinthe).

A few more clues are revealed through this conversation. The involvement of organic components points to another feature of *Mamuthek's Aperture*: it uses them to identify the type of creature to be summoned. It also highlights the involvement of Herrick Mendon and the possibility of romance; investigating him can yield another crop of clues. Like the other burglaries, this one suggests that the thieves were efficient, skilled, and looking for something in particular.

If the characters ask Caledon to list the items that were stolen, they will have gained the most valuable information of all. The items were used to power the summoning device, and Caledon's list reads like a roster of the most powerful underground inhabitants. Most of them were things that Caledon had agreed to take in trade from desperate adventurers, and he was experimenting with their properties in his preparations. The heroes might also discover that he actually has items in his shop that can be very effective against them. The items that were stolen include:
• A mummified hand from a troll
• Antennae from a rust monster
• The claw of a rast
• The horn of a minotaur
• The venomous stinger of a monstrous scorpion

Caledon the Root-Cutter   CR 7
XP 3,200
hp 60 (Area T: The Root-Cutter's Shop, "Caledon the Root-Cutter")

VISITING THE FINESMITH

Crenshaw the Finesmith is a master craftsman of detailed metalwork. He is also one of the victims of the thieves' guild. He had a large bag of powdered silver stolen from his floor vault in the Crafthall several nights ago. When he is asked to describe the incident, read or paraphrase the following:

"Whoever they were, it seems they knew what they were doing. The Watch saw nothing, and there is always a patrol somewhere in the Market. They left not a mark on the gate on the shop, nor did they damage the vault when they opened it. That vault has a lock of my own creation on it — the most secure lock I have known.

"They took all the coin — about 80 gold ducats and a bag of powdered silver that I use for casting custom items. Taking the silver seemed odd. It is not easily transacted, and several items were more valuable and no harder to liquidate: gold and silver wire, gold leaf, and a small quantity of mithral. All were untouched.

"I'm certain it has something to do with that witch, Bannon. She was in here just a week earlier buying powdered silver herself, and now she's gone off and left all this trouble in her place."

If the heroes request to see the vault, Crenshaw asks them to step outside while he opens it (Area **H-9**). It contains items jointly owned by him and Lord Angus, both raw materials and nearly finished products.

This conversation might suggest to the heroes that the thieves were well-organized, skilled, and under orders to steal certain items. Also, this is an important occurrence of powdered silver. Characters making a successful DC 15 Knowledge (arcana) or Spellcraft check will know that powdered silver is a material component used in several Abjuration spells, especially wards. In this instance, it is needed to establish the *magic circle* that is created when *Mamuthek's Aperture* is activated. The knowledge that Bannon purchased silver here may help the party understand the device's properties.

Crenshaw the Finesmith   CR 9
XP 6,400
hp 50 (Area H-9: The Finesmith, "Crenshaw the Finesmith")

LILITH'S THRALLS

Lilith has seduced three men of the Grey Citadel for the purpose of protecting and supporting her activities and those of Ebon Union, which is also under her control. Clever heroes will observe that the three men have several common characteristics: they have no family; they are not known as being especially romantic; and they all have workplaces with deep basements — and entrances to the underground caverns. The party may find out about these men from listening to rumors or receiving tips from Lord Angus, Rasputin, or other citizens.

THE SMITH

Ulf "Nine-Fingers" Ironfist is the master smith of the Ironworks. Lilith (in dwarven form) seduced him just after she took residence in the caverns. She needed his basement as an access point for her forays into the city to gather components for the operation of *Mamuthek's Aperture* and later to allow the thieves of the Ebon Union to do the same. Ulf believes she is a clan chief's daughter whose family has sworn to remain underground, where they feel dwarves belong. He thinks she plans to run away and join him on the surface, but for now he contents himself with periodic visits in the caves below the forge.

Ulf "Nine-Fingers" Ironfist   **CR 13**
XP 25,600
hp 63 (Area Q-4: The Foundry, "Ulf 'Nine-Fingers' Ironfist")

Speaking with employees at the forge (Area **Q**) might reveal certain clues that pertain to the mystery:

• Ulf has not taken up the hammer in several days (he is weakening, thanks to the repeat visits from the succubus).

• He does not spend as much time on the forge floor as he used to (he is often underground or in his quarters dreaming of his love).

• He has made a few foolish mistakes in the little work he does do, such as mixing ores improperly or using the wrong furnace (also a result of his lost levels).

• He busies himself with odd projects (such as reinforcing the door to the basement).

THE MERCHANT

Herrick Mendon is the merchant who manages the Crafthall and storehouse for Lord Angus. Lilith chose him as a victim because he knew the sources she would need for her material supplies and because, like Ulf Ironfist, his basement had an opening into the caverns. Mendon believes Lilith is an agent from a foreign guild, sent to gather information about Dun Eamon's markets and products, and she has promised him a lucrative position in the guild when they usurp control of the local economy. He has given up any information she has asked about, much of which is useless to her, but serves to conceal the important questions, such as where powdered silver can be found. They meet regularly in the basement storehouse.

Herrick Mendon   **CR 7**
XP 3,200
hp 39 (Area H-4: Mendon's Office, "Herrick Mendon")

Speaking with the tenant craftsmen upstairs (Area **H**) can shed some light on Mendon's odd behavior of late:

• He has been oddly forgiving in his collection of late rents (he profits more from Lilith's meeting than he does from skimming rent payments).

• He no longer harasses craftsmen about paying to draw the materials they need from the storehouse; he's more insistent that they get what they want and get out (he is nervous that site of his rendezvous might be discovered).

• He actually made a loan of a few silver coins to a man who asked in jest (he needed to clear his office to make it to a meeting with Lilith).

THE MILLER

Danver the Miller is the engineer who supervises the waterworks and runs the gristmill. He is a lecherous man whose weakness was easily identified and exploited by Lilith: women. She rarely appears to him in the same guise twice, and he is pleased with his apparent success with romance. Lilith needed access to his mill for an additional entrance to her caverns, and she also had him try to grind silver coins to supply her with powdered silver.

Danver the Miller   **CR 6**
XP 2,400
hp 27 (Area R: The Mill and Waterworks, "Danver the Miller")

The stout laborers who move all the grain to and from the mill (Area **R**) have noticed changes in Danver's personality of late and are willing to discuss them if asked:

• He does not heckle every farmer's daughter that enters the mill with a bushel of wheat. In fact, he now chides them for "letting him get away" (since meeting various forms of Lilith, his newfound charm has made him confident).

• He is hardly seen around the taverns and inns he used to frequent (most of his evenings spent preparing for and entertaining Lilith).

• He recently spent a large sum of money on the newest and gaudiest clothing and jewelry in Raiment Row.

ELINDA'S TRAIL OF CLUES

Despite her hurried departure, Elinda Bannon left a careful trail of clues to her great mistake and her current activities. The clues are deliberately cryptic; Elinda is quite vain and wished to leave what information she could in case she failed, but in such a way that it would not betray her error if she were successful. The clues are also geared toward those close to her — namely, Stump and the Angus brothers — so the heroes must work hard to gain the information for themselves.

Before she left her ruined library, Elinda left a single sheet of parchment with a note on it, actually enchanted with *secret page*. Lying across the drawers of her toppled desk, the page radiates mild Transmutation magic and reads:

> *Play chess*
> *Wind Papa's clock*
> *Clean birdcage*

Although the note reads like a "to do" list, these things are actually instructions on how to assemble three parts of a puzzle. Anyone who knows her well will recognize the connections: she loves to play chess (she plays with Cael once each week); she learned her first spells from her foster father (who never remembers to wind the clock she gave him); the birdcage is in the workshop (Stump and the brothers only know that the directions to the workshop are "in the desk").

In each of these locations (Areas **S**, **I-9**, and **L-9**, respectively; see Chapter Three), Elinda has hidden a small scrap of unmarked fabric. Each scrap radiates an aura of Transmutation magic and is actually one of three fragments of an amulet that Elinda recovered and hid using the *shrink item* spell. When the scraps of fabric are dropped, they transform into the three broken shards of the amulet and radiate residual Abjuration magic. The amulet was the device that held the succubus imprisoned on her home plane, a device that ceased to function and shattered into three parts when Lilith was called through *Mamuthek's Aperture*. Although its magic is gone, the amulet is engraved with the demon's name — Lilith, a name that is abhorrent to her (see dungeon Area **4-12** for Lilith's special vulnerabilities).

With each scrap of fabric is a small piece of parchment containing a short bit of poetry; Elinda intentionally disguised her advice so she could salvage her reputation. The three poems, if interpreted correctly, will reveal what little she understands about the device and its properties. Consider copying the poems onto separate sheets of paper as player handouts.

IN THE WORKSHOP

One scrap of fabric and a poem are hidden in Elinda's secret workshop (Area **L-9**). Stump and the Angus brothers only know that the directions to it are "in the desk." Under the lining of the birdcage where her owl familiar roosts is an envelope. In it is the scrap (a *shrunk item*, actually the left third of the amulet that bears the letters "LI") and the following poem:

> *Intent to reach across the void*
> *Great thoughts to proffer and collect*
> *Instead unpacked an Aperture*
> *That every cloud could not protect.*

With this poem, Elinda hopes the finder to realize that what she thought was a device for communication across the planes actually summoned a demon to her. She also alludes to the failure of silver wards — the lining of "every cloud." She capitalizes the word aperture in reference to *Mamuthek's Aperture*.

AT THE TEMPLE

In the courtyard at the Temple of Fortitude (Area **I-9**) is a section of alternating black and white tiles used for large-scale games of chess. A small shed nearby holds the game pieces and an envelope with Elinda's clue. The envelope holds the right third of the amulet (with the letters "TH") in *shrunk item* fabric form. A piece of parchment bears a short poem:

> *From stony beach to mountain peak*
> *To mighty marbled hall*
> *These building blocks of worlds,*
> *They choose*
> *From whence it comes to conquer all.*

In this poem, Elinda describes the role of minerals in deciding the source plane for the creatures summoned by *Mamuthek's Aperture*.

AT STUMP'S HOVEL

In the midst of Stump's cluttered shack (Area **S**) stands a finely crafted grandfather clock, a gift from Elinda to her foster father. In the case where the winding key is stored is another envelope. It contains the middle third of the amulet (with the letters "LI") in *shrunk item* fabric form, and another piece of poetry:

> *With the remnant of a thing that*
> *Once was living, choose the form*
> *Of the beckoned creature stepping*
> *From a worldly shimmering door.*

Here, Elinda describes the other component for the operation of *Mamuthek's Aperture*: an organic item to determine the creature summoned.

When the three pieces of the amulet are collected and the name "Lilith" is read near the sheet of paper from the desk, the three clues fade and a *secret page* is revealed:

> I know not what I have done, only that it is most frightening and unintentional. I fear that you read this now only because I have failed to set things right myself. In my attempt to communicate with beings from beyond out world, I have loosed a great evil upon our community. Wherever I must go now, I am sure that darkness waits for me. I can only hope for absolution in my success or forgiveness in my failure. I do not understand what manner of creature this is, only that the amulet you hold may be the only key to its destruction. Should I not return, you — whoever you are — must act to right my wrongs.
> — *Elinda Bannon*

Collectively, this information gives the heroes several important advantages. They can guess the identity of their ultimate foe (an evil being from another plane) and have gained a weapon to use against it (her true name). They can speculate about the involvement of *Mamuthek's Aperture* and how it works, and they can connect it to the burglaries. Also, they have some information that can help them begin to clear Elinda's name.

Chapter Three: The Grey Citadel Encounter Areas

Dun Eamon is a bustling, vibrant frontier city, too large and complex to detail completely. Thus, the areas that will most likely draw the heroes' attention during their investigation are described below. Most of the NPCs are simply good sources for rumors and other information, and others have links to potential further adventures. Areas in the city with a specific connection to the mystery include a reference to the Mystery Elements section in Chapter Two.

Area A: The Gatehouse

The party has no reason to linger here, but the unique nature of Dun Eamon's defenses deserves description. The River Eamon flows swiftly here, spreading out across the broad basalt spillway. Across the shallow ford, the mighty gatehouse of the Grey Citadel leers out of the drifting mists like an open maw. A steep ramp from the ford approaches it, and a dozen armored men with pikes and shields flank its base. A portcullis stands half-raised at the front of the gatehouse; beyond that, heavy ironbound doors stand open as well. The top of it bristles with ballistae and the steel caps of sentries.

A **mist watch constable** always accompanies the 9 **mist watch soldiers** and the **mist watch sergeant** that protect the gate. He questions every prospective visitor as to place of origin, duration of stay, and purpose of visit. He oversees the collecting of entrance taxes of 1 sp per beast and 1 sp per cart or carriage, which pay for upkeep of the streets. There is no charge for visitors on foot, but anyone with goods to trade must visit the Caravan Camp (**Area C**) and meet with Lord Angus' chief steward Semerion, who registers and taxes their goods. He warns the party that the use of magic, the open worship of dark gods, and the practice of slavery are all forbidden within the city walls, but requires no surrender or binding of weapons or other items.

Mist Watch Soldier (9)   **CR 1**
XP 400
hp 19 (Pathfinder Roleplaying Game GameMastery Guide, "Guard")

Mist Watch Sergeant   **CR 3**
XP 800
hp 34 (Pathfinder Roleplaying Game GameMastery Guide, "Guard Officer")

Mist Watch Constable   **CR 7**
XP 3,200
hp 49 (Pathfinder Roleplaying Game NPC Codex, "Constable")

The area just inside the gate always attracts more than its share of beggars, hired swords, and harlots, all waiting for caravans to enter or leave the city. Consider using the City Random Encounters Table in Chapter One as the party enters.

Area B: The Public Stables

Located adjacent to the Caravan Camp (Area **C**), this long wooden building houses the public stables and is identified by an iron sign that trails rust down the stone walls. The smell of dry hay, oiled leather, and horses is dominant inside the stables. The air is warm from the body heat of the animals, especially compared to the cold drizzle outside. Down the row, a powerful stallion kicks and snorts. Stabling options are as follows: 5 sp for 1 day; 3 gp for 1 week; 5 gp for 2 weeks. Extra rations of oats and vegetables are available for 1 sp per day and grooming is available for another 1 sp per day.

Tad does most of the grooming and feeding at the stables; his uncle **Edgar** does the mending and bookkeeping. In addition, both are paid informants — nobody knows more about who comes and goes. Each evening, Edgar meets with a member of the Ebon Union at the Hole, who then reports to Devlin, who reports to Lilith. Tad reports to both Rasputin and Bron Angus, although each knows about the other. By the time the heroes have found lodging, nearly everyone of consequence in town will know of their arrival.

The stables have one other secret, and the heroes might be the first to find it out. One of the horses — a tall, powerful stallion — is not a horse at all. It is a polymorphed man named **Weck**, originally a warrior from a far-off land who ran afoul of a powerful sorcerer while infiltrating his domain. He has been sold several times (his owners usually find him difficult to handle) and is currently owned by a wealthy merchant in the city. Edgar and Tad are unaware of this oddity.

A druid or ranger who makes a successful DC 10 Animal Empathy check will notice something distinctly odd and even unhorse-like about the stallion. Another character can do the same with a successful DC 25 Handle Animal check or DC 20 Ride check. Anyone else will simply see frantic snorting and pawing. Only the horse's vocal mechanism prevents Weck from communicating. He can understand Common perfectly well and is more than ready to play charades. A *speak with animals* or *detect thoughts* spell is also sufficient.

Once communication is established, Weck will plead with the party to restore him, offering them anything, including servitude, if they will do so. A DC 24 *dispel magic* spell returns him to his true form, including his non-magical armor, weapons, and supplies. If the *dispel magic* fails (and it may, given the party's level), he will beg to be purchased or stolen so the heroes might try again.

Once restored, Weck will be extremely loyal to his saviors. He will also be unwilling to ride a horse except in the most extreme circumstances.

Weck (Restored)   **CR 1**
XP 400
hp 19 (Pathfinder Roleplaying Game GameMastery Guide, "Guard")

Edgar & Tad

Edgar is a surly and bitter old man who runs the stables for Lord Angus only to settle his bar tabs and gambling debts.

Tad is Edgar's cheerful nephew, who has a room in the hayloft.

Edgar and Tad   **CR 1/2**
XP 200
hp 10 (Pathfinder Roleplaying Game GameMastery Guide, "Farmer")

The Grey Citadel
At Dun Eamon

Area C: The Caravan Camp

In the lower city, a wide area has been left clear of buildings for the maneuvering, loading, and unloading of the large merchant caravans that are always passing through the Grey Citadel. The stables (**Area B**) sit on one edge of the camp, handling care and feeding of the merchants' horse teams. Beyond the stables, a wide stone ramp leads to the upper city and the Market (**Area E**). Around the perimeter of the clearing, dozens of wagons are parked close together, many with tents slung between them.

The Caravan Camp is always a busy place. During the day, **caravan laborers** busily shift goods from the wagons to carts and handbarrows for delivery around the city, and replace them with the products the merchants have purchased from the local craftsmen. Some of the laborers are usually **acolytes** from the Temple of Fortitude (**Area I**). Any visitor with goods for trade is expected to visit **Semerion**, the Chief Steward of the Angus clan (who is always accompanied by a unit of the **Mist Watch**). He assesses the suitability of the materials and assigns a tax based on their value: 10% for foreign merchants, 3% for residents of Eamonvale.

At night, bonfires are lit and spits of meat and kettles of stew are hung at the edges. Kegs are procured and opened; fiddles, flutes, and drums are unpacked; and the singing, dancing, and gambling continue into the wee hours. The fierce rivalry between merchants of different trade guilds and dynasties often extends to their employees; fights are common here, as are contests of strength and skill such as wrestling, knife throwing, and lifting sacks of produce.

Most of the contraband transactions in the city take place here rather than in the Market. Greedy merchants often barter goods that are illicit under Angus laws, such as poisons, exotic spell components, narcotics, and slaves. Under cover of night, they buy stolen goods for a fraction of their value for resale in other cities. If the heroes wish to buy or sell any such goods, they will most likely be dealing with **Kinnan the Dark**.

A small, open shrine sits at the base of the slope leading to the Market. A small stone building with a small fireplace and a dozen cramped bunks, it is dedicated to the God of Roads, Note and is maintained by the wandering clerics of that faith. There is a good chance that **Brother Melph** is here offering healing and counseling services to travelers. The shrine is enchanted with a permanent magical effect providing temperature and illumination equivalent to a *tiny hut* spell.

Rasputin mingles freely here during the day, considering the value of information as it trickles in from the road and following leads regarding his lost niece.

Finally, the Caravan Camp is a gathering place for mercenaries seeking employment as **caravan guards**, messengers, and even simple thugs. They usually lounge around outside the stable building, boasting, drinking, and heckling the laborers until their coin runs out and they are forced to find menial work themselves.

Caravan Laborer CR 1/2
XP 200
hp 10 (Pathfinder Roleplaying Game GameMastery Guide, "Farmer")

Caravan Guard CR 1
XP 400
hp 16 (Pathfinder Roleplaying Game GameMastery Guide, "Caravan Guard")

Temple Acolyte CR 1/3
XP 135
hp 5 (Pathfinder Roleplaying Game NPC Codex, "Acolyte")

Mist Mage (10% chance) CR 5
XP 1,600
hp 33 (Pathfinder Roleplaying Game GameMastery Guide, "Battle Mage")

Mist Watch Soldier (9) CR 1
XP 400
hp 19 (Pathfinder Roleplaying Game GameMastery Guide, "Guard")

Mist Watch Sergeant CR 3
XP 800
hp 34 (Pathfinder Roleplaying Game GameMastery Guide, "Guard Officer")

Mist Watch Constable (25% chance) CR 7
XP 3,200
hp 49 (Pathfinder Roleplaying Game NPC Codex, "Constable")

The Mist Watch unit is composed of 9 soldiers and a sergeant, with a 25% chance for a constable and a 10% chance for a mist mage to be present.

Kinnan the Dark CR 3
XP 800
Elf swashbuckler (inspired blade) 4
NE Medium humanoid (elf)
Init +8; **Senses** low-light vision; Perception +8

AC 15, touch 13, flat-footed 12 (+2 armor, +2 Dex, +1 dodge)
hp 22 (4d10)
Fort +1, **Ref** +6, **Will** +0; +2 vs. enchantments
Defensive Abilities charmed life 3/day, nimble +1; Immune sleep
Speed 30 ft.

Melee mwk rapier +8 (1d6 + 4 Precision)
Special Attacks deeds (derring-do, dodging panache, kip-up, menacing swordplay, opportune parry and riposte, precise strike, swashbuckler initiative), panache (6)

Str 10, **Dex** 15, **Con** 10, **Int** 16, **Wis** 8, **Cha** 16
Base Atk +4; **CMB** +4; **CMD** 17
Feats Improved Initiative, Run, Weapon Focus (rapier)
Skills Acrobatics +2 (+6 to jump with a running start), Appraise +7, Bluff +10, Diplomacy +10, Intimidate +10, Knowledge (local) +10, Perception +8, Profession (merchant) +6, Sense Motive +6; **Racial Modifiers** +2 Perception, +2 Spellcraft to identify magic item properties
Languages Celestial, Common, Draconic, Elven, Sylvan
SQ dare (run like hell), elven magic, inspired panache
Other Gear leather armor, mwk rapier, platinum ring (worth 35 gp), 24 gp

Kinnan is called "the dark" because of his jet-black hair and dark eyes. He is every bit the charlatan, able to go from smiling and friendly to serious and threatening in the blink of an eye. Kinnan is independent, but he has ties with the Ebon Union through Rorin, the smuggler and fence found at the Hole.

Semerion CR 5
XP 1,600
Human expert 7
LG Medium humanoid (human)
Init +0; **Senses** Perception +1

AC 10, touch 10, flat-footed 10
hp 39 (7d8+7)
Fort +2, **Ref** +2, **Will** +6
Speed 30 ft.

Str 9, **Dex** 10, **Con** 11, **Int** 16, **Wis** 12, **Cha** 8

Base Atk +5; **CMB** +4; **CMD** 14
Feats Skill Focus (Appraise), Skill Focus (Knowledge [local]), Skill Focus (Profession [clerk]), Skill Focus (Profession [merchant]), Skill Focus (Profession [scribe])
Skills Appraise +16, Diplomacy +9, Knowledge (geography) +13, Knowledge (history) +13, Knowledge (local) +16, Knowledge (nobility) +13, Profession (clerk) +14, Profession (merchant) +14, Profession (scribe) +14, Sense Motive +11
Languages Common, Dwarven, Elven, High Boros

Semerion manages the flow of goods through Dun Eamon's markets.

Brother Melph   **CR 4**
XP 1,200
hp 33 (Appendix C: NPC Descriptions, "Brother Melph")

Brother Melph is a cheerful human priest of the God of Roads, Note who offers his clerical skills and traveling stories at the Caravan Camp. Brother Melph is one of several NPCs that can serve as a replacement characters or as a temporary addition to or permanent part of the party.

Rasputin   **CR 5**
XP 1,600
hp 27 (Appendix C: NPC Descriptions, "Rasputin")

Rasputin may question the party about its travels in hopes of finding new information about his niece, at your discretion.

Area D: The Market Tavern

This is one of the oldest stone buildings in the citadel, seated firmly on the bedrock slab that hosted the original trading post. It now stands on the edge of the market square, open all day and all night. The service here is not luxurious, but it is always friendly and reasonably priced. The food is hot and wholesome, the beer cold and plentiful, and the beds warm and dry. The menu attests to the concentration of dwarves in the community with its extensive selection of strong spirits and rich meads, as well as to the gnomes with several fine cheeses. Hostel style lodging is available at 1 sp for the dormitory and 5 sp for the bunkroom, with private rooms also available for 8 sp. The exterior doors and ground floor windows are sturdy and secure (Hardness 5; hp 20; Break [DC 23]; Disable Device [DC 25]). All interior doors here are locked (Hardness 5; hp 13; Break [DC 13]; Disable Device [DC 20]), except for unoccupied rooms and the dormitories.

Area D-1: Coat Hall

A short corridor leads from the front doors into the common room. Its walls are covered thickly with coats, cloaks, and rain capes hung on wooden pegs. Rows of boots and overshoes line the floor, and two large barrels hold cudgels and staves. Searching the garments in the hall yields 2d10 cp and 1d4 sp.

Area D-2: The Common Room

The largest room in the inn has an open-beam ceiling that reveals the second story rooms. It is nearly filled with trestle tables, and on each side a staircase leads to the upper level. Heavy iron chandeliers that are anchored to heavy oak beams that support the upper floor

Location D: The Market Tavern
also Timed Encounter 3-1: The Guild Strike
1 Square - 5 Feet

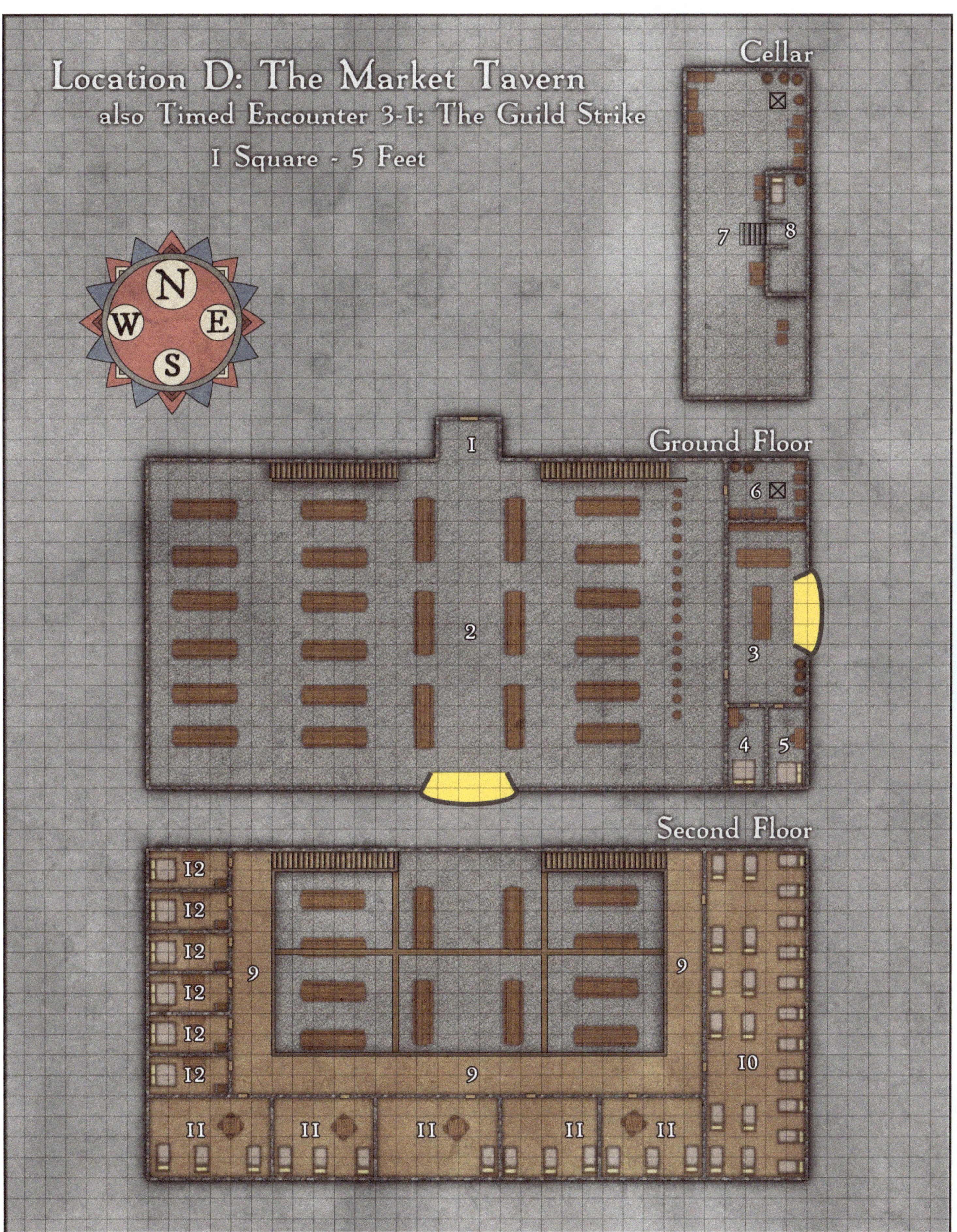

light the room. A long bar occupies one end; behind it are doors to the kitchen and cellar. Opposite the entry, an enormous fireplace heats the room, and in the far corner, an exit leads to a small woodlot. Other than the wee hours of the morning, dozens of customers and a continuous rumble of conversation are always in this room.

Area D-3: Kitchen

Through the door to the right of the bar is the kitchen, which is dominated by two huge tables, a pantry, and another fireplace. An iron cane holds numerous kettles and cauldrons over the hearth. The pantry is stocked with dry goods of all sorts, and on the top shelf, a box labeled "peppercorns" holds 4 *potions of cure light wounds*. Two doors lead from this room into the small apartments for the staff.

Area D-4: Fitch's Room

This room holds a small bed, a desk and chair, a chamber pot, and a washbasin. Fitch generally lives in squalor, a byproduct of running the tidy bar. His room is strewn with dirty mugs, clothing, and crumpled scraps of paper; he is in the process of writing his memoirs. In a locked chest are the more valuable trappings of his days as a dungeon delver.

The chest is locked (Hardness 5; hp 15; Break [DC 23]; Disable Device [DC 28]). It contains a partial map of a notorious dungeon (which you may use to introduce future adventures, if you choose), a suit of masterwork dwarven banded mail, a *+1 keen greataxe*, a *ring of protection +1*, a *potion of heroism*, an outline of his book, and a pouch with 85 gp.

Area D-5: Agatha's Room

This room has a canopy bed and a large desk, on which Agatha keeps the books for the tavern. The furnishings here are provincial but very tasteful; the proprietress wishes she could display her nice things in the common room, but she knows they would never last the night.

Area D-6: Taproom

The door to the left of the bar leads into a dim room where great casks sit on wooden racks. Also stored here are numerous smaller casks of spirits and bottles of wine. A trapdoor leads to the cellar, and a block and tackle is connected to the beam above to hoist the casks up from the cellar.

Area D-7: Cellar

The large cellar stores an extra cord of wood, large barrels of ale and cider, and crates of apples, potatoes, turnips, and carrots. A wooden loft holds sleeping quarters for Molly and Horace. A large rolling door opens onto the street behind, which is the setting for Timed Encounter 1.3: The Demons Attack (see Chapter Two).

Area D-8: The Loft

This wooden platform is raised off the damp floor and split into two small chambers, kept warm by the kitchen hearth overhead. Molly's room is tidy and simple, with a pallet bed heaped with furs and a wooden box for her meager possessions, which include a rag doll from her childhood and her mother's wedding veil. Horace's room is cluttered with junk that he scavenges from all over the city. He has numerous broken tools, chunks of scrap iron, and rejected projects from the Crafthall. He also has a rusted longsword and a helm from a suit of full plate.

Area D-9: The Galley

A sturdy railing protects intoxicated guests as they navigate one of two staircases to the gallery. A broad wooden walkway runs around three sides of the common room, lined with the doors to the guest quarters. The thick hemp ropes that support the chandeliers are anchored here.

Area D-10: The Dormitory

This large bunkroom is located on the upper floor. It is full of bunks stacked three high, and it echoes with the sound of snoring, night or day.

Area D-11: Small Bunkrooms

There are three of these rooms, which are more comfortably appointed than the dormitory. One is usually kept for individuals who want a bit more space but do not mind sharing. Agatha makes an effort to rent the others to groups, usually adventurers, mercenary companies, or the entourages of visiting merchants or dignitaries. Each one has six bunks, a table and chairs, a chamber pot, and a dressing screen.

Merchants of the Market

Tarsh the Cordwainer makes cord and rope with the help of his two sons. He brings his wares to market twice week and returns with raw materials. His regular travels bring him lots of news; he knows 1 rumor from the City Rumors Table (see Chapter Two).

Gurt Anford is a merchant of 10-foot poles; he carries a bundle of them on his back as he walks around the market. He is actually an expert craftsman and makes several poles that disassemble for packing. He can list endless uses for a 10-foot pole; his favorite is "for reaching things you can't reach with a 9-foot pole." Pole, 2 sp; collapsing pole, 1 gp.

Filip the Hatter (half-elf) has succumbed to the noxious fumes from the liquid mercury he uses to shape felt hats of all sorts. He is no longer sane and will often insist that he "has a hat that cries out" for a particular character's head and sit him or her down while he shapes it to fit. Hat or cap, 3 sp; the price triples for custom work.

Orin the Potter (gnome) is a skilled maker of clay pots, mugs, and other containers. He is very shaggy, nearly invisible behind his tangled beard, and spends all day at his pedal-driven pottery wheel muttering about how he should be given a shop in the Crafthall and how much he hates Herrick Mendon.

Oberlin is a juggler, acrobat, contortionist, and orator of colorful limericks who performs in the busy market. The heroes probably notice his flying props before they see him. He travels for most of the year and hears many stories; you may allow him to (a) know of the heroes and laud them with a fantastic tale, for which he will privately try to collect a fee, (b) give them a lead on a future adventure, or (c) drop a rumor or two regarding this adventure.

Dora and her three very attractive daughters (**Frieda**, **Maike**, and **Shara**) make and sell candles in front of their canopied cart. A peasant widow, Dora hopes to marry her girls well to merchants, nobles, or perhaps even successful adventurers. The girls are content to help their old mother dip candles and avoid the advances of the city's men.

Merchants   CR 1
XP 400
hp 13 (Pathfinder Roleplaying Game GameMastery Guide, "Shopkeep")

Area D-12: Private Rooms

These rooms are nicely if not lavishly decorated. Agatha prides herself on the décor and always hesitates before renting one to a filthy adventurer fresh off the road (she always makes a point of how nice the baths are!).

Area E: The Market

The central area of the Market is a sea of carts, wagons, tents, and even semi-permanent wooden structures. The occupants are numerous and diverse, local and foreign, and sell every item imaginable. Most of them are aggressive salesmen and skilled negotiators; they will generally offer prices 30% higher than the usual and be willing to negotiate down. Some of the merchants are listed below:

Area F: Raiment Row

This area, framed by a variety of carts, tents, wagons, and canopies, is one of several semi-permanent boulevards in the market. The trappers from the forest display their furs at one end; the weavers and dyers offer bulk cloth at the other; and the tailors, cobblers, and tanners line the avenue in between.

Nearly any garment can be found here, but the fact that Dun Eamon is a frontier city in a temperate rain forest ensures the popularity of sensible clothing. Furs, woolens, and waterproof goods can be bargained down to 10–25% below normal cost, while luxury goods such as silks and lace cost 10–25% above normal. There is a drain in the street here that leads to dungeon Area **1-1**.

The party may run into some acquaintances here. **Kelvin** and **Mert** (from Timed Encounter 1.3: The Demons Attack in Chapter Two)

Personalities of the Row

Other interesting occupants of Raiment Row (who can also supply information from the City Rumors Table found in Chapter Two) include:

Sabinna the Rug-Weaver is a toothless old gnome woman who weaves rugs and tapestries by hand. She is currently weaving a coat of arms for a local merchant and gladly takes commissions.

Alphonse specializes in a rare elven method of tanning hides that produces the supplest leather, which he stitches into customized, skin-tight garments.

Egan Taldo is a wily textile merchant — the man to see if one has rare fabrics to buy or sell. He is secretly in league with a foreign merchant guild and is highly suspicious of everyone.

Merchants   CR 1
XP 400
hp 13 (Pathfinder Roleplaying Game GameMastery Guide, "Shopkeep")

Mercy is a young orphan girl in a patchwork cloak who begs for fabric scraps on Raiment Row. With them, she makes colorful clothing for the poor and quilts to sell for food money.

Mercy   CR 1
XP 400
hp 13 (Pathfinder Roleplaying Game GameMastery Guide, "Beggar")

and **Logan the Furrier** both market their wares here and may have interesting rumors to pass along.

Logan the Furrier	CR 3

XP 800
hp 30 (Pathfinder Roleplaying Game GameMastery Guide, "Trapper")

Mert	CR 1/3

XP 135
hp 4 (Pathfinder Roleplaying Game NPC Codex, "Apprentice Jeweler")

Kelvin	CR 1

XP 400
hp 13 (Pathfinder Roleplaying Game GameMastery Guide, "Shopkeep")

AREA G: GROCER'S LANE

This strip of carts and wagons borders the side of the Market opposite Raiment Row. Its merchants are more temporary; many of them are crofters who come to sell their produce once a fortnight. Meats, fish, grains, breads, fruits, and vegetables can all be purchased here, as well as dried rations, imported spices, and beverages of many kinds. A drain in the street here leads to dungeon **Area 1-3**. Many colorful characters do business daily in Grocer's Lane:

GROCER'S LANE PERSONALITIES

Matilda is a large, red-faced woman in a bloodstained apron. She prepares and sells meat, fowl, and fish, as well as sausages and pickled organ meats. Her cart is right over the drain to facilitate cleanup; she knows the rumor about the claw marks and open grate.

Cedrix is a gaunt man who sells durable and easily preserved foods, including dried fruit, fish, and beef jerky; dry salamis; hard cheese; and unleavened bread. Most adventurers visit him before leaving town; he knows a rumor about the underground from them.

Aloysius is a well-traveled elf who markets exotic bottled wines and spirits from distant lands. He also has small casks of brandy, cider, and ale that he purchases from local farmers. He attracts attention by blowing fire with mouthfuls of high-proof alcohol (Range 5 ft.; Area: cone 5 ft. long; requires ignition source and ranged attack roll; flask 5 gp; 5 uses per flask).

Ephraim always has his pony cart laden with bundles of spices, both domestic and exotic. Some of his spices have medicinal properties, including one that has the effect of a *potion of cure light wounds* (25 gp, only 1 dose can be used per day).

Nik Ghoerkin makes delightful pickles from the wild cucurbits that grow in the forest. His pickles are inexpensive (6 cp per jar), but could fetch a high price in foreign lands where such things are unknown. He also sells pickled eggs, garlic, pork knuckles, and onions.

Merchants	CR 1

XP 400
hp 13 (Pathfinder Roleplaying Game GameMastery Guide, "Shopkeep")

AREA H: THE CRAFTHALL

An earlier Lord Angus built this long, wooden building to create both working and mercantile space for the city's craftsmen. It consists of a series of workshops facing each other across a wide corridor for the maneuvering of materials and products. Only the most capable and established artisans have shops here, and an appointment as an apprentice is the only way for a craftsman to gain entrance. Many of the products manufactured here are for export or are commissioned pieces for specific clients, and many of them are of excellent quality.

The building is a noisy roar of men's voices, clattering looms, and pounding tools. It is warm and dry here, and the smells of leather, wool, and freshly cut wood are thick in the air. The occupants are mostly men, all sturdy-looking laboring folk with leather aprons and rough, calloused hands. At night, the exterior doors to the Crafthall are securely locked (Hardness 5; hp 20; Break [DC 23]; Disable Device [DC 30]). All interior doors and shop gates are locked as well (Hardness 5; hp 13; Break [DC 13]; Disable Device [DC 20]).

The party may come here while investigating Mendon the Merchant or the burglary at the Finesmith's Shop. The craftsmen are generally willing to talk, as long as their work is not interrupted; see Mystery Elements in Chapter Two for their comments on Herrick Mendon and the tale of Crenshaw the Finesmith.

AREA H-1: THE COOPERAGE

In this shaving-strewn shop, casks and barrels of all sizes are manufactured, as well as wooden boxes and chests. A master and several apprentices work here, and they are capable of building secret compartments, false bottoms, and so on.

AREA H-2: CARPENTRY AND WOODWORK

All manner of wooden goods are fashioned here, from furniture to fine walking staves. The master here can make scroll tubes of oiled hardwood that are strong, light, and waterproof (2 gp).

AREA H-3: BOWYER & FLETCHER

Two brothers who excel in the manufacture of bows and arrows (but not crossbows) staff this shop. Magical bows and arrows are available here, as are specialty arrows (see Table). They know nearly everything pertaining to the wilderness area outside the city. They also make Arb Angus' personal hunting bow and arrows, and regard him very highly (paraphrase rumors to that effect).

SPECIALTY ARROWS

Item	Cost	Weight	Note
Hollow message arrow (20)	5 gp	3 lb	These arrows come with hollow shafts for holding a rolled sheet of paper
Whistling arrow (20)	2 gp	3 lb	See Pathfinder Roleplaying Game Ultimate Equipment
Glass vial arrow (5)	10 gp	1 lb	These arrowheads can carry one alchemical vial, potion, or dose of poison
Incendiary arrow (20)	10 gp	3 lb	See Pathfinder Player Companion: Ranged Tactics Toolbox

Gerg & Fej

Gerg and **Fej** spent their youth in the surrounding forest and are expert huntsmen; anyone sharing at least 1 hour with them or buying them a drink gains a +1 circumstance bonus to all subsequent Survival checks in the Eamonvale region.

Gerg and Fej	CR 5

XP 1,600
hp 45 (Pathfinder Roleplaying Game GameMastery Guide, "Monster Hunter")

Area H-4: Mendon's Office

In this small but finely appointed room, **Herrick Mendon** manages the entire Crafthall. He is employed by Arb Angus to purchase much of the raw material in bulk and resell it to the craftsmen; with the financial backing of the Lord's coffers, he can afford large quantities and makes a profit for Angus while selling it to shops at the normal rate. All the materials, both raw and finished, are catalogued by him and locked in the vast storeroom beneath the workshops. A locked trapdoor (1 in. thick; Hardness 5; hp 15; Break [DC 18]; Disable Device [DC 30]) reveals a narrow staircase to the storeroom (**Area H-12**).

Mendon is unscrupulous, miserly, and materialistic, but an excellent choice for the job he does. His appetite matches his purse, his girth is perhaps the greatest in the city, and he is almost always eating some delicate confection or exotic grilled treat.

Herrick Mendon   CR 7
XP 3,200
Human expert 9
LE Medium humanoid (human)
Init -4; **Senses** Perception -4

***

AC 12, touch 12, flat-footed 12 (+2 deflection)
hp 39 (9d8+18)
Fort +0, **Ref** -1, **Will** +2
Speed 30 ft.

***

Melee dagger +1/-4 (1d4-1/19-20)

***

Str 8, **Dex** 10, **Con** 12, **Int** 14, **Wis** 10, **Cha** 13
Base Atk +6; **CMB** +1; **CMD** 13
Feats Skill Focus (Appraise), Skill Focus (Bluff), Skill Focus (Diplomacy), Skill Focus (Knowledge [local]), Skill Focus (Knowledge [nobility]), Skill Focus (Profession [merchant])
Skills Appraise +13 (+15 for small or highly detailed items when using a magnifying glass, +15 on items valued by weight when using scales), Bluff +12, Diplomacy +12, Intimidate +9, Knowledge (local) +13, Knowledge (nobility) +13, Profession (merchant) +11, Ride +8, Sense Motive +8
Languages Common, Dwarven, Elven
Other Gear dagger, ring of protection +2, magnifying glass, merchant's scale, noble's outfit, 65 gp, 30 sp, keys to the Crafthall doors

Note: Herrick Mendon has accumulated 4 negative levels due to Lilith's embrace. The penalties have been factored in above (-4 to all d20 rolls and -20 hit points).

Area H-5: Leather Goods

This shop is geared toward the manufacture and sale of leather products including satchels and bags, clothing and armor (leather, studded, or hide). Elaborate book covers, scroll tubes, map cases, quivers, and scabbards are all available as well. They also manufacture the highly heat-resistant work clothing for the forges; for a 20% increase in price and weight, any leather clothing or armor can be made to provide resist fire 1.

Area H-6: Binder & Parchment Maker

A wizened old gnome and his assistants run this foul-smelling shop, where great vats of pulp simmer over red-hot braziers. The gnome offers parchment, paper, and books (including spellbooks) of many sizes, some with high quality latches or locks on the cover.

Area H-7: Tinsmith

Tin, bronze, copper, and other metals are shaped into implements and utensils in this hot, smoky shop. Cutlery, pots and pans, containers, and decorative coverings are all made here.

Area H-8: Weaver

Several massive looms clatter back and forth in this large area, manned by a dozen workers. Three supervisors oversee the blending of colors and patterns. Only large quantities of trade-quality fabric can be purchased here.

Area H-9: The Finesmith

Crenshaw the Finesmith avoids taking jewelry commissions, focusing instead on decorative items, weapon hilts, frames, book covers, fasteners, and any other item requiring intricate metalwork. He collaborates regularly with other craftsmen, adding their skill to his to produce the magnificent wares displayed in this small shop. His apprentices make jewelry settings for the gnomes in Area **H-10**. Crenshaw is a slender man with a bad stutter and a permanent squint from wearing his monocle. He is a master craftsman of all detailed metalwork and any craft that requires it.

Crenshaw was also the victim of one of the burglaries, which may be the reason that draws the party to the Crafthall. All of this powdered silver was stolen from the locked, trapped vault (see Side Box) built into the floor. See Mystery Elements in Chapter Two for his comments.

Crenshaw the Finesmith	CR 9

XP 6,400
Human expert 11
LG Medium humanoid (human)
Init +1; **Senses** Perception +0

AC 11, touch 11, flat-footed 10 (+1 Dex)
hp 50 (11d8)
Fort +2, **Ref** +4, **Will** +7
Speed 30 ft.

Melee dagger +9/+4 (1d4+1/19-20)

Str 12, **Dex** 12, **Con** 8, **Int** 16, **Wis** 10, **Cha** 9
Base Atk +8; **CMB** +9; **CMD** 20
Feats Skill Focus (Craft [armor]), Skill Focus (Craft [blacksmith]), Skill Focus (Craft [gemcutting]), Skill Focus (Craft [jewelry]), Skill Focus (Craft [locks]), Skill Focus (Craft [weapons]), Skill Focus (Knowledge [dungeoneering])
Skills Appraise +17 (+19 for small or highly detailed items when using a monocle), Craft (armor) +25, Craft (blacksmith)

+25, Craft (gemcutting) +25, Craft (jewelry) +25, Craft (locks) +25, Craft (weapons) +25, Disable Device +15, Knowledge (arcana) +17, Knowledge (dungeoneering) +23
Languages Common, Dwarven, Elven, Gnome
Other Gear dagger, all tools vest, traveler's any-tool, monocle, 3 keys to the floor vault

Area H-10: The Gemcutter's Shop

Entirely staffed by gnomes, the gemcutter's shop is a hushed and secretive place amid the clatter and bustle of the Crafthall. In addition to selling their own precious stones, the gnomes will consider buying stones as well, cut or uncut, provided they are worth at least 500 gp in their finished state.

Area H-11: The Lift

At the far end of the Crafthall is the huge lift used to move heavy loads of materials into and out of the storeroom. A sturdy gated railing to prevent accidents surrounds a 10-foot by 10-foot lift. That section of floor is reinforced with heavy beams and connected at each corner to block and tackle with thick hemp ropes. The ropes can be tied off to iron cleats for loading and unloading, but the lift is always stored in the lowered position. A successful DC 25 Strength check is required to raise the lift; up to 4 characters can cooperate on this check. One character must secure the lift. Should the lift fall on anyone, they must succeed on a DC 15 Reflex saving throw or take 11d6 bludgeoning damage. At night, a sturdy set of double doors (1 in. thick; Hardness 5; hp 20; Break [DC 23]; Disable Device [DC 30]; to **Area H-12**) are closed over the opening and padlocked by Mendon.

Area H-12: The Storeroom

This massive warehouse takes up the entire lower level of the Crafthall. All raw materials and finished goods are stored here: limber, bales of wool, refined metals, furniture, bolts of fabric, barrels, and boxes are all around. Half of this level is below ground, and a wide ramp leads up to double doors opening onto the Market. A staircase leads up to a trapdoor to Mendon's office (**Area H-4**), which is locked

Trapped Iron Floor Vault

Trapped Iron Floor Vault. 2 in. thick; Hardness 10; hp 60; Break (DC 28); Disable Device (DC 40; unique triple lock). The unique triple lock consists of three keys that must be turned in a particular order to avoid arming the trap.

Opening the vault without using the three keys in the proper order triggers a cascading *lightning bolt* trap.

Cascading Lightning Bolt Trap	CR 6

XP 2,400
Type magical; **Perception** DC 28; **Disable Device** DC 28 (inside the vault) DC 40 (outside the vault)
Trigger opening vault without using 3 keys in proper order; **Reset** automatic
Effect spell effect (three *lightning bolts* one after another in the same round, 6d6 damage each, Reflex DC 15 half each)

The vault contains 80 gp, 12 silver ingots worth 20 gp each, silver wire worth 20 gp, gold leaf worth 80 gp, gold wire worth 100 gp, six gold ingots worth 60 gp each, a platinum ingot worth 200 gp, an envelope of mithral chips worth 200 gp, six works in progress (sword hilts, latches, book binding, and so forth) worth 2d6 x 10 gp in materials.

from the other side. The large doors above the lift are also locked from above at night (see **Area H-11**).

Mendon keeps watch over an entrance to the underground caverns hidden in this storeroom. The passageway is concealed under the flagstones directly beneath the lift. As the lift is always stored in the lowered position and as the flagstones are not a good place to be while the lift is in use, the secret passageway is fairly safe. To discover the entrance, the party will need to open the large double doors above and raise the lift. With the lift raised, a successful DC 15 Perception check is needed to locate the loose paving stones in the floor. When the stones are lifted, a rush of moist, stale air is released—an indicator of the flooded crypt below. The opening leads to dungeon **Area 1-4**.

Area I: The Temple of Fortitude

The Temple sits in a large open section in the lower city. A majority of the population of the Grey Citadel worships the God of Strength, Strym, as do most of the hardy farmers, hunters, and trappers who live and work beyond the city walls. Strength, endurance, and perseverance are requisite qualities for survival in the harsh landscape of the frontier, and the congregation and clergy of the Temple of Fortitude embody such qualities and more. Part of the recent success of the Temple is due to the leadership of **Cael Angus**, the young Master and spiritual leader (see **Appendix C**). He has developed a way to support the Temple with a minimum of required tithes: while not engaged in training, meditation, or maintenance, **acolytes** from the Temple hire themselves out as stevedores in the Caravan Camp. The merchants are glad to have a workforce that is strong, diligent, and not too eager to head for the taverns, and the acolytes give most of their earnings to the Temple coffers.

While the investigation of the mystery may lead the party here, the Temple does not play a major role in this adventure. Enough information is provided here to support the plot, but mapping the area and developing further personalities for its inhabitants are up to you. In addition to the acolytes, a few **priests** are always on hand to deal with emergencies of faith or injury.

Cael Angus, Master of the Temple of Fortitude   CR 9
XP 6,400
hp 55 (Appendix C: NPC Descriptions, "Cael Angus Master of the Temple of Fortitude")

Temple Acolyte   CR 1/3
XP 135
hp 5 (Pathfinder Roleplaying Game NPC Codex, "Acolyte")

Priest of Strength   CR 3
XP 800
Human cleric 4
CG Medium humanoid (human)
Init +0; **Senses** Perception +6

AC 10, touch 10, flat-footed 10
hp 25 (4d8+4)
Fort +5, **Ref** +1, **Will** +6
Speed 30 ft.

Melee unarmed strike +6 (1d3+3)
Special Attacks channel positive energy 5/day (DC 14, 2d6)
Domain Spell-Like Abilities (CL 4th; concentration +6)
  5/day—strength surge (+2), touch of good (+2)
Cleric Spells Prepared (CL 4th; concentration +6)
  2nd—*bull's strength*[D], *hold person* (DC 14), *shield other*, *zone of truth* (DC 14)
  1st—*bless, bless water* (DC 13), *detect evil, protection from evil*[D], *sanctuary* (DC 13)

0 (at will)—*detect magic, detect poison, guidance, read magic*
D Domain spell; **Domains** Good, Strength

Str 16, **Dex** 10, **Con** 12, **Int** 8, **Wis** 15, **Cha** 14
Base Atk +3; **CMB** +6; **CMD** 16
Feats Cleave, Improved Unarmed Strike, Power Attack
Skills Heal +9, Knowledge (religion) +6, Perception +6
Languages Common
Other Gear wooden holy symbol

Special Abilities

Strength Surge (5/day) (Sp) Grant +2 to a melee attack or strength check.
Touch of Good +2 (5/day) (Sp) Grant +2 to skill checks, ability checks and saving throws for 1 rd.

Area I-1: The Entry Vault

This chamber is built from huge blocks of grey stone, but floored with imported marble. On the sides of the short corridor are six massive statues of the God of Strength, Strym, facing inward. Two of the six are actually **stone golems**, enchanted by an earlier priest to protect the Temple; they periodically rearrange themselves and the other, inert statues. They are activated by a command word known only to Cael or one of his ranking clerics, one of which is always in attendance. They also animate automatically if any of the holy relics are removed without Cael's authority, if a weapon is drawn in anger anywhere in the Temple, or if any magic other than that granted by the patron god is used there.

Stone Golem (2)   CR 11
XP 12,800
hp 107 (Pathfinder Roleplaying Game Bestiary, "Golem, Stone")

Area I-2: The Chamber of Worship

This vast room is bare of any decoration except for a massive symbol of the God of Strength, Strym opposite the entry. There are no pews or benches, only a bare stone floor on which to conduct the rituals and tests of strength and physical prowess that constitute the acts of faith for the devout. Wrestling matches, strength training, combat training, and sparring bouts are all held here; no activity is sacrilege unless it shows weakness under the gaze of the patron deity.

Columns run the length of the chamber, supporting the vaulted ceiling. Between the columns are doors leading to **Areas 3–9**. Above the doors, huge windows let the grey light filter in. A few acolytes are always here, either training or performing maintenance tasks and who can welcome the heroes and summon Master Cael at their request.

Area I-3: The Chapel

This small room is decorated with a few finely crafted tapestries of various trials of strength. A dozen stone benches are arranged before a simple altar. This chapel is reserved for silent meditation or important rituals.

Area I-4: The Dormitory

In this long, narrow room are the beds and personal effects of the Temple's acolytes. Each bunk has a rough woolen blanket and straw mattress, and the footlockers hold only the most basic personal items.

Area I-5: The Priest's Quarters

These simple rooms allow the clerics of the God of Strength, Strym space and privacy for their chosen studies and meditations. Each one holds a bed, wardrobe, washbasin, and chamber pot. Most have a small bookcase with the cleric's personal writings and a few treasured books detailing the many instances of manifestation of avatars of their deity. One bookcase is kept vacant for visiting clerics of the same (or even a sympathetic) faith.

Area I-6: Cael's Quarters

The Master's chamber is as stark as the rest of the Temple. He has a wardrobe with his ceremonial clothing and a large table covered with correspondence, research, and notes. A large chest holds his most precious holy icons and texts. He sleeps on the same type of straw mattress as the acolytes.

Area I-7: The Refectory

In this long chamber, the priests and acolytes prepare and eat their meals. Long tables and benches run down both sides of the room. A huge fireplace dominates one end of the room, including a roasting spit, bread ovens, and a smoking cabinet. The occupants of the Temple cook and clean for themselves, making food on long tables and washing in an enormous cauldron on the hearth. A trapdoor in the floor leads to the cellar, where dry goods are stored.

Area I-8: Storeroom

In this tiny, neat room the priests store all manner of training devices for use in the Chamber of Worship. Wooden weapons, padded armor, weights, climbing ropes, and all sorts of strength building aids can be found here.

Area I-9: The Courtyard

This enclosure provides another venue of meditation. It also hosts the Temple's vegetable and herb gardens. Several stone benches situated under fruit trees allow space for reflection. A black and white tile patio serves as a board for games of chess; the oversized game pieces are in a small shed (which also holds one of Elinda's clues, as described in the Mystery Elements section of Chapter Two).

Area J: The Garrison

The garrison is a large, two-story wooden building on a stone foundation. It is big enough to house, feed, and train the members of the Mist Watch. Bron and the high-ranking officers have quarters here, and the building also holds an armory and a jail.

The Garrison is not intimately involved in this adventure. It is a likely location for a meeting with **Bron Angus** (see **Appendix C** for his description) or a sure destination for heroes who make trouble in the city. It consists of several large dormitories, an armory, a training ground, a cell block, and a mess hall and quarters for the officers and commanders.

A Mist Watch patrol consists of 9 **mist watch soldiers**, 1 **mist watch sergeant**, with a 25% chance of 1 **constable** and a 10% chance of 1 **Mist Mage**.

Bron Angus, Captain of the Mist Watch   CR 11
XP 12,800
hp 94 (Appendix C: NPC Descriptions, "Bron Angus, Captain of the Mist Watch")

Mist Mage (10% chance)   CR 5
XP 1,600
hp 33 (Pathfinder Roleplaying Game GameMastery Guide, "Battle Mage")

Mist Watch Soldier (9)   CR 1
XP 400
hp 19 (Pathfinder Roleplaying Game GameMastery Guide, "Guard")

Mist Watch Sergeant   CR 3
XP 800
hp 34 (Pathfinder Roleplaying Game GameMastery Guide, "Guard Officer")

Mist Watch Constable (25% chance)   CR 7
XP 3,200
hp 49 (Pathfinder Roleplaying Game NPC Codex, "Constable")

Area K: The Keep

The castle and keep of the Angus clan are not integral to the plot of this adventure. This description offers a venue to meet with Lord Angus; any further exploration is beyond the scope of this module and left to you.

Area K-1: The Gatehouse

The gate usually stands open during the day, guarded by a Mist Watch patrol that consists of 9 **mist watch soldiers**, 1 **mist watch sergeant**, with a 25% chance of 1 **constable** and a 10% chance of 1 **Mist Mage**. A **steward** is always here as well, handling castle business and taking requests for audiences with Arb Angus. As often as not, however, Angus is here himself, meeting with his citizens in an informal manner, though important issues are discussed within the castle walls.

The Gatehouse is easily defended with an array of arrow slits, murder holes, two sets of ironclad doors, and a portcullis, which is closed at night. Use the description of the city gatehouse (**Area A**) for more details.

Mist Mage (10% chance)   CR 5
XP 1,600
hp 33 (Pathfinder Roleplaying Game GameMastery Guide, "Battle Mage")

Mist Watch Soldier (9)   CR 1
XP 400
hp 19 (Pathfinder Roleplaying Game GameMastery Guide, "Guard")

Mist Watch Sergeant   CR 3
XP 800
hp 34 (Pathfinder Roleplaying Game GameMastery Guide, "Guard Officer")

Mist Watch Constable (25% chance)   CR 7
XP 3,200
hp 49 (Pathfinder Roleplaying Game NPC Codex, "Constable")

Steward   CR 2
XP 600
hp 22 (Pathfinder Roleplaying Game NPC Codex, "Heir Apparent")

Arb Angus, Lord of Eamonvale   CR 13
XP 25,600
hp 73 (Appendix C: NPC Descriptions, "Arb Angus, Lord of Eamonvale")

Area L: The Wizard's Tower

Elinda's Bannon's tower is situated on the parapet wall just below where it joins the castle wall. Her family has lived there for several generations — for as long as they have been loyal servants of the ruling family. Elinda is the first generation in two centuries not to serve the Angus clan directly as a steward, bailiff, or in some other official role. Instead, she provides counsel to the brothers on the various elements of arcane magic and its relationship to government.

The tower itself has been heavily modified to suit Elinda's needs as a wizard. She keeps only a small apartment on the second floor; the rest is dedicated to her research. The entire tower is extensively warded against intrusion, as the heroes will likely find out if and when their investigation leads them here.

A wealth of treasure here might reward heroes that survive the defenses, but they will have to answer for it if Elinda is rescued (see Chapter Eight: Resolution).

A flight of stairs leads up to the parapet wall from the edge of the city neighborhoods. Citizens are not permitted on the wall, so the **Mist Watch lookouts** present the first line of defense for Elinda's tower. Heroes intending to enter must possess a writ of admittance from Lord Angus or be willing to approach using stealth under cover of darkness or distraction. Angus is not unwilling to authorize the heroes to enter if their investigation is proceeding well, but he warns them that he can do nothing about the wards.

Mist Watch Lookout (2)   **CR 1**
XP 400
hp 19 (Pathfinder Roleplaying Game GameMastery Guide, "Guard")

Area L-1: The Hallway of Doors

A locked iron door (2 in. thick; Hardness 10; hp 60; Break [DC 28]; Disable Device [DC 30]; radiates magic) seals the entrance to the tower. Opening the door by any means other than the single magical key (in Lilith's possession) arms all the traps on the approach to Elinda's apartments.

The lowest level of her tower has been reworked into a long, winding corridor divided into sections by normal wooden doors. This corridor is sprinkled with single-use traps that range from mildly embarrassing to potentially deadly. In some cases, the doors themselves are trapped; in others, the spaces between them are trapped. Each time a trap is triggered, a *magic mouth* (in the form of perfect, red female lips) appears to speak some command words. A Spellcraft check can be used to discern the spell as normal, but *dispel magic* attempts only eliminate the *magic mouth*, not the spell connected to the trap.

Stepping through the first wooden door triggers a *teleport* trap.

Teleport Trap   **CR 6**
XP 2,400
Type magical; **Perception** DC 30; **Disable Device** DC 30
Trigger location; **Reset** automatic
Effect spell effect (*teleport* to the center of the Market [Area E]; *disguise self* to change skin color purple; Will DC 17 negates)

The second door is unlocked, but when it is opened the *rock to mud to rock* trap on the floor in front of it triggers.

Rock to Mud to Rock Trap   **CR 5**
XP 1,600
Type magical; **Perception** DC 28; **Disable Device** DC 28
Trigger location; **Reset** automatic
Effect spell effect (*transmute rock to mud* spell, targets sink to waist depth, targets have one round to try to find some way out of the mud; beginning of next round the *transmute mud to rock* spell triggers, floor reforms into solid stone; Reflex DC 17 avoids)

The third door is unlocked and has an iron key hanging on a chain next to it. The key has a cloth tag on it which has "unwelcome" written on it. Reading the tag aloud triggers the *suggestion* trap on it.

Suggestion Trap   **CR 6**
XP 2,400
Type magical; **Perception** DC 28; **Disable Device** DC 28
Trigger command word; **Reset** automatic
Effect spell effect (*suggestion*); "go report your commendable activities here to the commander of the garrison"; Will DC 14 negates

The fourth door is protected with several *arcane eye* traps: one on the knob, one on the hinges, and one on the frame. These traps are not dangerous, but they are intended to help Elinda identify intruders.

Arcane Eye Trap   **CR 2**
XP 600
Type magical; **Perception** DC 22; **Disable Device** DC 22
Trigger location; **Reset** automatic
Effect spell effect (*arcane eye* and *silent image* "photograph" the room; silent images appear in Elinda's workshop [Area L-9])

The fifth door is unlocked but turning the knob activates a *maximized burning hands* trap placed on the door.

Maximized Burning Hands Trap   **CR 2**
XP 600
Type magical; **Perception** DC 26; **Disable Device** DC 26
Trigger location; **Reset** automatic
Effect spell effect (*maximized burning hands*); 20 fire damage; multiple targets (15 ft cone); Reflex DC 11 halves

The sixth door is unlocked and untrapped, but the floor beyond it hides a pit trap.

Pit Trap   **CR 5**
XP 2,400
Type magical and mechanical; **Perception** DC 20; **Disable Device** DC 20
Trigger location; **Reset** manual
Effect 20-ft fall into cistern (2d6 falling damage); DC 20 Reflex avoids; multiple targets (all targets in a 10-ft.-square area); apply drowning rules, heavy beam on chains (Atk + 15, 1d6 bludgeoning damage); triggers at beginning of second round; DC 15 + damage inflicted Reflex save avoids falling into pit; multiple targets (all targets on entry side of the pit), spell effect (*summon monster IV*); triggers at beginning of third round; 1d4 + 1 small water elementals appear in the cistern; duration (8 rounds)

Area L-2: The Stairwell

A spiral staircase leads upward from the end of the winding corridor. Additional traps could be placed on its steps, if desired.

Area L-3: Corridor

The hallway bisects the tower from the spiral staircase to a narrow window on the opposite side. On either side of the corridor are 2 doors. The staircase continues up to Area **L-8**.

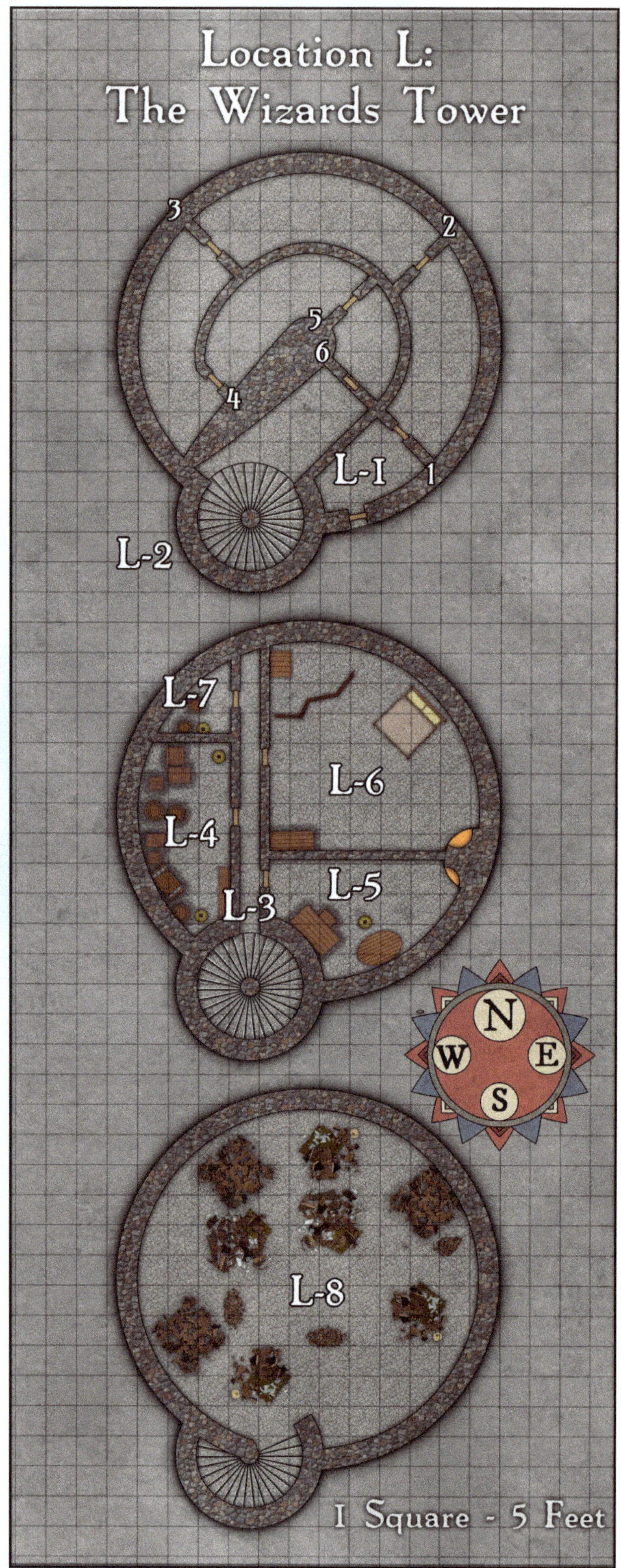

AREA L-4: THE SITTING ROOM

This is a simple, neat room in which Elinda entertains prospective clients and longtime friends. It holds comfortable horsehair chairs, potted plants, and a small bookcase filled with a few books on non-magical subjects. With the help of *unseen servants*, Elinda can rearrange this room for a dinner party when the mood strikes her.

On the wall amid several oil paintings of family members is a wooden plaque; it bears no inscription, only two brass hooks. This is where Elinda's foster father's *+1 keen shortsword* hung until she took it as she left (the other part of the matched pair is in **Area S: Stump's Hovel**). A successful DC 18 Perception check reveals that the lacquer is faded around the outline of a sheathed sword.

AREA L-5: THE KITCHEN

Elinda's kitchen is small but functional. A fireplace in a corner has an opening in the chimney to her bedchamber. A tall table and stools provide an area for food preparation and dining. A wooden pantry holds her food supplies, mostly dry goods bought in bulk for her long journeys. On the table are a full water skin, some small crusty loaves, and a cheese wrapped in wax that Elinda prepared for her mission but then left behind to save weight. Also scattered around are several open sacks and boxes of food, salted herring, nuts, and dried fruit — more evidence of her frantic packing.

AREA L-6: THE BEDCHAMBER

Elinda's bedchamber is back-to-back with the kitchen, sharing its chimney. She has an elegant canopy bed, a large wardrobe, a large chest, a dressing screen, and a washbasin.

The wardrobe is filled with her everyday working garments (leather breeches and linen shirts), her traveling clothes, and a few fine gowns. A dressmaker's mannequin stands inside wearing nothing but a non-magical leather cap with an iron band around it (she took the rest of her suit of magical leather armor when she left).

The locked chest (Hardness 5; hp 15; Break [DC 23]; Disable Device [DC 28]) contains Elinda's family heirlooms. In it are the symbols of office of previous agents of the Angus family. The chest contains the symbols of office of previous agents of the Angus family (an amulet, a circlet, a scepter, and so on), collectively worth 700 gp in materials alone and much more to an antiquarian with an interest in the region; a pouch with 500 gp; a large emerald (800 gp); a rod of solid platinum (200 gp); and a small pouch of mithral shavings (30 gp).

AREA L-7: PRIVY

A small chamber past the parlor holds a simple privy. A few books sit on a small stand; one of them is false and holds a *potion of neutralize poison*.

AREA L-8: THE LIBRARY

This room holds Elinda's extensive library, now in disarray from her battle with Lilith. The large, circular chamber is a picture of destruction. The finely carved bookshelves that once encircled it have been smashed into kindling, and book and papers are strewn in shin-deep piles from wall to wall. Visible amidst the wreckage are an ornate writing desk, a rolling ladder, a divan, and a sideboard, all upended and badly damaged. Many clues to the mystery can be found here, as well as the secret needed to find and unlock the door to Elinda's workshop. Sorting through the literature on the floor is a week's worth of work, and non-magical texts exist on every possible subject, in no particular order. Randomly generate the subject on any volume picked up off the floor, as appropriate to your campaign world. Other contents of the room, however, are more useful.

The sideboard has been overturned, but most of its contents, in crystal decanters, are intact (total value 300 gp). Elinda kept a valuable stock of spirits on hand for when her gnome mentor (Stump) could be talked into a visit. She also kept a few potions here for easy access; she took most of these when she left, but in her rush, she took the cognac and left a single *potion of cure serious wounds*.

The divan, once comfortably stuffed and upholstered in red velvet, now has a large "X" slashed into the middle cushion. Beneath the stuffing is a wooden panel that can be found by a character who makes a successful DC 18 Perception check with a recess that is best described as "a large 'T'-shaped indentation with a curved top and a dozen small holes on either side." This is where Elinda kept her crossbow and magical bolts, and she took them in a hurry when she left to pursue Lilith.

The greatest wealth of information can be found on the desk, which lies on its back in the middle of the room. A single sheet of paper, which radiates mild Transmutation magic, lies across the drawers (a hint that it was left after the desk was tipped). This is an important clue; see the Mystery Elements section in Chapter Two for a full description.

The desk also conceals the secret of Elinda's hidden workshop and is extensively trapped against intruders. The paneled front of the roll-top is stuck, but can be forced free with a successful DC 10 Strength check. Forcing the desk open breaks off the front knobs, so that the two tanglefoot bags mounted inside burst forth, automatically hitting the character or characters who forced the desk. A hidden catch that opens the desk without breaking the bags can be found with a successful DC 20 Perception check.

Once the top of the desk is opened, the assortment of quills, parchments, and spilled ink is a mess, but the blotting paper is the only thing that appears to have stayed in place. It is lightly stuck to the desktop with adhesive and comes free easily. On the underside are a few words in elegant script that read, "When nimble fingers come to pry, I beg them to stay, to answer why," and include a *sepia snake sigil* trap.

Sepia Snake Sigil Trap   **CR 4**
XP 1,200
Type magic; **Perception** DC 28; **Disable Device** DC 28
Trigger spell (sepia snake sigil); **Duration** 1d4 + 9 days;
    Reset none
Effect spell effect (*sepia snake sigil*); DC 14 Reflex save
    negates

On the panel below the blotter is a lock, which is broken, but the key hangs from a satin ribbon on a small nail inside the desk. If the key or any other sharp object is inserted into the keyhole, it bursts a bladder of grick brain juice, spraying the user. Using the key in this way does nothing to release the *arcane lock* that secures the panel.

Grick Brain Juice Trap   **CR 2**
XP 600
Type mechanical; **Perception** DC 20; **Disable Device** DC 25
Trigger location; **Reset** manual
Effect grick brain juice (paralysis); DC 13 Fortitude negates

When the panel is finally removed by magic or force, a carved message on the underside reads "Welcome" and triggers *explosive runes* that will be especially dangerous to anyone whose save is penalized or denied due to entanglement, immobilization, or paralysis.

Maximized Explosive Runes   **CR 7**
XP 3,200
Type magic; **Perception** DC 28; **Disable Device** DC 28
Trigger spell; **Reset** none
Effect spell effect (36 force damage); multiple targets (all
    creatures within 10 feet of the rune); Anyone next to the
    explosive runes takes the full damage with no saving throw;

any other creature within 10 feet of the *explosive runes* can make a DC 16 Reflex save for half damage

This arrangement may seem excessively frustrating (or deadly), but it is with good reason. Beneath the false top is one of a pair of *ring gates*, one of Elinda's most prized magical items. It is built into a wooden recess just the right size, and through it the stone floor of her workshop is visible. Her workshop is actually a tiny cottage located miles away in the middle of an impassable bog (see Area **L-9**). The other ring is built into the underside of a table in the workshop. When Elinda steps through the top of her desk, she drops to the floor in the workshop. She crafted a *tightfit belt* which allows her to use the *ring gate* more than once each day. She took this belt with her, so the heroes will need to find their own means of fitting through (**Note:** the limits of the *ring gate* may strand some or all of the heroes on either side, depending on their combined weight).

AREA L-9: THE WORKSHOP

Elinda's laboratory and workshop are hidden nearly 80 miles away from Dun Eamon. She keeps a small cottage (built with *fabricate* and *unseen servants*) in the middle of the Trackless Mire, a notorious peat bog that is inhospitable to all. No crofters or trappers cross its marshes, no predators hunt its moors; in fact, with the exception of its rich bird and insect life, nothing is there at all — truly a perfect place for a secret retreat. The floor is stone, the walls paneled in wood, and the roof is of thatch. Two closed windows and a well-made door keep out natural light; outside, a gentle wind rattles the shutters. Like the library, books and papers are strewn about, as well as bent and twisted metal, shattered glass, splashes of colored liquids, and a battered birdcage. The walls, floor, and ceiling are scored with sooty black lines in an irregular, feathery pattern.

If the heroes open the door or windows, they will see that they are no longer in the city, nor is it even visible. Instead, they see only a bleak moor covered with wind-blown heather and the occasional outcropping of rock. Travel across the moor is dangerous due to hidden caves, deep bogs, and sinkholes. It is 50 miles in any direction to the nearest settlement and 80 miles to Dun Eamon. No navigational landmarks are visible in the drifting mist.

Elinda's workshop was the place where she did most of her tinkering, both experimenting with ancient magical items and devising items of her own creation. She kept here the portion of her massive library that pertained to her current projects. On the wall are three wooden frames holding *silent images* that probably show the party struggling with the traps in **Area L-1**. These are invariably poor images and depict the party picking and scratching where they should not be. The frames can be destroyed, but nothing short of that removes the *images*.

Two long benches stand along opposite walls, covered with tools, dirty dishes, bits of broken mechanical components, and grease-stained notes. A table in the middle of the room (the one with the *ring gate* in the bottom) is covered with books, scrolls, loose papers, and wooden crates (of more papers). The birdcage is empty, but holds one of Elinda's clues described in the Mystery Elements section of Chapter Two. The clutter and destruction combine to make finding anything of value here difficult, but there is a treasure of several magic items. A successful DC 15 Perception check produces one of the following: *goggles of minute seeing*, *sustaining spoon* (in a dirty bowl), *wand of magic missiles* (CL 5, 6 charges), 5 *arcane scrolls* (*ray of enfeeblement, knock, fly, stoneskin, teleport*), 3 potions (*alter self, levitate, water breathing*).

Note: As Elinda is a student of all things magical, her workshop could conceivably hold any item. If a particular item would greatly benefit the heroes (providing an ability they lack), it can be easily inserted here in place of one of the items listed above. Elinda is not concerned if her wand, potions, and scrolls are used to facilitate her rescue, but her *ring gates* and other valuable items should be returned.

Area M: The Shrine of the Sun

In the corner of the market is a forgotten shrine to the Sun God. A traveling cleric decided that the people of the Grey Citadel needed more sunshine in their lives and built the shrine with the permission of the Angus family. Despite the cleric's resolve, the damp climate finally wore him down, and he abandoned his efforts and departed for sunnier realms.

The shrine holds a secret compartment that can be found with a successful DC 25 Perception check. It will only open if in direct sunlight (or equivalent magical effect) and in contact with a holy symbol of the Sun God. Inside are four *divine scrolls* of *cure moderate wounds.* Only the Angus brothers (and the original cleric) know about these items.

Area N: The Seer's Parlor

This tiny, shabby storefront is marked only by a large purple eye painted over door. Inside, **Amarathea the Seer** offers divinations, charms, and readings, including tarot, palmistry, and other forms. The shop is set in the lower city, near the Caravan Camp (**Area C**). Amarathea was one of the victims of the robberies, and this may be what leads the party here (see the Mystery Elements section in Chapter Two for more information).

Inside the shop, charms and tokens of every sort hang from the ceiling, prompting customers to duck low upon entry. A beaded curtain screens the back half of the shop, though flickering candles can be seen beyond it. In that area, threadbare cushions surround a small round table. Amarathea is seated on the far side of the table, which is covered by trays of small pebbles, carved runes, tarot cards, and bones. A flat, polished crystal lens sits on a bed of velvet in the center of the table: Amarathea's (non-magical) scrying stone.

Amarathea the Seer	**CR 6**

XP 2,400
Halfling adept 8
N Small humanoid (halfling)
Init +3; **Senses** Perception +5

AC 14, touch 14, flat-footed 11 (+3 Dex, +1 size)
hp 28 (8d6)
Fort +2, **Ref** +6, **Will** +10; +2 vs. fear
Speed 20 ft.

Seer Spell-Like Ability (CL 8th; concentration +11)
  1 / day—*divination*
Adept Spells Prepared (CL 8th; concentration +11)
  3rd—*scrying* (DC 17)
  2nd—*augury, locate object, see invisibility*
  1st—*command* (DC 14), *hypnotism* (DC 15), *identify, protection from evil*
  0 (at will)—*detect magic, ghost sound* (DC 13), *guidance*

Str 8, **Dex** 16, **Con** 8, **Int** 12, **Wis** 16, **Cha** 16
Base Atk +4; **CMB** +2; **CMD** 15
Feats Enlarge Spell, Skill Focus (Knowledge [arcana]), Skill Focus (Knowledge [planes]), Spell Focus (divination)
Skills Acrobatics +5 (+1 to jump), Climb +1, Knowledge (arcana) +15, Knowledge (planes) +15, Perception +5, Spellcraft +12; **Racial Modifiers** +2 Acrobatics, +2 Climb, +2 Perception
Languages Common, Gnome, Halfling

Amarathea is a shrunken old woman with her graying hair in a tight bun. Her gift has manifested itself in every generation in her home village due to a shattered *crystal ball* lying in the bottom of their well. Like each seer before her, Amarathea was cast out of the village before her visions could bring harm, and she eventually found her way to Dun Eamon. Her spell list is adjusted to represent her unique gift.

Whether the heroes come here investigating the mystery or on their own business, Amarathea insists on a "seeing." She tries to extract payment of 3 gp, but does the reading for free if refused; she does this periodically when "an aura is unusually strong." The reading can take whatever form the player wishes: palmistry, tarot, or anything else; Amarathea can use her supernatural divination ability with any of them. Some or all of the following can be applied to one character's reading or to several party members, or you can devise your own cryptic divinations:

"*You have a journey before you. Impulsive departure will send you down the road unprepared, but restraint will ensure you take with you what you need.*" (She sees their imminent progress into the caverns. She can see that the information that awaits them in investigating the city will help them below.)

"*Darkness reaches out to do you harm; only by remaining alert and on guard will you prevail.*" (She can see the intended assassination[s] by the Ebon Union, although not with any specific detail).

"*Your actions are mirrored by others; one who seems a foe may yet become a friend.*" (She can see that the efforts of the Band of the Crimson Mantle are parallel to those of the party. She also knows that one of them — Yelm the Barbarian — is not committed to the path of evil.)

Area O: The Hole

When this tavern opened several decades ago, the new owner valued it more than anything "in the whole world." In fact, the iron-lettered sign outside still reads "The Whole World Tavern." The first "W" hangs at an angle from a single nail, and these days, the place is better known as "the Hole."

This disreputable drinking establishment is located in the lower city. It provides cheap beer, watered wine, and day-old bread, plus a kettle of something like soup is usually on the fire. Vodrik, the grandson of the original owner and current proprietor, makes it his business to ignore everything that goes on in his bar. Thus, the Hole is the location of choice for illegal transactions, dark conspiracies, and secret meetings — probably the only reason it is still open. The exterior doors and ground floor windows are sturdy and secure and locked after-hours (2 in. thick; Hardness 5; hp 20; Break [DC 23]; Disable Device [DC 25]). All the interior doors are locked as well (1 in. thick; Hardness 5; hp 13; Break [DC 13]; Disable Device [DC20]).

Area O-1: The Barroom

This main room is always dark and smoky. Its low ceiling is thickly woven with cobwebs, and every floorboard and barstool creaks with age. A short bar and two large kegs stand on one wall, and a small fire smolders in a hearth at the back. The tables are round, allowing more privacy for the small groups of men that huddle there. Weapons are never collected at the door, and most customers leave their cloaks on, ready to run out at a moment's notice. The following are regular encounters at the Hole:

Area O-2: The Taproom

This small storeroom behind the bar is where Vodrik keeps (and waters down) the wine and ale. A small pantry of dry goods holds ingredients bought from the week-old bins in Grocer's Lane: sprouting potatoes, worm-eaten turnips, and stunted carrots better fit for horses than humans. A back door opens onto the alley behind the bar, and a narrow staircase leads up to the loft.

Area O-3: The Loft

Vodrik lives alone in this cramped room above the bar. A pallet bed, a pile of musty clothes, and a few dirty dishes are obvious. Hidden in the bedding are a purse with 185 gp and a *ring of swimming* given to him by his father (though neither of them were aware of its properties).

Area O-4: The Alley

Sometimes transactions take place behind the Hole in this refuse-choked alley. It is littered with smashed casks and rotting garbage and has 2d10 **rats** running about at any given time.

Rat (2d10)   CR 1/4
XP 100
hp 4 (Pathfinder Roleplaying Game Bestiary, "Rat, Common")

P: The Bathhouse

Note: This location includes a potentially lethal encounter with a guild assassin; character death is a strong possibility, and you may wish to modify this encounter accordingly.

The bathhouse is another of the Grey Citadel's unique institutions. Situated on the slope below the market, it takes advantage of a geothermal natural hot spring bubbling up from the volcanically active bedrock below the city. It is a gathering place for negotiating merchants, weary adventurers, and wayward lovers. Both public and private baths are available, as well as several services.

Baths: 5 sp per visit to the public bath, 2 gp per hour in a private room.
Refreshments: Food and drink available for private rooms only.
Laundry: 5 cp per client, undergarments only.
Massage: 1 sp per masseuse per hour, private rooms only.

Area P-1: The Entry

The main entrance to the baths is on the fringe of the market. Across a broad stone porch is a set of double doors, where one of the staff collects the fees and informs clients that no weapons larger than a dagger are permitted. Just inside are doors to the men's and women's dressing chambers and the main office and supply room. A corridor leads toward the back of the building and the private rooms.

Area P-2: The Office

The baths are run by a motherly old crone named **Dendra**, who seems to turn a blind eye to what goes on in the tubs but observes much more than is believed. She knows very little about Tabitha (see Area **P-6**, below). Her office is a simple affair, mostly dedicated to linens, with a small desk for bookkeeping. A staircase leads down to the laundry.

Dendra   CR 1
XP 400
hp 11 (Pathfinder Roleplaying Game GameMastery Guide, "Prostitute")

Area P-3: The Basement

In this steamy, stone-floored chamber, the hot water from the rubs above is used to do laundry for clients while they bathe. Any of the **bathhouse girls** who are not serving refreshments or providing massages upstairs are at work at the huge tubs. The girls have a distinct hierarchy: the newest ones do the hardest work, while the most established ones barely lift a finger. The talk here is mostly about the lack of business from Herrick Mendon (see the City Rumors Table in Chapter Two).

Barroom Personalities

Vodrik is the owner-operator of the Hole. He keeps a battleaxe under the counter and a *potion of bull's strength* among the bottles, more for self-preservation than for keeping order in his bar.

Vodrik   CR 3
XP 800
hp 23 (Pathfinder Roleplaying Game GameMastery Guide, "Barkeep")

Rorin is a fence and procurement agent for the Ebon Union; he finds buyers for their stolen goods and secures for them what is not worth the risk of stealing, such as food. He also maintains contact with Kinnan the Dark (see Area **C**).

Rorin   CR 2
XP 600
hp 20 (Pathfinder Campaign Setting: Isles of the Shackles, "Smuggler")

Yav is the local drunk and has been known to consume alcohol even while asleep in his usual chair near the fire. Every drink bought for him results in a rumor from the City Rumors Table (see Chapter Two) until he is too drunk to be coherent (after 1d6 more drinks than he has already consumed).

Yav   CR 1
XP 400
hp 23 (Pathfinder Roleplaying Game GameMastery Guide, "Drunkard")

Stump comes here to drink when his house gets tiresome. Unlike most of the clients, he listens carefully to everything said in his presence, regardless of how drunk he is.

Stump   CR 5
XP 1,600
hp 34 (Appendix C: NPC Descriptions, "Stump")

Drunken **Caravan Workers** are always present (2d4 of them).

Drunken Caravan Workers (2d4)   CR 1
XP 400
hp 23 (Pathfinder Roleplaying Game GameMastery Guide, "Drunkard")

Edgar comes in from the public stables each evening to sell information to Rorin.

Edgar   CR 1/2
XP 200
hp 10 (Pathfinder Roleplaying Game GameMastery Guide, "Farmer")

<table><tr><td>

Bathhouse Girl   CR 1
XP 400
hp 11 (*Pathfinder Roleplaying Game GameMastery Guide*, "Prostitute")

AREA P-4: THE DRESSING CHAMBERS

Here, clients change into the linen togas provided, putting their own garments into bags of netting to take into the public bath. An attendant is on hand to help clients undress and offer laundry services. The attendant in the men's chamber, a boy named **Ry**, is a thief as well, pilfering small coins from the client's pockets. If caught, he begs to be let off and may know an interesting rumor or two. A single door leads into the bath.

Ry   CR 1/2
XP 200
hp 5 (*Pathfinder Roleplaying Game GameMastery Guide*, "Pickpocket")

AREA P-5: THE PUBLIC BATH

A large, shallow pool occupies most of this torch-lit room. A ledge around the perimeter allows for seating, and the center of the pool is 4 feet deep. Steps descend from the edge nearest the door, and steaming water burbles from an iron pipe in one wall. At any given time, there are 3d8 occupants, 75% of whom are men. They converse in low voices or rest quietly, paying little attention to newcomers. If a conversation is initiated, bathers will know a random item from the City Rumors Table (see Chapter Two).

AREA P-6: PRIVATE BATHS

If a client expresses interest in a private room, an attendant is summoned from the laundry to escort him or her. The private rooms are small, with a round tub in the center of the floor, and are nicely furnished. An iron chandelier lights the room, a screen is provided for disrobing, and wooden planks are laid across the tub as a massage table. The attendants mention refreshments and massage services before leaving.

One of the masseuses is **Tabitha**, an assassin and member of the Ebon Union. If a single member of the party books a private bath any time after Timed Encounter 1.3: The Demons Attack (see Chapter Two), she sells or volunteers her "services" to take action against the lone character. She is fanatically loyal to the guild and eager to prove herself to Devlin.

Tabitha began working with the Ebon Union before they were expelled from their previous home; in fact, she was the one who traveled to the Grey Citadel and assessed the potential for the Ebon Union to set up an operation. She has told everyone that she is "looking for a new home for her several brothers" while "they handle selling the family farm." She serves Devlin by eliminating his rivals, as well as by distracting merchants and caravan guards. Rather than strike by force or lie in wait, she prefers to use her charms to get right under her victim's nose before dealing her deathblow. She is slim, dark-haired, and attractive.

Tabitha   CR 7
XP 3,200
Human assassin 3/unchained rogue 5
LE Medium humanoid (human)
Init +8; **Senses** Perception +10

AC 15, touch 15, flat-footed 10 (+4 Dex, +1 dodge)
hp 41 (8d8+5)
Fort +2, **Ref** +10, **Will** +1; +1 vs. poison
Defensive Abilities danger sense +1, evasion, improved uncanny dodge

</td><td>

Speed 30 ft.

Melee dagger +9 (1d4+4/19-20)
Special Attacks death attack (DC 15), sneak attack +5d6

Str 12, **Dex** 18, **Con** 10, **Int** 14, **Wis** 8, **Cha** 14
Base Atk +5; **CMB** +6; **CMD** 21
Feats Dodge, Improved Initiative, Mobility, Quick Draw, Run, Weapon Finesse
Skills Acrobatics +11 (+15 to jump with a running start), Bluff +13, Diplomacy +13, Disable Device +17, Disguise +13, Escape Artist +15, Perception +10, Sense Motive +10, Sleight of Hand +15, Stealth +15
Languages Common, Dwarven, Elven
SQ debilitating injury: bewildered, debilitating injury: disoriented, debilitating injury: hampered, poison use, rogue talents (quick disguise[APG], swift poison[APG]), trapfinding +2
Combat Gear blue whinnis (2); **Other Gear** dagger, silk robe with silk rope (10 ft.), 15 sp

Special Abilities

Death Attack (1d6+3 rnds, DC 15) (Ex) You can kill or paralyze for 1d6+3 rnds with a prepared sneak attack.
Debilitating Injury: Bewildered -2/-4 (Ex) Foe who takes sneak attack damage takes AC pen (more vs. striker) for 1 rd.
Debilitating Injury: Disoriented -2/-4 (Ex) Foe who takes sneak attack damage takes attack pen (more vs. striker) for 1 rd.
Debilitating Injury: Hampered (Ex) Foe who takes sneak attack damage has speed halved (and can't 5 ft step) for 1 rd.
Swift Poison (Ex) Poisoning a weapon becomes a move action.

Tactics: Tabitha waits, if possible, until the character is disrobed and enjoying the massage. After massaging (and studying) the character for 3 rounds, she attacks with the paralyze version of her death attack (unarmed, nonlethal). If this attack succeeds, and the character falls unconscious, she rolls the character off the boards and into the bath. Her robe is belted with a silk rope, which she removes and uses to bind the character's hands and feet. She holds him under the surface (tied, grappled, and pinned) until he drowns. Pending outside intervention, this character may be doomed, and Tabitha smiles quite evilly through the bubbles until he stops struggling. When he does, Tabitha removes the rope, collects her things, and slips out.

If the attack misses, Tabitha has a backup plan. She carries a small blade coated with blue whinnis poison. A character struck with a weapon coated with this poison must succeed on a DC 14 Fortitude saving throw or be poisoned. She attempts to wound the character and then defend herself until the first round has passed. If the character falls unconscious, Tabitha drowns him in the tub. If the character does not lose consciousness, Tabitha attempts to fight her way to the door and escape.

Blue Whinnis
Type poison (injury); **Save** Fortitude DC 14; **Frequency** 1/round for 2 rounds; **Cure** 1 save
Initial Effect 1 Con damage; **Secondary Effect** Unconsciousness for 1d3 hours

Needless to say, this encounter can complicate matters. If the character survives, he may (a) have a captive or (b) have to explain to the authorities why he killed his masseuse. If he did not survive the first attempt, it will appear he drowned in the bath, in which case Dendra contacts the Mist Watch and tries to minimize bad publicity. If

</td></tr></table>

he dies with an injury from the second attempt, the murder becomes very public. If a character is foolish enough to relinquish his weapons, remove his armor, *and* lie face down with his back to a total stranger, he may just deserve this fate!

AREA Q: THE IRONWORKS

This large stone building sits midway across the lower city, and its several chimneys constantly spouting smoke and fire make it easy to recognize. The renown of these ironworks is something with which the heroes should be familiar, for they are widely known as the finest in the realm. Harnessing the power of moving water to drive their bellows and regulate the cooling mechanisms, the ironworks of Dun Eamon have a more consistent temperature than most, and the quality metal goods they produce are widely sought. As with the Crafthall, the Angus family owns the building, and they grant the rights to work there to the most talented craftsmen. Ulf Ironfist is the best smith there and runs the ironworks for Lord Angus, who helps secure large quantities of quality ore at reasonable prices. The ringing of hammer and anvil and the shouts of workers can be heard from outside. Exterior doors (2 in. thick; Hardness 5; hp 20; Break [DC 23]; Disable Device [DC 25]) and ground floor windows are sturdy and secure. All interior doors here are locked (1 in. thick; Hardness 5; hp 13; Break [DC 13]; Disable Device [DC20]).

The Ironworks is a potentially exciting and lethal location for a fight. The heroes should have an opportunity to track a gang of housebreakers here on their way to the lair of the Ebon Union (see Timed Encounter 3.3, in Chapter Two). If the heroes accost them or are noticed, they fight rather than betray the secret of their location any further.

At some point, the heroes may investigate the Ironworks in connection with the mysterious events. The apprentices here revere Ulf's knowledge, but have no love for the wrath that arises when an important project is flawed or compromised. If the heroes can question an employee away from the master, they can relate information about Ulf's strange behavior (see the Mystery Elements section in Chapter Two).

AREA Q-1: ENTRANCE

A small, stone walled yard in front of the building provides a quiet place for workers to meet with a client. At any time, 1d3 **workers** are here, usually smoking their pipes and discussing forge practices. They each know 1 rumor from the City Rumors Table (see Chapter Two). In addition, they also know of Ulf's strange behavior, but only discuss it if questioned directly.

Worker (1d3)   **CR 4**
XP 1,200
hp 39 (Pathfinder Roleplaying Game NPC Codex, "Expert Blacksmith")

AREA Q-2: MAIN FLOOR

In this large, smoky room, a dozen men at anvils manufacture everything from horseshoes to axe heads. Grinding wheels, hand tools, and buckets of water and oil are arranged down both sides of the room, and the glowing mouths of the great forges gape on the back wall. A double door between the forges leads to the foundry; a single door at one end leads to the shop.

This area (as well as **Area Q-4**) is especially dangerous in combat. Coming in contact with the glowing coals in any of the forges deals 2d6 fire damage per round of contact. A number of items are left in the forges at any given time, and they are red-hot. Treat hot irons as

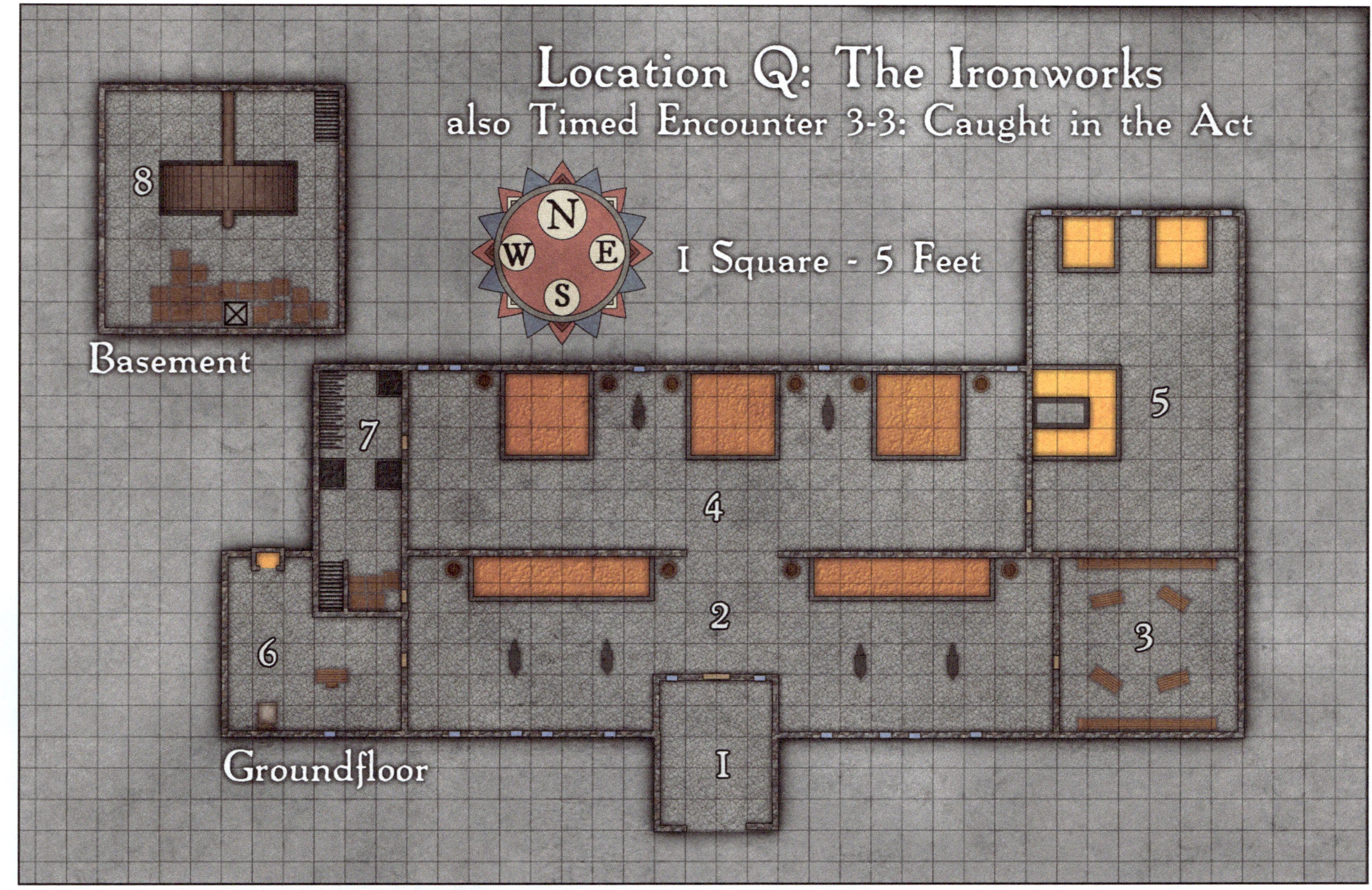

Location Q: The Ironworks
also Timed Encounter 3-3: Caught in the Act
1 Square - 5 Feet
N
W
E
S
Basement
8
Groundfloor
6
7
5
4
2
3
1

a longsword with the following modifications: –1 attack; the wielder must succeed on a DC 12 Fortitude save each round or suffer 1 fire damage; anyone wounded by an attack risks catching fire. Characters at risk of catching fire are allowed a DC 15 Reflex save to avoid this fate. If a character catches fire, they takes 1d6 points of damage immediately. In each subsequent round, the burning character must make another Reflex saving throw. Failure means they takes another 1d6 points of damage that round. Success means that the fire has gone out—that is, once he succeeds on his saving throw, he's no longer on fire. A character on fire may automatically extinguish the flames by jumping into enough water to douse themselves. If no body of water is at hand, rolling on the ground or smothering the fire with cloaks or the like permits the character another save with a +4 bonus.

AREA Q-3: THE SHOP

In this adjacent, windowless room, all the wares produced in the ironworks are for sale: tools, weapons, metal armor, and hardware. A dwarf named **Dregdim** runs the shop, and the door is locked (4 in. thick; Hardness 8; hp 40; Break [DC 25]; Disable Device [DC 35]) whenever he is away or in the foundry. The room also has a hidden floor vault.

The vault is incredibly secure (Hardness 10; hp 60; Break [DC 28]; Open Lock [DC 40]). It contains 1000 gp worth of precious metals that would only be useful to a metallurgist, and 200 gp in coins. All other items (such as mithral, finished magic items, and so forth) are locked in the Angus vault in the keep and catalogued for sale.

Dregdim   CR 4
XP 1,200
hp 39 (Pathfinder Roleplaying Game NPC Codex, "Expert
   Blacksmith")

AREA Q-4: THE FOUNDRY

This hot chamber is thick with fumes from smelted ores. All the mixing of metals is done here, as well as the casting of iron and steel. Several smaller forges stand back-to-back with the large ones in the other room. Ulf Ironfist and the other masters do their work here, where a larger range of furnace temperatures is available. Two huge anvils stand unused at one end of the room; at the other end, doors lead to the storeroom and Ulf's quarters. The forges here can be very dangerous during a fight (see **Area Q-2**, above).

When encountered at the ironworks, Ulf is usually in this room, supervising one project or another. Ulf is a strong, squat figure with a singed beard and a face that has been frequently scarred by flying slag. He is also missing the ring finger on his right hand, the result of an old foundry accident, and he hates being called "Ulf Nine-Fingers." Working with metal is his bread and butter; he has no time for anything else, including family or friends. He is the quintessential dwarf — gruff, deliberate, and resolute. He is the master smith of the ironworks, a lifetime craftsman, and a brilliant metallurgist. He oversees the efforts of a dozen forge laborers and also advises the other smiths and apprentices. Rarely, he will undertake a project himself, but only the most challenging (and lucrative) creations will entice him.

Ulf "Nine-Fingers" Ironfist   CR 13
XP 25,600
Dwarf expert 15
LG Medium humanoid (dwarf)
Init -6; **Senses** darkvision 60 ft.; Perception -6 (-4 to notice
   unusual stonework)

AC 11, touch 11, flat-footed 10 (+1 Dex)
hp 63 (15d8+30)
Fort +0, **Ref** -1, **Will** +3; +2 vs. poison, spells, and spell-like
   abilities

Defensive Abilities defensive training
Speed 20 ft.

Melee +2 warhammer +10/+5/+0 (1d8+5/×3)
Special Attacks hatred

Str 16, **Dex** 12, **Con** 15, **Int** 16, **Wis** 12, **Cha** 6
Base Atk +11; **CMB** +7 (+11 sunder); **CMD** 18 (22 vs. bull
   rush, 20 vs. sunder, 22 vs. trip)
Feats Combat Expertise, Greater Sunder, Improved Sunder,
   Power Attack, Skill Focus (Craft [armor]), Skill Focus (Craft
   [blacksmith]), Skill Focus (Craft [weapons]), Weapon Focus
   (warhammer)
Skills Acrobatics -6 (-10 to jump), Appraise +14 (+16 to
   assess nonmagical metals or gemstones), Bluff +9, Craft
   (armor) +22, Craft (blacksmith) +22, Craft (weapons) +22,
   Knowledge (arcana) +14, Knowledge (dungeoneering) +14,
   Knowledge (engineering) +14, Perception -6 (-4 to notice
   unusual stonework), Sense Motive +12, Spellcraft +14;
   Racial Modifiers +2 Appraise to assess nonmagical metals
   or gemstones, +2 Perception to notice unusual stonework
Languages Common, Dwarven, Gnome, Terran,
   Undercommon
Other Gear +2 warhammer, masterwork armorsmithing
   tools, masterwork blacksmithing tools, masterwork
   weaponsmithing tools

Note: Ulf has accumulated 7 negative levels due to Lilith's embrace. The penalties have been factored in above (-7 to all d20 rolls and -35 hit points).

AREA Q-5: THE GLASSWORKS

This small shop sits adjacent to the foundry room. It was built during the reign of Arb's father to maximize on the forge's waterwheel. His agents traveled far abroad to find the master craftsmen to design and operate the business, and the glass and crystal they produce is beyond compare. The dwarven smiths were not thrilled about keeping company with the foreign masters who work at their back door, but they give grudging respect to their ability.

Two **masters** and three **apprentices** work at the glassworks, which has one large furnace powered in the same manner as the forges, plus two smaller cooling furnaces. Shelves in the shop hold all manner of glassware and decorative items, plus stacks of valuable window-glass.

Apprentice (3)   CR 1/3
XP 135
hp 4 (Pathfinder Roleplaying Game NPC Codex, "Apprentice
   Jeweler")

Master (2)   CR 2
XP 600
hp 26 (Pathfinder Roleplaying Game GameMastery Guide,
   "Prisoner")

AREA Q-6: ULF'S APARTMENT

Ulf Ironfist keeps a neat, organized living space. A sturdy dwarf-sized bed and wardrobe occupy one wall; on the opposite wall is a small fireplace with an iron spit and kettle crane in it. In the middle of the room is a large wooden table with a stool. Books stacked on the table and on a small shelf at the far wall provide extensive resources on metallurgy, foundry practices, and iron working.

Area Q-7: Storeroom

This room houses large crates and hoppers filled with raw ores and also piles of unshaped iron rods. A door in the back leads downstairs to dungeon Area **1-6**. It is locked (2 in. thick; Hardness 7; hp 25; Break [DC 28]; Disable Device [DC 25]), and only Ulf Ironfist, Devlin, and Lilith have keys.

Area Q-8: The Basement

Hewn from dark stone, the forge's basement is oppressively hot, and the combined thunder of moving water and the wooden groan of the bellows is deafening. The upper half of a water wheel rises from the middle of the floor, churning and spraying icy water. On the wall opposite the rough stone stairs are stacks of wooden crates.

The crates conceal the opening to the underground network of tunnels. Ulf arranged them after Lilith first charmed him. Any character who makes a successful DC 20 Perception check finds that one of the largest crates is bolted to the stone floor and has a hinged top concealing a secret door. The bottom of this crate is missing, and a wooden ladder descends through the old drain to dungeon **Area 3-1**. Now that the drain no longer serves its purpose, several inches of water have pooled around the crates, which should indicate something is amiss.

Also, Ulf left himself a reminder of which tunnel to enter for his rendezvous with Lilith (he is notoriously forgetful). Any character who succeeds on a DC 15 Perception check notices that written on the wall above the crate, in Dwarven script, is the following note:

> *From house of iron toward the molten core,*
> *To embrace the Dwarf-maid I adore,*
> *Take the path at outstretched Dwarven arm,*
> *That brings back memories of Dwarven harm.*

The reference is to Ulf's missing ring finger on his right hand. When held at arm's length, the stump of his finger indicates the second tunnel from the right, the only one that leads into the cavern complex.

Area R: The Mill and Waterworks

This building sits in the lower city and taps an underground channel of the River Eamon. Its huge waterwheel drives several axles that provide power for the gristmill and the lumber saws. **Danver the Miller** is the engineer who supervises the operation and maintains the waterworks.

Lilith seduced Danver soon after Herrick Mendon. She wanted access to the city from more than one location, and the foundations of the waterworks are adjacent to Level 2 of the underground caverns. Yet these entrances are less frequently used because of the variety of molds and fungi that feed on the sawdust and grain washed from the mill. Only Lilith, Devlin, Gethrax, and a few thieves are willing to brave the hazards to use this entrance. The City Rumors Table (see Chapter Two) includes a sighting of Gethrax around the mill.

Danver is usually found moving between the sawmill and gristmill. The employees have noticed his odd behavior and are willing to talk about it (see the Mystery Elements section in Chapter Two).

Danver the Miller   CR 6
XP 2,400
Human expert 8
LN Medium humanoid (human)
Init -4; **Senses** Perception -5

AC 11, touch 11, flat-footed 10 (+1 Dex)
hp 27 (8d8+16)

Fort -2, **Ref** -2, **Will** +1
Speed 30 ft.

Melee dagger +1/-4 (1d4/19-20)

Str 10, **Dex** 13, **Con** 12, **Int** 12, **Wis** 11, **Cha** 9
Base Atk +6; **CMB** +1; **CMD** 12
Feats Skill Focus (Bluff), Skill Focus (Craft [carpentry]), Skill Focus (Diplomacy), Skill Focus (Knowledge [engineering]), Skill Focus (Profession [miller])
Skills Bluff +8, Craft (carpentry) +10, Diplomacy +8, Disguise +5, Knowledge (engineering) +12, Perception -5, Profession (miller) +9, Ride +7, Sense Motive +6
Languages Common, Dwarven
Other Gear dagger, masterwork engineering tools, cologne (6)

Note: Danver has accumulated 5 negative levels due to Lilith's embrace. The penalties have been factored in above (-5 to all d20 rolls and -25 hit points).

Danver fancies himself an attractive bachelor, though those days have long gone by. His education in engineering took place in a large city, where bright students could spend the evening hours with the women of their choice. He finds Dun Eamon to be too rough and unsophisticated and the women too "uptight." Any of the local women will characterize him as a "dirty old man." He is skinny and gaunt, his clothing is cheap but gaudy, and he usually smells overpoweringly of scented oils. He carries engineering tools (abacus, calipers, and so forth), and wears a tasteless wardrobe and overly strong cologne.

Area R-1: Sawmill

This half of the building houses the massive saws that process the timber from the forested slopes above the falls. The trees are floated over the falls in huge bundles — an awesome sight — and hauled up through the city from the landing. Most of the lumber produced is for construction in the city and in the outlying villages. Six men work here, moving cut and uncut timber and supervising the saws. A large, obvious trapdoor in the floor leads down to the waterworks below.

Worker (6)   CR 1
XP 400
hp 15 (Pathfinder Roleplaying Game GameMastery Guide, "Vagabond")

Area R-2: Gristmill

The other half of the mill holds one large and two small millstones, which grind most of the grain produced in the valley. Danver collects a measure of grain from each bushel he grinds; this grain supplies the city's reserves in the castle or is ground and sold to bakeries and households in Grocer's Lane (Area **G**). Four **men** monitor the grindstone and move heavy bags of grain to and from waiting carts.

An important clue awaits the heroes at the smallest millwheel. The grindstones had been separated and cleaned of all grain residues, then used at Lilith's suggestion to grind silver coins with which to ward *Mamuthek's Aperture*. The experiment damaged the wheel, and it has not been used to grind flour since then. A successful DC 18 Perception check reveals traces of silver powder on the floor around the stone; a successful DC 22 Strength check will separate the stones and reveal a silvery gouge around the circumference and a few coin fragments.

Worker (4)   CR 1
XP 400
hp 15 (Pathfinder Roleplaying Game GameMastery Guide, "Vagabond")

Area R-3: The Waterworks

This chamber is built into the bedrock of the island city. The floor is rough, un-worked stone. A channel allows water to rush through the base of the building where the massive wheel is suspended.

An entrance to the underground caverns can be found here, though seldom used. At the point where the axle passes through the stone foundation into the mill, a deep crack in the rock allows water to drain away. All the wastewater from the mill building eventually drains through this crack, which leads to dungeon Area **2-1**. All the sawdust and grain hulls are washed down through the crack as well; the rotten stench of stagnant water and fermentation wafts up through the crack on a warm breeze. To enter here, heroes must succeed on a DC 12 Acrobatics check, or take 1d6 bludgeoning damage from the moving cogs and axles.

Area S: Stump's Hovel

The old gnome adventurer **Stump** lives by himself near the Caravan Camp (Area **C**). Stump is a bitter, drunken old gnome and is completely unpleasant to deal with. His home is a run-down shack, mostly because his missing hand hinders him in making repairs. He lives on the profits of his last adventure and mostly contents himself with alcohol instead of companionship. Inside, a small fireplace warms the single room, which also contains a bed, wardrobe, table, stool, locked chest, and grandfather clock (which holds one of Elinda's clues as described in the Mystery Elements section of Chapter Two). Over the fireplace is a wooden plaque with two brass hooks — Stump's *+1 keen shortsword* hangs here. He fought with a matched pair in his adventuring days, but he gave the other one to Elinda after he lost his hand (an identical plaque hangs in her sitting room in Area **L-4**). The rest of his adventuring equipment is in the chest.

The chest is secured with a lock (1 in. thick; Hardness 5; hp 15; Break [DC 23]; Disable Device [DC 30]). It contains a masterwork light crossbow, 20 bolts, a *mithral shirt*, maps of several dungeon complexes, masterwork thieves' tools, and 3 *arcane scrolls* (*comprehend languages*, *knock*, *spider climb*; each caster level 3).

The heroes most likely come here for information about Elinda (although they might also approach Stump regarding the tunnels). He is troubled by her disappearance and by the deterioration of her reputation. He is very defensive of her and does not tolerate any insinuation of wrongdoing. If and when the heroes question him, he has little to offer. He can confirm her obsession with all things magical and mechanical; he knows that she left recently to pursue another artifact in far off lands and that she returned with it just a few days before her disappearance. In his opinion, she has never had any interest in summoning or had anything to do with it.

Stump	CR 5

XP 1,600
hp 34 (Appendix C: NPC Descriptions, "Stump")

Area T: The Root-Cutter's Shop

Caledon the Root-Cutter operates a small herbalist shop in the lower city. The druid makes and sells potions, poultices, and alchemical distillations and keeps a huge garden of exotic plants and herbs. He is usually willing to trade goods or services for his preparations, including exotic plant and animal substances.

Inside, baskets of ferns hang from overhead beams and the humid air is rich with smells of earth and organic matter. The floor is soft and mossy, the walls are covered in lichen, and potted plants clutter every available surface. A large brazier sits in the middle of the shop, with several small cauldrons suspended at different heights above it. His animal companion, the ancient wolf **Gareth**, usually sleeps curled around the base of the brazier. Caledon is most often seated at a counter opposite the door, trimming buds, docking roots, or scraping bark for his preparations. He will appear unaware of visitors until they speak, but he is merely allowing them to absorb the tranquility of his shop for as long as they like. He sells his products, but he is not concerned about money — usually, he will be willing to trade for any rare substances, especially those botanical in nature.

He keeps a stock of healing preparations on hand and ready for sale: a bowl of *goodberries* (x12, 1 gp each), *potions of cure light wounds* (x4, 50 gp each), *potions of cure moderate wounds* (x2, 300 gp each), a *potion of delay poison* (300 gp), and a *potion of neutralize poison* (750 gp). He also scribes *divine scrolls*: *hide from animals* (x2, 25 gp each, caster level 8), *speak with animals* (x2, 150 gp each, caster level 8), *speak with plants* (300 gp, caster level 8). He will prepare other potions and scrolls on request, but carefully considers the alignment of the user and possibly question his or her intent. He can distill poisons, but does not usually do so; using his herbalist skill, he can produce any of the plant-derived poisons.

He also offers alchemical items; use the standard pricing, but modify the description to reflect that his preparations are mostly derived from plants; he uses highly combustible sap for his alchemist's fire, distills digestive enzymes of carnivorous plants to yield acid, and so on. Some of these substances will be especially useful against Lilith's summoned creatures in the dungeon.

Caledon the Root-Cutter	CR 7

XP 3,200
Human druid 8
NG Medium humanoid (human)
Init +2; **Senses** Perception +4

AC 18, touch 12, flat-footed 16 (+6 armor, +2 Dex)
hp 60 (8d8+24)
Fort +8, **Ref** +4, **Will** +10; +4 vs. fey and plant-targeted effects
Speed 30 ft. (20 ft. in armor)

Melee club +5/+0 (1d6-1)
Special Attacks wild shape 3/day
Druid Spells Prepared (CL 8th; concentration +12)
  4th—*command plants* (DC 18), *cure serious wounds, reincarnate*
  3rd—*cure moderate wounds, neutralize poison, remove disease, speak with plants*
  2nd—*animal messenger, delay poison, lesser restoration, wood shape* (DC 16)
  1st—*cure light wounds, cure light wounds, cure light wounds, goodberry, shillelagh* (DC 15)
  0 (at will)—*detect magic, detect poison, guidance, mending*

Str 8, **Dex** 14, **Con** 14, **Int** 10, **Wis** 18, **Cha** 12
Base Atk +6; **CMB** +5; **CMD** 17
Feats Brew Potion, Maximize Spell, Natural Spell, Scribe Scroll, Toughness
Skills Acrobatics -1 (-5 to jump), Craft (alchemy) +13, Handle Animal +12, Heal +17, Knowledge (nature) +13, Profession (herbalist) +15, Survival +17
Languages Common, Druidic
SQ nature bond (wolf named Gareth), nature sense, trackless step, wild empathy +9, woodland stride
Combat Gear healer's kit; **Other Gear** +2 hide armor, club, alchemist's lab

Gareth	CR —

XP —
Wolf
N Large animal
Init +2; **Senses** low-light vision, scent; Perception +6

AC 19, touch 11, flat-footed 17 (+2 Dex, +8 natural, -1 size)

hp 74 (7d8+42)
Fort +10, **Ref** +7, **Will** +3 (+4 morale bonus vs. enchantment
  effects)
Defensive Abilities evasion
Speed 50 ft.

Melee bite +10 (2d6+9 plus trip)
Space 10 ft.; **Reach** 5 ft.

Str 23, **Dex** 15, **Con** 20, **Int** 2, **Wis** 12, **Cha** 6
Base Atk +5; **CMB** +12; **CMD** 24 (28 vs. trip)
Feats Improved Natural Attack (bite), Power Attack, Share
  Feature (woodland stride), Toughness
Tricks Attack, Attack Any Target, Come, Down, Fetch,
  Fighting, Heel, Seek, Stay, Track
Skills Acrobatics +2 (+10 to jump), Perception +6, Stealth +6,
  Survival +1 (+5 when tracking by scent); **Racial Modifiers**
  +4 Survival when tracking by scent
SQ attack any target, come, devotion, fetch, fighting, heel,
  seek, track, woodland stride

Note: Caledon is one of the people visited by Ebon Union thieves
seeking components for *Mamuthek's Aperture*; the robbery and
Caledon's reaction are described in the Mystery Elements section of
Chapter Two.

Area U: The Waterfront

The Citadel has a small gate at the edge nearest the pool at the base
of the waterfall. This gate is not so heavily guarded as the main gates,
but it would be very difficult to access unnoticed. A few citizens make
their living fishing in the deep pool, and the large bales of lumber that
are floated over the falls from upstream are retrieved here and hauled
to the sawmill.

Beneath one of the moss-covered docks is a **lizardfolk youth** (See
the Wilderness Encounters Appendix and the City Rumors Table in
Chapter Two for additional material). A successful DC 15 Survival
check identifies the nature of the tracks in the mud and leads the
party to the space under the dock. The young creature is injured,
half-starved, and frightened of its uncertain fate and the possibility of
punishment on return to its village. Returning it to its village can be
beneficial to the party, but the citizens of Dun Eamon would kill the
child if given the opportunity.

Lizardfolk Youth   CR 1
XP 400
hp 11 (currently 4) (Pathfinder Roleplaying Game Bestiary,
  "Lizardfolk")

Chapter Four: Level 1 — Tales From the Crypt

This is the uppermost level of the subterranean caverns below Dun Eamon, although direct routes to lower levels exist and the party will not necessarily come here first. Half of the level is made up of refuse-filled sewer tunnels; the other half is a flooded crypt. Rats, gricks, and an otyugh populate the sewers. The crypt is home to a small band of morlocks displaced from their home below and a rast called by Lilith. There are also a wight and two dangerous traps capable of producing dozens of undead.

The tombs date from a great battle fought in the valley long ago and nearly forgotten. The people of the valley buried their heroes at the base of the castle, an area that was later covered over to make room for the Market. The remains interred here include heroes of several races, a great holy warrior, and an ancestor of the Angus clan.

Area 1-1: Entry Chamber — Raiment Row Drain

This stinking pit is awash in dark water and choked with rotting piles of garbage and discarded fabric. Dim light filters down from the drain 20 feet above, and in the watery reflections, a passage can be seen leading into darkness. One wall is made of mortared stone, and a section seems to have collapsed, revealing an entrance to the crypt. Gethrax's *box o' darkness* traps (see Area **1-9**) are positioned so that entering the crypt without triggering them is impossible. The piles of fabric cast off from Raiment Row above help to conceal this chamber's

---

Level 1: Tales From The Crypt

Entrances: The drain in Raiment Row empties into **Area 1-1**. The drain in Grocer's Lane empties into **Area 1-3**. A tunnel from **Area H-12** in the Crafthall leads to **Area 1-4**.

Exits: Area 1-7 opens into the waterfall well in **Area 2-24**. A tunnel in **Area 1-6** leads to **Area 3-9**. The unstable floor in **Area 1-16** may collapse, dumping characters into **Area 2-6**.

Wandering Monsters: Very few wandering monsters are on this level; most keep to their lairs or defend their food source. Check for wandering monster encounters every hour or after any loud event, although only the grick or the rast will investigate noise with food in mind.

1d20	Encounter
1	**Morlocks** (1d2, scavenging for food, subtract from **Area 1-10**)
2	**Rats** (2d6, subtract from **Area 1-2**)
3	**Dire Rats** (1d6 + 1, subtract from **Area 1-4**)
4	**Grick** or **Rast** from lairs on this level.
5	**Ebon Union Thug**
6–20	No Encounter

Morlock (1d2)	CR 2
XP 600
hp 22 (Pathfinder Roleplaying Game Bestiary, "Morlock")

Rat (2d6)	CR 1/4
XP 100
hp 4 (Pathfinder Roleplaying Game Bestiary, "Rat, Common")

Dire Rat (1d6 + 1)	CR 1/3
XP 135
hp 5 (Pathfinder Roleplaying Game Bestiary, "Rat, Dire")

Grick	CR 3
XP 800
hp 27 (Pathfinder Roleplaying Game Bestiary 2, "Grick")

Rast	CR 5
XP 1,600
hp 51 (Pathfinder Roleplaying Game Bestiary 2, "Rast")

Ebon Union Thug	CR 1
XP 400
hp 16 (Pathfinder Roleplaying Game GameMastery Guide, "Street Thug")

Detections: The whole level radiates faint evil. The *box o' darkness* (see **Appendix B**) traps in the corridors of **Area 1-9** cause detections aimed in their direction to indicate not only evil but hopeless despair as well.

Continuous Effects: The natural caverns and tunnels are shin-deep in stinking black water; the crypt corridors are only inches deep. Any character taking the charge action or who moves more than double their movement speed is subject to tripping over a hidden obstacle. The character must succeed on a DC 12 Reflex saving throw or fall prone and take 1d3 bludgeoning damage. Any character that falls prone for any reason on this level has a 10% chance (per immersion) of contracting filth fever. Dropped items require a DC 15 Perception check to recover. A thorough search beneath the water reveals 1d3 gp worth of coins (mostly silver and copper) per minute of sifting through muck, which also requires a test for disease. Unless the heroes have a light source with them, the entire level is in near total darkness.

Standard Features: In the sewage caverns, the walls are of rough stone and the floor is a combination of loose cobblestones, sand, and garbage. The overhead clearance is 10 feet in the tunnels and 15 feet in the rooms. In the crypt, the walls are of mortared stone and the floors are flagstone. All doors are of stone (4 in. thick; Hardness 8; hp 60; Break [DC 28]; Disable Device [DC 30]) and open inward. The ceilings are 10 feet high and barrel-vaulted.

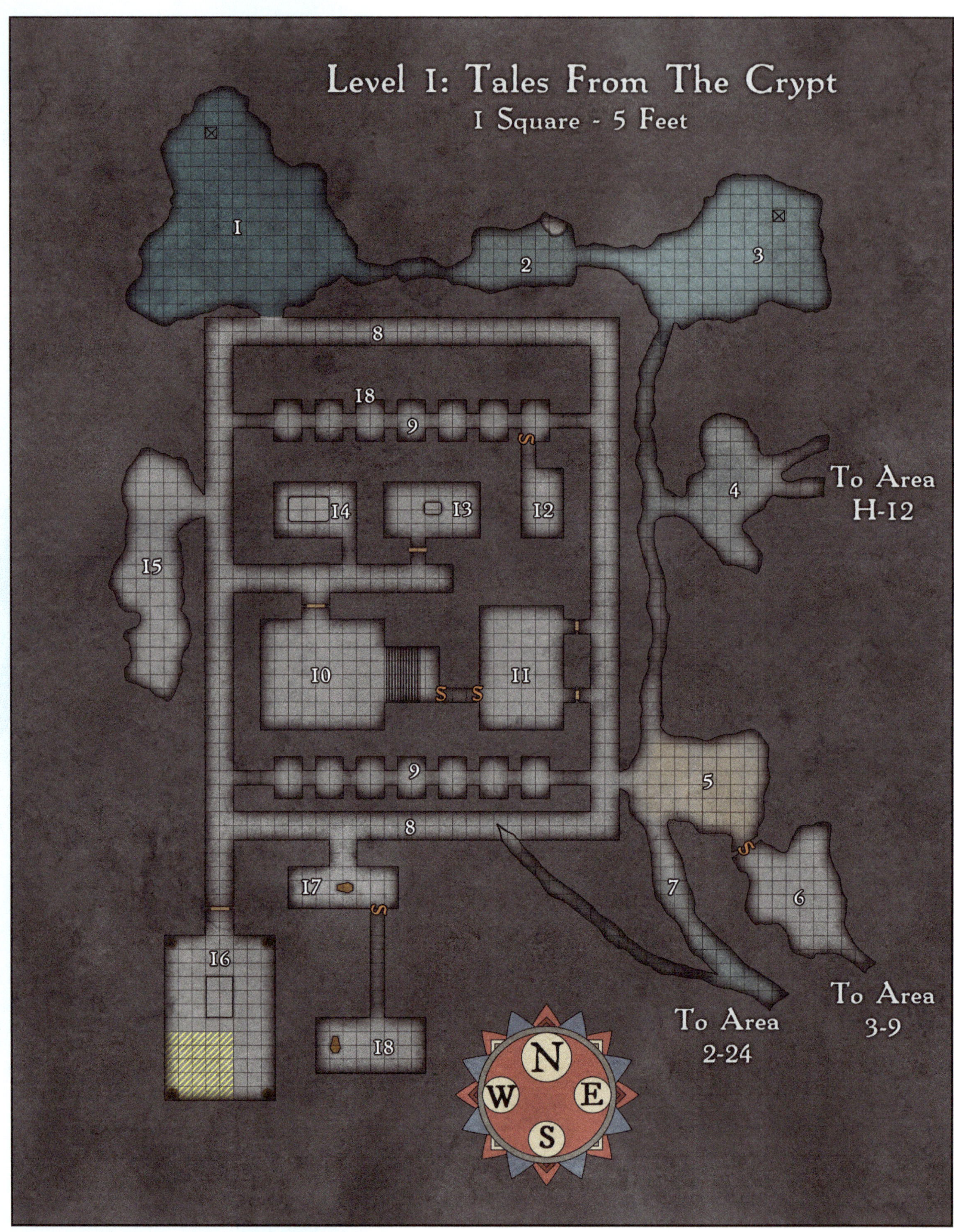

Level I: Tales From The Crypt
I Square - 5 Feet
I
2
3
8
I8
9
I5
I4
I3
I2
I0
II
9
8
I7
I6
I8
4
To Area
H-I2
5
7
6
To Area
2-24
To Area
3-9
N
W
E
S

occupant: an **otyugh**. This muck-dweller hides beneath piles of rotten cloth and wears a *cloak of resistance +1*. If the cloak isn't washed before being worn, the wearer will be subject to filth fever.

Otyugh CR 4
XP 1,200
hp 39 (Pathfinder Roleplaying Game Bestiary, "Otyugh")

Tactics: This otyugh knows there is something special about its cloak and has grown brash. It attacks any creature entering its lair, although it does wait to attack until the heroes move to investigate one of the openings. Noticing the otyugh before it surprises the heroes requires a successful DC 20 Perception check.

Area 1-2: The Rat Cave

The water is only ankle-deep in this oblong chamber, and the bits of trash floating about show signs of being chewed. With the water shallow and the food plentiful, 20 **rats** have taken up residence in this room. Their lair is deep in the shadows on a rock ledge 10 feet off the ground. Climbing to the ledge requires a DC 15 Climb check; the climber is most likely attacked upon arrival. The ledge is barely big enough for 1 Medium-size or 2 Small characters. A *potion of spider climb* is hidden near the back in a pile of droppings — an adventurer had been trying to use it to escape the otyugh and dropped it when he was surprised by a face full of rats.

Rat (20) CR 1/4
XP 100
hp 4 (Pathfinder Roleplaying Game Bestiary, "Rat, Common")

Tactics: Unless the player declares that their character is attempting to move stealthily, the rats prepare an attack action and leap onto the hero when they peek over the edge. Staying on the wall when this happens requires a DC 15 Reflex saving throw.

Area 1-3: Entry Chamber – Grocer's Lane Drain

Situated right below Grocer's Lane, this chamber collects all the rotten produce from the Market above. The squirming of maggots is audible, and the stench brings bile to the throat of any character passing through. If anyone falls prone in this area, double the chance of contracting filth fever. Lurking near the exit tunnel are 2 **gricks**, one on either side. Submerged in the corner of the area opposite the entrance are 2 bodies (an Ebon Union Cutpurse who failed to make it back home safely one night, and a beggar who refused to inform for the Ebon Union). On the Cutpurse, there are 2 daggers, an entrails-stained set of leather armor, a pouch of caltrops, a pouch with 6 gp and 20 sp, and a masterwork shortsword. There is a secret compartment in the shortsword's hilt that can be noted with a successful DC 18 Perception check. The hilt contains a slip of paper which reads "green first", a clue relating to a trap in **Area 3-22**. On the beggar is a signet ring worth 150 gp, or 450 gp if returned to the beggar's family in a far-off land of your choosing.

Grick (2) CR 3
XP 800
hp 27 (Pathfinder Roleplaying Game Bestiary 2, "Grick")

Tactics: The gricks lurk on either side of the entry (the light from the drain sometimes lures prey into their lair). They lash out from hiding, attempting to surprise the first two heroes. The gricks can be seen with a successful DC 16 Perception check. They instinctively

fight until slain, abandoning a prone character for one still moving.

Area 1-4: Entry Chamber – The Crafthall Tunnel

This small room has a raised floor that is mostly free of water. Bones are scattered all over, and at the base of one wall is a pile of broken pottery and glass. At the back of the room are two deep cracks in the wall. This room is the arrival point of a long tunnel from the basement of the Crafthall (**Area H-12**). It is infested with 8 **dire rats**, which the thieves have learned to distract with sugary sweets such as jam and honey. Upon arrival, they smash a jar or two against the far wall and slip past the rats while they eat. The rats' lair in one of the cracks contains their non-combatant young (2d6 **rats**). Within in this crack there is also a chewed satchel containing a chewed roll of blank parchment, a pouch with 28 gp, a thunderstone and an unopened jar of strawberry jam that acts as a *potion of cure light wounds*. The resulting sugar toxicity from consuming the jam imparts a -1 Dexterity penalty for the next 3 hours or until the next meal. The other crack leads to the passage to the Crafthall.

Dire Rat (8) CR 1/3
XP 135
hp 5 (Pathfinder Roleplaying Game Bestiary, "Rat, Dire")

Rat (2d6) CR 1/4
XP 100
hp 4 (Pathfinder Roleplaying Game Bestiary, "Rat, Common")

Tactics: The dire rats attack as soon as they are aware of beings approaching their lair, unless they are distracted with sweets. When 75% of them are killed, the remaining rats back into their lair to defend their offspring.

Area 1-5: Stirges and Secrets

Most of this room has a relatively dry sandy floor. Obvious tracks lead across it from a deep fissure on one wall into the murky water of the natural corridor. A few burned scraps of rag lie scattered around the room. One of the walls is of mortared stone, which has collapsed to reveal a chamber beyond. Allow the party to make a DC 15 Perception check to hear the quiet buzzing of 6 **stirges** in the crevices of the ceiling above. Immediately lighting the oily rags keeps them at bay; otherwise, they attack the party just after they arrive. Wedged in a crack in the ceiling, 12 rat corpses can be found in what appears be the stirges' larder. One of the rats is noticeably heavier than the others as it has a string of pearls worth 900 gp in its belly.

In the crack on the wall is a pivoting stone door with a pair of iron rings at the base (1 in. thick; Hardness 8; hp 50; Break [DC 30]; Perception [DC 22]; Strength check [DC 26] to open, Strength check [DC 12]) using poles for leverage. This door hides the entrance to a cavern used by the Ebon Union as a stop on their way to their lair on Level 3.

The collapsed stone wall leads to **Area 1-8**. Stepping through it will probably trigger a trap in **Area 1-9**.

Stirge (6) CR 1/2
XP 200
hp 5 (Pathfinder Roleplaying Game Bestiary, "Stirge")

Tactics: The stirges attack as soon as they have reason to believe there is prey below — note that they may react to the skeletons that result from the trap in **Area 1-9**, depending on the party's location when the trap is triggered. The only thing that deters them is smoke;

if the oily rags are lit or some other smoke is introduced, the stirges retreat into the cracks.

AREA 1-6: THE READY ROOM

Compared to the foul mess that is unavoidable elsewhere, this small cavern is nearly livable. A pile of rags looks like it could be a bed, and a few crates arranged in a corner have several candle stubs and dirty cups on them. A faint spot of light touches one wall. At the back, a low tunnel descends into darkness. There is a 10% chance per hour that an Ebon Union individual or group arrives; randomly determine which direction they are heading and use the profile from the Ebon Union section of **Appendix C**. Check for this possibility as soon as the heroes arrive.

This is the staging area for the Ebon Union's forays into the city. They usually rest here after the climb up from their lair or stockpile supplies here to be carried down. A hairline crack in the ceiling allows whatever sunlight or moonlight exists above to filter down, where a mirror reflects it into the room so the thieves can establish the hour of the day. The tunnel in the back leads down to **Area 3-9**.

A sack with 5 rations and 3 bottles of wine (8 gp each) wrapped in cloth sits on a table. Also on the makeshift table is a deck of playing cards that have been magically treated to resist moisture and dirt (possibly valued as high as 1,000 gp, but only worth so much to a handful of people, easily mistaken for more powerful magical cards). The mirror jammed in the ceiling is made of silver and tortoise shell. This mirror is worth 35 gp.

AREA 1-7: OUTFLOW TUNNEL

This tunnel slopes down toward the sound of rushing water. Some distance down it picks up the drainage from **Area 1-8**. It eventually leads to the huge waterfall well described in **Area 2-24**.

AREA 1-8: PERIMETER CORRIDOR

The first time the heroes enter this area from either **Area 1-1** or **1-5**, they almost certainly trigger a trap left in **Area 1-9** by Gethrax (refer to this area for complete details).

This corridor is 10 feet wide and runs all the way around the tomb complex. The walls are breached at three places, leading to **Areas 1-1**, **1-5**, and **1-15**. In one corridor, a wide crack at floor level drains away water toward **Area 1-7**. Only a Small character could fit through this tunnel and would be subject to disease, but halfway down is a corroded tin box containing a garnet necklace worth 360 gp.

AREA 1-9: CRYPT CORRIDORS

Burial niches in both walls dominate this long narrow corridor. They are lined up head to toe from one end to the other and are stacked three high. In most of them are ancient corpses, no longer clad in flesh, but still wearing armor and sometimes clutching weapons. These are the long-dead heroes of the near-forgotten war that threatened the

valley. They were loyal defenders of the island city when it came under siege and so were buried here near the keep's gate to guard it for eternity. Thieves have already scavenged most of this area, so only a few bits of treasure remain. In one burial niche is a stone statue in place of a corpse; the stone wall behind it conceals a secret door (2 in. thick; Hardness 4; hp 30; Perception [DC 28]; Break [DC 18], Disable Device [DC 30]) to Area **1-12**. In the other burial niche and scattered around on the floor there are two rusty daggers, a light steel shield and 250 sp.

Read the following as the party approaches within 50 feet of either *box o' darkness* (see **Appendix B**) trap:

> As you move into the corridor, a strange sound reaches your ears. It sounds like the cries of happy children playing and the cheerful notes of a wind-up music box.
>
> *[If the party can see the box at the end of 5 rounds, add:]*
>
> The top of the box pops open on hidden hinges, and a one-inch figure rotates slowly inside. The cheerful music slowly winds to a stop, the pitch falling off in a tuneless moan. A thick, oily mist begins to seep from the box, spreading out around you, and the figure rotates to face you as the music dies out. It is a reaper in black, bearing a scythe. All around you, the dead begin to stir...

Box o' Darkness Trap   **CR 4**
XP 1,200

Type magic; **Perception** DC 28; **Disable Device** DC 28
Trigger good-aligned humanoid coming within a 50-ft. radius;
  Reset none
Effect When triggered, they begin to play a pleasant tune
  as would a child's music box, and the sound of laughing
  children can be heard. After five rounds, the music slows,
  and thick black fog seeps out of the box, expanding to cover
  a 50-foot radius. This area receives the effects of a *desecrate*
  spell followed by *animate dead* cast at 15th level. Then, 15
  HD of undead are raised from that area (if available). The
  trap magically converts the surrounding 20-foot area into
  unhallowed ground for up to 30 hours. The DC to resist
  negative channeled energy within this area gains a +3
  profane bonus. Every undead creature entering a *desecrated*
  area gains a +1 profane bonus on all attack rolls, damage
  rolls, and saving throws. An undead creature created within
  or summoned into such an area gains +1 hit points per HD.

These portable magical traps were designed by evil priests to hamper the efforts of good-aligned creatures. Gethrax placed them to further secure the caverns against the righteous, and he felt (rightly) that the Crypt below the Market was the most accessible area. Parties are likely surprised by the first one and may even be holding it when the top pops open and the evil mists seep out. If the heroes keep their wits about them, they may react quickly enough to minimize the effect of the second one — by moving it, consecrating the area, or perhaps some other creative solution.

The traps are armed when wound up, and from then on are triggered by the approach of any good-aligned humanoid within 50 feet. On the bottom of the box is an engraved sigil (see also Area **3-17** and the Wilderness Encounters Appendix) that may lead the party to the powerful creator of the *boxes o' darkness* in a later quest.

Desecrated Skeleton   **CR 1/3**
XP 135

hp 5 (Pathfinder Roleplaying Game Bestiary, "Skeleton")

AREA 1-10: CHAPEL

This room appears to have been a place of worship at some point, complete with curtained altar. Unless the heroes have taken steps to infiltrate the room, 6 **morlocks** leap up and grab their weapons as the door opens. If the heroes enter through the secret corridor from Area **1-11**, they emerge behind a tapestry and have a good chance to surprise the creatures. Two of them are hidden beneath the altar and will almost certainly surprise the heroes regardless of which way they come in.

The chapel was included in the tomb to represent the dominant belief system in the valley at the time; feel free to use any non-evil deity, forgotten or otherwise. The chapel was taken over by **Bashrib's** morlock band when they were displaced by the arrival of the Ebon Union. A ranger, gnome, dwarf, or other character with a reasonable background may recognize that morlocks tend to dwell much deeper in the earth, coming this close to the surface only to raid or scavenge but not to build a lair. Most of their treasure is in a large locked chest (1 in. thick; Hardness 5; hp 15; Break [DC 23]; Disable Device [DC 25]) in the corner, but a few items are in Area **1-11**. Bashrib carries the key to this chest around his neck.

Within the chest there are 180 gp, 260 sp, 3 pieces of uncut amber (worth 80 gp, 95 gp, and 110 gp respectively), a silver-plated dagger with a turquoise and jet handle (worth 380 gp), and an ivory statue of a horse (worth 65 gp). Within the room there is a mildewed tapestry (used as bedding) with gold thread in it worth 250 gp. Behind the altar tapestries, a secret door can be found with a DC 15 Perception check. The door opens easily, leads through a passageway to Area **1-11** and has a disgusting treasure of its own: 3 silver bowls (12 gp each, or 24 gp if sold to a temple of the appropriate deity) that the morlocks use as chamber pots.

If any of the morlocks survive the encounter, they might be convinced to share some of what they know about the dungeon. They might be charmed, intimidated, or even tortured; let the role-playing abilities of the players determine what their characters learn. If Bashrib survives, he attempts to barter for his survival with information, perhaps even agreeing to guide the party through the parts of the dungeon he knows. All of the morlocks are familiar with Level 3; their lair used to be in Area **3-29**, the troll cave.

Morlock (7)   **CR 2**
XP 600

hp 22 (Pathfinder Roleplaying Game Bestiary, "Morlock")

Bashrib the Barbarian   **CR 5**
XP 1,600

hp 57 (Appendix A: New Creatures, "Bashrib the Barbarian")

Tactics: Crouched in the center of the chapel are 6 morlocks, squabbling over food scraps. The 7th, a female, is spending quality time under the altar with Bashrib the Barbarian, the leader and dominant male. The morlocks in the open grab their weapons and attack the heroes as they enter, although the party may be able to surprise them. While most morlocks are equipped with spiked bone clubs, a few do wield spears. Regardless of how the fight begins, the chief and his mate wait two rounds before leaping out and attacking the heroes closest to the altar, preferably ones with their backs turned to the altar. Bashrib is very irate at having his snuggling time interrupted and immediately flies into a rage.

AREA 1-11: MEMORIAL

This rectangular room is devoid of furnishings save for a bed of furs made up in a corner. The walls are exquisitely carved in bas-relief and depict an epic battle between an allied force of humans, dwarves, and gnomes and a great evil horde of orcs and orc-kin. These carvings are

a tribute to the epic battle for the valley in which so many great heroes lost their lives. The carvings themselves are worth several thousand gold pieces each, but the logistics of removing them are complicated, as each panel weighs thousands of pounds and was actually carved in this room. Of course, the citizens will not take kindly to their relics being removed, even if they have forgotten that they exist. A secret door (1 in. thick; Hardness 5; hp 20; Break [DC 23]; Disable Device [DC 20]; Perception [DC 20]) leads to **Area 1-10**. A few items of the morlocks' treasure are hidden in the stinking furs. This includes a silver pitcher (matches the chalices in the tunnel, worth 80 gp or 160 gp if sold to a temple of the appropriated deity), and a pouch with 11 moonstones. Of these moonstones, four are worth 40 gp, another four are worth 50 gp, two are worth 60 gp, and one is worth 70 gp.

AREA 1-12: HIDDEN BURIAL VAULT

The craftsmen who built the tombs created this hidden vault. In addition to the great heroes who fell in battle, scores of commoners died, and the stonemasons were allowed to place a stone statue in the vault to represent their dead. Regardless, they created this small antechamber behind a secret door to honor the dead of the lower classes. Hundreds of skulls line the walls in great pules, and a number of items of treasure (clearly those of common folk) were left with the dead in keeping with various belief systems. These items include 12 clay jugs of stale beer (1 sp for the jugs), 7 bottles of fine wine (8 gp each), 3 bottles of not-so-fine wine (worthless), 2 sets of high quality artisan's tools (55 gp each), silver holy symbol of a good-aligned deity (25 gp), and a small oak cask of several hundred-year old unblended

"cask-strength" whiskey (80 gp, or 2,000 gp if sold to a collector or master distiller).

The vault is reached by squeezing through a trapped passage behind a secret door (2 in. thick; Hardness 8; hp 40; Break [DC 30]; Open Lock [DC 25]; Perception [DC 22]) in the stone carving of a craftsman in **Area 1-9**. Upon opening the door, the falling block trap makes a melee attack roll against the targets directly below it.

Falling Block Trap   CR 5
XP 1,600
Type mechanical; **Perception** DC 20; **Disable Device** DC 20
Trigger location; **Reset** manual
Effect Atk +15 melee (10′ stone block; 6d6); multiple targets (all targets in a 10-ft. square)

AREA 1-13: DWARVEN BURIAL VAULT

The door to this area is locked (4 in. thick; Hardness 8; hp 80; Break [DC 30]; Disable Device [DC 35]) and trapped. Upon opening the door, a field of spikes drops from the ceiling as a character enters the room.

Falling Spike Trap   CR 5
XP 1,600
Type mechanical; **Perception** DC 20; **Disable Device** DC 20
Trigger location; **Reset** manual
Effect Atk +15 melee (field of spikes; 6d6); multiple targets (all targets in a 10-ft. square)

This room is decorated with beautiful carvings and graceful stone arches. The burial niches that line these walls are slightly shorter than the ones in the other corridors, and a large stone casket dominates the center of the room.

This tomb is dedicated to the many dwarves that fell in the great battle, and their leaders and heroes are buried here. Ten dwarven warriors lie in rotted robes holding dwarven greataxes across their chests. The central casket is the tomb of the dwarf lord Gedgrath; his name and title are carved on the lid in dwarven script. Removing the lid requires a DC 24 Strength check. Gedgrath is lying in state here. His items and the weapons of the other dwarves make up the treasure. This includes 10 dwarven greataxes (300 gp), masterwork dwarven plate armor (1,800 gp), jewel-encrusted masterwork greataxe (820 gp), and a mithral crown studded with fire opals (5,500 gp). If the party brings all of these items to the dwarven market at once, questions might be raised as to how these items were acquired.

AREA 1-14: GNOME BURIAL VAULT

The door to this vault has been smashed to rubble. Inside are a large marble slab and a few burial niches, but the bones of the dead lie scattered on the ground. The air is noticeably colder in this chamber, which has already been looted. It is a tribute to the gnome heroes of the great battle; the marble slab has their story and the history of the battle inscribed on it, which may be of interest to bards. It could also make reference to the villains' stronghold that was sealed but never cleansed; this detail is left to your discretion for further development. A patch of **brown mold** and a pitiful treasure of 1 sp per party member both wait in the corner.

Brown Mold   CR 2
XP 600
Brown mold feeds on warmth, drawing heat from anything
    around it. It normally comes in patches 5 feet in diameter,
    and the temperature is always cold in a 30-foot radius
    around it. Living creatures within 5 feet of it take 3d6 points
    of nonlethal cold damage. Fire brought within 5 feet of
    brown mold causes the mold to instantly double in size. Cold
    damage, such as from a *cone of cold*, instantly destroys it.

AREA 1-15: THE RAST'S LAIR

This rough-walled stone chamber is lit by an unseen source. A **rast** dwells in a smaller cave to one side of the main room. Lilith called it after she had the Ebon Union rob the herbalist's shop; if the heroes have not already made the connection, they may realize that a rast's claw was one of the stolen items, but only if they can identify the creature. It attacks fearlessly and relentlessly as soon as the party enters its lair. The rast's treasure (a red *potion of fire breath*, a blue *potion of fly*, and a green *potion of gaseous form*) is the source of the light and hovers at the ceiling of the smaller chamber (15 feet up; describe them as you would colored light bulbs). If the treasure is not restrained, it will float upwards at a rate of 1 foot per round.

The rast hovers in the smaller section of the cave until the party enters, possibly drawn by the light of the potion. It attempts to paralyze as many opponents as possible before selecting one to feed on, and this unlucky hero gets grappled as the rast tries to drag him or her away while the rest of the party watches helplessly. If surrounded in close combat, the rast rises to the ceiling and actively targets opponents with its Paralyzing Gaze until the odds are evened.

Rast   CR 5
XP 1,600
hp 51 (Pathfinder Roleplaying Game Bestiary 2, "Rast")

AREA 1-16: ANGUS TOMB

The doors to this chamber are locked (4 in. thick; Hardness 8; hp 70; Break [DC 30]; Disable Device [DC 35]).

Double doors give way into a vault at the end of the corridor. A large casket sits in the center of the rectangular room, unadorned except for some carved script on the lid. Rotting tapestries hang from brass rods on all four walls, and brass braziers stand empty in all four corners. The brazier in the southwest corner seems to be leaning at an off angle. This room is the final resting place of the Lord Angus who marshaled the army and masterminded the defense of the citadel during the war. He was laid to rest in a place of honor, and for many weeks, mourners passed around his tomb. The worn path in the floor can be noticed with a DC 18 Perception check. The inscription on the lid reads:

> *Colm Angus*
> *Lord of Eamonvale*
> *Slain on the Ramparts*
> *For the Sake of his People*
> *Let None Disturb his Rest*

A great hunter, he was buried with a treasure of his personal hunting weapons, although the *Sword of Angus* was passed on through his heirs to Arb. The tomb can be opened with a successful DC 20 Strength check. The tomb contains 4 brass braziers (worth 20 gp each), a masterwork composite longbow (Strength +3), and 16 *+1 arrows*.

The brazier in the southwest corner leans because the floor it sits on is ready to collapse. This weakness can be identified by a successful DC 20 Knowledge (engineering) or Craft (stonemasonry) check. Any weight greater than 150 pounds on a 10-foot by 10-foot square around the brazier will trigger a collapse. The floor in a 25-foot by 25-foot area in the corner buckles momentarily before collapsing. Treat characters in the triggering area as being in the bury zone and characters elsewhere in the collapse area as being in the slide zone of a collapse.

Collapse   CR 8
XP 4,800
Characters in the bury zone of a cave-in take 8d6 points of
    damage, or half that amount if they make a DC 15 Reflex
    save. They are subsequently buried. Characters in the slide
    zone take 3d6 points of damage, or no damage at all if they
    make a DC 15 Reflex save. Characters in the slide zone who
    fail their saves are buried.
Characters take 1d6 points of nonlethal damage per minute
    while buried. If such a character falls unconscious, he must
    make a DC 15 Constitution check each minute. If it fails, he
    takes 1d6 points of lethal damage each minute until freed or
    dead.
Characters who aren't buried can dig out their friends. In 1
    minute, using only her hands, a character can clear rocks
    and debris equal to five times her heavy load limit. The
    amount of loose stone that fills a 5-foot-by-5-foot area weighs
    1 ton (2,000 pounds). Armed with an appropriate tool, such
    as a pick, crowbar, or shovel, a digger can clear loose stone
    twice as quickly as by hand. A buried character can attempt
    to free himself with a DC 25 Strength check.

The collapse spills some or all of the party into **Area 2-6**, which has its own nasty surprises.

Area 1-17: The Paladin's Cenotaph

No doors restrict access to this small room. It holds only a large marble tomb raised off the floor on a slab of granite. An inscription on the pedestal reads:

The citizens of Eamonvale were unwilling to see Roark buried here because of the manner of his death. The cenotaph was placed to commemorate his death, but the heir to the Angus lordship buried his body in a secret chamber anyway. The "tomb" is actually a block of solid marble carved to represent a burial vault and it does not "open."

Roark was a paladin from the distant north who heeded the call of the imperiled valley and rode to aid the defense. A cadre of powerful necromancers and undead beings led the invaders, and a wight fatally wounded Roark even as he struck it down. He bade the citizens prepare a consecrated grave for him as he struggled with the curse. They laid him down before the injuries claimed him, and even as he passed, his spirit struggled against the spawn within. His soul remains trapped within the husk of his body, barely holding the wight impulse at bay, and as the evil influences on this level have increased his grip on undeath has been slipping.

Nothing here indicates that Roark is anywhere in this room, but a DC 25 Perception check reveals a secret door (4 in. thick; Hardness 10; hp 60; Break [DC 28]; Open Lock [DC 35]) disguised as stone, but formed of iron on the inside. Behind it lies Roark's tomb, hidden from would-be grave robbers in hopes that what he might become would never see the light of day.

Area 1-18: The Paladin's Tomb

This room is small and simple — no tapestries, no carvings, no furnishings. A marker in the stone floor indicates that it is the final resting place of **Roark the Righteous**. The lid to Roark's tomb is massively heavy, requiring a DC 30 Strength check to open it. If the lid is pried off the floor vault, it shifts the fragile balance of good and evil, tipping the scales against Roark's spirit and freeing the undead creature he should have become ages ago. Information from the memorial statue in **Area 1-17** and in the read-aloud text below should hint at the necessary means to defeat the wight.

The powerful spirit of Roark's living self is nearly able to keep the wight from animating his corpse. When Roark the Wight is active, any shift in the balance of positive and negative energy affects him. Sources of positive divine energy such as *bless, consecrate, prayer,* or holy water (or others at your discretion) allow Roark's spirit to subdue the undead impulse and disable but not destroy the wight. Similarly, introducing negative energy reinforces the wight's dominance over the remains; for each spell powered by negative energy cast on or around the wight, it requires one additional positive spell to restore the balance and return Roark to a pile of bones. Destroying the wight destroys Roark as well, but an extensive quest may allow Roark's spirit to be salvaged and laid to rest. This development is up to you.

Roark the Righteous   CR 7
XP 3,200
hp 60 (Appendix A: New Creatures, "Roark the Righteous")

The wight abandons the shield and attacks with either its slam or its sword (50% chance of either) until killed, turned, or overcome by Roark's spirit. Based on the clues on the statue and in the text block, the heroes may be able to help Roark overcome the wight and return his own corpse to the tomb. The pedestal says "Bless Him," and a *bless* or other intervention introduces enough divine energy to allow Roark to regain control of his remains and fling them back into the burial recess. The heroes must still return the lid to its original position, and the wight only remains subdued temporarily; the party may still need the find a permanent solution.

Chapter Five: Level 2 — Fungus Among Us

This is the second level below the surface, although it can be reached directly via the tunnel below the Mill. The caverns here were carved by the force of moving water and still tend to be more wet than dry. The steady flow of organic waste from the mill has spawned a great deal of botanical and fungal growth on this level — some of it quite intelligent. Among the vegetable denizens of the swampy caverns are a shambling mound and some assassin vines, and non-botanical life abounds in the form of monstrous cave crayfish and comical (but deadly) dire frogs. Lilith's summoned rust monsters are here as well. The most dangerous occupant is Gethrax, one of Lilith's allies, who makes his lair here to be close to the surface.

The hazards here generally keep the thieves from passing through, but Lilith and Devlin use this level to access the surface from time to time. Several adventurers seeking bounties on the demons penetrated this far into the dungeon before meeting their ends. As the plants have little use for the bodies beyond nourishment, the possessions of the fallen make up most of the treasure here.

Area 2-1: Entry Chamber — The Millworks Basement

This wedge-shaped cavern has tunnels leading to other areas on Level 2 and one leading to **Area R-3** in the mill. A pool of stagnant, stinking water in the corner conceals a water-filled tunnel (see **Area 2-15**) leading to **Area 2-16**.

Level 2: Fungus Among Us

Entrances: This level has only one surface access point: a slimy tunnel winding down from the basement of the mill. The unstable floor in **Area 1-16** may collapse, dumping the characters in **Area 2-6**. A passage from **Area 1-7** arrives in **Area 2-24**, the waterfall room.

Exits: The waterfall room in **Area 2-24** has an underground river that flows out to **Level 4**. A secret passage in **Area 2-17** leads to **Area 3-9**. If the heroes were to bring down the ceiling in **Area 2-6**, they could climb up to **Area 1-16**.

Wandering Monsters: Many of the creatures on this level are plants and tend to wait rather than actively look for their prey. A few of the creatures, however, do move about — check for a wandering monster encounter every hour or after any loud event.

1d20	Encounter
1–2	**Bats** (2d6, subtract from **Area 2-2**)
3–4	**Rats** (2d6, subtract from **Area 2-23**)
5	**Dire rats** (1d6 + 1, subtract from **Area 2-5**)
6	**Gethrax** (from **Area 2-17**)
7	**Sogrin the Ogre** (from **Area 2-16**)
8	**Rust Monster** (1, subtract from **Area 2-10**)
9–20	No Encounter

Bat (2d6)   CR 1/8
XP 50
hp 2 (Pathfinder Roleplaying Game Bestiary, "Bat, Common")

Rat (2d6)   CR 1/4
XP 100
hp 4 (Pathfinder Roleplaying Game Bestiary, "Rat, Common")

Dire Rat (1d6 + 1)   CR 1/3
XP 135
hp 5 (Pathfinder Roleplaying Game Bestiary, "Rat, Dire")

Gethrax   CR 9
XP 6,400
hp 75 (Area 2-17: The Dead Man's Party, "Gethrax")

Sogrin the Ogre   CR 3
XP 800
hp 30 **(currently 14)** (Pathfinder Roleplaying Game Bestiary, "Ogre")

Rust Monster   CR 3
XP 800
hp 27 (Pathfinder Roleplaying Game Bestiary, "Rust Monster")

Detections: The level has a strong life force, but neither good nor evil seems to dominate it... rather, hunger is the driving force of these creatures. The lair of Gethrax the antipaladin radiates potent evil.

Continuous Effects: This level is a major drainage for the city, and the constant flow of runoff and nutrients ensures that the caves and corridors are always full of water and slime. Any character taking the charge action or who moves more than double their movement speed is subject to tripping over a hidden obstacle. The character must succeed on a DC 12 Reflex saving throw or fall prone, taking no damage thanks to the thick moss growing everywhere. Enough luminescent fungi are scattered throughout this level that the overall lighting is the equivalent of dim light.

Standard Features: The walls here are of rough, unworked stone, and the floor and ceiling are uneven and studded with stalactites and stalagmites. Tunnels are generally rounded with water trickling down the middle; rooms have pools of standing water with thick carpets of bright green algae. Secret doors on this level are actually curtains of moss and fungus. Overhead clearance is 10 feet in the tunnels and 15 feet in the caverns, measured from the water level (some caverns have pools that go much deeper).

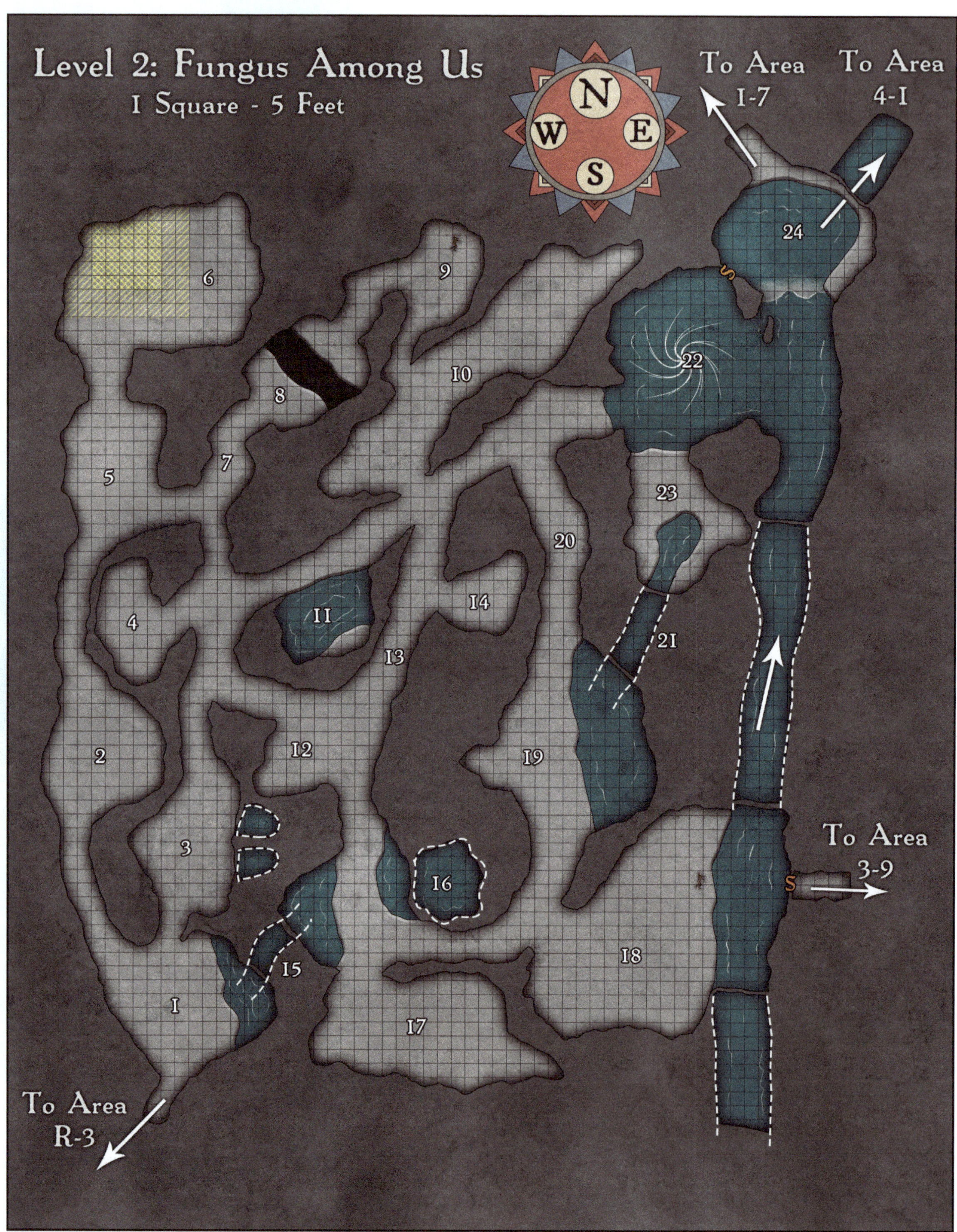

Level 2: Fungus Among Us
1 Square - 5 Feet
N
W
E
S
To Area I-7
To Area 4-1
To Area 3-9
To Area R-3
1
2
3
4
5
6
7
8
9
10
11
12
13
14
15
16
17
18
19
20
21
22
23
24

Area 2-2: Going Batty

This cave holds a relatively harmless surprise for the party — 40 **bats**. As soon as they are disturbed by loud noise, attacks, or major changes in their environment, the bats take flight, wheel crazily around the party for a few moments, and fly off into some other part of the cave. They inflict superficial injuries, spread lots of guano, and alert Gethrax (**Area 2-17**) to the intruders.

Bat (40)   CR 1/8
XP 50
hp 2 (Pathfinder Roleplaying Game Bestiary, "Bat, Common")

Area 2-3: Albino Cave Crayfish

Consider each character's encumbrance before running this encounter.

Glowing blue fungi on the ceiling light this long, narrow cavern. The floor is flat for the first time and is covered with a spongy layer of mossy growth. A trickle of water is heard at the far end. That flat surface in this area is not actually the cavern floor, but a floating bed of moss on the surface of a pool of stagnant water. There, they will encounter the **monstrous crayfish** that live in the pool, not to mention the potential of drowning as a result of armor or encumbrance. With a successful DC 24 Perception check, adventurers can discern the true nature of the floor. A safe passage through can then be discerned with a successful DC 22 Survival check. Failing this, the heaviest members of the party will likely fall through the surface of the moss bed to be trapped underneath. When a creature weighing 200 pounds or more attempts to cross the cave, their square gives way. The creature must make a DC 25 Reflex saving throw. On a fail, the mossy blanket closes over the hero's head as they fall trapping them in darkness. In order to find their way to the original hole, the hero must make a DC 15 Perception check and a DC 10 Swim check to climb out. An alternative is to make a new hole; in this case, treat the carpet of moss as having hardness 5 and 4 hit points per 5-foot section. Characters under the moss can tear a hole with a DC 24 Strength check. Other heroes may attempt to assist, but they are subject to the 200-pound weight limit. Dispersing body weight by slithering on one's belly or using long or flat objects (ladders, large weapons, and so forth) increases the limit to 300 pounds; doing both increases it to 400 pounds. Several previous adventurers have died here, and a rich treasure awaits surviving explorers of the pool. Underneath the blanket of moss, adventurers can find a breastplate, a longsword, 4 *+1 arrows*, a jar of *restorative ointment*, and a pouch with 49 gp.

Monstrous Crayfish (2)   CR 3
XP 800
hp 26 (Tome of Horrors Complete, "Crayfish, Monstrous")

Tactics: When the first character enters the pool, the crayfish leave their holes and approach slowly. They wait 1 full round after the fall and then attempt to flank a single opponent until another becomes available. They fight until reduced to 25% of their original hit points before retreating into their deep holes (treat as three-quarters cover).

Area 2-4:
And Then There Were Two

The pale, blubbery creature crouched here is a **dretch** and should look familiar from the party's adventures in the city above. It is scratching strange circles in the sand... that is, it is luring in the party to use its *stinking cloud* ability. Hiding nearby is another **dretch** that can be spotted with a DC 19 Perception check.

Dretch (2)   CR 2
XP 600
hp 18 (Pathfinder Roleplaying Game Bestiary, "Demon, Dretch")

Area 2-5: Dire rats

This area seems to have been set up as a camp of some sort. The remains of a small fire and a few chewed bones are tucked up against the back wall, and some tatters of woolen cloth may have once been a bedroll. This cave is home to 8 hungry **dire rats** that are dangerous on their own and even more so if they strike while the party is suffering the effects of the collapse in **Area 2-6**. In a small hollow behind the shredded bedroll is their nest; they keep their treasure here, still on the back of a dungeoneer who failed to return to the surface. The dungeoneer is wearing a backpack with a set of linen clothes, 3 torches, a shortsword, a scroll tube with 3 *arcane scrolls* (*mirror image*, *spectral hand*, and *floating disk*), and a coin purse containing 32 pp.

Dire Rat (8)   CR 1/3
XP 135
hp 5 (Pathfinder Roleplaying Game Bestiary, "Rat, Dire")

Tactics: The dire rats are defensive of their lair, although no young are present at this time. They fight aggressively until 75% of them are killed, at which point they flee into the caverns to seek another home.

Area 2-6: Bring the House Down

This chamber is different from any other on this level in that a portion of its roof is constructed of mortared stone. This section supports **Area 1-16** above, although not very well. Any loud noise, concussion of applied force (striking, leaning, pushing, and so on) against the columns or ceiling will bring it down on top of the heroes. See **Area 1-16** for damage and opportunities to recognize the danger. The damage zones are larger here; however, use the entire collapse area as the bury zone and a 10-foot perimeter beyond that as the slide zone. The instability of the pillars can be noticed with a DC 20 Knowledge (engineering) or Craft (stonemasonry) check. There is a very good chance that the party will enter this room from above!

If the **dire rats** in **Area 2-5** have not already been dealt with in some manner, they investigate the collapse. This encounter may hamper the rescue of pinned characters or deal lethal damage to an already injured party, so allow 2 or more rounds before the rats arrive.

Area 2-7: Just A Fun Guy

Hidden among the multitudes of mushrooms and fungi that cling to the walls of the corridor is a **violet fungus**. It is well fed and inactive and does not attack the party unless alerted by the **shriekers** in **Area 2-8** or attacked. Noticing it among the other fungi requires a DC 18 Perception check.

Violet Fungus   CR 3
XP 800
hp 30 (Pathfinder Roleplaying Game Bestiary, "Fungus, Violet")

Tactics: This fungus does not attack the party on sight. If it is attacked or if it hears the shriekers in **Area 2-8**, it moves as fast as it can to attack. Its primitive, fungal instincts kick in, and it fights until destroyed.

Area 2-8: The 'Shroom Room

This narrow cave is split by a fissure so deep that the bottom is beyond the reach of the party's lights. Tunnel openings are on both sides of the fissure. The entire room is densely populated with slimy fungi; a particularly tall purple variety dominates the north side. Some of the tall purple mushrooms are **shriekers**, with 2 **violet fungi** hidden at the edges of the chasm. The chasm is 10 feet wide. A failed attempt to jump the chasm requires a DC 18 Reflex saving throw to avoid being lost in the fissure. The landing on either side is slick, requiring a DC 12 Reflex saving throw to avoid falling prone; failure by more than 5 results in 1d3 bludgeoning damage.

For the purposes of this adventure, the fissure is bottomless, and any character or item falling into it is lost. Alternatively, you may use it to integrate other dungeon areas or place a river at the bottom that drains into **Area 2-24**.

Lying under a mound of fungal growth is the body of an independent burglar who fatefully tried his hand at dungeon delving; his belongings make up the treasure for this area. The treasure can be spotted with a DC 20 Perception check. The mound contains a chain shirt, a dagger, a velvet envelope containing 3 silver and emerald hairpins worth 1,200 gp, a gold bracelet worth 60 gp, and a pouch containing 18 gp and 20 sp.

Violet Fungus (2)　　　　　　　　　　　　　　　**CR 3**
XP 800
hp 30 (Pathfinder Roleplaying Game Bestiary, "Fungus, Violet")

Shrieker　　　　　　　　　　　　　　　　　　　**CR –**
XP –
This human-sized purple mushroom emits a piercing sound
　　that lasts for 1d3 rounds whenever there is movement or a
　　light source within 10 feet. This shriek makes it impossible
　　to hear any other sound within 50 feet. The sound attracts
　　nearby creatures that are disposed to investigate it. Some
　　creatures that live near shriekers learn that this noise
　　means there is food or an intruder nearby.

Tactics: The shriekers here react to any light or movement within 10 feet or anywhere on their side of the fissure. If some party members are more inclined or equipped than others to jump the fissure, this probably means that the party is split up for this encounter. The distribution of heroes between the two sides is especially important if the violet fungus from Area **2-7** has not been killed; it will arrive after 3 rounds. All of these fungi fight (and shriek) instinctively until killed.

AREA 2-9: THE LITTLE MADMAN

This small cave has two tunnels at one end. In the corner furthest from the tunnel entrances lies a crumpled body. The robes are tattered and dirty, but even from a distance they seem to be the colors of the Band of the Crimson Mantle. This is the body of Dresden the Mad (unless you have chosen to alter these events). When the Band engaged the rust monsters from **Area 2-10**, Dresden got separated from the group. The other members had far more to fear from the creatures, and they fled with their metal items, leaving the little gnome to his fate. Rust stains are around his body, and he has been scavenged of all metal items, but his remaining equipment makes up the treasure for this area. Note that any loud noises may attract the rust monsters from next door. On his body is a sling, a pouch of rocks, a *potion of fire breath*, a *potion of gaseous form*, and 2 *arcane scrolls* (*haste* and *knock*).

AREA 2-10: RUST MONSTERS

Bits of wood and leather stained with rust litter the floor in this long, narrow room. Two domed, earth-colored creatures with the appearance of large beetles burst from a burrow at the far end and rush toward the heroes as they enter. These **rust monsters** are more of Lilith's called creatures (although they are normal, not fiendish) that she turned loose in the caverns to guard against intruders. Their treasure is entirely non-metal and is mostly buried in their burrow, which can be noticed with a DC 15 Perception check. Within the burrow is 50 feet of silk rope, a jeweled leather belt with no buckle worth 160 gp, and 4 worthless weapon hafts and handles (improvised clubs).

Rust Monster (2)　　　　　　　　　　　　　　　**CR 3**
XP 800
hp 27 (Pathfinder Roleplaying Game Bestiary, "Rust Monster")

Tactics: The rust monsters rush directly toward the largest source of metal in the party, although they do not attack the same target if several similar volumes of metal are present. They do not pursue fleeing adventurers if a meal of rusted metal is available. If both are reduced to 25% of their original hit points or if one is killed, they flee.

AREA 2-11: THE ORACLE FROGS

On the right side of this tunnel is a large, dark pool of water. Sitting on a stone ledge at the back are three very large, placid-looking frogs. Their eyes swivel to watch the heroes as they walk past. A few coins are visible in the murky pool below the ledge. These **dire frogs** possess rudimentary intelligence and a gift for extra-sensory visions. They answer one question per character, per day, to a maximum of three per day. Before a question is answered, an item worth at least 1 gp must be tossed into the pool below the frogs. The pool is full of the frogs' treasure, but it is trapped with a curse that follows anyone who steals from it. At the bottom of the pool is a *potion of cat's grace*, a flask of oil, a silver hand mirror worth 11gp, a drinking horn with gold and lapis lazuli trim worth 65 gp, and a collection of 78 gp and 130 sp.

Bestow Curse Trap　　　　　　　　　　　　　　**CR 4**
XP 1,200
Type magic; **Perception** DC 28; **Disable Device** DC 28
Trigger removal of items from pool; **Reset** automatic
Effect spell effect (*bestow curse*); curse functions as per the
　　spell *bestow curse*, although you are free to use more colorful
　　curses, such as "can only eat insects" or "can only speak in
　　single syllables"; Will DC 18 negates

If attacked, the dire frogs fight until killed. They are unwilling to leave the dungeon voluntarily and resist any attempts to capture them. If the party is a single character of any size or is made up of 3 or fewer Small characters, there is a 20% chance that the frogs will be hungry and attack on sight.

Giant Dire Frog (3)　　　　　　　　　　　　　　**CR 3**
XP 800
hp 50 (Tome of Horrors Complete, "Frog, Giant Dire")

Collective Oracle (Sp): These three dire frogs have a unique
　　shared ability to perform minor acts of clairvoyance and
　　fortune telling. They answer a maximum of 3 questions per
　　day, but only 1 question per character per day. All three
　　frogs must be alive and together to answer questions. Treat
　　the questions as *divinations* with a 70% chance of accuracy.
　　The answers are limited by the frogs' vocal capabilities and
　　will always consist of three syllables, one from each frog. For
　　example, asking about a mysterious cave in which lurks a
　　dangerous, plant-based creature might result in an answer
　　such as *"vines... bring... death."* Simple questions such as
　　"Who are you?" still count toward the daily limit and produce
　　simple answers such as *"We... are... frogs."* There is a 50%
　　chance that the syllables / words are in the wrong order and
　　require deciphering by the asker.

Tactics: The dire frogs only fight if attacked. Any other activity is met with total apathy. If an opportunity to escape a fight is possible, they take it; otherwise, they fight to the best of their ability until dead.

AREA 2-12: AWWWWW, RATS!

A huge pile of rotten plant matter and flotsam has washed up in a sandy corner of this room. The 10 **rats** have hollowed out a nest in the pile of garbage, which also conceals their treasure. Within the pile of garbage, a coin purse containing 4 pp, 11 gp, and 54 sp can be found. In addition, a mummified human hand bearing the tattoo of a dragon (actually the icon of a distant cult) can be found.

Rat (10) CR 1/4
XP 100
hp 4 (Pathfinder Roleplaying Game Bestiary, "Rat, Common")

Tactics: These rats are more likely to flee than fight, although they attack any creature between them and the mouth of their cave for 1 or 2 rounds on their way out.

AREA 2-13: ASSASSIN VINES

This corridor has an unusually low ceiling. Up ahead, backlit by a purple glow, is a pile of something on the ground — bodies. More specifically, the remains of bodies: bones, armor, weapons, and baggage lie strewn across the corridor, surrounded by hundreds of tiny mushrooms of every color. The 2 **assassin vines** that dwell on the ceiling of this corridor do not strike until the remains of their victims have attracted the party. Detecting them before they attack requires a DC 20 Perception check. Their treasure is spread over the length of the corridor, along with the remains of the deceased owners. This includes a suit of half plate with skeletal remains still inside, a 50-foot length of hemp rope that will break if a load greater than 100 pounds is place on it, and a *ring of climbing* (still on a finger inside a gauntlet). The glow from down the tunnel originates in **Area 2-14**.

Assassin Vine (2) CR 3
XP 800
hp 30 (Pathfinder Roleplaying Game Bestiary, "Assassin Vine")

Tactics: As soon as one or more creatures enter the corridor below them, the vines attack, lashing out with their tough vines. They immediately attempt to use their improved grab/constrict ability and may try to hoist up a grabbed character.

AREA 2-14: A COZY HOLLOW

This small alcove is just big enough for the party to enter. Light is provided by clumps of phosphorescent fungus and the floor is relatively dry, providing a good place for a break.

A DC 15 Perception check reveals an etched sigil on the wall of this cave: the stylized initials "E.B." Elinda Bannon spent a few hours here when she passed through several days ago.

AREA 2-15: UNDERWATER TUNNEL

This underwater tunnel connects **Areas 2-1** and **2-16**. Passing through it safely requires three DC 15 Swim checks or a swim speed. Only Medium or smaller creatures may attempt it. Halfway through it is the treasure of an unsuccessful swimmer, though the skeleton has long-since washed away. The treasure is a solid gold bust of a merchant patriarch from a nearby kingdom wrapped in canvas. It is worth 900 gp although it is possibly worth more to the merchant house.

AREA 2-16: AN OGRE'S TEARS

A motionless pool of dark water stands on either side of the tunnel, with a narrow gravel path leading between. A water-filled tunnel (see **Area 2-15**) connects one of the pools with **Area 2-1**. A slab of rock at the back of the other does not quite touch the surface of the water, leaving a small pocket of air and darkness beyond. Deep, heavy sobbing can be heard from within this watery cave. This is the hiding place of **Sogrin**, an ogre wounded by Gethrax. He ventured into the caverns from downriver looking for a new lair, but the antipaladin was not very accepting of his new neighbor. Sogrin goes on the defensive as soon as the party approaches, but only fights if pressed. A gunnysack is tied to his belt. Within the gunny sack there is a *potion of cure moderate wounds*, a *potion a cure serious wounds*, a pouch containing 60 gp, 50 sp, and a dead rat.

Sogrin the Ogre   **CR 3**
XP 800

hp 30 (currently 14) (Pathfinder Roleplaying Game Bestiary,
"Ogre")

Tactics: Sogrin is wounded from his last fight and does not feel like
another one just yet. He tries to frighten the party with loud, smelly
bellowing and false lunges with his club spear. A DC 15 Sense Motive
check reveals that he is only feinting with his weapons. If given the
opportunity, he flees past the party and hides elsewhere. He is not
above making peace with the heroes and even considers joining them
to fight Gethrax, if they make such an offer. How long he stays and his
overall disposition as an NPC is up to you.

AREA 2-17: THE DEAD MAN'S PARTY

This low-ceilinged cavern stinks of fresh death and the salty-
sweet odor of blood. In one corner is the source of the stench: a pile
of eviscerated corpses under a cloud of black flies. This is the lair of
Gethrax, the powerful antipaladin. He visits the city regularly, causing
havoc here and there and retuning with news for his patron, Lilith. He
has also trapped Level **1** with his *box o' darkness* traps (see **Appendix
B**), a device crafted by a sinister order. He waits, invisible and bathed in
blood, in the far corner behind the bodies. He may know that the party
is coming from the bats in **Area 2-2** or from various other events or
loud noises. His items are the only treasure here. The *ring of invisibility*
and the hand wearing it must be bathed in still-warm blood once a week
otherwise it ceases to function for the current user.

This area is desecrated, the DC to resist negative channeled energy
within this area gains a +3 profane bonus. Every undead creature
entering a *desecrated* area gains a +1 profane bonus on all attack rolls,
damage rolls, and saving throws. An undead creature created within
or summoned into such an area gains +1 hit points per HD. The bodies
(beggars, drunks, harlots, and other "unmissed" types) are the results
of Gethrax's deranged anatomical exploration and his blood rituals.
Each corpse has a chunk of black stone in its eye socket — they are
prepared to be *animated*, and a DC 15 Spellcraft check reveals this.

Gethrax   **CR 9**
XP 6,400
Human antipaladin 10
CE Medium humanoid (human)
Init +1; **Senses** Perception +0
Aura cowardice (10 ft.), despair (10 ft.)

AC 19, touch 10, flat-footed 19 (+9 armor)
hp 75 (10d10+20)
Fort +12, **Ref** +7, **Will** +10
Immune disease
Speed 30 ft. (20 ft. in armor)

Melee +1 mighty cleaving falchion +14/+9 (2d4+5/18-20)
Special Attacks channel negative energy 4/day (DC 18, 5d6),
    smite good 4/day (+3 attack and AC, +10 damage)
Antipaladin Spell-Like Abilities (CL 10th; concentration
    +13)
    At will—*detect good*
Antipaladin Spells Prepared (CL 7th; concentration +10)
    3rd—*animate dead*
    2nd—*bull's strength, silence* (DC 15)
    1st—*bane* (DC 14), *cause fear* (DC 14), *death knell* (DC 14)

Str 16, **Dex** 12, **Con** 14, **Int** 8, **Wis** 10, **Cha** 16
Base Atk +10; **CMB** +13 (+15 sunder); **CMD** 24 (26 vs.
    sunder)
Feats Cleave, Cleaving Finish, Great Cleave, Improved

Cleaving Finish, Improved Sunder, Power Attack
Skills Acrobatics -5 (-9 to jump), Knowledge (religion) +12,
    Ride +8, Stealth +8
Languages Common
SQ cruelties (cursed, nauseated, sickened), fiendish boon
    (weapon +2, 2/day), touch of corruption 8/day (5d6)
Combat Gear ring of invisibility; **Other Gear** +2 splint mail,
    +1 mighty cleaving falchion, box o' darkness

Special Abilities

Aura of Cowardice -4 (10 ft.) (Su) Enemies in aura are not
    Immune to fear and take -4 to saves vs. fear effects.
Aura of Despair -2 (10 ft.) (Su) Enemies in aura take a -2 to
    all saves.

Description: Gethrax was a mercenary fighter who signed on with
an evil warband that was hired to hamper the efforts of a holy crusade
against a cult of evil priests. Thanks to Gethrax's leadership, the
band of paladins and clerics was destroyed before they reached the
cult's fortress deep in the Stoneheart Mountains. His success with the
mercenaries and his obvious lust for carnage won him a position in the
cult, and he began learning their dark arts for himself. His wanderings
have spread evil far wide in the name of his order, and his pact with
Lilith has made him even more dangerous. He serves as her eyes and
ears in the city and in the Ebon Union, and he has no compunction
about killing for her or anyone else. Eventually, he hopes that her
takeover of Dun Eamon will be advantageous for his secret sect.

Tactics: Gethrax prefers to use his *ring of invisibility* to surprise
his victims. He waits invisibly at the rear of his chamber, behind the
pile of corpses. When the party is at least partially distracted by the
corpses, he casts *animate dead* on the pile, creating **zombies** and
skeletons from the freshest corpses. As long as undead are functional,
Gethrax continues to cast spells such as *bane* and *silence* until the party
discovers him (although they can hear him clearly). If all the undead
are destroyed (or are about to be), Gethrax turns visible and attacks, a
terrible apparition in gore-caked armor. He chooses escape over death
if possible, but if given no opportunity for escape, he spends his final
round winding up his last *box o' darkness* trap. This *box* animates 2
more skeletons in the area (see Area **1-9** for a description of the *box
o' darkness* trap). While the skeletons attack, Gethrax turns invisible
and tries to escape.

Desecrated Skeleton (6)   **CR 1/3**
XP 135

hp 5 (Pathfinder Roleplaying Game Bestiary, "Skeleton")

Desecrated Zombie (4)   **CR 1/2**
XP 200

hp 13 (Pathfinder Roleplaying Game Bestiary, "Zombie")

AREA 2-18: THE RIVER ROOM

A powerful underground river flows along the back wall of this
cavern, and a body lies near it. Across the swift flowing river is a
secret door that leads to Level 3, where the Ebon Union has their
lair. A small ledge on the far side of the river holds a tunnel entrance
that the thieves use to come and go from their lair. It is concealed by
drooping strands of algae but is not otherwise secured. The tunnel
entrance can be spotted by a DC 18 Perception check. The door opens
easily. One must cross the river to gain access; the river is 10 feet wide
at this point and flows at a rate of 40 feet per round toward **Area 2-22**.
The river can be crossed with a DC 15 Swim check.

The thief (whose body holds this room's treasure) was headed for
the door when Gethrax surprised him in an unusually malicious mood.
The presence of his corpse may help the heroes locate the secret door.

On the thief's body there is a leather pack containing a jeweled ebony inkpot and pen (40 gp), gold hourglass (100 gp), empty map case with inlaid mother-of-pearl (35 gp), a set of thieves' tools, 50 ft. of silk rope, a grappling hook, 2 daggers, a set leather armor, 2 pouches of caltrops, and a coin pouch containing 6 gp and 10 sp.

AREA 2-19: DARKMANTLES

The corridor widens here, and there is a deep pool of murky water on one side, and a small alcove on the other. A shovel and a crowbar lie half-buried in the middle of the soggy floor. The tools are the leavings of an ill-fated pair of fortune-seekers whose bodies in the pool make up the treasure. Nearby there is a shield, a morningstar, a hooded lantern, and a coin purse containing 18 gp and 20 sp. A group of 4 **darkmantles** on the ceiling await the heroes' investigation of the pool, the chamber, or the odd debris, although they are stationed directly above the tools. From the pool, an underwater passage (see **Area 2-21**) leads to **Area 2-23**.

Darkmantle (4)   **CR 1**
XP 400
hp 15 (Pathfinder Roleplaying Game Bestiary, "Darkmantle")

Tactics: The darkmantles hang hidden over the center of the chamber, requiring a DC 20 Perception check to see (if they are being looked for). If a character enters the center of the area at any time, the darkmantles release their grip on the ceiling and attack. If the initial attacks miss, they use their *darkness* ability to cover their flight back to the ceiling for another attempt. All of these creatures fight until slain. A character whose vision is obscured by darkmantles or by darkness may find that they are prone to accident. Each round, each character should make a DC 12 Reflex saving throw to avoid falling prone (15% chance of falling into pool) and suffering 1d4 bludgeoning damage. The low DC represents that only the clumsiest or unluckiest character will stagger into a wall with a darkmantle on their head!

AREA 2-20: SLIMED

This low tunnel has many stalactites hanging from the ceiling. In addition to the water dripping down, a **green slime** waits here to drop onto unsuspecting parties, usually attacking the second or third person to pass under it. That character immediately notices a burning sensation on exposed flesh as the wet, slimy mass falls from above. A previous victim lies nearly completely buried in the tunnel with a few bits of treasure. The body requires a DC 18 Perception check to notice. The body has a handaxe, a *potion of invisibility*, and a coin pouch containing 8 gp and 20 sp.

Green Slime   **CR 4**
XP 1,200
This dungeon peril is a dangerous variety of normal slime. Green slime devours flesh and organic materials on contact and is even capable of dissolving metal. Bright green, wet, and sticky, it clings to walls, floors, and ceilings in patches, reproducing as it consumes organic matter. It drops from walls and ceilings when it detects movement (and possible food) below.

A single 5-foot square of green slime deals 1d6 points of Constitution damage per round while it devours flesh. On the first round of contact, the slime can be scraped off a creature (destroying the scraping device), but after that it must be frozen, burned, or cut away (dealing damage to the victim as well). Anything that deals cold or fire damage, sunlight, or a *remove disease* spell destroys a patch of green slime. Against wood or metal, green slime deals 2d6 points of damage per round, ignoring metal's hardness but not that of wood. It does not harm stone.

AREA 2-21: UNDERWATER TUNNEL

This tunnel is full of black water and connects **Area 2-19** to **Area 2-23**. Passing through it safely requires three DC 15 Swim checks or a swim speed. Only Medium or smaller creatures may attempt it. Characters arriving in **Area 2-23** break the surface in the middle of a very large pile of rats.

AREA 2-22: THE BIG POOL

A great pool of murky water dominates this large cavern. Piles of debris and driftwood are piled up around the edges, where the sheer walls come right down to the water. On the far wall, a swift current runs across the pool to an exit tunnel and pours over what could only be a giant waterfall. A small cave is next to the inlet of the river, but standing water isolates it from the sandy beach at the tunnel entrance.

This pool leads to the exits from this level, but it is difficult to navigate. The fast moving river current keeps the pool flowing in a whirlpool motion; thus, crossing the room is not easy. Creatures falling into the pool are swept into the reach of the **shambling mound** that dwells here or into the current and then pulls over the falls. A secret door to **Area 2-24** is not hard to locate or open, but to reach it, the party must find a way across the water. The door can be spotted with a DC 15 Perception check. This secret door is located 20 feet above water level on the wall opposite the entrance tunnels. The wind generated in **Area 2-24** causes the tendrils of slime that conceal the door to move about — that is what the party should notice. Getting to the door requires a DC 20 Climb check; falling into the pool results in being swept back toward the shambling mound. Also, a narrow ledge begins at the far edge of the waterfall and leads to another exit, but the logistics of crossing the swift current at the edge of the waterfall are complicated.

The shambling mound lurks between the entrance tunnel and the mouth of **Area 2-23** and may be mistaken for another logjam of floating debris. A DC 26 Perception check reveals the true nature of the debris. Despite the name, the creature no longer shambles; it is rooted to the bottom of the pool lest it be swept over the falls. Still, its reach threatens the exits of both tunnels, and nearly everything coming downstream gets swept once around the whirlpool, so it has grown big and lazy. Any treasure the creature might have possessed has been washed away by the swift current (although a great amount of wealth awaits in **Area 2-23**).

Accessing the secret door is the easiest way into **Area 2-24** (although not many options are available once there). The whirlpool, which flows counterclockwise at a rate of 20 feet per round, must be crossed to reach the door. The whirlpool effect in the big pool carries floating objects into the currently naturally (and over the falls!).

An alternative is to cross the river current to the far side of the waterfall and find the small ledge there. Doing so requires some way to stay afloat (floatation, a raft, magic, and so on) and a way to maneuver across the river. The current flows at a rate of 40 feet per round. The walls are smooth up to 3 feet above water level and are then rough and covered with slimy protrusions from there up to the ceiling.

Immobile Shambling Mound   **CR 6**
XP 2,400
hp 67 (Pathfinder Roleplaying Game Bestiary, "Shambling Mound")

Tactics: The shambling mound has learned the value of patience in waiting for its meals to be delivered by the river current. It waits for the heroes to enter the room, either by the water or perhaps by picking

their way across the rafts of driftwood that conceal the beast itself! It cannot move or flee, although clever heroes may decide to apply their energy to dislodging it and forcing it over the falls (which requires 20 points of damage to its underwater extremities).

Area 2-23:
Rats, Rats, and More Rats

This area, a small cave on the edge of a great pool of water, is simply full of 20 **rats**. Area effect spells, oil, and acid are far more effective ways of dealing with their numbers than killing them one by one. Either way, their treasure, which is buried in the corner, can only be accessed if they are all neutralized. The treasure contains an ebony coffer (150 gp) wrapped in canvas containing 24 three-ounce platinum bars (90 gp each) stamped with the mark of a foreign merchant house. Revealing these in the city may have complex political results, but any development is up you. An underwater passage (see **Area 2-21**) leads to **Area 2-23**.

Rat (20)   **CR 1/4**
XP 100
hp 4 (Pathfinder Roleplaying Game Bestiary, "Rat, Common")

Tactics: These rats are threatened regularly by the shambling mound and so are easily panicked. As soon as they notice an infiltrator, they rush into a clawing, biting frenzy that does not subside until they are all killed. They do not pursue a character underwater or into the reach of the shambling mound.

Area 2-24: Waterfall Well

This cavern is shaped like a cylinder, nearly 150 feet from top to bottom. The roar of falling water makes conversation in this area impossible, and the air is full of spray. A huge waterfall rushes over a precipice halfway up, crashing 80 feet down to a churning pool. Opposite that, a smaller waterfall exits a small tunnel and trickles down the slimy wall. A narrow ledge looks like it connects the exit of the small tunnel to the edge of the large waterfall. The water below swirls and eddies before flowing out through a large tunnel opening.

This is the final area on this level. The waterfall flows into a deep well leading to Level **4**, while a rough path leads to a tunnel to **Area 1-7**. A fall from (or being swept over) this waterfall results in 5d6 bludgeoning damage. A character in the pool at the base should be required to begin checking for drowning after half the normal time, due to the incredible force of water involved. Characters in the pool must struggle to escape the force of the waterfall; a DC 18 Swim check is required to stay afloat and suffer only 1d3 bludgeoning damage. Failing this check requires another check immediately to avoid going under. After 2d4 rounds, objects in the pool are swept downstream toward **Area 4-1**.

CHAPTER SIX: LEVEL 3 – A RIVER RUNS THROUGH IT

This is the third level below the surface, although it may be reached by a direct tunnel from the Ironworks (**Area Q**). Be aware that parties who arrive here via **Levels 1** and **2** will have most likely gained a level. Those parties need less recovery time between encounters, while parties coming directly from the surface will find the creatures, traps, and lack of neutral ground here very challenging indeed. The level is made up of the lair of the Ebon Union in an abandoned gnome gatehouse and the tunnels by which it is approached. The tunnels are filled with dangerous creatures, some placed by thieves and others naturally occurring. Opponents on this level include gricks, giant spiders, mephits, and an enormous squid. Also present are Lilith's abyssal troll and the bulk of the Ebon Union, including their master, Devlin.

A mighty underground river dominates the level, cutting it in half. The approach to the lair of the Ebon Union crosses it several

LEVEL 3: A RIVER RUNS THROUGH IT

Entrances: The basement of the Ironworks (**Area Q-8**) has a secret passage to **Area 3-1**. Tunnels from **Area 1-6** and **Area 2-18** converge in Area **3-9**.

Exits: The river flows over a waterfall to **Area 4-1**. The passage from **Area 3-29** leads to **Area 4-3**.

Wandering Monsters: Most of the creatures on this level have lairs and move around very little. As a result, most of the wandering monster encounters are with minor creatures or with thieves on their way in or out of the lair. Roll 1d20 every hour, or after a loud event.

1d20	Encounter
1–2	**Dire rats** (1d6 + 1, subtract from **Area 3-5**)
3–4	Ebon Union Thief (**Burglar**, **Shifter**, or **Cutpurse**)
5–6	Ebon Union Gang (1d4 **thugs**, 1d4 **knives** plus 1 or 2 **bolts** or **nets**)
7	**Giant Spider** (1, subtract from Area **3-11**)
8–20	No Encounter

Dire Rat (1d6 + 1)   CR 1/3
XP 135
hp 5 (Pathfinder Roleplaying Game Bestiary, "Rat, Dire")

Ebon Union Bolt   CR 3
XP 800
hp 22 (Pathfinder Roleplaying Game GameMastery Guide, "Dealer")

Ebon Union Burglar   CR 2
XP 600
hp 16 (Pathfinder Roleplaying Game GameMastery Guide, "Burglar")

Ebon Union Cutpurse   CR 1/2
XP 200
hp 10 (Pathfinder Roleplaying Game NPC Codex, "Cutpurse")

Ebon Union Knife   CR 1/2
XP 200
hp 5 (Pathfinder Roleplaying Game GameMastery Guide, "Pickpocket")

Ebon Union Net   CR 3
XP 800
hp 30 (Pathfinder Roleplaying Game GameMastery Guide, "Slaver")

Ebon Union Shifter   CR 2
XP 600
hp 20 (Pathfinder Campaign Setting: Isles of the Shackles, "Smuggler")

Ebon Union Thug   CR 1
XP 400
hp 16 (Pathfinder Roleplaying Game GameMastery Guide, "Street Thug")

Giant Spider   CR 1
XP 400
hp 16 (Pathfinder Roleplaying Game Bestiary, "Spider, Giant")

Shielding: The deep gnome stronghold is shielded with lead barriers. No magical detection or transportation is possible through the perimeter walls. The trap corridor is shielded as well, preventing detection and transportation magic within it.

Detections: The level radiates evil, although not to any overpowering degree.

Continuous Effects: The tunnels here are mostly dry, the water having drained off into the river. The reflected sunlight from the surface is far behind, as is the phosphorescent fungal growth; unless the party provides its own light, this area is in total darkness. The exception are the areas occupied by the Ebon Union, which are lit with torches or small fires and are considered to be in dim light.

Standard Features: In the tunnels, the walls, floors, and ceilings are all rough, unworked stone. These tunnels and chambers average 10 feet high, unless otherwise indicated. The river gorge is 100 feet from ceiling to water level on average, and the depth of the river averages 15 feet. The lair of the Ebon Union features the exquisite craftsmanship of the deep gnomes: flawlessly fitted stone floors and walls with smooth stone ceilings. In these areas, overhead clearance is only 7 feet high, unless otherwise indicated. All interior doors are of worked stone (4 in. thick; Hardness 8; hp 60; Break [DC 28]; Disable Device [DC 30]) and open inward.

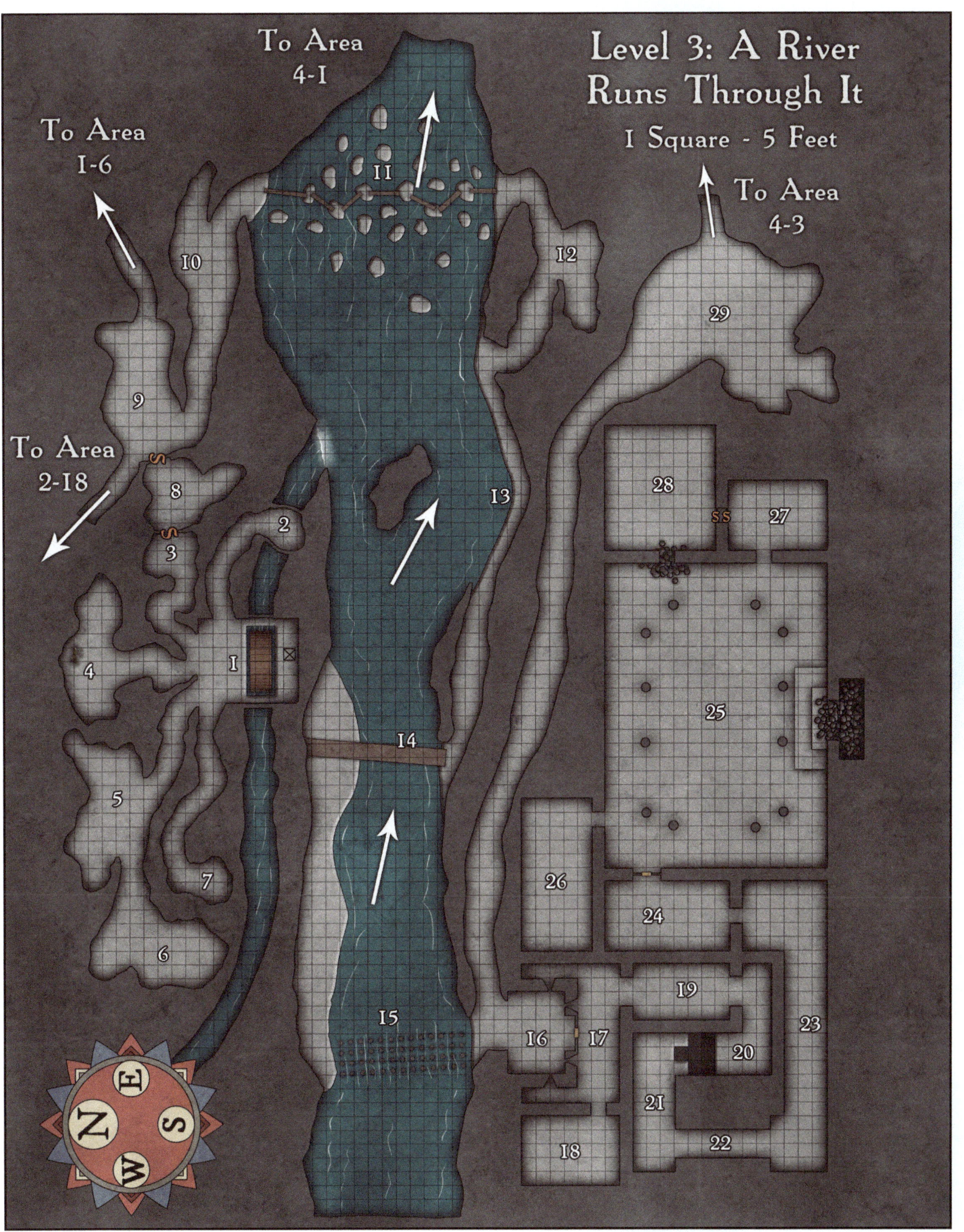

To Area 4-1
To Area 1-6
To Area 2-18
Level 3: A River Runs Through It
1 Square - 5 Feet
To Area 4-3
10
9
8
3
2
1
4
5
7
6
11
12
13
14
15
29
28
27
25
26
24
19
23
20
16
17
21
22
18
N
E
S
W

times, and some form of trap or creature protects the crossings. The gnome gatehouse once protected the entrance to the gnomes' great underground city, but the entry tunnel has collapsed, leaving a handful of rooms and the gnomes' deadly trap corridor to be inhabited by the thieves' guild.

AREA 3-1: ENTRY CHAMBER — THE IRONWORKS TUNNEL

Descent into this spray-dampened chamber lands the heroes on a stone ledge. A sluice channel has been carved into the floor to carry fast-moving icy water through the room, powering the huge waterwheel. Past the thundering wheel, there is a matching ledge on the opposite side of the channel. The sluice is one of several powerful waterways that flow through the bedrock beneath the city. The builders of the forge cut this room out of the stone to access its forceful current to power their wheel, which drives the bellows and water pumps for the forges above. The party must slip through the narrow spaces around the thundering waterwheel and over the sluice itself to proceed; this route requires a successful DC 15 Acrobatics check. Ropes, poles, ladders, or other items can be used to reduce the difficulty of this check.

The water in the sluice moves at a rate of 40 feet per round. Any character falling in is swept through a low tunnel to be expelled high over the river; falling into the river this way inflicts 4d6 points of bludgeoning damage. They are then swept downstream into **Area 4-1**, passing below Area **3-11** on the way. A character falling into the sluice upstream from the wheel have the added pleasure of being crushed before falling into the river, suffering 4d10 bludgeoning damage without a save.

The far side of the room is the same 10-foot wide ledge as the area at the base of the ladder. From here, 5 tunnels lead off in various directions. A poem that Ulf Ironfist carved on the wall upstairs in **Area Q-8** reveals which on to take — the second from the right. The others lead to various dangerous traps and encounters that are not without reward, but do not take the heroes any closer to their goal.

AREA 3-2: A WILD RIDE

This tunnel seems to dead-end as the party moves around a corner. The end of the tunnel actually occupies the space directly over the sluice tunnel from **Area 3-1**. A trap here drops characters directly into the fast-moving flow and carries them swiftly to be expelled in a long free-fall into the river gorge near **Area 3-13**. Falling into the river in this way inflicts 4d6 points of bludgeoning damage. Characters are then swept downstream into **Area 4-1**, passing below **Area 3-11** on the way.

Hidden Sluice Trap   CR 1
XP 400
Type mechanical; **Perception** DC 20; **Disable Device** DC 20
Trigger location; **Reset** manual
Effect fall into fast moving current and over waterfall; DC 20 Reflex avoids; multiple targets (all targets in a 10-ft.-square area)

AREA 3-3: SECRET DOOR

This small round chamber appears completely empty, but it hides the secret door (2 in. thick; Hardness 4; hp 30; Perception [DC 28]; Break [DC 18]; Disable Device [DC 30]) to the location of the romantic union between Lilith and some of her victims. The ground is covered with loose stone rubble (from carving the doors).

AREA 3-4: STIRGE CAVE

A collection of 7 leathery-skinned **stirges** hang near the ceiling of this chamber. The blood-drained corpse of a guild prisoner lies bound at the back of the area, the result of a painful interrogation process involving the bloodsucking beasts. He is dressed in common clothing, but an astute character might notice his boots are unusually well made with a DC 20 Perception check. In hidden compartments in the heels of his boots are the items the Ebon Union was after — the only treasure here. The hidden compartments can be found with a DC 22 Perception check. The compartment contains 3 uncut sapphires (worth 250 gp, 225 gp, and 200 gp) alongside a tiny map with landmarks but no names, except for a drawing of a gem labeled "Temple of the Azure Eye".

Stirge (7)   CR 1/2
XP 200
hp 5 (Pathfinder Roleplaying Game Bestiary, "Stirge")

Tactics: The stirges attack as soon as they have reason to believe there is prey below. They are deterred only by smoke; if it is introduced, they retreat to another area.

AREA 3-5: DIRE RATS

This small side-chamber is empty, but a deep hole in the back wall ends in shadows. It is full of 8 **dire rats**, their non-combatant young **rats**, and a few bits of treasure. Near the rats is a human ear with a pearl earring worth 120 gp alongside a silvered dagger.

Dire Rat (8)   CR 1/3
XP 135
hp 5 (Pathfinder Roleplaying Game Bestiary, "Rat, Dire")

Rat (2d6)   CR 1/4
XP 100
hp 4 (Pathfinder Roleplaying Game Bestiary, "Rat, Common")

Tactics: The dire rats attack as soon as someone begins exploring the entrance to their lair, most likely flying into the face of a single curious explorer. When 75% of them are killed, the remaining rats back into their lair and defend their offspring or flee into the dungeon.

AREA 3-6: YELLOW MOLD

This room smells dry and musty and is bare of anything of interest except for a small, fungus-covered chest in the corner. The chest is contaminated with **yellow mold** just waiting to be disturbed, but the contents are worth the risk. The chest (Hardness 5; hp 5; Break [DC 17]; Disable Device [DC 30]) was left as an emergency cache by a party of adventurers that did not survive to retrieve it. The chest contains 2 flasks of *alchemist's fire*, 4 flasks of oil, hooded lantern, 5 *sunrods*, 5 *tindertwigs*, 10 torches, 50 ft. of silk rope, 200 ft. of cotton cord, a clay jug of water (stale), and 4 *potions of cure light wounds*.

Yellow Mold   CR 6
XP 2,400
If disturbed, a 5-foot square of this mold bursts forth with a cloud of poisonous spores. All within 10 feet of the mold must make a DC 15 Fortitude save or take 1d3 points of Constitution damage. Another DC 15 Fortitude save is required once per round for the next 5 rounds, to avoid taking 1d3 points of Constitution damage each round. A successful Fortitude save ends this effect. Fire destroys yellow mold, and sunlight renders it dormant.

Area 3-7: Pit Trap

The tunnel appears to dead-end as the party turns a corner. In actuality, the last few feet of the corridor conceal a trap in the form of a concealed pit.

Pit Trap CR 2
XP 600
Type mechanical; **Perception** DC 20; **Disable Device** DC 20
Trigger location; **Reset** manual
Effect 40-ft.-deep pit (4d6 falling damage); DC 20 Reflex
  avoids; multiple targets (all targets in a 10-ft.-square area)

Area 3-8: The Love Shack

This area is at the end of the second tunnel from the right in **Area 3-1**: the only one of the five that leads somewhere productive. The tunnel opens into a small cavern that is musky with the smell of incense. Near the back, dozens of candles surround a pile of luxurious pillows and cushions and a small alabaster table. A complex mechanism of iron bars and latches is mounted to large slabs of rock that cover the tunnel entrances.

This chamber is one of the locations of the covert trysts between Lilith and Ulf Ironfist. Ulf manufactured the secret doors for Lilith to protect their cozy little hideaway. If the heroes come directly from the Ironworks, they are looking at the back of it; if they came from **Level 1** or **2**, they probably detected it from outside.

The alabaster table weighs 90 lbs. and is worth 800 gp if taken by the party. The jade incense burner alongside a box of imported incense are worth 550 gp together. The silk pillows are worth 7 gp each and a jug of strong high quality dwarven mead worth 8 gp can also be found.

Area 3-9: Entry Chamber — Tunnels from Level 1 and 2

If the party descends to this level from **Level 1** or **2**, this is the chamber that it enters. The Ebon Union uses it as a storeroom and staging area, especially when they coordinate activities from more than one location. A rough map of Dun Eamon is sketched on one wall in chalk; the locations of the burglaries, the garrison, the tavern, and all the entrances to the underground are clearly marked. A well-made secret door (2 in. thick; Hardness 4; hp 30; Perception [DC 28]; Break [DC 18], Disable Device [DC 30]) conceals the exit to **Area 3-8** and the Ironworks access point.

Area 3-10: Grick Lair

At this point, the narrow tunnel splits into two that seem to run parallel. A DC 10 Perception check allows the party to notice several sets of assorted tracks leading up the left-hand passage. A DC 15 Survival check reveals flaws in the tracks: a dwarven stride is too long, a footprint is reversed, and so forth. An unusually intelligent pair of **gricks** that dwell here has intentionally laid these tracks. Fewer visible tracks go down the right-hand tunnel due to a smaller quantity of dust.

The passage to the left narrows to little more than a crack that is long enough for the whole party to squeeze into. In the back of the crack is a pile of grisly human remains, mostly lower legs and feet with boots and shows held on by entrails and strips of flesh. The gricks use these to lure prey into their lair.

Once the party is inside, the gricks strike at the last party member in line. Their lair is on a hidden ledge above the chamber and can be

spotted with a DC 25 Perception check. On the ledge with the gricks is the body of a recent victim, a thief from the Ebon Union. The corpse possesses a *charm of silence* (see **Appendix B**) that the gricks have integrated into their tactics. The remaining treasure is stored on the ledge behind the creatures, a masterwork shortsword and a large pack of powdered silver worth 45 gp.

Grick (2) CR 3
XP 800
hp 27 (Pathfinder Roleplaying Game Bestiary 2, "Grick")

Tactics: The gricks strike as soon as they judge the party has fully entered the chamber. The smaller grick lowers the corpse of the thief, using its area of *silence* to envelop the last character in line. The large one attempts to grapple the character and drag it up onto the ledge. Once the victim is on the ledge and silenced, both creatures turn to the attack. Unless that character can find a way to announce his plight to his comrades, he may not last long against both creatures.

Area 3-11: Cavern of Spires

The smooth walled tunnel opens abruptly into a huge cavern here, roughly 100 feet across. The floor drops away over a steep cliff a few feet into the cavern, and whatever lies below is hidden by thick mist. Several dozen rough stone spires rise up from the mist, a series of stone islands in a sea of grey fog. On the opposite side of the cavern, a small ledge is visible, as well as a narrow tunnel entrance. Heavy wooden beams have been laid across the tops of the spires, forming a makeshift walkway that leads to the mouth of the other tunnel. The sound of roaring water is heard from far below.

This area has been adapted by the thieves' guild to serve as the outer line of defense for their lair. The carefully laid board walkway is a trap rigged to collapse under the weight of intruders, spilling them into the web of the 8 **giant spiders** imported from the forests outside the city.

Giant Spider (8) CR 1
XP 400
hp 16 (Pathfinder Roleplaying Game Bestiary, "Spider, Giant")

Collapsing Beam Trap CR 1
XP 400
Type mechanical; **Perception** DC 20; **Disable Device** DC 20
Trigger location; **Reset** manual
Effect The 4-inch square beams have been rigged to collapse.
  The first two beams are secure, but the third has been
  hollowed out; it appears the same as the others from above,
  but can only hold 150 pounds before snapping. A DC 18
  Reflex saving throw allows a character to leap toward the
  nearest spire, with a DC 15 Strength check required to grab
  the edge.
Characters in the spider web can attempt to escape from the
  webs with a DC 18 Escape Artist check or to break free with
  a DC 24 Strength check. The webs have hardness 5 and 4 hit
  points per 5-foot section. Grabbing a spire or lowered item
  gives a +5 bonus to an Escape Artist or break attempt. Treat
  creatures in it as entangled. The rest of the beams are secure.

The spiders' treasure is kept at the base of a large spire in the center of the chasm, along with the body of its previous owner, which can be noticed with a DC 15 Perception check — a guild thief who had stopped off for a few pints after a heist one night and took a bad step while returning to the lair. The body is wearing leather armor and is equipped with a shortsword, a dagger, a satchel containing pouch of silver dust worth 15 gp, a coin purse (8 gp, 19 sp, and 12 cp), a tobacco pipe, and a silver flask half full with cheap brandy worth 12 gp. In the bottom of the flask are 3 jade beads worth 12 gp each.

Crossing the cavern by leaping from stone to stone is possible, as many of the thieves do. This method requires a series of DC 15 Acrobatics checks. A failed check requires another DC 15 Reflex saving throw to avoid a fall. Characters must make one check for each jump attempt, and 7 attempts are required to cross the cavern. When the thieves must carry heavy objects across the chasm, they retrieve the boards stored in **Area 3-12**. The surface of the fog lies 10 feet below the tops of the spires, the spiders' webs are 10 feet below that, and another 60 feet further down is the rushing underground river. Characters falling into the river take 3d6 bludgeoning damage, with an extra 1d6 piercing damage if they manage to fall from the tops of the spires. The river carries them through a low tunnel to **Area 4-1**.

Area 3-12: Storage Cave

This area is full of flea-infested grain sacks, empty casks, and other junk. The thieves store things here on the off chance they might come in handy. Several 10-foot beams kept here are used for carrying heavy items across the chasm in **Area 3-11**.

Also present in this area is the body of Tell, Elinda Bannon's owl familiar. Tell was killed elsewhere in the dungeon and Esme brought his body here (see **Area 3-13**).

Area 3-13: Mephit Gallery

The claustrophobic tunnel gives way to a narrow ledge that snakes along the cliff, high above the fog-shrouded river. The ledge is two feet wide and can be traversed without incident, provided the heroes are not distracted by combat or other events. During combat on the ledge, treat any critical miss as a stumble; stumbling characters must make a DC 12 Reflex saving throw to avoid a fall as described below.

After making DC 15 Perception checks, the characters hear the sound of flapping wings, like some flying creature swooping through the darkness. The creature is **Esme**, a dust mephit. Her history is intertwined with the other creatures in this encounter: a pair of fire mephitis named **Iktor** and **Vlaus**, who have prepared a trap for the party. Characters falling from the ledge into the river take 4d6 bludgeoning damage and are swept over the waterfall into Area **4-1**, passing below **Area 3-11** on the way.

They have a small treasure stored on top of the isolated rock spire where they harass adventurers and thieves from out of reach. On top of the rock spire is an *everburning torch*, a *potion of water breathing*, a half melted silver ingot worth 60 gp, and 35 gp painted to appear like copper. Esme has no desire to attack the characters, only to watch them or something else die. She likes to get to know the victims of an imminent accident or ambush, and she approaches the party if permitted.

Esme's obsession with death has kept her from leaving the other mephits, though she despises them for their mischievous attitudes. They manage to create enough carnage to fulfill her requirement for death, but she would just as happily watch them die as well. The party intrigues her, and she flies about pestering them about their acts of violence and asking how painful various deaths were until they reach the halfway point of the ledge. She stops suddenly and informs the party, "Oh, um, the others will try to kill you now," and flies away to watch the show.

Esme CR 3
XP 800
hp 19 (Pathfinder Roleplaying Game Bestiary, "Mephit, Dust")

Iktor and Vlaus CR 3
XP 800
hp 19 (Pathfinder Roleplaying Game Bestiary, "Mephit, Fire")

Swinging Boulder Trap CR 3
XP 800
Type mechanical; **Perception** DC 20; **Disable Device** DC 24
Trigger location; **Reset** manual
Effect +6 ranged (2d6+4 [x4], rocks, crit x3); the rocks blend with the color of the rock and can be detected with a DC 25 Perception check; anyone struck with a rock must make an immediate DC 18 Reflex saving throw for half damage; passing the save by 5 or more results in no damage; anyone suffering full damage from a rock must make a DC 15 Fortitude save or fall from the ledge, although adjacent characters may attempt to assist or catch a falling character (adjudicate the fall on the following round, and use initiative between characters to see if they can assist in time)

Tactics: Iktor and Vlaus attack from their prepared position on top of a tall spire in the middle of the river gorge. The spire is 30 feet away, and the fiery little figures can be seen dancing in excitement on the top. On the first round of combat, they release chained rocks to swing into the ledge where the heroes stand, hoping to reduce their numbers and have a good laugh. The boulders continue to swing, coming close to the ledge every other round but losing momentum at a rate of two feet per round (impact on round 1, two feet away on round 3, four feet away on round 5, and so on), and they could be used by heroes to cross to the mephits' spire. On subsequent rounds, the mephits use *heat metal* on armored heroes, then *scorching ray*, and finally their breath weapons. They do not engage the heroes in melee unless they appear badly weakened. If they lose more than 75% of their hit points or if any mephit dies, the rest flee.

Esme, as indicated, bears no ill will toward the party, but she does hope that they either kill something in a spectacular fashion or die excitingly themselves. She can actually be a quite morbid little cheerleader throughout the conflict. She fights back if attacked, but does not flee if there is no immediate danger to her; she would rather watch the dying mephits/heroes expire.

Development: Esme, Iktor, and Vlaus were called using *Mamuthek's Aperture* (see **Appendix B**). Lilith used a chip of obsidian as the material component, hoping for a fire elemental or something equivalent. Instead, she got Iktor and Vlaus, much to her disappointment. Esme was drawn into the bargain because of the layer of dust that Lilith failed to remove from the obsidian. Furious, Lilith expelled the mephits from the lowest level of the dungeon, warning them to stay out of her way and not to attack or hinder the Ebon Union. The mephits have followed her orders out of fear, although they periodically "help" one of the thieves to his death. They know that Lilith's lair is on **Level 4**, but they are not aware of the greater plot or the events in the city. Esme, if she survives, can relate much of this information to the party; she thinks it unimportant, but she has no reason to withhold it. She may also accompany the heroes if they tolerate her company, as she sees them as a good source of death and suffering.

AREA 3-14:
BRIDGE OVER FOGGY WATERS

Nothing is unusual or dangerous about this sturdy hemp bridge, although it sways and creaks ominously with every step. On the far side, an iron ladder of individual rungs has been bolted to the wall. It descends to a narrow, gravelly beach at water level. This beach runs only one direction: along the chasm wall toward **Area 3-15**.

AREA 3-15: CALAMARI, ANYONE?

The beach narrows and disappears near the evidence of a bridge that once spanned the underground river. The waterway is wide, swift, and shallow, swirling around stone pylons that are arranged in rows of four all the way across. A large barrel of some stinking liquid stands on the beach with a bucket next to it, and a matching barrel is visible across the river.

This is the ruin of a gnome bridge. Identifying it as such with a successful DC 15 Knowledge (engineering) or Craft (stonemasonry) check may tell the heroes that they are close to the stronghold . The defender of this area is a **giant squid**. It lives in the swift-moving water downstream from the bridge, hanging on to the pylons with its tentacles to resist the force of the water. The barrels contain a strong tanning solution that the squid finds unpleasant. By flinging a bucket of it into the water upstream, the heroes can compel the squid to protect its sensory organs and thus sneak by. This has no effect on the squid during combat, when hunger overcomes instinct.

Hopping from one pylon to the next is easy. A character using a double move needs no checks to cross the remains of the bridge. Moving faster than that or charging requires a DC 12 Acrobatics check each round. Failing this check requires a DC 12 Reflex saving throw to avoid falling. The river is 50 feet wide at this point, so it should take most characters two or three rounds to cross in this manner. During combat on the pylons, a critical miss should be treated as a stumble as in **Area 3-13**; a stumbling character must make a DC 12 Reflex saving throw to avoid a fall. Anyone suffering a critical hit from the squid should check as well with a DC 15 Reflex saving throw to avoid falling.

Giant Squid CR 9
XP 6,400
hp 102 (Pathfinder Roleplaying Game Bestiary, "Squid, Giant")

Tactics: The squid attacks as soon as there are characters halfway across the pylons. Two of its eight tentacles are committed to holding itself in position against the current; it uses its arms for attacking. The tentacles holding on to the pylons can be located with a DC 15 Perception and can be attacked normally as per the called shot rules. Each arm can take 3 points of slashing damage before being severed, and any excess damage is not carried over to the creature's total hit points. Piercing and bludgeoning weapons deal damage to the

creature's total hit points. Each time one of these tentacles is severed, the squid reallocates one of its remaining tentacles on its initiative. If both anchoring tentacles are severed before the squid's initiative, it tumbles away downstream.

On the far side of the bridge, the tunnel turns back downstream toward **Area 3-29**, and **Area 3-16** is readily visible just ahead.

Area 3-16: Entry Alcove

This small area is carved from solid rock and adorned with images of gnome culture. If the party has not yet encountered any thieves on this level, the alcove is unthreatened. If a randomly encountered guild member or members survived, then four **Bolts** man **Area 3-17**. An iron door (2 in. thick; Hardness 10; hp 60; Break [DC 28]; Disable Device [DC 30]) protects the entrance to the gnome's gatehouse.

Ebon Union Bolt (4)   **CR 3**
XP 800
hp 22 (Pathfinder Roleplaying Game GameMastery Guide, "Dealer")

Area 3-17: Gatehouse

If the party has engaged thieves on this level but allowed survivors to escape, they have returned to their lair with a report and the level of security has increased. If Devlin learns (presumably from survivors)

that a party of adventurers is making its way down the tunnels, he posts 4 **Bolts** in this area (though they tend to post a single lookout and retire to **Area 3-18**). Subtract these thieves from the total in **Area 3-25**. Devlin keeps the heightened watch for 24 hours or until he has reason to believe the threat has passed. The thieves fire their crossbows at anyone not announcing themselves as loyal servants of the Ebon Union. If the sentries do not know the interlopers, they summon reinforcements and Devlin from within the lair.

Ebon Union Bolt (4)   **CR 3**
XP 800
hp 22 (Pathfinder Roleplaying Game GameMastery Guide, "Dealer")

Tactics: If the crossbowmen are here, then the party is expected. As soon as they become aware of the characters, the crossbowmen set up a lethal crossfire from the arrow slits, focusing on anyone trying to open the door. If the door opens, one of them tries to escape into **Area 3-19** to go warn Devlin, while the others cover his retreat. If half of them are killed, the others withdraw through the series of traps to make a report and prepare for the party as a group.

Area 3-18: Guardroom

This room used to house a small unit of gnome guards to man the gatehouse, but now it is set up to accommodate a few thieves who might be assigned to watch the entrance. An upturned crate serves as a card table, and numerous empty bottles are strewn around the room. The deck of cards has six aces.

AREA 3-19: BUT IN DWARF-SCRIPT, GNOME BEGINS WITH

This rectangular room is lit by a soft, ambient glow. Stone tiles etched with letters and strange, unrecognizable icons cover most of the floor. A large slab of marble set into one wall bears an inscription, with something scrawled next to it in charcoal. In this chamber is the first of several traps and puzzles the heroes must overcome to gain access to the Ebon Union's lair. Since the lair is in the gatehouse of an ancient deep gnome stronghold, the engineers found it easier to recondition some of the gnome traps rather than create their own.

The floor here is divided into a series of stone tiles, each with a different letter or symbol on it. The letters come from every alphabet imaginable: Dwarven, Elven, Common, Infernal, Celestial, and so on. Only certain tiles can bear the weight of a person, and a riddle on the wall indicates which ones. On a marble slab recessed into the wall are four lines of text in Gnome, using the Dwarven script. On the wall next to the marble slab, someone has written the Common translation in charcoal.

> *To find the way to city deep*
> *Follow host into his keep*
> *But tread with caution lest you name*
> *An enemy and lose the game.*

This fairly straightforward riddle suggests that the tiles that spell out the name of the host are safe, which they are. The heroes, however, must puzzle out whose stronghold they are in. The party can do this by considering the text, analyzing the craftsmanship of the chamber, or by recalling rumors from the city. Skills such as Craft (stonemasonry), Knowledge (history), and Linguistics may be useful, as well as spells such as *tongues*. Furthermore, the answer ("gnome") must be translated back into Gnome and spelled out using the Dwarven runes on the floor.

If any tiles other than the Dwarven runes that spell out "gnome" in Gnome are touched, the trap is triggered. When an incorrect tile is stepped on, all the tiles in a 5-foot square area around the triggering tile collapse into a pit, including any otherwise correct tiles. The tiles are 6 inches square, and to step on one without touching the surrounding tiles requires a DC 15 Acrobatics check. Moving across the room requires three such checks. The bottom of the pit is hidden by magical *darkness* and *silence*.

Tile Pit Trap   CR 2
XP 600
Type mechanical; **Perception** DC 21; **Disable Device** DC 25
Trigger location; **Reset** manual
Effect 40-ft.-deep pit (4d6 falling damage); DC 35 Reflex
    avoids; the high save DC represents the fact that the
    character must land solely on another appropriate tile

AREA 3-20: ILLUSIONARY HALLWAY PINCUSHION TRAP

This rectangular chamber is lit like the first. There is a pit in the floor whose bottom is lost in darkness. On the far side of the pit is the doorway in the wall, surrounded by age-tarnished spikes. There is

no ledge at the threshold, only the hallways beyond. In this area, it is the illusions for which gnomes are notorious that present a trap to be overcome. The doorway and corridor image is an illusion; that space on the wall is actually solid stone covered in sharp spikes. The visible spikes are illusions as well, for they cover the actual doorways to the corridors, one on either side of the spike field. The most likely initial response is a running jump into the concealed spikes. The only way in is to jump through the illusionary spikes and land in the hallway. The illusion can be broken with a successful DC 18 Will saving throw.

The jump itself is not very difficult, but the consequences are dangerous. The pit is 10 feet across and 15 feet wide (the width of the area). A DC 15 Acrobatics check allows a character to clear the pit. If a character hits the real spikes, she suffers 1d4 hits, each dealing 1d4+2 points of damage, and must make a Strength or Climb check (DC 12 +1 per successful spike hit) to hold on to the spikes. Leaping into the illusionary spikes sends a character skidding into the hallway beyond. Falling into the pit (because of a failed Acrobatics check or failure to hang onto the spikes) results in 4d6 points of damage. The bottom of the pit is hidden by magical *darkness* and *silence*.

Pit Trap   CR 2
XP 600
Type mechanical; **Perception** DC 0; **Disable Device** DC 20
Trigger location; **Reset** none
Effect 40-ft.-deep pit (4d6 falling damage); DC 20 Reflex
    avoids

Spiked Trap   CR 2
XP 600
Type mechanical; **Perception** DC 20; **Disable Device** DC 20
Trigger location; **Reset** none
Effect spikes (Atk +10 melee, 1d4 spikes for 1d4+2 damage
    each); DC 26 Reflex for half

AREA 3-21: DISASSEMBLED TRAP

This area is cluttered with shattered chunks of stone, bent iron rods, gears, and vicious-looking blades. There is a doorway on the far side of the rubble. The engineers of the Ebon Union were unable to devise the function and application of this trap and had to destroy it. A character with Knowledge (engineering) can spend several minutes here examining the debris to gain a +1 insight bonus when dealing with mechanical traps of gnome origin.

AREA 3-22: SHOCKING DEVELOPMENTS

This stretch of hallway is floored with simple grey and green marble tiles. There are 50 of them, in 10 rows of five, set in no obvious pattern or order. Scrawled charcoal writing in Common is on the wall, but there is corresponding Gnome script. A door is at the far end. This open expanse of hallway is trapped, and the charcoal writing on the wall again reminds the thieves (some of whom are not especially sharp) how to enter safely. The black scrawl near the door reads:

> *Foolish feet that walk astray*
> *Bring bolts of lightning from the floor*
> *Escape a frightening crisping — go*
> *Where every other went before*

Perhaps this is some gnome riddle used to grant safe passage, but when the Ebon Union restored it to operation for their purposes, such trivialities were done away with and they periodically reset the tiles in a completely random fashion. What is important is the arrangement of the pressure-plate triggers beneath the tiles, which are still arranged in the original gnome layout: a checkerboard grid. The clue in the rhyme is "where *every other* went before," meaning that *every other* tile is trapped, regardless of color. By starting directly opposite the entrance and skipping every other tile, a character can proceed unharmed with no checks at all. The first tile opposite the door is green and all the others in that row are grey; the party may have found a scrap of paper in **Area 1-3** that refers to this. There are an equal number of grey and green tiles because they used to be laid out in the checkerboard pattern, so counting tiles may help solve the puzzle (25 of each color). Analyzing the trap can also reveal the secret, but any failed Disable Device check in this regard triggers the trap and delivers the lightning shock if the tile is actually trapped underneath.

Shocking Floor Trap   CR 9
XP 6,400
Type magic; **Perception** DC 26; **Disable Device** DC 26
Trigger proximity (alarm); **Reset** automatic
Effect spell effect (shocking grasp, Atk +9 melee touch [4d6
    electricity damage]); multiple targets (every other 2-ft. x 2-ft.
    section of floor)

AREA 3-23: GNOME BARBEQUE

This corridor is longer and narrower than most, tiled rather simply compared to the last chamber. The air smells thickly of something aged and earthy, and the corridor turns a corner at the far end. The area beneath the floor is filled with natural gas, and a character making a DC 15 Knowledge (nature) check might recognize it as smelling like swamp gas. The simple stone tiles have wide cracks in between, which allow the gas to seep up. If an open flame is carried over the tiles, the gas is ignited and flares up between the cracks in a spectacular wall of flame.

The gnomes had solved their problem with the sensitivity of the gas by applying the effects of a *quench* spell to the entire corridor, which is still in effect. Any character stepping through the doorway from **Area 3-22** is subject to the effects, and all non-magical fires on their person (torches, lanterns, candles, and so forth) are extinguished. The spell cannot affect magic items and magical fires. Conveniently, this allows parties to proceed safely into the darkness without igniting the gas.

Yet the *quench* only extinguishes open flames, not sparks. If a character attempts to relight their torch with a tinderbox or otherwise creates a source of ignition, the gas explodes, causing 6d6 fire damage to all within the chamber. Only characters within half of their movement of either door may attempt a save.

Natural Gas Trap   CR 4
XP 1,200
Type mechanical; **Perception** DC 20; **Disable Device** DC 25
Trigger location; **Reset** automatic
Effect ball of flame (6d6 fire damage); DC 15 Reflex for half

AREA 3-24: ANTECHAMBER

The chamber at the end of the series of trapped hallways is wider by several feet and is unlit. A large iron door (2 in. thick; Hardness 10; hp 60; Break [DC 28]; Disable Device [DC 30]) is on one side. Stacked against the walls are several long poles, a few polearms, ladders, coils of rope, and some small casks and crates. This is the anteroom to the gnomes' gate chamber (**Area 3-25**). The only treasure is the collection of items that the Ebon Union needs only during their forays to the surface or items they have not yet brought into their lair. This includes a canvas bundle with two rapiers and two glaives, two 100-ft. coils of hemp rope, 20 torches, a cord of firewood, a miner's pick, a shovel, two buckets, and a cask of ale worth 10 gp.

AREA 3-25: GATES TO THE DEEP

This chamber was the focal point of the old gnome stronghold, as it held the massive stone gates to their underground community. In events that may or may not have been connected to the gnomes' departure, the tunnel beyond the gates collapsed, sealing off access to their city and isolating the gatehouse complex. The gatehouse stood empty for untold years before being discovered by the Ebon Union. The room is easily three times the height of the corridor that approaches it, and massive, ornately carved columns support its vaulted ceiling. A stone ledge runs all the way around the room at a height of 10 feet. On one wall, a pair of enormous doors stands wide open, revealing piles of rock and rubble beyond. The chamber is obviously in use as a makeshift dormitory and mess hall; pallet beds, hammocks, trestle tables, and cooking fires contrast sharply with the stately stone edifices.

This room is a significant encounter, most likely a showdown with the core of the Ebon Union (5 **thugs**, 5 **knives**, 6 **bolts**, 2 **nets**, 2 **cutpurses**, a **shifter**, and a **burglar**) and **Devlin**. If any Bolts were killed in Area **2-17**, subtract them from those found here. Do not subtract any thieves killed elsewhere in the dungeon, as it is assumed that they were coming or going on business in the city. This group represents the number that can be found here at any given time. If the Ebon Union is expecting trouble (probably because a thief escaped a previous encounter and made it back), they have used the time to prepare a nice welcome for the party. If the party manages a stealthy approach to the lair (that is, without encountering any thieves or triggering any of the traps in Areas **3-19, 20, 22, 23**), they may catch the thieves at rest and off their guard. The encounter is structured based on the high probability of the former; if the party achieves complete surprise, a few modifications may be necessary. There is a chance that the party may attempt to infiltrate one or more characters into the thieves' guild — see the Ebon Union section of the **Appendix C** for details on the process.

If the thieves are aware of the heroes' approach, they take up positions in hiding around the room and in adjacent chambers. The Bolts and Nets occupy the high ledge, hidden by shadows, pillars, or piles of trash and bedding. The Knives are hidden around the lower portion of the room, under tables, in beds, behind crates, and so on. The possessions of the various combatants of this room constitute the treasure.

Ebon Union Bolt (6)   CR 3
XP 800
hp 22 (Pathfinder Roleplaying Game GameMastery Guide,
    "Dealer")

Ebon Union Burglar   CR 2
XP 600
hp 16 (Pathfinder Roleplaying Game GameMastery Guide,
    "Burglar")

Ebon Union Cutpurse (2)   CR 1/2
XP 200
hp 10 (Pathfinder Roleplaying Game NPC Codex, "Cutpurse")

Ebon Union Knife (5)   CR 1/2
XP 200
hp 5 (Pathfinder Roleplaying Game GameMastery Guide,
    "Pickpocket")

Ebon Union Net (2)   CR 3
XP 800
hp 30 (Pathfinder Roleplaying Game GameMastery Guide, "Slaver")

Ebon Union Shifter   CR 2
XP 600
hp 20 (Pathfinder Campaign Setting: Isles of the Shackles,
    "Smuggler")

Ebon Union Thug (5) — CR 1

XP 400

hp 16 (Pathfinder Roleplaying Game GameMastery Guide, "Street Thug")

Devlin, Master of the Ebon Union — CR 7

XP 3,200

Human unchained rogue 8

NE Medium humanoid (human)

Init +8; **Senses** Perception +11

AC 18, touch 14, flat-footed 14 (+4 armor, +4 Dex)

hp 52 (8d8+16)

Fort +3, **Ref** +10, **Will** +2

Defensive Abilities danger sense +2, evasion, improved uncanny dodge

Speed 30 ft.

Melee +1 keen rapier +9/+4 (1d6+5/15-20), mwk short sword +9/+4 (1d6-1/19-20)

Special Attacks sneak attack +4d6

Str 8, **Dex** 18, **Con** 12, **Int** 14, **Wis** 10, **Cha** 14

Base Atk +6; **CMB** +5; **CMD** 19

Feats Improved Initiative, Improved Two-weapon Fighting, Quick Draw, Skill Focus (Bluff), Two-weapon Fighting, Weapon Finesse

Skills Acrobatics +15, Appraise +13, Bluff +16, Diplomacy +13, Disable Device +21, Escape Artist +15, Intimidate +13, Perception +11, Sense Motive +11, Sleight of Hand +15, Stealth +20

Languages Common, Elven, Undercommon

SQ debilitating injury: bewildered, debilitating injury: disoriented, debilitating injury: hampered, rogue talents (coax information, eerie disappearance [full round action, 60 feet], false attacker, fast stealth), trapfinding +4

Combat Gear potion of invisibility; **Other Gear** +1 shadow studded leather, +1 keen rapier, mwk short sword, masterwork thieves' tools

Special Abilities

Coax information (Ex) Can use Bluff or Diplomacy to force an opponent to act friendly.

Debilitating Injury: Bewildered -2/-4 (Ex) Foe who takes sneak attack damage takes AC pen (more vs. striker) for 1 rd.

Debilitating Injury: Disoriented -2/-4 (Ex) Foe who takes sneak attack damage takes attack pen (more vs. striker) for 1 rd.

Debilitating Injury: Hampered (Ex) Foe who takes sneak attack damage has speed halved (and can't 5 ft step) for 1 rd.

Eerie Disappearance (Ex) Move up to speed to cover/ concealment, Stealth to Hide, Demoralize foes that lost track of you.

False Attacker (immediate action) (Ex) Attack from hiding, Bluff check to deceive foe into thinking another foe was the attacker.

Description: Devlin inherited leadership of the Ebon Union after the organization was devastated by the inquisition of a group of paladins, lawful priests, and ambitious adventurers. The previous guildmaster and his lieutenants were killed, and many of the thieves were incarcerated for their crimes or returned to petty thievery and extortion. Of the small group that remained together and fled the city, Devlin was the most charismatic and held the highest rank. The group subsisted on highway robbery for a time before settling under Dun Eamon (a portion of the gang remains in the Eamonvale wilderness; see the **Appendix D**). Despite the fact that he had few men and almost no resources, Devlin's tactical instinct and clever plans have helped turn the Ebon Union into an efficient and wealthy organization. He has impressed upon his men the value of preparation and teamwork and taught them that abandoning a heist before it turns sour is sometimes best. In return, he demands ultimate loyalty from his men and punishes turncoats and skimmers ruthlessly. The men respect and obey him and would die before betraying him or their brothers.

Devlin is a slender, dark-haired man with a smooth voice and an aura of cool confidence. He will always attempt to talk instead of fight during a transaction, but when the deal is too far gone to salvage, his rapier is as quick as his tongue and as sharp as his mind.

Tactics: The thieves of the Ebon Union are very likely aware of the party's approach, either from encountering them elsewhere in the dungeon, engaging them in Area **3-16**, or by listening to the various sounds resulting from the triggering of traps along the corridor. If this is the case, the Bolts and Nets take up positions in hiding around the gallery in the chamber requiring a DC 19 Perception check to notice. The Knives hide around the bases of the columns and amid the pallet beds and other furnishings on the floor requiring a DC 17 Perception check to notice. If the party achieves surprise, the thieves are scattered about sleeping, playing cards, drinking, or training. In either case, they respond to the party's entrance immediately, attempting to gain a surprise round of missile fire and net dropping before entering melee and attempting to flank as many heroes as possible. The Thugs and the other specialists enter from Area **3-26** to join the fray. Devlin enters from Area **3-27**, along with any unique NPCs who may have survived previous encounters, such as **Kubris**, **Thurf**, or **Gulik**. This development increases the difficulty of this encounter; consider having these NPCs advance and become recurring villains instead. If Tabitha survived, she is not present, but rather stayed in the city.

Devlin is a skilled swordsman, but he prefers to escape alive if possible. He joins the fight in such a way as to minimize his apparent ability if he has a clear shot at the exit corridor (he does not want to be targeted as the leader if the battle is going poorly). If death is imminent and his escape is blocked, only a heroic death will do. The other thieves flee or surrender if two-thirds of them are killed or if the heroes kill more than double their own number in a single round. Realistically, the party will have trouble defeating the thieves if they are allowed to establish flanking positions. If the heroes use the doorway to protect their flanks and cast area effect spells to deal damage, the thieves should not present an undefeatable challenge. The only treasure in this area is the equipment of the thieves; the rest is hidden away in Area **3-28**.

Development: The further exploration of the gnome tunnels beyond the rubble-choked gates is a possibility, but the results of such a venture are left to you (see Resolution).

Area 3-26: Chapel

This room was clearly a religious fixture of some type, but it now serves as more of a kitchen. Crates and barrels are stacked near an altar, several strings of vegetables are hung in place of ruined tapestries, and a large barrier now serves as a scummy stewpot. This room was originally a shrine to a gnome god, either a recognizable deity or one long forgotten, at your discretion. It has now been modified to serve as the Ebon Union's primary cooking and food storage area. The dry goods that are stored here are of poor quality and are aged well past freshness, but several cases of salted meats make the stews worth eating. The brazier is the only treasure in the room and is worth 200 gp.

Area 3-27: Private Quarters

Devlin has taken for himself the quarters that were once given to the commander of the gnome garrison. A few of the items here are valuable bits of treasure that serve enough of a purpose to be kept out of the hoard. The room features running water, piped in by some unknown gnome method, although the receiving basin is shattered and replaced with a wooden tub. Devlin's sleeping arrangements consist of a massive pile of 10 silken pillows draped with two bolts of valuable fabric stolen during the days of highway banditry. A large table dominates the room's center and holds several maps of the city and the surrounding wilderness, a magnifying lens, scales, and a pair of oil lamps. The magnifying glass, oil lamps, and pillows are worth 7 gp each. The bolts of fabric are slightly soiled and worth 30 gp each. A secret (Perception DC 28; Break DC 18) leads to **Area-28**.

Area 3-28: The Hoard

This room is dirty and filled with rubble except for a raised platform in the back corner. Piled upon this platform are the ill-gotten gains of dozens of heists: stacks of shining silver coins, gem-encrusted serving pieces, and gold-embroidered tapestries. Stacked around the bottom of the platform are two wooden chests, canvas wrapped bundles, a large mirror, a small casket trimmed in silver, and several other items of exquisite beauty, exemplary craftsmanship, and, presumably, great value. The treasure is dominated by silver coin (of which there is simply a lot) and unique or hard-to-market items; the simple serving pieces and jewelry have already been fenced. The chests are trapped to protect their contents from the prying fingers of greedy thieves as well as from outsiders.

Large Chest's Poison Dart Volley Trap CR 2
Type mechanical; **Perception** DC 20; **Disable Device** DC 15
Trigger location; **Reset** none
Effect poison darts (Atk +10 ranged, 1d3 plus poison [large scorpion venom]); multiple targets (all targets in a 10-ft.-square area)

Large Scorpion Venom
Type poison (injury); **Save** Fortitude DC 17; **Frequency** 1/round for 6 rounds; **Cure** 1 save
Effect 1d2 Str damage

The large chest contains 978 gp, a leather belt worth 15 gp that contains concealed pouches holding 8 gold bars worth 20 gp each, a wooden case holding 30 small silver bars worth 5 gp each, an iron box with 25 pp, and two small platinum bars worth 50 gp each.

Small Chest's Poison Latch Needle Trap CR 3
XP 800
Type mechanical; **Perception** DC 20; **Disable Device** DC 20
Trigger touch; **Reset** none
Effect Atk +5 melee (1 damage plus poison [giant wasp poison])

Giant Wasp Poison
Price 210 gp
Type poison (injury); **Save** Fortitude DC 18; **Frequency** 1/round for 6 rounds; **Cure** 1 save
Effect 1d2 Dex damage

The small chest contains an assortment of 50 agates, azurite, turquoise, and other gems worth 10 gp each. In addition, the chest also contains 10 bloodstone and quartz gems worth 50 gp each.

Silver-Trimmed Casket Curse Trap   CR 4
XP 1,200
Type magic; **Perception** DC 28; **Disable Device** DC 28
Trigger opening the casket; **Reset** automatic
Effect spell effect (*bestow curse*, -6 Wisdom); Will DC 19
    negates

The silver-trimmed casket is cursed. The casket contains the mummified remains of an infant prince from an ancient desert kingdom wearing a hammered-gold death mask with garnet eyes worth 1,500 gp. The casket itself is worth 900 gp.

Treasure: The treasure horde contains a masterwork greatsword, a set of masterwork half-plate with a winged helm, a canvas bundle containing a silvered short sword with amethysts in the cross guard (580 gp), a canvas bundle containing a curtain of glass beads and freshwater pearls (1,000 gp), a canvas bundle containing four bolts of trade-grade silk (100 gp each), a canvas bundle containing two bolts of exquisite silk (200 gp each), a full-length mirror in ivory frame (60 lbs., 750 gp), a silver pitcher (35 gp), a silver serving platter (20 gp), six lead-crystal goblets in wooden case (15 gp each, or 100 gp for entire set), two gold marriage goblets (50 gp each), a gold-rimmed bowl (28 gp), a set of six jeweled masquerade masks (wolf 90 gp, lion 95 gp, hawk 100 gp, bull 100 gp, unicorn 105 gp, dragon 110 gp), and 6,780 sp.

AREA 3-29:
TOUGHER THAN THE AVERAGE TROLL

This cavern is one of the largest on this level, with several smaller caves and a tunnel exiting the far side. A huge, black-skinned humanoid beast is digging in the sandy floor at the base of a crack in the wall, as if it were looking for something. Roll immediately to establish awareness. This **abyssal troll** was called from the Abyss after Lilith obtained the items from the Seer's Parlor and the Root-Cutter's Shop. She placed it at the edge of **Level 3** to protect her domain and to keep thieves from wandering down into her lair. The **Band of the Crimson Mantle** (see **Appendix C**) is hiding here, injured and cornered by the troll. For this encounter, they are all at 50% of their maximum hit points. Unless you choose to do otherwise, Dresden the Mad has already been killed (his body may have been found on **Level 2**). They take advantage of the party's arrival to escape, taking some cheap shots at them on the way.

Abyssal Troll   CR 6
XP 2,400
hp 63 (Appendix A: New Creatures, "Troll, Abyssal")

Pratchett   CR 4
XP 1,200
hp 28 (currently 13) (Appendix C: NPC Descriptions, "Pratchett")

Isidra   CR 4
XP 1,200
hp 24 (currently 11) (Appendix C: NPC Descriptions, "Isidra")

Yelm   CR 4
XP 1,200
hp 48 (currently 23) (Appendix C: NPC Descriptions, "Yelm")

Tactics: The troll is easily distracted from his project and attacks as soon as he becomes aware of the party. He ignores the fleeing Band and continues to attack the heroes until killed.

The Band of the Crimson Mantle has been pinned in the small cave for several hours, recovering and monitoring the troll's activities. As soon as the troll leaves the opening of the cave (most likely to fight the party), the Band grabs its possession and races for the tunnel exit to **Level 4**. On the way, it targets the party with a few minor attacks, such as a crossbow bolt from Pratchett and a *bane* spell from Isidra, mostly adding insult to whatever injuries the troll is inflicting. Unless the party goes to great lengths to stop the Band, it successfully exits the area.

Development: The Band of the Crimson Mantle has proven to be cruel, cowardly, and evil, but Yelm still has an opportunity to redeem himself. If the party has lost members or is in need of NPC support, you may consider having Yelm desert the Band and join the party. If this is the case, Yelm turns from his flight and attacks the troll from behind (he is not inclined to run from a good fight and has been less than enthusiastic about Pratchett's leadership of the Band). This premise can be used to introduce Yelm as a new character or NPC. The extra muscle will be of use on **Level 4**, and this is an easy way to replace casualties or add hirelings without the party needing to revisit the surface. Consider the party's past dealings with the Band when determining the outcome of this development. If the party is faring well, Yelm flees with the rest of the Band.

Chapter Seven: Level 4 — Mamuthek's Managerie

This is the lowest known level of the underground network of caverns and rivers. It is smaller than the others, but populated with more powerful creatures. The terrible products of Lilith's experimentation with *Mamuthek's Aperture* are here: an Abyssal minotaur, a cursed treant, dretches, howlers, and the usual dungeon vermin. Lilith awaits the party with role-playing and combat challenges.

Area 4-1: Twin Falls

Two powerful waterfalls crash from considerable height to churn the pool below into brown foam. Bits of driftwood and debris float at the edges of the pool. A small, sandy beach on one side of the chamber features a water-carved corridor leading into the rock wall. The water flows out through a low, dark tunnel. The sandy beach leads into Lilith's lair, passing several of her powerful minions on the way. Following the river leads past two additional beaches, one of which has an entrance to the lair. Being swept over either of these waterfalls has the same results as the one in **Area 2-24**.

Area 4-2: Dire Rats

A chorus of hissing squeaks can be heard from within a small side-cavern. Above those sounds, the crunching of bone and the popping of ligaments is audible. In a grisly display of scavenger appetite, the 6 **dire rats** here are dismembering the bloated corpse of an adventurer that washed down from somewhere upriver (at your discretion, this corpse and its items could be replaced with the body and items of a party member lost in one of the rivers on a previous level). The adventurer's body is torn, waterlogged, and distended with the gaseous byproducts of advanced decay. In its smelly pouches is the treasure of this chamber: a *potion of cure serious wounds*, a packet of *dust of tracelessness*, a chain shirt, a battleaxe, a masterwork shortbow, a quiver with 10 arrows, and a pouch with 35 gp.

Dire Rat (6) CR 1/3
XP 135
hp 5 (Pathfinder Roleplaying Game Bestiary, "Rat, Dire")

Area 4-3: Entry Chamber — Tunnel from Level 3

The floor of this chamber is flat and sandy, with a great confusion of tracks pointing in every direction. A tunnel exits into darkness on one side and another gives way to a corridor on the opposite side that branches in two directions. This room is empty of anything of interest except for two clues. Only an expert can analyze the tracks on the floor. With a successful DC 28 Survival check, they reveal the presence of howlers, dretches, and humanoids (the remnants of the Band of the Crimson Mantle), but not which direction they went or how long ago. Carved on the wall near the corridor entrance is another "EB" sigil from Elinda Bannon. Finding the mark requires a successful DC 15 Perception check.

Level 4: Mamuthek's Menagerie

Entrances: The river from **Area 2-24** flows through a low tunnel to **Area 4-1**. A river from Level **3** flows over a falls into **Area 4-1** as well. A tunnel from **Area 3-29** leads to **Area 4-3**.

Exits: The only exit from this level leads out of the underground caverns and into the gorge below the city. The river that flows through this level joins the flow of the waterfalls that spill from around the island city and falls several hundred feet into a deep pool.

Wandering Monsters: With the exception of a few minor creatures, the denizens of this level stick to their respective areas. Check on 1d20 for wandering monsters only every two hours; loud events do not produce any special interest, but they do warn the occupants of the trespassers' presence.

1d20	Encounter
1–2	Screaming, demonic bellowing or mad gibbering noises
3–4	**Dire rats** (1d4, subtract from **Area 4-2**)
5–6	**Dretches** (1d2, subtract from **Area 4-8**)
7–20	No Encounter

Dire Rat (1d4) CR 1/3
XP 135
hp 5 (Pathfinder Roleplaying Game Bestiary, "Rat, Dire")

Dretch (1d2) CR 2
XP 600
hp 18 (Pathfinder Roleplaying Game Bestiary, "Demon, Dretch")

Shielding: No areas are shielded on this level, but Lilith wears an *amulet of proof against detection and location* that shields her alignment and true nature.

Detections: The entire level radiates evil and chaos. The demonic auras of the various Abyssal creatures and the foul acts that have taken place here saturate the place with a palpable aura of darkness. The cursed treant in Area **4-6** radiates an aura of desperation and anguish.

Continuous Effects: These lowest caverns are mostly dry. Unless the party provides its own light source, the area is in total darkness.

Standard Features: The walls and ceilings are rough with stalactites and mineral formations. The floor is covered with sand from the river and is generally dry. Overhead clearance is 10 feet unless otherwise indicated.

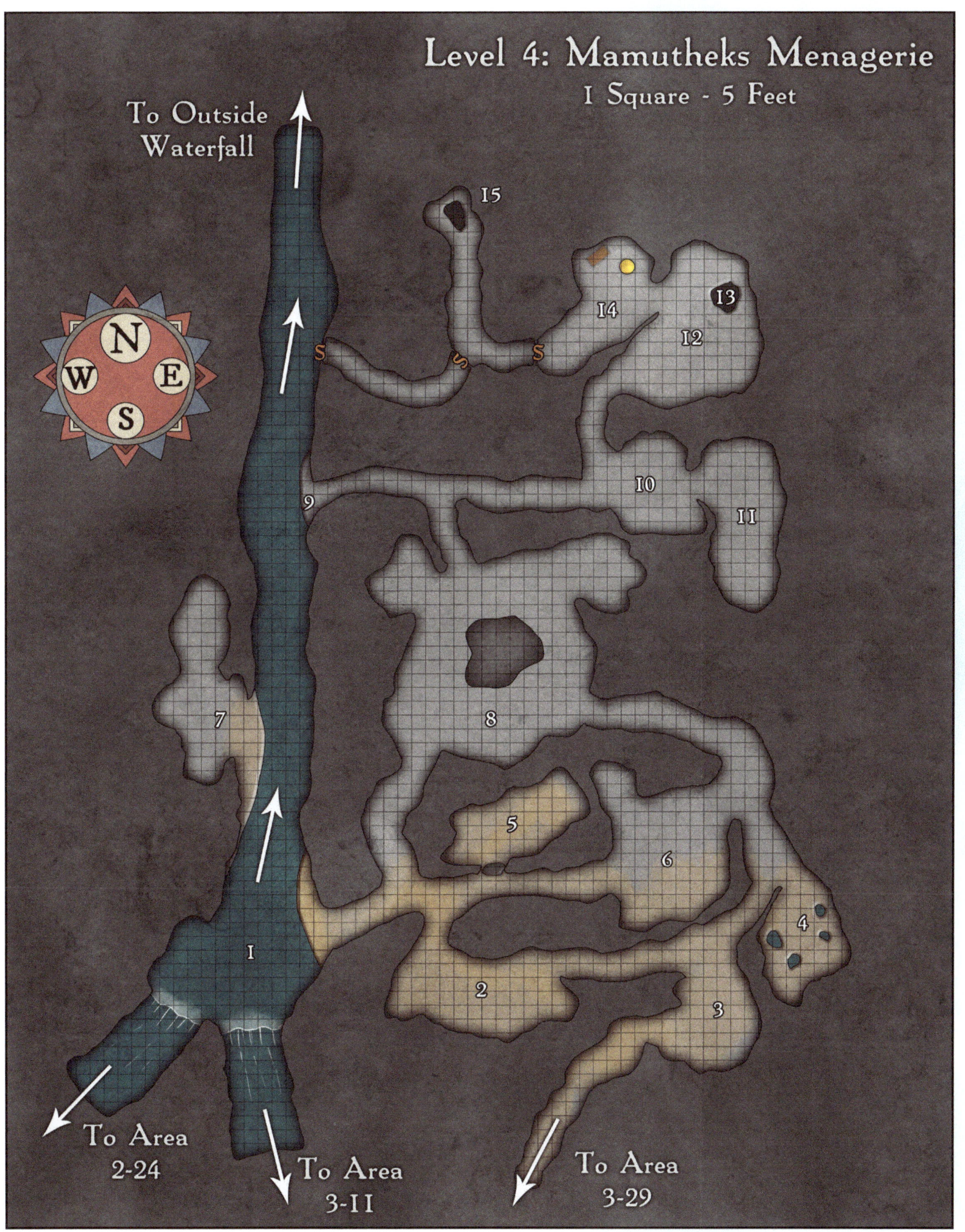

Level 4: Mamutheks Menagerie
1 Square - 5 Feet
To Outside Waterfall
N
W
E
S
15
14
13
12
10
11
9
7
8
5
6
4
1
2
3
To Area 2-24
To Area 3-11
To Area 3-29

Area 4-4:
Knock, Knock Ooze There

This room is vaguely wedge-shaped, and puddles of water cover the floor in places. Water also drips from every stalactite, making a chorus of dripping tones. The drips seem to fall especially heavily from a crack in the ceiling toward the rear. The crack in the ceiling is far too small to fit through without magic alterations (Tiny or smaller creatures only). It goes nowhere of importance, unless you wish to insert a connecting passage for future development. It probably engages the interest of the heroes long enough to allow the **gray ooze** in the corner to attack. Its treasure is scattered on the ground where it lay: 20 glass marbles and a set of *eyes of the eagle* without frames.

Gray Ooze CR 4
XP 1,200
hp 50 (Pathfinder Roleplaying Game Bestiary, "Ooze, Gray")

Area 4-5: Who Let the Dogs Out?

A heavy stone block rests against what appears to be an opening in the tunnel wall. Marks in the sand indicate that the block was dragged there and wedged into the crack. A faint scratching can be heard from somewhere behind the stone. With the help of the Abyssal minotaur, Lilith keeps a pair of **howlers** penned up in this small cave. The heroes may be tempted to move the boulder and explore the cave. Moving the huge stone requires a successful DC 26 Strength check, and multiple characters can collaborate on this effort. Using levers, digging pits, and so on can help as well; add a +2 insight bonus for each such innovation. While the party is so engaged, the howlers within hide themselves among their "toys" — a collection of driftwood and grisly body parts. They prepare a charge action for the round the stone falls away, and complete the action unless they see their beloved mistress Lilith or the minotaur, who has thumped them badly in the past.

Howler (2) CR 3
XP 800
hp 30 (Pathfinder Roleplaying Game Bestiary 2, "Howler")

Tactics: Unless the howlers see one of the two figures mentioned above, they attack immediately and fight hungrily until killed. They are hidden when the stone is removed and burst forth immediately to achieve surprise, if possible.

Area 4-6: Only You
Can Prevent Forest Fires

This cavern is lit from within by a flickering yellow light. An odd groaning can be heard, punctuated periodically by a mighty bellow and the sound of heavy logs crashing onto stone. The chamber is home to what may be the most bizarre creature called by *Mamuthek's Aperture*. Lilith very much wanted a fire elemental to guard her lair (and keep it warm). She tried accessing the Elemental Plane of Fire the first time with a chunk of obsidian, but this material produced the mephits in Area **3-13**, to her disappointment. In her next attempt, she endeavored to put a live flame on the tray of the summoning device, including a tiny sliver of wood to fuel it. Because of the wood included on the tray, her results were far from desirable.

Shurr'arrin CR 10
XP 9,600

Flame-Spawned Treant
CN Huge outsider (plant, elemental, extraplanar, fire)
Init +0; **Senses** darkvision 60 ft., low-light vision; Perception +16
Aura fiery aura (5 ft., DC 21)

AC 24, touch 8, flat-footed 24 (+16 natural, -2 size)
hp 114 (12d8+60)
Fort +13, **Ref** +4, **Will** +9
Defensive Abilities modified regeneration; **DR** 10/magic and slashing; **Immune** bleed, critical hits, fire, flanking, precision damage, plant traits
Weaknesses vulnerability to cold, vulnerability to fire
Speed 30 ft.

Melee 2 slams +17 (2d6+9/19-20)
Ranged rock +8 (2d6+13)
Space 15 ft.; **Reach** 15 ft.
Special Attacks burn, rock throwing (180 ft.), trample (2d6+13, DC 25)

Str 29, **Dex** 10, **Con** 21, **Int** 12, **Wis** 16, **Cha** 13
Base Atk +9; **CMB** +20 (+22 sunder); **CMD** 30 (32 vs. sunder)
Feats Alertness, Improved Critical (slam), Improved Sunder, Iron Will, Power Attack, Weapon Focus (slam)
Skills Diplomacy +9, Intimidate +9, Knowledge (nature) +9, Perception +16, Sense Motive +9, Stealth -8 (+8 in forests); **Racial Modifiers** +16 Stealth in forests
Languages Common, Ignan, Sylvan, Treant; treespeech
SQ animate trees, double damage against objects

Special Abilities

Animate Trees (At will) (Sp) Animate any trees in 180 ft at will, controlling up to two at a time.
Burn (DC 21) (Ex) A flame-spawned creature deals fire damage with any natural attack. Those hit by a flame-spawned creature 's natural attack must succeed on a Reflex save or catch on fire. The flame burns for 1d4 rounds. A burning creature can take a move action to p
Fiery Aura (5 ft., DC 21) (Ex) You have a fiery aura and anyone within a set distance must succeed on a Fortitude save or take the listed fire damage from the intense heat. The save DC is Constitution-based. Combustibles automatically catch fire if they contact you.

Description: **Shurr'arrin** is an ancient treant that once ruled as the lord of a great forest. He raised an army to defend against a cult of fire worshippers, but he was defeated and his forest burned. As punishment for his insolence, the elemental priest that led the cult cursed him and banished him to the Elemental Plane of Fire, where he remained until Lilith's summons drew him through the *Aperture*. His curse is a heinous one: he is immune to fire and the damage caused by it, but not immune to the resultant pain. A second curse makes extinguishing his burning limbs once they are alight impossible — something that happened immediately following his arrival on the Elemental Plane of Fire. He has been imprisoned there for unknown eons, always burning but never consumed. Shurr'arrin is now thoroughly insane from lifetimes of agonizing pain and now acts without reason. He looks like an enormous tree engulfed in raging flames.

Tactics: Shurr'arrin is completely insane and attacks as soon as he is aware of something upon which he can vent his anguish. As he charges, allow the party a DC 18 Perception to make out his garbled moaning in a mix of Treant, Ignan, and Common: "*Let me die... why won't I burn... just let me die...*"

The party may try to amend his condition. A *remove curse* spell lifts the curse that keeps him burning but does not actually extinguish the flames — that must be done by some other means, such as immersion in water or a *quench* spell. The greater curse that renders him immune to flame but not to pain requires more extensive efforts to break, such as a *break enchantment* spell — the exact nature of this curse is up to you.

Extinguishing the flames does nothing to restore Shurr'arrin's sanity, although once extinguished he may break off the attack and act randomly instead. Restoring his mind requires a *restoration* or similar spell. If no efforts are taken to help him, he fights ferociously until killed (by means other than fire).

AREA 4-7: STIRGES

This small cavern is reachable only by following the river (more likely by drifting down it) to the small beach on one shore. The cave is filled with 8 **stirges**, one of which has a bracelet stuck on its neck — this treasure can be removed only after death. The bracelet is made of gold with a single emerald charm worth 1,200 gp.

Stirge (8)   **CR 1/2**
XP 200
hp 5 (Pathfinder Roleplaying Game Bestiary, "Stirge")

Tactics: The stirges attack as soon as they realize they are not alone. They fight until 5 of them are killed or until smoke is introduced. Randomize the ones that flee the area to see if one of them wears the bracelet.

Development: At your discretion, this chamber could contain an access tunnel to some point inside the Angus keep.

AREA 4-8: DRETCH PIT

Fires dot this large, circular cavern, surrounding an uneven platform made of lashed driftwood and planks that occupies the center of the room. The shadowed mouths of several smaller caverns and recesses are visible. A low murmuring comes from below the wooden panels. This is the chamber that turned Elinda Bannon around to look for another way in — the home of the Lilith's 8 **dretches** and their "caretaker," an **abyssal minotaur**. The side caverns house the minotaur's lair and the remnants of the **Band of the Crimson Mantle** (see **Appendix C**). The dretches are in the pit, where they are kept out of the way and out of trouble until Lilith looses them in the city. If the minotaur has his way (see below), the strength of the boards figures in the combat here. Treat the entire assembly as having Hardness 2, hp 5, Break DC 10. Walking on any part of the wooden covering requires a DC 15 Acrobatics check to keep weight distributed evenly; landing or being otherwise forced onto the trap increases the difficulty to a DC 20 Acrobatics check. Increase both of these DCs by +1 for each 50 pounds of total weight, including any equipment. Failure results in structural collapse, although a DC 22 Reflex saving throw may be attempted to get back on solid ground. The pit is 20 feet deep, dealing 2d6 bludgeoning damage on a fall, and full of dretches.

Collapsing Floor   **CR 2**
XP 600
Type mechanical; **Perception** DC 20; **Disable Device** DC 25
Trigger location; **Reset** repair
Effect 20-foot fall (2d6); multiple targets (all creatures in 10 ft. area); DC 22 Reflex save avoids

Dretch (8)   **CR 2**
XP 600
hp 18 (Pathfinder Roleplaying Game Bestiary, "Demon, Dretch")

Abyssal Minotaur   **CR 6**
XP 2,400
hp 57 (Pathfinder Roleplaying Game Bestiary, "Half-Fiend Minotaur")

Description: Describe the minotaur in such a way that its fiendish nature is obvious — flaming hooves, glowing eyes, and so on. If the players jump to the conclusion that this is the "demon" their characters have sought, then humor them; such assumptions may come back to haunt them!

Tactics: The minotaur waits to attack until the pit distracts the party's attention, if possible. When it does attack, it initiates the combat by selecting a character standing close to the edge of the pit as a target for a bull rush attempt. If the bull rush is successful, the hero

is forced onto the flimsy wooden covering as described above. Unless the hero is remarkably dexterous or lightly equipped, they most likely fall through to face the dretches. If given a choice, the minotaur bull rushes a heavily armored warrior instead of a rogue or spellcaster. As the combat progresses, it may attempt another bull rush if a character is foolish enough to get between it and the edge of the pit.

The dretches in the pit attack zealously as soon as an opponent is present, although they cannot get out of the pit alone. They attempt to use their number to surround individuals.

Development: At whatever point the side caverns are explored, the party finds any survivors of the Band of the Crimson Mantle held prisoner there. This may include Pratchett, Isidra, and possible Yelm, or none of them, depending on what was done with the encounter in **Area 3-29**. They are unconscious (regardless of arrival time) and buried up to their necks in the sand. They have only 20% of their hit points left, and Isidra has no spells. Their weapons are buried at their feet and all their other items are still on their persons. Without healing and rest, they will do the party little good, but dispatching them or leaving them to die on their own should be considered an evil act, as they currently pose no threat. Their interactions with the party over the course of the adventure and the party's general alignment should factor into an interesting quandary. This turn of events presents a good role-playing challenge, especially if the party is divided on what to do.

If allowed to survive and recover, Pratchett resents any implied obligation to the heroes, but does not attempt to challenge them unless the odds favor him. Isidra has seen death up close and is more intrigued by it than ever; she has no gratitude or animosity and does not challenge the party. Yelm nobly regards himself indebted to the heroes if they save him, although he is shamed by his defeat and wishes to redeem himself. This moment allows another opportunity for him to join the party as a replacement character or NPC. Generally, the Band presents no threat if they are allowed to leave — consider it a temporary truce in what might become an ongoing rivalry.

AREA 4-9: BEACH

This small beach is the only way to bypass **Area 4-8** and its dangerous tenants. While there is no inherent danger on the beach or in the tunnel leading away from it, overshooting the landing can be quite deadly. This is the last stop on the underground river before it exits the caverns and joins the massive waterfalls thundering down from overhead. Beyond the beach, there is no dry ground — only rock-walled tunnel and water rushing at 40 feet per round. Being washed over the falls in this manner results in 14d6 bludgeoning damage, with no save. The usual rules for drowning apply to any survivors.

AREA 4-10: ALARMS

In this area, Lilith has placed *alarm* spells to secure her inner sanctum. An audible version is placed at the exit of the tunnel from **Areas 4-8** and **4-9**, and a mental version is placed at the tunnel opening leading to **Area 4-12**.

AREA 4-11: THE GARBAGE DISPOSAL

This small chamber is splattered with shattered bodies and reeks like a charnel house. Creatures of unrecognizable nature have been torn limb from limb, their entrails strewn about among splinters of bone and bits of fur. Not all of Lilith's summonings have produced creatures that were willing or able to serve her dark purposes. The minotaur from **Area 4-8** provides the service of eliminating them from her affairs. The room has the effects of a *stinking cloud* spell, causing nausea; any afflicted must use their action each round to retch. An affected creature may attempt a DC 15 Fortitude saving throw at the end of its turn, ending the effect on a success.

AREA 4-12: LILITH

This is the inner sanctum of **Lilith**, the succubus demon. The encounter needs to be modified if the party managed to avoid all creature encounters, alarms, and traps on this level, which is unlikely. The unworked stone walls of this chamber are nearly invisible beneath its opulent furnishings. A silken canopy is slung overhead between stalactites, and the mysterious light source above it is tinted pale yellow. Piles of cushions are strewn carelessly about, and a luxurious round bed is centered against the far wall. An iron cage hangs from the ceiling with a wilted female form inside.

The figure locked in the cage is really Lilith using her Change Shape ability. The cage requires a DC 25 Disable Device check to unlock. Unless the party has prior history in Dun Eamon, they have never met the real Elinda Bannon and have no reason to doubt that she should be here. She wears Elinda's *amulet of proof against detection and location*, so the heroes will be unable to sense her chaotic evil nature. Some of Elinda's other items are still in her pack, opposite the cage, and might be useful if a battle ensues. These stolen items are listed as the treasure for this area but Elinda would like to see them again. The fact that the heroes came here hoping to find the missing wizard and the cinematically heroic nature of the rescue may aid in Lilith's deception as well.

If the heroes did good detective work in the city above, however, they may suspect that some form of shape shifting seductress is at work. They may also have the knowledge needed to trap Lilith in a lie, but to do so will require role-playing cleverness. The following encounter is critical to the outcome of the adventure, so play out the scene carefully.

The party may or may not realize that the real Elinda Bannon is still in danger. Her prison is a deep hidden pit (**Area 4-13**) beneath the plush bedding in this chamber. The pit can be found with a successful DC 18 Perception check.

Playing Lilith: Lilith feigns unconsciousness until disturbed, when she will "awake" and is overjoyed to find that her saviors have arrived. She demands to know if they have destroyed "the demon," which the party may or may not believe has been accomplished. She also insists that the party escort her from the dungeon quickly so that she may deliver a warning to Lord Angus. Use the following text, or ad-lib your own.

"Thank Jamboor[*the god/goddess of magic in your campaign*]! I had given up hope of ever seeing sunlight again! Who are you? Please, tell me you have defeated that foul, otherworldly creature! Regardless, we must make haste to the surface. I fear a most sinister plot is brewing between the outsiders and those they have possessed in the city. Lord Angus and all of Dun Eamon are in grave peril: I must speak with him immediately!"

Already, Lilith has made one small slip — she has not spent enough time on the surface to know that the sun never really shines in the Grey Citadel. She makes several more as time goes on, but only attentive heroes can catch them. Even the persona she adopts is that of a waifish damsel-in-distress — an image that Elinda has intentionally projected since her capture; yet the players may have learned enough about Elinda to doubt this image. The party might also be able to trap Lilith with a few careful questions regarding people in her life, such as Stump or the Angus brothers. Their ability to do so depends on how they phrase their questions and how much Lilith may have learned in the city. Elinda Bannon has been deliberately vague during her imprisonment, hoping that such an opportunity would arise. This encounter can be as role-playing oriented as the group wishes, within the limits of your creativity and flexibility.

Some parties may be satisfied at this point and head immediately for home, but most will have a few more questions, giving Lilith a few more chances to give herself away. Her responses on the issue of:

Her capture: "*The hell-spawn took me near the river gorge [**Level 3**] as I prepared my spells. I could go no further, and I had exhausted all my resources.*"

The troll in **Area 3-29** subdued Elinda, but she was backtracking to try to bypass the minotaur in **Area 4-8**. The party may have found her "EB" sigil in Area **4-3**.

Her route: "*I descended through the basement of the forge building and crossed the river before approaching the falls.*"

When pressed, Lilith recites the route she used most often, but the party may have found Elinda's sigil in **Area 2-14**. Again, clever questioning can trap Lilith in her masquerade.

Her level of responsibility: "*I am entirely at fault! It was my own tragic fixation with magical devices — I did not have the power to control the creature I summoned.*"

If the heroes pursue this conversation, they may realize that Lilith does not know that Elinda was only trying to communicate, not summon.

Her trail of clues: "*I am glad such a capable party as yourselves came to my aid and was able to interpret them.*"

Lilith does not know what the actual clues were. Depending on how the heroes word their questions, they may be able to catch her in a lie.

The nature of "the demon": "*A savage creature from the lower planes. Terrible and horned, it is, and resistant to normal weapons and some spells.*"

Lilith would like the party to believe that they killed the demon, so she describes the Abyssal minotaur from **Area 4-8**. This tactic may arouse suspicion if the heroes (a) followed up the theft of minotaur body parts from Caledon's shop or (b) have established a strong case in favor of a demonic seductress.

The Ebon Union: "*A gang of smugglers and brigands has a lair down here. I believe they have been corrupted by the demon and bent to his will.*"

This is essentially the truth as Elinda would know it.

Lilith CR 7

XP 3,200

hp 84 (Pathfinder Roleplaying Game Bestiary, "Demon, Succubus")

Like many creatures of the lower planes, Lilith has an inherent weakness: she is vulnerable to the sound of her true name. As a shapechanger, she has many identities, but her own name may be used to invoke unfavorable or even deadly forces against her; in fact, it was her name that was used in the amulet that bound her in a demon prince's prison until *Mamuthek's Aperture* released her. Invoking her name as a free action in addition to an attack or spellcasting attempt increases the chance of success; give a +1 divine bonus to that character's attack rolls or effective caster level. This bonus represents that Lilith is cowed and momentarily more susceptible to damage. The bonus lasts for the duration of the attacker's turn and is not cumulative. If her name is invoked as part of an Abjuration spell (such as *magic circle* or *banishment*) or an Enchantment spell (such as *command* or *confusion*), Lilith's spell resistance in negated entirely. Her name counts as something she hates for the purpose of *dismissal* and *banishment* spells.

Description: Lilith is a power-hungry schemer, not terribly surprising for one of the more duplicitous demons of the Abyss. She is unique in the number of enemies she has amassed among the demon princes, however, and in the number of factions that want her dead for reasons best left to future development. As a result, she is determined never to return to the underworld, especially when life on the Material Plane is so enjoyable. To those ends, she is very deliberate about how she uses the artifact. She is cunning, deceitful, and manipulative to the utmost and should be played as a shrewd, calculating villain. When not masquerading as another female humanoid, she prefers a form that features straight dark hair and green eyes, with alabaster skin and ideal human proportions.

Tactics: If the heroes confront Lilith with her deception, she attempts to excuse her errors with the intensity of her experiences. If that fails, she tries to *charm* the most powerful male party member, saying to him, "How can you doubt me? I am in as much danger as any of you!" If she can get one or more party members to support her, she makes an attempt to flee toward the surface and escape. Also, if the party runs across a powerful foe, she takes advantage of the distraction and flees. She tries to lead the chase through areas where she knows her minions to dwell and fights if escape is not an option.

If combat ensues or if it benefits her escape, Lilith begins with Elinda's *wand of magic missiles*. She is willing to use *ethereal jaunt*, but not *teleport*, as she has many enemies and a large bounty on the Astral Plane.

Lilith knows that she is effectively cornered here and imagines that many if not all of her summoned creatures have been defeated. Her intention is to convince the party to escort her to the surface, where she hopes to escape into a crowd. If they do not contest her identity, she insists that they pack up the artifact (in **Area 4-14**), "lest it fall into evil hands," and depart immediately. Once released from her cage, she also retrieves a satchel with Elinda's spellbooks (from **Area 4-14**) and a backpack with her other items (see below). In the bottom of the satchel are several material components meant for use with the artifact. If Lilith is given the opportunity, she combines the giant constrictor snakeskin with the last of the Abyssal ore to call (she hopes) an Abyssal giant constrictor snake (see **Area 4-14**).

If the party is thoroughly convinced that Lilith is Elinda, she could follow through on her request to be escorted all the way to Arb Angus, whom she then tries to seduce and *charm*. If she can accomplish this feat, her conquest of the Grey Citadel will be nearly complete, and the characters will have failed in their quest, at least for now. These events and their repercussions are beyond the scope of this adventure, although the material is present to adapt to such an eventuality. Such elaborate twists are left to your discretion.

The treasure on Lilith's person includes Elinda's crossbow, 10 (subtract 1d6) *+2 bolts*; 2 *screaming bolts*; 2 *sleep bolts*; *+1 keen short sword*; *wand of magic missile* (14 charges remaining, caster level 7), a dagger, a backpack with 3 day's rations, a waterskin, and a blanket.

AREA 4-13: PRISON PIT

The real **Elinda Bannon** still needs to be rescued. She is bound in a deep pit beneath the bedding in **Area 4-12**. The opening can be seen with a successful DC 18 Perception check. The pit has a narrow mouth, but widens as it descends into a conical chamber that is 30 feet high at the entrance and 60 feet in diameter. A magical *darkness* effect is centered in the chamber, leaving a 10-foot perimeter of normal (but also dark) conditions. Elinda is badly injured and without spells, and she is guarded by another of Lilith's summoned creatures, an **abyssal giant scorpion**.

Elinda Bannon is unconscious, regardless of when the party finds her. She has 6 hit points and no spells prepared. Her familiar was killed elsewhere in the dungeon (see **Area 3-12**). She has her armor, rings, and circlet, but her weapons, wand, amulet, and spellbooks are in Lilith's possession.

Abyssal Giant Scorpion　　　　　　　　　　**CR 4**
XP 1,200
hp 37 (Appendix A: New Creautures, "Scorpion, Abyssal Giant")

Elinda Bannon　　　　　　　　　　　　　　　**CR 8**
XP 4,800
hp 57 (currently 6) (Appendix C: NPC Descriptions, "Elinda Bannon")

No spells remaining, missing gear

Tactics: The scorpion lurks on the far edge of the magical *darkness*, out of sight of the party. It waits to attack until the pit or the prisoner distracts the heroes in some way. After that, it knows no restraint.

AREA 4-14: SUMMONING CHAMBER

A thinly wrought sphere of golden metal sits on a four-legged stand in the center of the room. Lines of soot trace the stone walls and floor of this chamber. A table against one wall is cluttered with odd bits of junk, chipped rocks, and vials of liquid. This area is the resting place of *Mamuthek's Aperture* (see **Appendix B**), the ancient artifact that called Lilith and began the saga that is presumably about to come to an end, one way or another.

A secret door (2 in. thick; Hardness 4; hp 30; Perception [DC 25]; Break [DC 18]; Disable Device [DC 30]) on the far wall leads to an escape tunnel for Lilith and a final trap for the party. Among the treasure on the table is a satchel with Elinda's spellbooks (see **Appendix C**) and some potential material triggers — the remains of what was stolen from the civilians on the surface. Among the items are a mummified feline paw (of a tiger), a carefully rolled snakeskin (from a giant constrictor), and a bleached skull (of an ape). These are all normal animals; Lilith has already used the more exotic components to call her troll, minotaur, and so on. Also in the satchel are the leftover mineral samples — a few chunks of Abyssal ore, the Astral moonstone, and the vial of Elysian soil. These components, plus any other items the heroes may have with them can be used to activate the artifact. Lilith is temporarily out of powdered silver, and she knows better than to call fiendish creatures with the *magic circle* to buy her time to *charm* them. The heroes might have silver of their own, or they may be willing to call an unbound creature... The possibilities are numerous, depending on how much the heroes know (or thinks they know) about the artifact.

The use of the *Aperture* in or after whatever conflict develops between Lilith and the party can shift the balance of power considerably. If Lilith is permitted to use the artifact, she calls an Abyssal constrictor with the last chips of ore and the snakeskin. If the heroes choose to use the device, they might end up with an Elysian tiger, or something far more bizarre, or nothing at all: the products of *Mamuthek's Aperture* are entirely left your discretion.

AREA 4-15: PIT TRAP

The door opens to reveal a tunnel that is visible in dim light for a few feet and then disappears into inky blackness. The secret door in **Area 4-14** has another secret door (2 in. thick; Hardness 4; hp 30; Perception [DC 25]; Break [DC 18]; Disable Device [DC 20]) just beyond it that hides the true exit tunnel. This tunnel leads to the river channel, but there is no beach or dry ground. Lilith uses this tunnel to exit her lair and then fly up to **Area 4-1**. The more obvious tunnel continues past the second secret door to a concealed pit trap that is hidden in magical darkness. Characters running after Lilith may be taken in by the false corridor and could fall to their deaths without a bit of restraint.

Concealed Pit Trap　　　　　　　　　　　**CR 5**
XP 1,600
Type mechanical; **Perception** DC 35; **Disable Device** DC 20
Trigger location; **Reset** manual
Effect 100-ft.-deep pit (10d6 falling damage); DC 20 Reflex avoids; multiple targets (all targets in a 10-ft.-square area)

CHAPTER EIGHT: RESOLUTION, REWARDS, AND DEVELOPMENT

When the heroes emerge from the tunnels having eliminated the demonic threat and rescued the wizard, throngs of cheering crowds await them. Experience rewards should be finalized and booty sorted out (remember that some items of treasure may cause reactions if used in the city). A job well done — but not necessarily the end of the adventure...

Lord Angus pays out the agreed upon reward of 2,000 gp in full. If the party can prove that the demons were much more powerful than the dretches and howlers that terrorized the surface, he readily doubles the reward; if the party can prove that the underground caverns are free of thieves, demons, undead, and all other threats, he triples the reward.

If Elinda was rescued, she may be willing to reward the party with one or two custom minor magic items, but such work is not easily undertaken. First, her lab and library must be restored, and the process of gathering materials and making preparations may lead the heroes on yet another quest. Her gratitude is unconditional, but her services may depend on how thoroughly the heroes looted her tower and their willingness to return her items stolen by Lilith. Ulf Ironfist is similarly willing to craft weapons or armor for the party or collaborate with Elinda on one magical weapon or suit of armor. They are willing to absorb up to 6,000 gp worth of costs to create an item or items. The party must handle any further costs.

If *Mamuthek's Aperture* was retrieved, the party now has the responsibility of deciding what to do with it. If Elinda was successfully rescued, she will certainly factor into that discussion, as will Arb Angus, who feels it is his responsibility to keep it from doing harm again. A quest to destroy it could result, or a trip to deliver it to some inaccessible place or noble order for safekeeping.

After the party has dealt with the threat of Lilith and her demons, other threats may possibly be left underground. Gethrax, the Ebon Union, the *box o' darkness* traps, and even the naturally occurring predators of the underground should be dealt with to ensure the city's safety. Even after the dungeon is cleared, thieves certainly remain in the city — and quite likely a few demons as well. Continued service to Lord Angus as he begins to restore order is a definite possibility. If Lilith, Gethrax, Devlin, or the Band of the Crimson Mantle survive, they could easily become recurring antagonists, especially if the party stays in the area.

After encountering Gethrax and his *box o' darkness* devices, the party most likely has the clues needed to pursue the destruction of his necromantic order, following a trail of *boxes* and seeking out their fortress-temple in the Stoneheart Mountains. Cael Angus and the Temple of Fortitude might sponsor such a venture.

Even after the Ebon Union is ousted from the caverns, they may yet present a threat. If Devlin is allowed to escape, he returns to lead the highwaymen in the forest, if they still exist. If Tabitha or any of the other guild agents escaped, they may continue to haunt the party as well.

The ancient gnome stronghold beneath the city still beckons. An extensive (and expensive) excavation project would require the services of engineers and laborers, but the potential wealth of the gnome ruins is tempting. Alternatively, the gnomes might still occupy their underground city and might request (or require) the party's assistance in dealing with an external subterranean threat.

Several citizens still suffer from the damage inflicted by Lilith and might need advanced healing that only comes at the end of the specific holy quest. The citizens hope that the party might stay nearby, and they continue to treat them as heroes. Indeed, it should be difficult for a character to pay for a meal with her own coin or empty her glass without it being refilled within moments. The party should have time to rest, recover, and reap the benefits of being the heroes of the Grey Citadel.

Appendix A: New Creatures

Bashrib the Barbarian — CR 5
XP 1,600
Morlock barbarian 3
NE Medium monstrous humanoid
Init +8; **Senses** darkvision 120 ft., scent; Perception +10

AC 15, touch 14, flat-footed 11 (+4 Dex, +1 natural)
hp 57 (6 HD; 3d10+3d12+21)
Fort +7, **Ref** +10, **Will** +5; +2 morale bonus vs. spells, supernatural abilities, and spell-like abilities while raging but must resist all spells, even allies'
Defensive Abilities trap sense +1, uncanny dodge; **Immune** disease, poison
Weaknesses light blindness
Speed 50 ft., climb 30 ft.

Melee light hammer +8 (1d4+2, warhammer +8/+3 (1d8+4/×3) or bite +5 (1d4+2)
Special Attacks leap attack, rage (11 rounds/day), rage power (superstition +2), sneak attack +1d6, swarming

---

Str 19, **Dex** 18, **Con** 17, **Int** 8, **Wis** 12, **Cha** 8
Base Atk +6; **CMB** +10; **CMD** 24
Feats Improved Initiative, Lightning Reflexes, Two-weapon Fighting
Skills Acrobatics +16 (+24 to jump), Climb +24, Intimidate +6, Perception +10, Stealth +13 (+17 in caverns); **Racial Modifiers** +8 Acrobatics, +16 Climb, +4 Stealth in caverns
Languages Undercommon
SQ expert climber, fast movement
Other Gear light hammer, warhammer, jade necklace (worth 85 gp)

Special Abilities

Leap Attack (Ex) Make an attack at any point during a jump.
Rage (11 rounds/day) (Ex) +4 Str, +4 Con, +2 to Will saves, -2 to AC when enraged.
Superstition +2 (Ex) While raging, gain bonus to save vs. magic, but must resist all spells, even allies.
Swarming (Ex) Can share a square with another member of race. If both attack the same foe, they are flanked.

Roark the Righteous — CR 7
XP 3,200
Sword wight
LE Medium undead
Init +1; **Senses** darkvision 60 ft.; Perception +15

AC 22, touch 10, flat-footed 22 (+8 armor, +4 natural)
hp 60 (8d8+24)
Fort +4, **Ref** +3, **Will** +7
Defensive Abilities channel resistance +4; **Immune** undead traits; **Resist** fire 10
Speed 30 ft. (20 ft. in armor)

Melee frost brand +11/+6 (2d6+4/19-20 plus energy drain and 1d6 cold) or
slam +2 (1d4 plus energy drain)
Special Attacks energy drain (1 level, DC 16)

Str 12, **Dex** 12, **Con** —, **Int** 11, **Wis** 13, **Cha** 15
Base Atk +6; **CMB** +7; **CMD** 18
Feats Blind-fight, Heavy Armor Proficiency, Shield Proficiency, Skill Focus (Perception), Toughness, Weapon Focus (greatsword)
Skills Acrobatics +3 (-5 to jump), Climb +6, Perception +15, Stealth +6
SQ sword channel
Other Gear +1 splint mail, heavy steel shield, frost brand

Special Abilities

Sword Channel (Ex) Energy drain functions through melee weapons.

Scorpion, Abyssal Giant — CR 4
XP 1,200
Fiendish giant scorpion
CE Large vermin
Init +0; **Senses** darkvision 60 ft., tremorsense 60 ft.; Perception +4

AC 16, touch 9, flat-footed 16 (+7 natural, -1 size)
hp 37 (5d8+15)
Fort +7, **Ref** +1, **Will** +1
DR 5/good; **Immune** mind-affecting effects; **Resist** cold 10, fire 10; **SR** 9
Speed 50 ft.

Melee 2 claws +6 (1d6+4 plus grab), sting +6 (1d6+4)
Space 10 ft.; **Reach** 10 ft.
Special Attacks constrict (1d6+4), poison, smite good

Str 19, **Dex** 10, **Con** 16, **Int** —, **Wis** 10, **Cha** 2
Base Atk +3; **CMB** +8 (+12 grapple); **CMD** 18
Skills Acrobatics +0 (+8 to jump), Climb +8, Perception +4, Stealth +0; **Racial Modifiers** +4 Climb, +4 Perception, +4 Stealth

Special Abilities

Poison: Sting - injury (DC 17) (Ex) Poison—Injury; **save** Fort DC 17; **frequency** 1/round for 6 roundsds; **effect** 1d2 Str; **cure** 1 save.

Troll, Abyssal — CR 6
XP 2,400
CE Large humanoid (giant)
Init +2; **Senses** darkvision 60 ft., low-light vision, scent; Perception +8

AC 16, touch 11, flat-footed 14 (+2 Dex, +5 natural, -1 size)
hp 63 (6d8+36); regeneration 5 (acid or fire)
Fort +11, **Ref** +4, **Will** +3
DR 5/good; **Resist** cold 10, fire 10; **SR** 11
Speed 30 ft.

Melee bite +8 (1d8+5), 2 claws +8 (1d6+5)
Space 10 ft.; **Reach** 10 ft.
Special Attacks rend (2 claws, 1d6+7), smite good

Str 21, **Dex** 14, **Con** 23, **Int** 6, **Wis** 9, **Cha** 6
Base Atk +4; **CMB** +10; **CMD** 22
Feats Intimidating Prowess, Iron Will, Skill Focus (Perception)
Skills Intimidate +9, Perception +8
Languages Giant

Appendix B: New Magic Items

Mamuthek's Aperture

Aura moderate conjuration; **CL** 11th; **Weight** 20 lbs.; **Slot** —;
Price 163,350 gp

A power-hungry summoner named Mamuthek created this ancient device (see Adventure Background in the Introduction). It is formed of thin gold bands that pivot on tiny rivets and can be collapsed into a small wooden box (6 in. x 8 in. x 12 in.) or expanded to create a globe of interwoven strips. When unfolded, it sits on a four-legged stand and looks deceivingly flimsy. A small gold plate hangs from the top of the globe from four fine chains. When activated (by giving it a gentle spin), the globe accelerates to blinding speed, opening an aperture to another plane of existence and calling a creature (or creatures) as per the *planar binding* spell. The device can call up to 16 HD worth of creatures or a single creature of no more than 16 HD.

The plate is used for determining both the source plane and target creature to be called. A mineral placed on the tray determines the plane on which the gate opens; this includes minerals from alternate Material Planes and Inner or Outer planes. A piece of organic matter placed on the tray determines the nature of the creature called; there is no limit on how long the organic material has been lifeless or how large it must be. If both organic and mineral materials are provided, the artifact will attempt to locate a creature of that type on that plane. For example, a chunk of ore from the Abyss and the top of a minotaur's horn will produce an Abyssal minotaur, if one exists. If no material is provided when the device is activated, it attempts to locate the last being it contacted and retrieve it again, regardless of how much time has passed since the previous activation.

Mamuthek's Aperture does not force any action or obligation on the creature beyond a compulsion to step through. Called creatures with 6 or fewer HD cannot resist; creature with more than 6 HD can resist the compulsion with a DC 18 Will saving throw. Around the equator of the golden globe is a shallow tray that can be used to establish a ward against the creature. If filled with powdered silver (25 gp worth per use), a circle of protection is created to ward against the alignment of the called creature. If this is used, treat it as a *magic circle* as described in the *lesser planar binding* spell. If the creature successfully passes a SR roll, makes a successful Charisma check, or uses dimensional travel, or if the operator does not supply powdered silver before activating the device, the called creature is not contained and is free to act as it wishes.

If the creature is contained, the service agreement may be negotiated as normal. If it has the opportunity or if no task is assigned, the creature may return by activating the artifact while inside the globe, but this is only possible before the device is used to call another creature. Also, creatures called using *Mamuthek's Aperture* are never forced to return, even after completing the service; there is no maximum duration, and a creature can stay and act independently if it so desires.

Several liabilities exist in this faulted artifact. The lack of obligation on the part of the creature puts the user at risk. Also, the inability to send a called creature back has resulted in the introduction of some very powerful beings to the Material Plane over the years.

Note: Called creatures do not disappear when slain; their bodies figure into the events of **The Grey Citadel**.

Feats Craft Wondrous Item, *magic circle*, *planar binding*; **Cost** 81,850 gp

Charm of Silence

Aura faint illusion; **CL** 3rd; **Weight** —; **Slot** neck; **Price** 2,400 gp

This small charm is worn on a non-magical chain around the neck. It consists of an onyx stone within a tiny silver globe that can be opened to expose the charm. When the onyx is exposed, it projects an area effect identical to the *silence* spell, except that the radius is limited to 10 feet. The area of silence prevails until the globe is closed and the onyx is concealed or the charm is removed (**Note:** the death of the wearer does not end the effect). The charm of silence can be activated only once per day; once it is deactivated, it cannot be used again for 24 hours, regardless of how much time has passed since the original activation.

Feats Craft Wondrous Item, *silence*; **Cost** 1,200 gp

Box o' Darkness

Aura faint necromancy; **CL** 5th; **Weight** 1 lbs.; **Slot** none; **Price** 11,250 gp

The *box o' darkness* trap is used by Gethrax to protect his lair in dungeon Level 1. (**Note:** The *box o' darkness* traps featured in this adventure are much more powerful [15th level]; the one described here is the 5th level "standard" version.) While it is a magical item (created by Gethrax's unholy order), it is also considered a trap and its effects are fully described in Area **1-9** (see Chapter Four). The heroes should continue to encounter these items if they pursue the cult that manufactures them.

The traps are armed when wound up and from then on are triggered by the approach of any good-aligned humanoid within 20 feet. When triggered, they begin to play a pleasant tune as would a child's music box, and the sound of laughing children can be heard. After 5 rounds, the music slows and thick black fog seeps out of the box, expanding to cover a 20-foot radius. This area receives the effects of a *desecrate* spell, followed by *animate dead*, both cast at 5th level; 5 HD of undead are raised from that area (if available) and receive +1 hit point and a +1 bonus to attack, damage, and saving throw rolls. Check to turn undead in this area suffer a -3 penalty for the duration of the *desecrate* spell (10 hours). On the bottom of the box is an engraved sigil that may be able to lead the party to the powerful creator of the devices in a later quest.

Box o' Darkness Trap   **CR 4**
XP 1,200
Type magic; **Perception** DC 28; **Disable Device** DC 28
Trigger good-aligned humanoid coming within a 20-ft. radius;
Reset none
Effect When triggered, they begin to play a pleasant tune
as would a child's music box, and the sound of laughing
children can be heard. After five rounds, the music slows,
and thick black fog seeps out of the box, expanding to cover
a 20-foot radius. This area receives the effects of a *desecrate*
spell followed by *animate dead* cast at 5th level. Then, 5
HD of undead are raised from that area (if available). The
trap magically converts the surrounding 20-foot area into
unhallowed ground for up to 10 hours. The DC to resist
negative channeled energy within this area gains a +3
profane bonus. Every undead creature entering a *desecrated*
area gains a +1 profane bonus on all attack rolls, damage
rolls, and saving throws. An undead creature created within
or summoned into such an area gains +1 hit points per HD.
Feats Craft Wondrous Item, *animate dead*, *desecrate*; **Cost** 5,750 gp

Appendix C: NPC Descriptions

Many of the important power figures and influential people of Dun Eamon may be found in several different locations or may be encountered frequently enough that their profiles need regular reference. Listed below are the profiles for the primary NPCs of the adventure. Their backgrounds are detailed so they can be paraphrased in part when the heroes inquire about them during their investigation. The primary villains (Gethrax, Devlin, and Lilith) are encountered in more predictable locations; their profiles are found in their encounter areas.

The Angus Clan

The three Angus brothers share the responsibilities of leadership in Dun Eamon and are regarded by most to be just and capable.

Arb Angus, Lord of Eamonvale

Arb Angus, Lord of Eamonvale   CR 13
XP 25,600
Human aristocrat 6/cavalier 8
LG Medium humanoid (human)
Init +1; **Senses** Perception +19

AC 19, touch 14, flat-footed 18 (+5 armor, +3 deflection, +1 Dex)
hp 71 (14 HD; 6d8+8d10)
Fort +8, **Ref** +5, **Will** +9
Speed 30 ft.

Melee mwk short sword +14/+9/+4 (1d6+1/19-20) or
  Sword of Angus +15/+10/+5 (1d10+3/17-20 plus 2d6 vs. evil)
Ranged mwk composite longbow +14/+9/+4 (1d8+1/×3)
Special Attacks banner +2, cavalier's charge, challenge 3/day (+8 damage, +3 morale bonus to CMB and attacks of opportunity), tactician 2/day (Blood for the Empire, 7 rounds)

Str 13, **Dex** 13, **Con** 10, **Int** 10, **Wis** 14, **Cha** 17
Base Atk +12; **CMB** +13; **CMD** 27
Feats Blood For The Empire, Exotic Weapon Proficiency (bastard sword), Leadership, Mounted Archery, Mounted Combat, Point-Blank Shot, Precise Shot, Rapid Shot, Ride-by Attack, Spirited Charge, Step Up
Skills Bluff +7, Climb +5, Diplomacy +20, Handle Animal +20, Intimidate +7, Knowledge (local) +4, Knowledge (nature) +4, Perception +19, Profession (barrister) +6, Ride +18, Sense Motive +19 (+23 to detect bluffs and sense enchantment effects affecting a creature's behavior), Survival +6, Swim +5
Languages Common
SQ expert trainer +4, mobile wall, mount, order of the scales, seek retribution
Other Gear *Sword of Angus* (+2 holy keen bastard sword), arrows (20), mwk composite longbow (+1 Str), mwk short sword, bracers of armor +5, ring of protection +3, amulet of the angus crest, emerald signet ring (worth 500 gp), gold band of lordship

Special Abilities

Banner +2/+1 (60 ft.) (Ex) Allies within 60 ft. who can see your banner gain +2 save vs. fear & +1 to hit while charging.
Blood for the Empire When attacking target damaged by ally last round, +2 to attack and weapon damage, 1 round *haste* when ally dies.
Scale's Challenge +8 (3/day) (Ex) +8 to damage target, -2 AC vs. others when used, +3 to CMB and AoO.
Seek Retribution (8 rounds, 1/day) (Ex) +3 competence bonus on Atk, Dmg, & opposed checks.
Step Up When a foe makes a 5 ft step away from you, you can move 5 ft to follow them.
Tactician (Blood for the Empire, 7 rds, 2/day) (Ex) Grant the use of one of your teamwork bonus feats to all allies within 30 ft.

Description: Arb Angus is a tall, robust man with thick brown hair and a well-trimmed beard. Despite his social rank, he disdains ceremonial dress and usually wears simple clothing of high quality leather and wool. The only indicator of his lordship is the unadorned gold circlet on his brow and the ancestral Angus blade on his hip.

The eldest of the three Angus brothers, Arb rules Eamonvale, a remote river gorge in a temperate rain forest. He inherited title and land from his father, and the region has developed well under his reign. He is young, having just entered his 30th year, and he rules with the confidence and vigor of youth tempered by the strict discipline and wisdom of his father. His policies on trade and tax ensure a place for the local farmers and craftsmen in the economy, and his strict prohibition on foreign guild influence has drawn much controversy. While many abroad would see him overthrown, he is well-loved by his citizens.

His youth was spent in close contact with his brothers, engaged with the activities of aristocratic life. He is a skilled hunter and falconer and a competent horseman, but he never adjusted well to courtly life and is always quick to dispense with etiquette if such can be done without offense. He trusts his brothers implicitly, and they are involved in every important decision he makes. It is known that he does not intend to take a wife until later in life, but that has not stopped Elinda Bannon from being drawn to him.

While in the city, he spends as little time in the Keep as possible. He often speaks with craftsmen and merchants around the Market or stops to listen to a traveling minstrel and share a pint in a tavern. He can be encountered nearly anywhere in the citadel.

Bron Angus, Cpt. of the Mist Watch

Bron Angus, Captain of the Mist Watch   CR 11
XP 12,800
Human aristocrat 4/fighter 8
LG Medium humanoid (human)
Init +7; **Senses** Perception -1

AC 24, touch 13, flat-footed 21 (+8 armor, +3 Dex, +3 shield)
hp 94 (12 HD; 4d8+8d10+32)
Fort +9, **Ref** +6, **Will** +5 (+2 vs. fear)
Speed 30 ft.

Melee +1 heavy shield bash +15/+10 (2d6+2), +2 keen longsword +15/+10/+5 (1d8+8/17-20) or
  +2 keen longsword +19/+14/+9 (1d8+8/17-20)
Special Attacks weapon training (heavy blades +1)

Str 16, **Dex** 17, **Con** 14, **Int** 10, **Wis** 8, **Cha** 12
Base Atk +11; **CMB** +14; **CMD** 27
Feats Bashing Finish, Greater Weapon Focus (longsword), Improved Initiative, Improved Shield Bash, Improved Two-weapon Fighting, Leadership, Shield Master, Shield Slam, Skill Focus (Profession [soldier]), Two-weapon Fighting, Weapon Focus (longsword), Weapon Specialization (longsword)
Skills Bluff +5, Climb +4, Diplomacy +16, Handle Animal +5, Intimidate +16, Knowledge (local) +4, Profession (soldier)

+20, Ride +4, Sense Motive +3, Survival +3, Swim +4
Languages Common
SQ armor training 2
Other Gear +2 chainmail, +1 bashing spiked heavy steel
   shield, +2 keen longsword, chain of command, signal horn

Special Abilities

Bashing Finish Whenever you score a critical hit with a
   melee weapon, you can shield bash the same target as a free
   action.
Shield Master No off-hand penalties for shield bashes, add a
   shield's enhancement bonus to attack rolls.
Shield Slam Shield Bash attack gives a free bull rush on a hit.

Description: Bron Angus is tall and slim, tightly strung with wiry
muscle from training with the Watch. His brown hair is cropped shirt,
and he wears a handlebar moustache to age his appearance. He is almost
never seen out of his uniform of mail, blue tabard, and grey cape.

Three years younger than his brother Arb, Bron is the captain of the
Mist Watch. As a young man, Bron's father apprenticed him to his uncle,
who was a mercenary captain. He traveled extensively until his father's
death and became wise in the ways of war and the nuances of command.
He operates with his father's strictness, but lacks the compassion that
ensured his brother's success. Despite his grim personality and apparent
lack of emotion, Bron is passionate about his duty to the city, and this
commitment has won him the extreme loyalty of his men.

Bron is being actively sought as a husband by many of the wealthy
maidens of the citadel and surrounding region, especially those whose
merchant fathers have financial interests at stake. He avoids their
advances on the pretense that a commander's duty is to his men and
his city, but in reality, he is badly smitten with Elinda Bannon. Only
his knowledge of her affection for his older brother Arb and his deep
respect for him keeps Bron from acting.

Bron is fanatical about his work and spends nearly every waking
hour at it. He meets regularly with the officers of the Watch in their
mess, trains recruits personally in the garrison yard, and can often be
seen striding purposefully along the ramparts of the citadel, inspecting
his men. He also lingers at the gates, measuring those who come and
go under jurisdiction.

Cael Angus,
Master of the Temple of Fortitude

Cael Angus, Master of the Temple of Fortitude CR 9
XP 6,400
Human aristocrat 2/cleric 8
CG Medium humanoid (human)
Init +0; **Senses** Perception +13

AC 13, touch 10, flat-footed 13 (+3 armor)
hp 55 (10d8+10)
Fort +7, **Ref** +2, **Will** +12
DR 5/evil
Speed 30 ft.

Melee +2 holy gauntlet +12/+7 (1d3+5 plus 2d6 vs. evil)
Special Attacks channel positive energy 5/day (DC 16, 4d6),
   holy lance (4 rounds, 1/day), might of the gods (+8, 8 rounds/
   day)
Domain Spell-Like Abilities (CL 8th; concentration +11)
   6/day—strength surge (+4), touch of good (+4)
Cleric Spells Prepared (CL 8th; concentration +11)
   4th—*air walk, holy smite*[D] (DC 17), *neutralize poison*
   3rd—*dispel magic, magic circle against evil*[D], *prayer,*
   remove disease, wind wall

2nd—*bull's strength*[D], *calm emotions* (DC 15), *hold person*
   (DC 15), *shield other, zone of truth* (DC 15)
1st—*bless, bless water* (DC 14), *deathwatch, detect evil,*
   protection from evil[D], *sanctuary* (DC 14)
0 (at will)—*detect magic, detect poison, guidance, read magic*
D Domain spell; **Domains** Good, Strength

Str 16, **Dex** 10, **Con** 12, **Int** 8, **Wis** 16, **Cha** 14
Base Atk +7; **CMB** +10; **CMD** 20
Feats Cleave, Cleaving Finish, Great Cleave, Improved
   Cleaving Finish, Improved Unarmed Strike, Power Attack
Skills Diplomacy +6, Heal +16, Knowledge (arcana) +3,
   Knowledge (local) +3, Knowledge (religion) +12, Perception
   +13, Sense Motive +7, Spellcraft +3
Languages Common
Other Gear +2 holy gauntlet, bracers of armor +3, mantle of
   faith, wooden holy symbol

Special Abilities

Holy Lance (4 rounds, 1/day) (Su) Touched weapon
   temporarily becomes holy.
Might of the Gods (8 rounds/day) (Su) Add your cleric level
   to your STR for checks.
Strength Surge (6/day) (Sp) Grant +4 to a melee attack or
   strength check.
Touch of Good +4 (6/day) (Sp) Grant +4 to skill checks,
   ability checks and saving throws for 1 rd.

Description: Cael Angus is a short, barrel-chested youth. His head
is shorn in the tonsure of his order, and he is rarely seen in other than
his coarse brown robes. His arms bulge with powerful muscles, and he
wears thick leather armbands gilded with the icons of his faith.

Cael is the master of the Temple of Fortitude, the favored place of
worship in the Grey Citadel. While many other religions are practiced
openly, most of the citizens are devoted to the God of Strength, Strym.
Cael and his priesthood minister to the needs of the locals and also venture
out to the mines, lumber camps, and farms that surround the city. He has
discovered a means by which the Temple can sustain itself on minimum
tithes: while not at prayer or training, the burly acolytes hire themselves
out as laborers and stevedores to visiting merchant caravans.

The youngest brother of the Angus clan entered the priesthood at
the temple at an early age and proved to be an excellent study and
devoted acolyte. Cael rose quickly in the clergy, and before his 20th
year, he took over the duties of and law to rest the aging head priest.
Now 25, Cael is responsible for the spiritual well-being of hundreds
of citizens. His devotion to his god is the only force that exceeds his
devotion to his older brothers, whom he admires greatly.

Cael leaves the citadel only on the direst business. He can usually
be found at the Temple of Fortitude, where his time is divided between
meditation, mentoring his acolytes, and meeting with his congregation.
He also moves freely about the city, overseeing the activities of the
laborers, making house calls, and considering the rants of the prophets
in the marketplace.

Key Independents

These characters are some of the more powerful or notorious citizens,
for one reason or another. Elinda, currently missing, is not encountered
until the end of the adventure. Fitch, Brother Melph, Rasputin, and
Stump all have their roles to play in the development of the mystery,
but once those encounters are completed (or deleted), these NPCs are
available to replace a deceased character or act as henchmen; with
minor modifications to the adventure, any or all of them could serve
as pre-generated characters. The Band of the Crimson Mantle is an
adventuring party whose efforts will rival those of the heroes.

ELINDA

Elinda Bannon   **CR 8**
XP 4,800
Human loremaster 2/wizard 7
LG Medium humanoid (human)
Init +2; **Senses** Perception -1

AC 17, touch 15, flat-footed 15 (+2 armor, +3 deflection, +2 Dex)
hp 57 (9d6+25)
Fort +4, **Ref** +5, **Will** +5
Speed 30 ft. (20 ft.)

Melee +1 keen short sword +1 (1d6+1/17-20) or
  dagger +4 (1d4/19-20)
Ranged javelin of lightning +2 (1d6) or
  light crossbow +6 (1d8/19-20)
Special Attacks hand of the apprentice (7/day)
Wizard Spells Prepared (CL 9th; concentration +13)
  5th—*teleport*
  4th—*maximized magic missile, scrying* (DC 18), *stoneskin*
  3rd—*dispel magic, lightning bolt* (DC 17), *shrink item* (DC 17), *stinking cloud* (DC 17)
  2nd—*cat's grace, invisibility, locate object, minor image* (DC 16), *rope trick*
  1st—*identify, mage armor, magic missile, magic missile, obscuring mist*
  0 (at will)—*detect magic, light, mage hand, read magic*

Str 10, **Dex** 14, **Con** 12, **Int** 18, **Wis** 8, **Cha** 14
Base Atk +4; **CMB** +4; **CMD** 19
Feats Combat Casting, Craft Magic Arms & Armor, Craft Wand, Craft Wondrous Item, Maximize Spell, Scribe Scroll, Skill Focus (Knowledge [arcana]), Skill Focus (Knowledge [engineering]), Toughness
Skills Acrobatics -1 (-5 to jump), Appraise +8, Craft (armor) +16, Craft (jewelry) +16, Craft (weapons) +16, Diplomacy +6, Fly +3, Knowledge (arcana) +20, Knowledge (engineering) +20, Linguistics +8 (+13 to understand messages written in incomplete, archaic, or exotic forms), Spellcraft +16, Use Magic Device +14
Languages Celestial, Common, Draconic, Dwarven, Elven, Gnome
SQ arcane bond (familiar), lore, secret (secret health)
Combat Gear +2 crossbow bolts (10), javelin of lightning, screaming bolt (2), wand of magic missile; **Other Gear** +1 silken ceremonial armor, +1 keen short sword, sleep arrow (2), crossbow bolts (10), dagger, light crossbow, amulet of proof against detection and location, helm of comprehend languages and read magic, ring of protection +3, ring of sustenance, backpack, bedroll, belt pouch, flint and steel, ink, inkpen, mess kit, spell component pouch, spellbook, trail rations (5), waterskin

Special Abilities

Hand of the Apprentice (7/day) (Su) As a standard action, throw melee weapon (use Int instead of Dex) and instantly returns.

Note: Elinda's spell list represents her "traveling" assortment; when working at home, she focuses much more on divination spells.
Elinda's Spellbooks: All spells prepared, plus all 1st- and 2nd-level wizard spells from *Pathfinder Roleplaying Game Core Rulebook*, *explosive runes, nondetection, sepia snake sigil, tongues, illusory script, fly, secret page, remove curse, arcane eye, improved invisibility, adjustable polymorph, feeblemind, wall of force* and *passwall*.

Note: Elinda's magic items are extensive, as is fitting for her background, and scattered throughout this adventure. The heroes are likely to encounter some of these items in the hands of the villain. While Elinda does not mind her items being used to facilitate her rescue, she expects them to be returned and offers to craft something especially for the party. These items are NOT part of the demon's "treasure."

Description: Elinda is a tall, slender beauty with thick brown hair, usually braided to keep it from interfering with her tinkering. Her clothing is always simple and of the highest quality. When she travels, she favors sensible outfits of blouses and trousers, while at home and about town she wears the clothes of a craftsman, including a leather apron laden with tools and smudged with soot and grease.

Elinda is an artificer, a wizard who focuses her studies on the construction and use of ancient magical devices and artifacts. She travels widely in search of relics and spends a great deal of time sifting through rotting times for obscure clues and references to the resting places of powerful magical items. She has great skill in the creation of magical items as well, although she considers that to be merely a means by which to fund her continual research, the expansion of her library, and her acquisition of rare treasures. She often collaborates with the craftsmen of the city, especially weaponsmiths, as the city's forges are the best for miles around and can produce enchantment-quality blades with ease.

Elinda grew up in the Grey Citadel, for her father was the chief steward of the previous lord. She spent her childhood with the three brothers and all are very close, although their adult lives have led them down different paths. She longs to wed herself to Arb, the eldest of the brothers, but she thinks she lacks the femininity to attract him (in reality, he feels his duties to his citizens prevent him from taking a wife). Bron, the middle brother, is badly smitten with Elinda, but keeps his distance out of respect for his older brother. Her relationship with Cael is the strongest, and they play a weekly game of checkers at the temple.

When she is not traveling, Elinda can usually be found in her apartments in a tower on the curtain wall of the citadel, where she has a large library in addition to a modest living space. She visits the brothers regularly and also spends a fair bit of time at the forges, conferring with the masters on metallurgy and technique.

RASPUTIN

Rasputin   **CR 5**
XP 1,600
Half-elf bard 6
CN Medium humanoid (elf, human)
Init +2; **Senses** low-light vision; Perception +11

AC 14, touch 12, flat-footed 12 (+2 armor, +2 Dex)
hp 27 (6d8)
Fort +1, **Ref** +7, **Will** +5; +2 vs. enchantments, +4 vs. bardic performance, language-dependent, and sonic
Immune sleep
Speed 30 ft.

Melee +1 returning dagger +7 (1d4+2/19-20) or
  dagger +6 (1d4+1/19-20) or
  mwk dagger +7 (1d4+1/19-20) or
  rapier +6 (1d6+1/18-20)
Special Attacks bardic performance 18 rounds/day (countersong, distraction, fascinate [DC 17], inspire competence +2, inspire courage +2, suggestion [DC 17])
Bard Spells Known (CL 6th; concentration +10)
  2nd (4/day)—*cat's grace, cure moderate wounds, detect thoughts* (DC 16), *invisibility*
  1st (5/day)—*charm person* (DC 15), *cure light wounds,*

hypnotism (DC 15), *unseen servant*
0 (at will)—*dancing lights, detect magic, ghost sound* (DC 14),
mage hand, prestidigitation, read magic

Str 12, **Dex** 14, **Con** 8, **Int** 13, **Wis** 10, **Cha** 18
Base Atk +4; **CMB** +5; **CMD** 17
Feats Point-Blank Shot, Precise Shot, Skill Focus (Perform
  [string instruments]), Weapon Finesse
Skills Acrobatics +11, Appraise +10, Intimidate +13,
  Perception +11, Perform (sing) +13, Perform (string
  instruments) +16, Sleight of Hand +11; **Racial Modifiers** +2
  Perception
Languages Common, Elven, Undercommon
SQ bardic knowledge +3, elf blood, lore master 1/day, versatile
  performances (sing, string)
Other Gear +1 returning dagger, dagger, dagger, mwk
  dagger, mwk dagger, rapier, bracers of armor +2, balalaika,
  cards, dice, entertainer's outfit, juggler's kit, monkey named
  Vlado, hacksilver (worth 90 gp), 54 gp, 22 sp, 18 cp

Special Abilities

Lore Master (1/day) (Ex) Can take 10 on any trained
  knowledge checks. Activate to take 20 as a standard action.
Versatile Performance (Singing) +13 (Ex) You may
  substitute the final value of your Perform: Sing skill for Bluff
  or Sense Motive checks
Versatile Performance (String Instruments) +16 (Ex)
  You may substitute the final value of your Perform: String
  Instruments skill for Bluff or Diplomacy checks

Vlado   CR 1/4
XP 100
hp 4 (Pathfinder Roleplaying Game Bestiary, "Monkey")

Other Gear Vest, fez, hurdy-gurdy, tin cup

Description: Rasputin is a half-elf minstrel of dark complexion
and slender build. His foreign heritage is evident in his dress and
grooming; he favors loose, colorful silk clothing and has thick side-
whiskers and long hair.

He is popular around the city, known for performing sleight-of-
hand tricks for the local children and pulling bouquets from his sleeve
for blushing ladies. His balalaika is always at hand and his repertoire
ranges from tear-jerking romantic ballads to bawdy folk songs,
but some carry special messages, for Rasputin is an information
merchant. He conceals his information in his lyrics so that only their
intended listener may recognize them, and he divulges the requested
information only after payment has been made to his tip jar, which is
managed by his monkey Vlado. In addition to gathering and selling
information, Rasputin often serves as a coordinator and go-between
for illicit business deals and is willing to violate the city's trade
policies, so long as it doesn't involve murder, dark magic, or slavery.

His youth was spent on the road with a troupe of entertainers, and
in addition to his music, he possesses considerable skill as a blade
thrower — a skill he prefers to keep secret until it is needed. Concealed
beneath his cheerful personality is the driving force in his life: an
unfulfilled promise he made to an older brother who lay dying after a
bandit raid. His brother's child Elisabeta, a rare beauty with a talent for
dance, had been abducted during the fighting, surely destined for the
slave markets of the arid south. Rasputin pursued and dispatched the
band of highwaymen with a vengeance, but not before his niece was
sold to a gang of slavers. Since then, Rasputin has drifted from city to
city, investigating every brothel and pleasure den and infiltrating the
highest royal houses to examine their harems.

He has stayed in the Grey Citadel for several months now, waiting
out the winter, saving traveling funds, and talking with merchants and
caravan laborers coming in from the trade roads. He can usually be
found by day in the Caravan Camp and performs most evenings at the
Market Tavern.

Brother Melph

Brother Melph   CR 4
XP 1,200
Human cleric 5
NG Medium humanoid (human)
Init +2; **Senses** Perception +4

AC 14, touch 11, flat-footed 13 (+3 armor, +1 Dex)
hp 33 (5d8+10)
Fort +5, **Ref** +3, **Will** +8
Speed 40 ft.

Melee +1 quarterstaff +4 (1d6+1)
Special Attacks channel positive energy 6/day (DC 15, 3d6)
Domain Spell-Like Abilities (CL 5th; concentration +9)
  7/day—bit of luck
Cleric Spells Prepared (CL 5th; concentration +9)
  3rd—*dispel magic, fly*[D], *prayer*
  2nd—*aid*[D], *bull's strength, consecrate, hold person* (DC 16)
  1st—*bless, bless water* (DC 15), *entropic shield,
  longstrider*[D], *sanctuary* (DC 15)
  0 (at will)—*create water, detect magic, guidance, light*
  D Domain spell; **Domains** Luck, Travel

Str 10, **Dex** 14, **Con** 13, **Int** 8, **Wis** 18, **Cha** 12
Base Atk +3; **CMB** +3; **CMD** 15
Feats Combat Casting, Extra Channel, Improved Channel,
  Turn Undead
Skills Knowledge (religion) +7, Spellcraft +7
Languages Common
SQ agile feet (7/day)
Other Gear mwk studded leather, +1 quarterstaff, backpack,
  bedroll, belt pouch, candle (10), everburning torch, flint and
  steel, hemp rope (50 ft.), holy text, mess kit, pot, soap, spell
  component pouch, torch (10), trail rations (5), waterskin,
  wooden holy symbol

Special Abilities

Agile Feet (7/day) (Su) For 1 round, you ignore difficult
  terrain.
Bit of Luck (7/day) (Sp) Target takes the higher of 2d20 for
  a d20 roll.
Turn Undead (DC 15) Your Channel Energy can make
  undead in 30 ft flee for 1 min.

For many of the crofters and trappers of Eamonvale, he is the only
man of the cloth to visit with any regularity, and he has been present
at a great many births, deaths, weddings, harvest festivals, and barn
raisings in the valley. Those who know him are always glad to see
him, for he invariably brings news from afar and a new story or joke.
His traveling companions are often surprised by his wry wit, just as
his enemies are surprised by his agility and whirling attacks with his
unassuming walking staff.

A compulsive wanderer, he rarely settles in one location for long
unless his services are needed. Nobody knows where he comes from
originally, and when asked about his homeland, he responds, "Origins
and destinations are unimportant... it is the journey that matters."

Melph can be encountered outside of Dun Eamon (see the
Wilderness Encounters Appendix), as well as in the Caravan Camp.

FITCH

Fitch the Barman CR 4
XP 1,200
Dwarf fighter 5
LG Medium humanoid (dwarf)
Init +1; **Senses** darkvision 60 ft.; Perception +0 (+2 to notice unusual stonework)

AC 19, touch 12, flat-footed 18 (+7 armor, +1 deflection, +1 Dex)
hp 48 (5d10+20)
Fort +7, **Ref** +2, **Will** +1 (+1 vs. fear); +2 vs. poison, spells, and spell-like abilities
Defensive Abilities defensive training
Speed 20 ft.

Melee +1 keen greataxe +11 (1d12+8/19-20/×3) or
  sap +8 (1d6+3 nonlethal)
Special Attacks hatred, weapon training (axes +1)

Str 16, **Dex** 13, **Con** 16, **Int** 12, **Wis** 10, **Cha** 8
Base Atk +5; **CMB** +8; **CMD** 20 (24 vs. bull rush, 24 vs. trip)
Feats Cleave, Cleaving Finish, Great Cleave, Power Attack, Weapon Focus (greataxe), Weapon Specialization (greataxe)
Skills Acrobatics -3 (-7 to jump), Appraise +1 (+3 to assess nonmagical metals or gemstones), Climb +7, Knowledge (engineering) +9, Perception +0 (+2 to notice unusual stonework), Profession (barkeep) +8; **Racial Modifiers** +2 Appraise to assess nonmagical metals or gemstones, +2 Perception to notice unusual stonework
Languages Common, Dwarven, Undercommon
SQ armor training 1
Combat Gear potion of *heroism*; **Other Gear** mwk banded mail, +1 keen greataxe, sap, ring of protection +1, 85 gp

Description: Fitch is the barkeep, a grizzled, broad-shouldered, dwarf who says nothing but heard everything. He usually wears a coarse woolen shirt and trousers, but his armor is kept oiled and locked away should it be needed.

His services at the bar are varied, but mostly relate to pulling pints and keeping inventory for the extensive cellars. Customers regard him as trustworthy, mostly because he is rarely heard to speak a word to anyone. The safety of the Market Tavern, its staff, and its customers is of utmost importance to him. He is especially fond of Molly and Horace, the two young folks that work at the Tavern, as they are without family, and he has none of his own. He maintains a friendship with Stump, a compatriot and former business partner who frequents the bar.

Fitch is a retired adventurer. He traveled the land as a young dwarf, fighting wars, crusading against goblinkind, and delving deep into perilous dungeons. The patrons at the Market Tavern have learned, however, that those are not days he likes to revisit, and he is very hesitant to discuss adventuring with anyone. He does not even discuss them with Stump, who was the leader of their adventuring band. He is content with his current life and prefers to keep his previous one a secret.

Fitch is almost always encountered at the Market Tavern, although he can be found during the slow hours in the market looking out for exotic spirits with which to stock the shelves.

STUMP

Stump CR 5
XP 1,600
Gnome arcane trickster 2/unchained rogue 1/wizard 3
N Small humanoid (gnome)
Init +2; **Senses** low-light vision; Perception +10

AC 17, touch 13, flat-footed 15 (+4 armor, +2 Dex, +1 size)
hp 34 (6 HD; 5d6+1d8+12)
Fort +4, **Ref** +6, **Will** +3; +2 vs. illusions
Defensive Abilities defensive training
Speed 20 ft.

Melee +1 keen short sword +6 (1d4+1/17-20) or
  wizard hook +6 (1d3+1)
Ranged mwk light crossbow +6 (1d6/19-20)
Special Attacks hand of the apprentice (6/day), hatred, sneak attack +3d6
Spell-Like Abilities (CL 6th; concentration +7)
  1/day—*dancing lights, ghost sound* (DC 12), *prestidigitation, speak with animals*
Wizard Spells Prepared (CL 5th; concentration +8)
  3rd—*dispel magic, swipe*
  2nd—*acid arrow, invisibility, knock*
  1st—*mage armor, magic missile, protection from evil, reduce person* (DC 14)
  0 (at will)—*detect magic, light, mage hand, read magic*

Str 10, **Dex** 14, **Con** 15, **Int** 16, **Wis** 8, **Cha** 12
Base Atk +2; **CMB** +1; **CMD** 13
Feats Accomplished Sneak Attacker, Arcane Armor Training, Combat Casting, Scribe Scroll, Weapon Finesse
Skills Acrobatics +6 (+2 to jump), Appraise +7, Craft (alchemy) +14, Disable Device +14, Escape Artist +9, Knowledge (arcana) +10, Knowledge (history) +7, Perception +10, Sleight of Hand +11, Spellcraft +7, Stealth +15, Use Magic Device +5; **Racial Modifiers** +2 Craft (alchemy), +2 Perception
Languages Common, Draconic, Elven, Gnome, Sylvan, Undercommon
SQ arcane bond (wizard hook), gnome magic, ranged legerdemain, trapfinding +1
Combat Gear scroll of comprehend languages (CL 3rd), scroll of knock, scroll of spider climb; **Other Gear** mithral shirt, +1 keen short sword, wizard hook, crossbow bolts (20), mwk light crossbow, masterwork thieves' tools, prosthetic hand, spellbook

Special Abilities

Arcane Armor Training Swift action: -10% arcane spell failure due to armor.
Hand of the Apprentice (6/day) (Su) As a standard action, throw melee weapon (use Int instead of Dex) and instantly returns.
Ranged Legerdemain (Su) Can use Disable Device or Sleight of Hand from 30 ft away, but +5 DC.

Description: Stump is an aging, unpleasant gnome with short grey hair and thick eyebrows and beard. His left hand is missing at the wrist and has been replaced with a steel spike. He bathes infrequently and usually smells like alcohol.

Stump's gnomish cheer has gone out of him and been replaced with bitterness and resignation; he takes joy only in monitoring the success of his adopted daughter, Elinda Bannon. Most of the citizens regard him as a sad old drunk, not knowing the truth of his past. He also maintains contact with Fitch, the barman at the Market Tavern. Fitch is an old adventuring partner of his and one of the only survivors of the expedition that cost him his hand. He periodically gives advice to Lord Angus, who respects his wisdom and experience in foreign lands.

Stump has explored some of the most notorious dungeons in the land. His academic dedication and mastery of ancient tongues served him well in such endeavors, and he achieved renown to such a degree that he was able to pick and choose from lucrative financial offers from some very powerful figures. His last expedition as a dungeon guide met with great tragedy, and Stump was one of three survivors of a party of twenty. The failure of that outing compromised his reputation, but the booty allowed him to retire comfortably in the valley.

Stump can be encountered at the Market Tavern or at the Hole, but spends most of his time drinking and sulking in his run-down hovel.

The Band of the Crimson Mantle

This group of adventurers has been in Dun Eamon only a few days longer than the party. They are greedy and unscrupulous, but not all of them are necessarily evil. The heroes may clash with them above and beneath the ground as they investigate the mystery surrounding the underground caverns. Because Dun Eamon is a city of adventure on a busy trade route, some of the locals may know of the Band; the background information is provided as rumor material as well as a role-playing aid. The Band has adopted a red cloak as its symbol, although the members wear theirs in different fashions. Since joining forces, the Band has established a system of common phrases for communication, represented by the Innuendo skill.

Pratchett

Pratchett   **CR 4**
XP 1,200
Half-elf unchained rogue 5
NE Medium humanoid (elf, human)
Init +3; **Senses** low-light vision; Perception +10

AC 18, touch 13, flat-footed 15 (+5 armor, +3 Dex)
hp 28 (5d8+5)
Fort +2, **Ref** +7, **Will** +1; +2 vs. enchantments
Defensive Abilities danger sense +1, evasion, uncanny dodge; **Immune** sleep
Speed 30 ft. (20 ft. in armor)

Melee sap +6 (1d6-1 nonlethal) or
    short sword +6 (1d6+3/19-20)
Ranged +2 light crossbow +8 (1d8+2/19-20)
Special Attacks sneak attack +3d6

Str 8, **Dex** 17, **Con** 12, **Int** 14, **Wis** 10, **Cha** 14
Base Atk +3; **CMB** +2; **CMD** 15
Feats Point-Blank Shot, Precise Shot, Rapid Reload, Skill Focus (Disable Device), Weapon Finesse
Skills Acrobatics +8 (+4 to jump), Appraise +10, Bluff +10, Climb +4, Diplomacy +10, Disable Device +13, Linguistics +10, Perception +10, Sleight of Hand +8, Stealth +8, Use Magic Device +10; **Racial Modifiers** +2 Perception
Languages Abyssal, Celestial, Common, Draconic, Dwarven, Elven, Gnome, Infernal, Undercommon
SQ debilitating injury: bewildered, debilitating injury: disoriented, debilitating injury: hampered, elf blood, rogue talents (deadly range, swift poison), trapfinding +2
Combat Gear purple worm poison (16); **Other Gear** +1 mithral chain shirt, +2 light crossbow, crossbow bolts (20), sap, short sword, backpack, grappling bolt, silk rope (50 ft.), thieves' tools, trail rations (2), waterskin, garnet (worth 100 gp) x2, garnet (worth 120 gp), garnet (worth 90 gp), 65 gp, 18 sp, map to his secret cache of supplies and treasure (difficulty, location, and value to be determined by DM)

Special Abilities

Debilitating Injury: Bewildered -2/-4 (Ex) Foe who takes sneak attack damage takes AC pen (more vs. striker) for 1 rd.
Debilitating Injury: Disoriented -2/-4 (Ex) Foe who takes sneak attack damage takes attack pen (more vs. striker) for 1 rd.
Debilitating Injury: Hampered (Ex) Foe who takes sneak attack damage has speed halved (and can't 5 ft step) for 1 rd.

Description: Pratchett is a handsome half-elf with wavy black hair and bright eyes. He wears his sword and crimson cape in the most dashing manner he can imagine, but his bravado is sometimes transparent, allowing his greed and lust for power to show through.

Pratchett was an orphan raised by a band of thieves in a distant city. He spent his youth lifting merchant purses and holding up caravans, but he was always dissatisfied with his share of the booty. After he was caught skimming a few coins from a stolen pouch, he fled before an assassin's blade could end his career. He decided that adventuring rather than thievery was the way to make money, and he formed his own company. His years at the bottom of the pecking order led him to crave authority; he does not tolerate any threat to his leadership. It is rumored that the Band's last fighter lost sight of who was really in charge and fell victim to a poisoned crossbow bolt. Money matters most to Pratchett; he cares nothing for his companions or his clients. Other adventuring parties drive down profits and take away jobs; therefore, they are competition and must be harassed and handicapped by any means possible.

Pratchett knows that Dresden is completely unstable and would gladly replace him, but he needs an arcane spellcaster and does not mind paying him in shiny knick-knacks. He sees Isidra as a harmless eccentric who is good in a fight and can heal the party, and her obsession with death distracts her from the treasure and its distribution. He known Yelm is a great fighter, and the only pay he requires is enough cash for drinks and another fight.

Isidra

Isidra   **CR 4**
XP 1,200
Human cleric 5
NE Medium humanoid (human)
Init +0; **Senses** Perception +9

AC 19, touch 11, flat-footed 19 (+6 armor, +1 deflection, +2 shield)
hp 24 (5d8+1)
Fort +3, **Ref** +1, **Will** +8
Speed 30 ft. (20 ft. in armor)

Melee heavy mace +4 (1d8+1)
Special Attacks channel negative energy 6/day (DC 13, 3d6), death's kiss 7/day
Domain Spell-Like Abilities (CL 5th; concentration +9)
    7/day—touch of evil (2 rounds)
Cleric Spells Prepared (CL 5th; concentration +9)
    3rd—*animate dead*[D], *cure serious wounds, dispel magic*
    2nd—*bull's strength, cure moderate wounds, ghoul touch*[D] (DC 17), *hold person* (DC 16)
    1st—*bane* (DC 15), *cause fear*[D] (DC 16), *cure light wounds, deathwatch, doom* (DC 16)
    0 (at will)—*detect magic, guidance, light, read magic*
    D Domain spell; **Domains** Evil, Death (Undead subdomain)

Str 12, **Dex** 10, **Con** 8, **Int** 14, **Wis** 18, **Cha** 13
Base Atk +3; **CMB** +4; **CMD** 15

Feats Command Undead, Extra Channel, Spell Focus
(necromancy), Undead Master[UM]
Skills Acrobatics -3 (-7 to jump), Knowledge (arcana) +10,
Knowledge (religion) +10, Perception +9, Sense Motive +12,
Spellcraft +10
Languages Abyssal, Common, Necronomus
Combat Gear potion of cure light wounds (3), scroll of gentle
repose (CL 5th), scroll of speak with dead (CL 5th); **Other
Gear** +1 scale mail, +1 unholy reliquary light steel shield,
heavy mace, ring of protection +1, mummified hand of a
small child, trail rations (2), silver necklace with three tiny
black pearls (worth 800 gp), 32 gp, 18 sp

Special Abilities

Death's Kiss (2 rounds, 7/day) (Su) Melee touch attack
makes target count as undead for positive/negative energy
healing/harming
Touch of Evil (2 rounds, 7/day) (Sp) With a melee touch
attack, target is sickened and counted as good-aligned for the
purpose of [Evil] spells.

Note: Isidra's armor was a gift from her mentor. Unlike most
magical armor, this suit of scale mail will only adapt to a new owner's
race/build/gender if both the armor and the new wearer are immersed
in unholy water. It is currently in the form of a revealing bustier and
corset, a scale skirt, bracers, and leggings.
Description: Isidra is a pale, slender woman who might have been
beautiful if it was not for her dark, sunken eyes and sardonic smile.
She wears black robes over her armor, and her crimson mantle is the
only color on her person.
Isidra's upbringing was happy at first, but later led her down the
dark path she now treads. Her parents, caretakers at a small cemetery,
were slain when they stumbled into a Priest of Death robbing bodies
for his rituals. The evil cleric took over the position of caretaker and
became Isidra's only family. He raised her and schooled her in the
dark arts of necromancy, and she grew morbid and detached through
lack of contact with living beings. When the villagers mobbed up
and razed the cleric's dwelling, she escaped, returning later to the
smoldering ruins. She heard her mentor's cries for her, but could only
sit and watch with fascination as death took him. She fled one crime
scene after another until she found the Band; they needed a healer,
and they usually managed to leave a pleasant trail of corpses wherever
they went...
Isidra is starting to realize that Pratchett is just using her, but she
does not care enough about money to be concerned. She ignores Yelm;
his carefree approach to life is why she prefers the company of the
dead. She leaves Dresden in his own little world, but is concerned that
her chosen path may drive her to the same fate.

DRESDEN "THE MAD"

Dresden "the Mad"　　　　　　　　　　　　　　　　　**CR 4**
XP 1,200
Gnome sorcerer 5
CN Small humanoid (gnome)
Init +2; **Senses** low-light vision; Perception +1

AC 13, touch 13, flat-footed 11 (+2 Dex, +1 size)
hp 43 (5d6+25)
Fort +5, **Ref** +3, **Will** +1; +2 bonus vs. fear effects, +2 vs.
illusions
Defensive Abilities defensive training; **Resist** acid 10
Speed 20 ft.

Melee dagger +1 (1d3-2/19-20)
Ranged sling +5 (1d3-2)

Special Attacks hatred
Spell-Like Abilities (CL 5th; concentration +9)
1/day—*dancing lights, ghost sound* (DC 15), *prestidigitation,
speak with animals*
Bloodline Spell-Like Abilities (CL 5th; concentration +9)
7/day—*elemental ray* (1d6+2 acid)
Sorcerer Spells Known (CL 5th; concentration +9)
2nd (5/day)—*acid arrow, invisibility, scorching ray* (acid)
1st (7/day)—*burning hands* (acid) (DC 15), *color spray* (DC
16), *grease, mage armor, magic missile*
0 (at will)—*detect magic, flare* (DC 14), *ghost sound* (DC 15),
mage hand, prestidigitation, read magic
Bloodline Elemental (earth)

Str 7, **Dex** 14, **Con** 18, **Int** 7, **Wis** 8, **Cha** 18
Base Atk +2; **CMB** -1; **CMD** 11
Feats Combat Casting, Eschew Materials, Glimpse Beyond,
Heighten Spell
Skills Acrobatics +2 (-2 to jump), Knowledge (arcana) +2,
Knowledge (planes) +2 (+4 to identify vulnerabilities and
powers of evil outsiders, this check can be made untrained),
Linguistics -1, Perception +1, Spellcraft +2, Use Magic
Device +8; **Racial Modifiers** +2 Perception
Languages Common, Gnome, Sylvan, Terran
SQ bloodline arcana (change energy damage spells to match
bloodline energy), gnome magic
Combat Gear potion of fire breath, potion of gaseous form,
scroll of haste, scroll of knock; **Other Gear** dagger, sling,
sling bullets (30), ring of feather falling, assorted rocks (his
"friends"), flask, trail rations (2)

Special Abilities

Bloodline Arcana: Elemental (Ex) You may change any
energy spell to use Acid energy.
Elemental Ray (1d6+2 acid, 7/day) (Sp) As a standard
action, ranged touch attack deals damage to foe.

Description: Dresden is thin and scrawny, and he usually stands by
himself, mumbling and casting about wild glances. The stone "toad
familiar" nestled in his mangy hair, his rotten teeth, and his bizarre
personality make him a thoroughly unpleasant individual. His red
cloak has been fashioned into a loose toga and is torn and ridden with
lice, much to Pratchett's disgust.
Not all arcanists adapt well to the power they control, especially
when the power comes from within. Dresden is one such case,
dangerously unbalanced and unpredictable.
He was born in a quiet little gnome village that was completely
unprepared to have a sorcerer in its midst. Dresden spent many
childhood hours alone, talking to rocks and experimenting with his
powers. The explosive destruction of his parents' house was the result
of one such experiment. He miraculously escaped unharmed and was
seen skipping into the woods holding a conversation with only himself.
Since then, he has found employment on and off as an adventuring
spellcaster, but as his grip with reality slips, work becomes harder
to find. Dresden speaks almost exclusively in Terran, although it is
unknown how or why he learned that language. He is mischievous and
sadistic and uses his spells to heckle and annoy people.
Only Pratchett seems able to communicate effectively with him,
which Dresden tolerates because it keeps him from having to deal
with other people. He finds Yelm and Isidra to be very dull because
they do not seem to be a part of the world in which he currently lives.
Note: Dresden does not survive the events of *The Grey Citadel*.

Yelm

Yelm   CR 4
XP 1,200
Human barbarian 5
CN Medium humanoid (human)
Init +2; **Senses** Perception +9

AC 18, touch 12, flat-footed 16 (+6 armor, +2 Dex)
hp 48 (5d12+15)
Fort +6, **Ref** +3, **Will** +2
Defensive Abilities improved uncanny dodge, trap sense +1
Speed 40 ft. (30 ft. in armor)

Melee +1 mighty cleaving greatsword +9 (2d6+5/19-20)
Ranged throwing axe +7 (1d6+3)
Special Attacks rage (14 rounds/day), rage powers (animal fury, auspicious mark)

Str 17, **Dex** 14, **Con** 14, **Int** 10, **Wis** 12, **Cha** 8
Base Atk +5; **CMB** +8; **CMD** 20
Feats Cleave, Furious Focus, Power Attack, Reckless Rage
Skills Acrobatics +5, Handle Animal +7, Perception +9, Ride +5, Survival +9
Languages Common
SQ fast movement
Combat Gear oil (2); **Other Gear** chainmail, +1 mighty cleaving greatsword, throwing axe (4), backpack, hemp rope (50 ft.), kilt, kumis wineskin, whiskey, torch (6), trail rations (5), hacksilver armband (worth 8 gp), silver neck torc (worth 20 gp), silver trimmed drinking horn (worth 12 gp), 25 gp, 16 sp

Special Abilities

Animal Fury (Ex) Gain a d4 bite attack while raging
Auspicious Mark (1/rage) (Su) Use 2 rage as a swift action, gain +1d6 to a d20 roll.
Rage (14 rounds/day) (Ex) +4 Str, +4 Con, +2 to Will saves, -2 to AC when enraged.

Description: Yelm is a tall, powerful man with a booming voice and a fierce look in his green eyes. His long red hair is braided into his thick beard, and intricate blue tattoos cover half of his face and most of his body. His red swath of cloth is worn in a primitive but functional fashion, loosely pleated around him and held with a thick leather belt.

Yelm has been many things in his life — wandering barbarian, slave, pit fighter, caravan guard, beggar, soldier, wilderness guide, prisoner, outlaw, gambler, and more. Yet he has come to realize there are only two activities he truly enjoys: drinking and fighting. Those two activities can keep him in plenty of trouble, and he needs the Band to stay out of it. He is not evil, but he is immoral and unruly. He has no tolerance for weakness or cowardice and always prefers a stand-up fight to sneaking about in the dark.

Yelm will likely follow Pratchett as long as he finds things to fight and gives him money to drink, although he does not approve of some of the leader's methods. He looks on Isidra as a challenge and is always trying to get her to find a bit more enjoyment in life. He leaves Dresden in his own world, but is tempted to put the little madman out of everyone's misery.

The Mist Watch

The maintenance of law and order in and around the Grey Citadel is the responsibility of the Mist Watch. The force is made up of career soldiers, citizen militia, and wilderness outriders. There is no law of mandatory service for the citizens, but any man living within the city walls is subject to conscription in times of war.

Bron Angus is the Captain of the Watch and has been highly successful despite his young age. His experiences as a young man in a mercenary company taught him to be intolerant of sloth, insolence, and drunkenness, and his strict orders have resulted in an elite fighting force. The members of the Mist Watch are trained to a basic level with all weapons and tactics, but many of them have additional areas of expertise. All the Watchmen are rotated through various duty stations to avoid boredom and complacency.

Some specialists do exist within the ranks of the Watch: cavalry units known as **Outriders**, **Lookouts** manning the city walls, **Woodsmen** patrolling the wilderness areas of the valley, and the **Mist Mages** supporting the Watch with arcane magic.

Outriders patrol the wilderness surrounding the citadel, on the lookout for brigands and threatening monsters. They are always accompanied by a **Warden** when outside the city. See the Wilderness Encounters Appendix for outrider profiles.

Woodsmen are skilled hunters and trackers that patrol the thick woods beyond the reach of mounted patrols and act as scouts in time of war. See the Wilderness Encounters Appendix for their profiles.

Common patrols are as follows:

Mist Watch City Patrol: 9 guards, 1 guard officer, 25% chance of 1 constable, 10% chance of 1 Mist Mage

Mist Watch Night Patrol: 9 guards, 1 guard officer, 50% chance of 1 constable, 25% chance of 1 Mist Mage; add torches.

Mist Watch Mounted Patrol: 7 Outriders, 1 Warden, 10% chance of 1 Woodsman with horse.

The Ebon Union

The Ebon Union is a displaced guild of criminals and cutthroats. They were ousted one year previous to this adventure from their lair in the city of Reme (or any convenient urban location in your campaign world) by a coalition of adventurers and city guardsmen. Devlin, the highest ranking survivor, took the remnants of the gang and fled into the wilderness, where they survived as highwaymen for several months (the party may have even encountered their bandit gangs in the past). The approach of autumn and a taste for the luxuries of city life finally drove them to seek out a new home. The aspiring assassin Tabitha was one of several outriders sent to seek out a potential home for the guild. When she investigated the rumors of a gnome fortress below Dun Eamon, she knew the Ebon Union had found a place to make its new home. Some of the Union did not fancy a life underground — they remained in the wilderness under command of the ranger Hobark and are described in the Wilderness Encounters Appendix.

The Ebon Union has developed a unique character through its trials of the past year, and some of its members that made the transition are very specialized. A few of them (called **Nets**) became adept with the net during their escapades as bandits, hiding in trees and using weighted nets to drag horsemen to the ground. These experts have found their nets to be useful in the city as well, especially for taking uncooperative merchants or rogues into custody for a "discussion" with Devlin. Their crossbowmen (known as **Bolts**) developed remarkable accuracy while providing cover fire for raids on merchant caravan camps, and these thieves now provide cover from the rooftops while the burglars are at work. The booty of their caravan raids needed to be marketed, so a number of fences (**Shifters**) exist within the organization. Thanks to the heavily restricted trade sanctions in Dun Eamon, these scoundrels have also found continued demand for their skills. Thieves with more traditional skills (**Burglars** and **Cutpurses**) supply the guild with its most consistent income.

The Union's lair is in the fortified gatehouse of a long-abandoned gnome stronghold on the Level 3 of the underground cavern complex. The thieves dwell in the darkness much of the time, and they have adapted to their surroundings. Treat all members of the Ebon Union as having low-light vision; this ability is lost if they spend a day or more above ground in the daylight. The thieves have specific orders regarding the secrecy of their location and a number of locations in the city that they can use as staging points for their entries and exits from the sewers.

The Ebon Union is very conscious of any investigation the party conducts, and their eyes and ears all over the city keep them informed of the heroes' progress. As the adventure progresses, Timed Encounter 3.1 (see Chapter Two) and a possible assassination attempt at the Bathhouse (Area **P**; see Chapter Three) represent the Union's efforts to protect its identity and activities. Allow the Ebon Union to react to the heroes' actions, especially if they encounter thieves and allow them to escape — the Ebon Union is quick to exploit any information the survivors can provide about party composition and abilities. Similarly, if any thieves survive encounters with the party in the dungeon, the thieves in the lair in Area **3-25** (see Chapter Six) are prepared for the group's arrival.

Ebon Union Bolt   CR 3
XP 800
hp 22 (Pathfinder Roleplaying Game GameMastery Guide, "Dealer")

Ebon Union Burglar   CR 2
XP 600
hp 16 (Pathfinder Roleplaying Game GameMastery Guide, "Burglar")

Ebon Union Cutpurse   CR 1/2
XP 200
hp 10 (Pathfinder Roleplaying Game NPC Codex, "Cutpurse")

Ebon Union Knife   CR 1/2
XP 200
hp 5 (Pathfinder Roleplaying Game GameMastery Guide, "Pickpocket")

Ebon Union Net   CR 3
XP 800
hp 30 (Pathfinder Roleplaying Game GameMastery Guide, "Slaver")

Ebon Union Shifter   CR 2
XP 600
hp 20 (Pathfinder Campaign Setting: Isles of the Shackles, "Smuggler")

Ebon Union Thug   CR 1
XP 400
hp 16 (Pathfinder Roleplaying Game GameMastery Guide, "Street Thug")

Note: The party might possibly try to infiltrate one or more of its members into the Ebon Union. This strategy is not unreasonable — after all, the Ebon Union would rather have the local rogues contributing to its coffers than working against it. The process is not easy, however. First, they must make contact with a representative, which can be done by detaining a randomly encountered member or approaching one of the guild agents (such as Rorin, Kinnan the Dark, or Edgar). They require a heist of the character's choosing that must yield a profit of at least 200 gp, with all of the profits going to the guild. The applicant is then rewarded with a cloth token and a vague set of directions to the lair (enter the market drain and follow the flow of the water, cross and re-cross the river, and so on). If the applicant survives the trip, he must surrender his personal treasure to the guild hoard for "safe-keeping."

Devlin is very untrusting of new recruits — the character can expect several dangerous assignments before he is fully accepted. This is a complicated plot development that is not fully accommodated by the adventure text, so you may choose not to allow it to occur. Infiltration is unlikely after the group begins an investigation into the robberies or tangles with any of the thieves.

The profiles of Devlin and his lieutenants are detailed in the locations or events in which they are encountered:

Edgar at the Public Stables (Area **B**).
Molly at the Market Tavern (Area **D**).
Rorin at the Hole (Area **O**).
Tabitha at the Bathhouse (Area **P**).
Kubris and **Thurf** in Timed Encounter 3.1 (see Chapter Two).
Gulik in Timed Encounter 3.3 (see Chapter Two).
Devlin in dungeon Area **3-25**.

Appendix D: Wilderness Encounters

This Appendix details the wilderness areas around the city of Dun Eamon. It is presented separately because it is not crucial to the main adventure. DMs are encouraged to set the Grey Citadel in their own world and to use wilderness encounters appropriate to their own campaign. The following information is provided either as a more fleshed out campaign setting or as source material for you to cut and paste and use as you will in your own setting to expand upon the main adventure contained in this book.

The Grey Citadel is located in a remote area, many miles from anywhere of note. This most likely means — if you are using this material to detail the trip to Dun Eamon — that the heroes will spend a few days (and nights) en route to the city on whatever business has drawn them there. These encounters should help impart the flavor of the various creatures, conditions, and organizations that make the frontier such a dangerous place to adventure.

A few of these encounters have ties to the plot as detailed in the city, but none of them are critical to the success of the adventure, so feel free to run as few or as many of these as desired or to save them for future adventures in Eamonvale. They have been geared toward the party levels indicated for the adventure, with a few exceptions, but their treasure generally reflects the poor economy of the frontier wilderness. Some of them (notably the lizardfolk and highwaymen lairs) may need additional development and/or mapping.

The wilderness surrounding Dun Eamon is mostly forested mountain slopes, although some areas feature steep rocky bluffs, trackless moors, or boggy hollows. For extended wilderness adventuring in Eamonvale, supplement the following information with encounters from *Pathfinder Roleplaying Game Core Rulebook*. Use the Forest and Mountains portions, as well as the Civilized Areas section while on the trade road. Three encounter tables are provided below: one for trade road traffic, one for wilderness encounters, and for use at night in either location.

In addition to the road and wilderness encounters, two other regions of note are found in Eamonvale. One is the Trackless Mire, a vast blanket bog that is utterly inhospitable. It is covered with hidden sinkholes, quickmud, limestone fissures, caverns, and easily confused landmarks, making it a lethal place for adventuring. The wizard Elinda Bannon keeps a secret workshop here (see Area **L-9** in Chapter Two). There are no encounters of importance in this desolate area.

The other type of encounter region is the village, of which there are several scattered every 10 or 12 miles along the road. These small communities are almost exclusively made up of farmers, trappers, and shepherds. A village of 100 citizens or more has a magistrate and a small militia; the most influential citizens usually administrate the smaller ones. Encounters in these small communities might also include caravans, mounted patrols, and woodsmen.

The Surrounding Wilderness

The River Eamon flows down out of the Stoneheart Mountains, first through snow-fed mountain streams, then crashing down through rocky gorges and finally calming and widening as it flows across the lowland plains toward the sea. The region surrounding the river valley (known as Eamonvale) is governed from the city of Dun Eamon, as described below. The authority of the Lord of Eamonvale extends from the river's headwaters in the rugged mountains to the edge of the grasslands that stretch endlessly away from the foothills of the Stonehearts. Encounters in the region immediately surrounding the city are described in this chapter.

The trade road runs from the more civilized lowlands over the forbidding peaks of the Stoneheart Mountains into exotic distant lands. Merchant traffic is consistent on the road for as long as the mountain passes are open, but it peaks during the summer and fall seasons, when rivers are down and the first snow has not yet fallen. Even after the merchant trade across the mountains has fallen off for the season, local hunters, trappers, farmers, craftsmen, and adventurers still travel to the Grey Citadel with regularity, so the trade road is never without encounters.

Some of the regions that frame the trade road are desolate and uninhabited, but most of the Eamonvale region is alive with animal life and dotted with small settlements. Wandering off the road is not advised by anyone who knows the area — bandits, highwaymen, and humanoid tribes are always nearby. Outrider patrols from Dun Eamon travel the tradeways and police the villages and hamlets, but even they do not wander far from the road.

Wilderness Weather

Weather in Eamonvale is commonly chilly, damp, and grey. Assume that at any given time there is some combination of light fog and mist in the air, which has the same effect as the weather described in the city. Treat any encounter as taking place in partial concealment; any existing concealment factor is increased to the next category. Heavier fog and rain are included on the encounter tables and described below.

Heavy Fog: Heavy fog obscures all vision beyond 5 feet, including darkvision. Creatures 5 feet away have concealment. Heavy fog lasts 1d4 hours.

Rain: Rain reduces visibility ranges by half, resulting in a –4 penalty on Perception checks. Rain automatically extinguishes unprotected flames (candles, torches, and the like) and imposes a –4 penalty on ranged attacks. These rainstorms last for 2d4 hours.

Downpour: A strong but short-lived cloudburst combines the effects of rain and fog as described above. These storms only last for 1d4 hours.

Exposure is a danger in the wilderness as well. Apply nonlethal damage as described in the "Cold Dangers" section of the *Pathfinder Roleplaying Game Core Rulebook* to any character that becomes soaked as a result of rain or is dressed for very warm weather (toga, linen robes, loincloth, and such). Fortitude saves (DC 15 +1 per previous check) should be made every 4 hours to avoid 1d6 points of nonlethal damage. DC 15 Survival checks or proper clothing (winter clothing, rain cloaks, and the like) can help reduce the danger (+2 bonus to Fortitude save), as can stopping to camp and build a fire.

Encounters on the Trade Road

The trade road is a wide boulevard of crushed gravel spotted with periodic potholes and washouts. It is 20 feet wide in most places, with a 5-foot wide grassy verge on either side. Beyond the verge, the landscape varies from rocky gorge to thick forest to steep precipice, and often the terrain beyond the road is invisible in the drifting mist. For encounters on the road, roll 1d20 every hour.

1d20	Encounter
1 (unique)	**Logan the Furrier**
2 (unique)	Fallen Messenger
3 (unique)	**Brother Melph**
4–5	Merchant Caravan
6 (unique)	**Kamvase,** Wandering Minstrel
7–8	Lizardfolk Hunters or Hobark's Highwaymen
9–10	Outrider Patrol

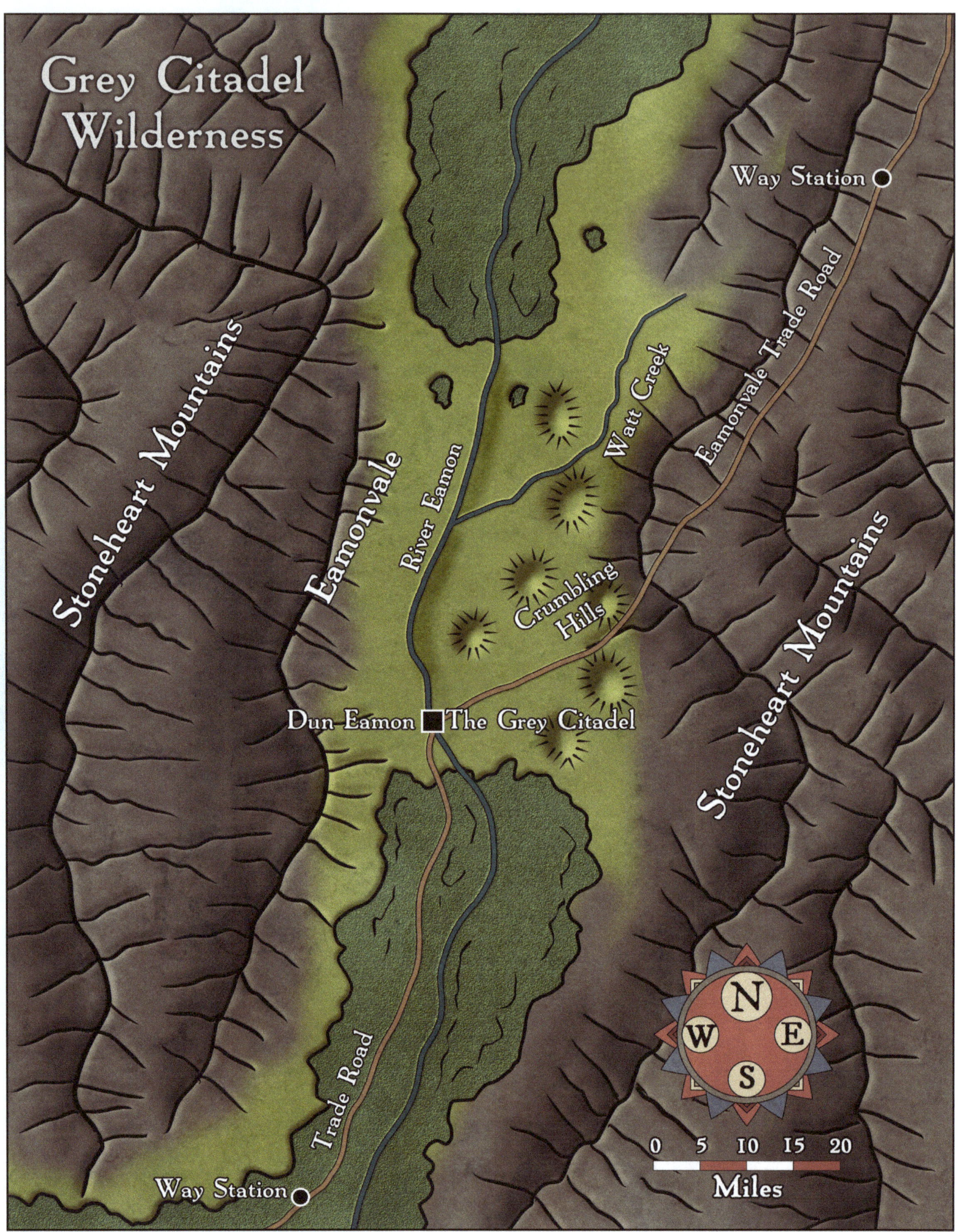

Grey Citadel Wilderness
Stoneheart Mountains
Stoneheart Mountains
Way Station
Way Station
Eamonvale Trade Road
Eamonvale
River Eamon
Watt Creek
Crumbling Hills
Dun Eamon
The Grey Citadel
Trade Road
N
W
E
S
0 5 10 15 20
Miles

1d20	Encounter
11	Heavy Fog
12	Rain
13	Downpour
14–20	No Encounter

LOGAN THE FURRIER

Logan is a typical trapper who lays his trap lines along the wooded mountain creeks around the city. When encountered, he appears with an enormous bundle of furs slung across his back, a canvas bag at his side, and a spear in his hand. He uses the trade road for travel to and from the city's market, where he sells his tanned skins in Raiment Row. He has a small shack up in the hills where he does his own tanning and curing. He visits the Grey Citadel once or twice each week and can give the party a rumor or two from the City Rumors Table (see Chapter Two), most likely dealing with the demons or some other current event, but it may be slightly inaccurate due to the word of mouth process his rumors usually come by.

If Logan is encountered at night, the party comes upon his small roadside camp. Day or night, he is always ready to share a few words of gossip, directions, or idle conversation. He is especially eager to trade a pipe of his cheap, coarse tobacco for a pinch of some exotic imported variety, he touts the quality of the local product in hopes of an exchange.

Logan the Furrier   **CR 3**
XP 800
hp 30 (Pathfinder Roleplaying Game GameMastery Guide, "Trapper")

FALLEN MESSENGER

At the beginning of the encounter, a large furry creature can be seen on the slope below the trade road tearing at something clothed in fabric. The creature in this encounter is a brown bear, a powerful omnivore common in these mountains. This one is scavenging from the corpse of a murdered messenger, although the party initially has no way of knowing this. The bear fights if threatened, but other options include distracting the bear with another food source or luring it away.

The body, which is already cold, is that of a messenger from a large temple of a good-aligned deity in a lowland city. The message was intended for Cael Angus, Master of the Temple of Fortitude in Dun Eamon. Gethrax and a few bandits from the highwayman gang murdered the messenger to keep his message from reaching the city. With a DC 10 heal check, an examination of the body reveals that not all of the acolyte's injuries are from the bear's meal — he has several sword wounds as well. The message is contained in the side bar.

An odd icon follows the message (the heroes may encounter this sigil in dungeon Areas **1-9** and **2-17**). It is the mark of a powerful cadre of necromancers whose temple is hidden deep in the mountains, although only a bard of great experience or a learned sage would recognize it.

Brown Bear   **CR 4**
XP 1,200
hp 42 (Pathfinder Roleplaying Game Bestiary, "Bear, Brown")

Treasure: On the messenger's body are a *potion of cure light wounds* and a ruby ring (250 gp).

BROTHER MELPH

The party encounters this young man on the trade road, mostly likely as he strides purposefully toward Dun Eamon with a light pack and sturdy staff. Brother Melph is an itinerant wanderer and a priest of the God of Roads, Note. He is returning to the city from his usual journey through the valley, stopping in at taverns and roadside inns to offer healing, counseling, and news. For many of the more remote villages, he is the only man of the cloth that visits with any regularity. The party may meet him eventually (or again) in the Caravan Camp at Dun Eamon. He is available as a replacement or surrogate party member. He can usually be heard whistling before he can be seen. He was in Dun Eamon fairly recently and so might be able to share a slightly out-of-date rumor from the City Rumors Table (see Chapter Two). Brother Melph can be encountered any time of day, but only along the road. If encountered at night, he is not camped, but he may come striding along in the darkness on the road he knows so well.

Brother Melph   **CR 4**
XP 1,200
hp 33 (Appendix C: NPC Descriptions, "Brother Melph")

MERCHANT CARAVAN

Up ahead, a number of wagons have convened at a broad turnout in the road. Horsemen are present, clad in fine clothing in the colors of the wagons. These horsemen are young aristocrats and courtiers, the arrogant sons of noble merchant houses learning the ways of caravans. The caravan master is an elderly man who spent his life in service to the house; he is skilled and competent, but allows himself to be bullied by the young nobles. In addition to the cargo of textiles and spices, they carry a few passengers — wealthy women and their servant girls on their way to join their husbands at a distant trading emporium. The encounter with the merchant caravan can be handled in several different ways (or in each of these ways at different times, or with different caravans).

• The young aristocrats insist that the party wait in the road until their caravan has gotten underway and moved on. Any objection is seen as a challenge to their authority and any insult is read as an affront to the dignity of the merchant house and a personal assault. They may issue a challenge to a fencing match, a test of skill, or some other duel, while the caravan master and guards roll their eyes and look the other way.

• The party comes upon the caravan just after highwaymen have attacked it. Several people are injured; two wranglers are dead. The master and the passengers are eager to pay for additional escorts, but without their purses they can only pay in promises. The young noblemen are adamant about needing no assistance and may even go so far as to accuse the party of being in league with the bandits.

• The party comes upon the caravan while highwaymen are attacking it. If the party makes the young nobles look bad, the accusations of being allied with the bandits may still come out, as does the request for an escort.

• The heroes find the caravan as they make camp for the night and are invited to join for a meal and a drink. In the morning, the arrogant nobles accuse the characters of stealing goods from the wagons, which one of them has actually left for his allies in the highwayman gang. The heroes must defuse the situation and possibly reveal the traitor.

Young Nobles (4) CR 1
XP 400
hp 19 (Pathfinder Roleplaying Game NPC Codex, "Squire")

Caravan Laborer CR 1/2
XP 200
hp 10 (Pathfinder Roleplaying Game GameMastery Guide, "Farmer")

Caravan Guard CR 1
XP 400
hp 16 (Pathfinder Roleplaying Game GameMastery Guide, "Caravan Guard")

Caravan Master CR 5
XP 1,600
hp 31 (Pathfinder Roleplaying Game GameMastery Guide, "Traveling Merchant")

Noblewomen (3) CR 1/2
XP 200
hp 7 (Pathfinder Roleplaying Game NPC Codex, "Princess")

Treasure: In addition to the NPCs' items, the caravan holds a cargo of textiles, spires, and other trade goods worth hundreds of gold pieces on the open market, but is fairly worthless to adventurers without good mercantile contracts, trade agreements, and bartering ability.

Kamvase, Wandering Minstrel

From a distance, the party hears the idle strumming of a lute and a lilting, melodic voice. Upon sighting the party, a chubby halfling seated on a boulder shifts his ballad to one that features the heroes as the subject:
"...when mighty adventurers come around, the beasties tremble 'pon the ground, and soft swoons many a winsome lass, and men are quick to raise their glass... Well met, travelers!"

This is **Kamvase**, a halfling bard with a larcenous streak. Many welcome his company on the road, only to find their purses lightened and the minstrel nowhere in sight when they turn around. He is eager to share the road with a powerful party, mostly for his protection, but also to relieve them of a few choice items.

Kamvase readily shares his plentiful music and his limited wine and cheese if it looks like the heroes will accept his company. If they do, he waits until they are camped to make his move. When watches are distributed, he accepts one on his own, if the party is agreeable. If a character shares a watch with him, he uses his lute and soft singing to lull the hero to sleep (using a *sleep* spell). If confronted with accusations, he simply feigns innocence, calling his spell a lullaby. If given a moment with the entire party asleep, he quickly pinches a few small items and makes off into the woods (he avoids large or obvious things such as swords, preferring something that will not be missed immediately). The party's reactions may be diverse, depending on what was stolen from whom. The item may be lost forever, the DM may choose to allow a manhunt, or Kamvase could surface again in Dun Eamon. When in the city, Kamvase usually makes contact with Kinnan the Dark at the Caravan Camp to liquidate his ill-gotten gains (see Area **C**, in Chapter Three).

Kamvase CR 2
XP 600
Halfling bard 3
CN Small humanoid (halfling)
Init +3; **Senses** Perception +7

AC 17, touch 15, flat-footed 14 (+2 armor, +1 deflection, +3 Dex, +1 size)
hp 20 (3d8+6)
Fort +3, **Ref** +7, **Will** +3; +4 vs. bardic performance, language-dependent, and sonic, +2 vs. fear
Speed 20 ft.

Melee short sword +2 (1d4-1/19-20)
Ranged sling +6 (1d3-1)
Special Attacks bardic performance 11 rounds/day (countersong, distraction, fascinate [DC 14], inspire competence +2, inspire courage +1)
Bard Spells Known (CL 3rd; concentration +6)
1st (4/day)—*charm person* (DC 14), *expeditious retreat, innocence, sleep* (DC 14)
0 (at will)—*daze* (DC 13), *detect magic, ghost sound* (DC 13), *mage hand, prestidigitation, read magic*

Str 8, **Dex** 16, **Con** 13, **Int** 12, **Wis** 8, **Cha** 17
Base Atk +2; **CMB** +0; **CMD** 14
Feats Point-Blank Shot, Rapid Shot
Skills Acrobatics +5 (+1 to jump), Appraise +7, Climb +1, Perception +7, Perform (sing) +9, Perform (string instruments) +11, Sense Motive +5, Sleight of Hand +9, Stealth +13; **Racial Modifiers** +2 Acrobatics, +2 Climb, +2 Perception
Languages Common, Elven, Halfling
SQ bardic knowledge +1, versatile performance (string)
Other Gear leather armor, short sword, sling, sling bullets (30), ring of protection +1, masterwork lute, gold ring (worth 45 gp), 35 gp, 22 sp

Special Abilities

Versatile Performance (String Instruments) +11 (Ex)
You may substitute the final value of your Perform: String Instruments skill for Bluff or Diplomacy checks

Lizardfolk Hunters

Through the mists that drift across the road ahead of the heroes, a ghostly shape appears momentarily and then disappears just as quickly. A low, hissing cry rises and falls somewhere amidst the fog-shrouded trees. If characters succeed at a DC 20 Perception check, they notice that the creature walked upright like a human, but was much taller and balanced itself with a thick, serpentine tail.

The figure crossing the road was a lone **lizardfolk hunter**, but his hunting party is just ahead of him in the forest. If the heroes engage the hunters, use the profiles in the Lizardfolk Valley description and be sure to include the limited visibility rules from the Conditions in the City section of Chapter One. The hunting party does not respond immediately to an attack on the straggler, preferring to sacrifice him to enhance their own attack on the characters. If they are successfully shadowed or tracked, they lead the characters back to their lair, described in the Lizardfolk Valley section, below. If the party is accompanied by the lizardfolk youth described in Area **U** (see Chapter Two), the hunters are more receptive to negotiations and may escort the party to their village, but they do not lower their guard. The lizardfolk are most active upriver of the city, where their lair is located; downriver of the city, this encounter should be replaced with Hobark's Highwaymen.

Lizardfolk Hunter (6)   CR 1
XP 400

hp 11 (Pathfinder Roleplaying Game Bestiary, "Lizardfolk")

Treasure: These lizardfolk carry only their weapons.

Highwayman Gang

A band of highwaymen have prepared an ambush on a lonely stretch of the trade road. Their leader Hobark is with them. Some are mounted, others armed with nets or crossbows. They attack any party that does not obviously outnumber or overpower them. This encounter might be used effectively with the merchant caravan encounter, providing the additional consideration of non-combatants to defend and work around. It may turn into a dangerous running battle in the form of a high-speed chase on foot or horseback through the damp, foggy woodland. The highwaymen are most active south of the city, where their lair is located; north of the city, this encounter should be replaced with the Lizardfolk Hunters. The stats below describe the standard compliment of bandits for an ambush.

Hobark   CR 6
XP 2,400

hp 53 (Pathfinder Roleplaying Game GameMastery Guide, "Highwayman")

Bolt (4)   CR 3
XP 800

hp 22 (Pathfinder Roleplaying Game GameMastery Guide, "Dealer")

Net (3)   CR 3
XP 800

hp 30 (Pathfinder Roleplaying Game GameMastery Guide, "Slaver")

Rider (6)   CR 1/2
XP 200

hp 11 (Pathfinder Roleplaying Game GameMastery Guide, "Bandit")

Tactics: The Bolts take up positions on either side of the road to bait the party into approaching the ambush site and can be noticed with a DC 19 Perception check. The Nets, who can be noticed with a DC 19 Perception check, hide in trees above and just in front of the crossbow positions, holding their actions until chargers pass below them, when they attack with their nets. The Riders wait on either side of the road behind the crossbowmen to sweep into the road in a countercharge or to surround fallen heroes.

Hobark accompanies the horsemen, but he is quick to leave his horse and attack on foot unless an entire party is mounted.

Treasure: The bandits have several pouches of coin from this day's raids, worth 120 gp and 200 sp.

Outrider Patrol

The mounted outrider patrols originate in Dun Eamon and are charged with protecting the trade road and the travelers on it as they approach the city. They have a range of roughly 50 miles in any direction — rarely more than a day's ride from the city. There are exceptions to this limit, such as when the outriders are on specific business: i.e., responding to a crisis or escorting a diplomat, priest, or magistrate. When out of the city, they prefer to billet themselves in a village tavern, a home, or a barn, but they are equipped to camp outdoors if no other option is available. A writ from Lord Angus gives them authority over most citizens of the valley, although they cannot overrule an appointed agent of Lord Angus (such as a magistrate) unless circumstances are extreme.

Outrider patrols travel in groups of eight, one of whom is a Warden. They wear the livery of the Angus clan (blue and grey tabards over mail) and carry blue banners at their lance tips. They are obliged to stop every group of travelers when they enter the valley and inquire about their destination, business intentions, and length of stay. They also assess a party's composition and include it in their report when they return to the city. Their high rate of travel ensures that most visitors to the region are expected by the time they arrive in Dun Eamon. In extreme circumstances, the Warden may dispatch two riders to return at full speed to request further support or deliver important information.

The outriders are not at leisure to discuss current events in the city, although they have been instructed to be on the lookout for capable adventurers that might be of use to the community. An DC 20 Diplomacy check to gather information, perhaps with a bonus for someone of military bearing, might prompt the Warden to infer that events are afoot in the city that might result in lucrative adventures for the party.

Outrider (7)   CR 1
XP 400

hp 19 (Pathfinder Roleplaying Game NPC Codex, "Squire")

Warden   CR 5
XP 1,600

hp 42 (Pathfinder Roleplaying Game GameMastery Guide, "Cavalry")

Valley Woodsman: There is a 15% chance that a valley woodsman on horseback accompanies any outrider patrol.

Valley Woodsman   CR 3
XP 800

hp 30 (Pathfinder Roleplaying Game GameMastery Guide, "Trapper")

Encounters

Off the Trade Road

If the heroes choose to leave the relative safety of the road, they may already be tracking one of the preceding factions. If they are wandering aimlessly or looking for a place to camp, use the following table to determine their encounter, rolling 1d20.

1d20	Encounter
1	Bernya the Nymph
2–4	Wolf Pack
5–6	Giant Boar
7–8	Shaw, Valley Woodsman
9–10	Lizardfolk Valley or Highwaymen's Camp
11	Heavy Fog
12	Rain
13	Downpour
14–20	No Encounter

Bernya the Nymph

The party most likely encounters **Bernya the nymph** standing on a tree limb over the road, challenging their passage with an arrow set to her bowstring. Bernya is one of several fey creatures that dwell in the misty forests of Eamonvale, but she is unique among her kind. She is troubled by her past and by the unrest in the valley, and her class levels and her attitude are unlike that of any other nymph. She usually contents herself with monitoring the passage of adventuring bands and merchant caravans, but periodically her rage boils over and she confronts a party openly, demanding to know its business in the valley. This reaction is more likely if the party shows evidence of evil tendencies or travels with servants or thralls, and she attacks without notice if any party obviously keeps slaves. She reacts the same when encountered at night.

Several human generations ago, a band of slavers came to the valley. They raided the outlying villages and readily dispatched or evaded the militias that opposed them. Internal affairs kept the Angus clan from mounting an efficient defense, and many of the citizens retreated to within the city walls. Bernya and a few farmers and woodsmen fought against the slavers, but their efforts were ineffective, and the band prepared to leave the valley with its human cargo. During a final, desperate attack on the slaver's camp, Bernya was badly injured and taken as a prize slave herself, bound and masked to contain her beauty.

A small group of woodsmen and adventurers attacked the caravan repeatedly as it wound its way out of the mountains, eventually managing to free the nymph. She joined their guerilla band, vowing that she would not rest until all the slaves had been freed and the slavers dispatched. They eventually completed the task and eliminated the slavers, but by the time Bernya returned from the pursuit across distant lands, she was unable to return to the life she had known. She has sworn to keep that kind of evil from arising in her domain again.

Bernya the Nymph CR 8
XP 4,800
Nymph ranger 3
CG Medium fey
Init +5; **Senses** low-light vision; Perception +17
Aura blinding beauty (30 ft., DC 21, currently DC 16)

AC 26, touch 23, flat-footed 20 (+3 armor, +7 deflection, +5 Dex, +1 dodge)
hp 92 (11 HD; 8d6+3d10+47)
Fort +16, **Ref** +21, **Will** +19
DR 10/cold iron
Speed 30 ft., swim 20 ft.

Melee kukri +12/+7 (1d4/18-20) or
  mwk scimitar +13/+8 (1d6+5/18-20)
Ranged mwk longbow +13/+8 (1d8/×3)
Special Attacks combat style (two-weapon combat), favored enemy (humans +2), stunning glance
Spell-Like Abilities (CL 8th; concentration +15)
  1/day—*dimension door*
Druid Spells Prepared (CL 7th; concentration +10)
  4th—*dispel magic*
  3rd—*call lightning* (DC 16), *cure moderate wounds, neutralize poison*
  2nd—*barkskin, delay poison, hold animal* (DC 15), *share language* (DC 15)
  1st—*cure light wounds, cure light wounds, faerie fire, obscuring mist, pass without trace*
  0 (at will)—*detect magic, know direction, light, purify food and drink* (DC 13)

Str 10, **Dex** 21, **Con** 18, **Int** 16, **Wis** 17, **Cha** 25
Base Atk +7; **CMB** +12; **CMD** 30
Feats Agile Maneuvers, Combat Casting, Dervish Dance, Dodge, Endurance, Iron Will, Two-weapon Fighting, Weapon Finesse
Skills Diplomacy +18, Escape Artist +15, Handle Animal +18, Heal +14, Knowledge (local) +11, Knowledge (nature) +14, Perception +17, Perform (dance) +12, Sense Motive +17, Stealth +18, Survival +17, Swim +18
Languages Common, Sylvan
SQ favored terrain (forest +2), inspiration, track +1, unearthly grace, wild empathy +24
Other Gear studded leather, arrows (20), kukri, mwk longbow, mwk scimitar

Special Abilities

Blinding Beauty (DC 21, currently DC 16) (Su) Blind humanoids in 30 ft if they look at the nymph (Fort neg). Can suppress as a free action.
Inspiration (Su) Chosen creature gains +4 to Will saves and Craft/Perform checks while carries a mark of favor.
Stunning Glance (DC 21, currently unusable) (Su) As a standard action can stun one creature in 30 ft for 2d4 rds (Fort neg).

Unearthly Grace (Su) This creature adds her Charisma modifier as a racial bonus on all her saving throws, and as a deflection bonus to her Armor Class.

Description: Bernya is a stunningly beautiful creature, but the scars of her battles against the slavers mar both her appearance and her persona. Her hair is dirty and tangled, her face is smudged with dirt, and a long scar cross from below her right eye to the corner of her jaw. She wears bloodstained armor and carries an ash bow, a scimitar, and a kukri knife — souvenirs of the defeated southern slave raiders.

Animal Companion: Two wolves of Lassilim's pack almost always accompany Bernya while she patrols the wilderness.

Wolf (2)   **CR 1**
XP 400
hp 13 (Pathfinder Roleplaying Game Bestiary, "Wolf")

Note: Bernya's *stunning glance* nymph special attack is unusable in her current condition due to her downtrodden attitude and disfiguring scars. Those who would normally be subject to her deadly appearance are distracted by her troubled nature. She is still extremely striking, and her *blinding beauty* functions as normal, but with a reduced save DC. Bernya's bonus against her favored enemy is a result of her deep-seated rage, cold determination, and intuition, rather than being indicative of any special familiarity or training.

WOLF PACK

Many packs of wolves roam the forests around Dun Eamon, but two are uniquely large and powerful. A dire wolf named **Gorian** leads one pack; a celestial dire wolf named **Lassilim** leads the other. Lassilim's pack has allied itself with Bernya and assists her in seeking balance in the woodlands. Gorian and his wolf pack want to force the human hunters and farmers out of the area so that the beasts might once again dominate the mountain slopes, with Gorian himself as lord of the realm.

The heroes have an equal chance of encountering either wolf pack, as well as the chance of encountering a non-aligned pack of normal wolves. Lassilim's pack does not attack the party unless provoked or asked to do so by Bernya. Gorian's pack attacks immediately, trying to kill or drive off any trespassers in "their" realm. The other wolf packs size up the party before attacking, and usually try to separate a weaker member from the group and chase him or her into the mist.

1d20	Wolf Pack Encounter
1–5	4d4 + 4 **wolves** plus **Gorian**, a dire wolf
6–10	3d4 + 4 **wolves** plus **Lassilim**, a celestial dire wolf
11–19	3d4 + 4 **wolves**
20	Gorian's pack *and* Lassilim's pack

Wolf   **CR 1**
XP 400
hp 13 (Pathfinder Roleplaying Game Bestiary, "Wolf")

Gorian   **CR 3**
XP 800
hp 37 (Pathfinder Roleplaying Game Bestiary, "Wolf, Dire")

Lassilim   **CR 4**
XP 1,200
Celestial dire wolf
N Large animal
Init +2; **Senses** darkvision 60 ft., low-light vision, scent;

Perception +10

AC 14, touch 11, flat-footed 12 (+2 Dex, +3 natural, -1 size)
hp 37 (5d8+15)
Fort +7, **Ref** +6, **Will** +2
DR 5/evil; **Resist** acid 10, cold 10, electricity 10; **SR** 9
Speed 50 ft.

Melee bite +7 (1d8+6 plus trip)
Space 10 ft.; **Reach** 5 ft.
Special Attacks smite evil

Str 19, **Dex** 15, **Con** 17, **Int** 2, **Wis** 12, **Cha** 10
Base Atk +3; **CMB** +8; **CMD** 20 (24 vs. trip)
Feats Run, Skill Focus (Perception), Weapon Focus (bite)
Skills Acrobatics +2 (+6 to jump with a running start, +10 to jump), Perception +10, Stealth +3, Survival +1 (+5 when tracking by scent); **Racial Modifiers** +4 Survival when tracking by scent

LIZARDFOLK VALLEY

Exploring beyond the trade road, rescuing the lost lizardfolk child from the city, or tracking the lizardfolk hunting party may lead the heroes here — to the lair of the lizardfolk tribe. This area is a deep gorge with a geothermal hot spring at the rear. The warm water flows under a bridge at the road, where the party might feel a warm breeze blowing out of the valley. The reptilian humanoids occupy a small village at the back of the valley, but have extensively trapped the entire area.

They arrived only a few years before the events of this adventure. The Angus clan has always kept a zero tolerance policy on slavery and allows no person in bondage across the ford. A slave caravan managed to pass off its human cargo as servants, but they had also been carrying a number of lizardfolk, captives from the distant south. The reptilian humanoids were not doing well in the cold mountain environment, nor had they adjusted well to captivity, so they were clubbed and left to die outside the city. They made their way into the forest, where they managed to scavenge and hunt enough to survive.

When they discovered the hot springs in the small valley, their chances for survival and their quality of living increased. The temperature was reminiscent of their tropical home, and the mineral rich plant life supported numerous small creatures for them to hunt and trap. The small tribe has flourished here, built a village, and begun to explore the mountain slopes and venture in disguise into the city nearby. Still, they dream of returning to their tropical home in the south, but they cannot begin to plan such a journey and are content to stay where they are for now. They have no connection to the events of the adventure.

The lizardfolk have found plenty of time to establish their presence in the area, and the village is well defended by cunning traps and ambushes, most of which use fungal poisons. There is a 20% chance that a trap is watched by a group of lizardfolk hunters.

Poisoned Punji Pit Trap   **CR 4**
XP 1,600
Type mechanical; **Perception** DC 20; **Disable Device** DC 20
Trigger location; **Reset** manual
Effect 10-ft.-deep pit (1d6 falling damage); punji sticks (Atk +10 melee, 1d4 spikes per target for 1d4+2 damage each plus poison [blistercap spore]); Reflex DC 20 negates; multiple targets (all targets in a 10-ft.-square area)

Poisoned Pit Trap   **CR 1**
XP 400
Type mechanical; **Perception** DC 20; **Disable Device** DC 20

Trigger location; **Reset** manual
Effect 20-ft.-deep pit (2d6 falling damage plus poison
[blistercap spore]); DC 20 Reflex avoids; multiple targets (all
targets in a 10-ft.-square area)

Poison Dart Volley Trap   CR 4
XP 1,600
Type mechanical; **Perception** DC 20; **Disable Device** DC 15
  Trigger location; **Reset** repair
Effect poison darts (Atk +10 ranged, 1d3 plus poison
[blistercap spore]); multiple targets (all targets in a 10-ft.-
square area)

Blistercap Spore
Type poison, contact; **Save** Fortitude DC 20; **Frequency** 1/
  round for 6 rounds; **Cure** 2 consecutive saves.
Initial Effect: 1d2 Dex drain and 1 Con drain
Secondary Effect: Sickened for 1 minute

Chief Ank'M'Tak   CR 13
XP 25,600
hp 95 (Pathfinder Roleplaying Game Monster Codex,
  "Lizardfolk Clutch Mother")

Description: Chief Ank'M'Tak wears a loincloth of snakeskin
pierced with pins, brooches, and other jewelry. His totem staff
is rumored to give him the power of his defeated enemies. He is
powerfully built and carries himself with pride. His only concerns are
for the survival and growth of his tribe.

Shaman Shar'M'No   CR 12
XP 19,200
hp 97 (Pathfinder Roleplaying Game Monster Codex,
  "Lizardfolk Sorcerer")

Description: Shar'M'No wears a ragged robe stolen from a traveler.
His is the only one in the tribe to wear humanoid clothing and stands
out as such. He is smaller that Ank'M'Tak and often looks around
with paranoia, hissing under his breath. He covets the chief's position
and wishes to overthrow him.

Lizardfolk Hunter (20)   CR 1
XP 400
hp 11 (Pathfinder Roleplaying Game Bestiary, "Lizardfolk")

Description: These lizardfolk are prepared for battle; they carry
only their weapons and wear only loincloths ornamented with shells
and bones.
  Lizardfolk Non-Combatants (10): The village is home to a
number of elderly or infant lizardfolk who do not take part in any

conflict. The elders have the respect of the tribe, and the young cannot survive without the hunters to provide them with food.

Tactics: The shaman Shar'M'No has advised Chief Ank'M'Tak that the extraction of information from (and eventual roasting of) captives is critical to survival, so they do not attack sentient beings on sight. When the lizardfolk do encounter humanoids, they attempt to take them prisoners and deliver them to their village for a meeting with their leaders.

There is a 20% chance that a party of lizardfolk hunters is watching any of the traps in the valley, as the traps do not kill or permanently detain most creatures. These hunters assess the danger of the trapped creature and either move to surround it or send for reinforcements from the village. The lizardfolk attempt to time their attack so that it takes advantage of whichever trap the party has triggered. Most of their traps involve poison, so they focus on heroes who remain standing. They attack those characters with their javelins at range and then close to melee. When in close combat, they fight defensively against anyone who appears to be succumbing to the poison's effects, as they are under orders to bring survivors in if possible.

When the lizardfolk fight as a tribe, the hunters throw their javelins as they close in and then rush into melee with their morningstars. The Chief and the shaman stand back and support the tribe with their spells, using their weapons if a threat comes near. If Chief Ank'M'Tak is wounded, weakened, or otherwise vulnerable, Shar'M'No tries to kill him, ensuring his place as leader. If the heroes notice this act, they may intervene and win the Chief's favor.

If the party gains access to the village, as prisoners or otherwise, the chief and shaman take an audience with them. Should the party stumble onto the camp, the hunters immediately move to surround it, but do not attack without orders from Ank'M'Tak. The Chief questions the heroes as to their motives and attempts to ascertain the threat level. If the heroes can use their Diplomacy skills effectively and pass a DC 20 Diplomacy check, they might learn of the tribe's desire to return to their native jungles. The shaman covets the leadership of the tribe and tries desperately (and often successfully) to influence the Chief's decisions. A gift to the tribe improves relations considerably, while insults and threats are not taken well. Depending on the heroes' actions, the Chief may offer to trade with them, challenge them to a trial, or simply order the tribe to kill them. A test of strength and hunting prowess might be called on to settle any issue that might arise — the party must enter the valley and defeat an equal number of lizardfolk hunters, including the chief… without the use of their equipment!

If the party arrives at the village as a result of making contact with the lost lizardfolk youngster from Area **U** in Dun Eamon (see Chapter Two), reactions may be very different. The tribe is grateful to have the child returned, but they immediately subject the youngster to harsh reprimands and interrogation to ensure that he acted without fear and battled well while in the city. If the party supports this image, the young creature receives only the rebuke. If the party reports that it was hiding in fear, a harsh punishment is in order. Alternatively, the heroes could be asked or required by the tribe to determine the fate of the youngster when they visit the city.

Regardless of how the youngster fares, the Chief and shaman both thank the heroes and offer them sanctuary. If the lizardfolk village remains in the valley, the heroes have a place where they can rest and store supplies. At the DM's discretion, the leaders may approach the party with their desire to leave the valley and return to their ancestral homeland, which could become an involved process. The shaman continues to covet the Chief's position and conspire against him, and the heroes might become pawns in his clever schemes as their relations with the tribe progress.

Highwaymen's Camp

The highwaymen are camped on a high bluff above the road. The camp consists of a few dozen tents, dugouts, and temporary shacks, plus two wagons stolen from merchant caravans. Several fire pits are scattered about, as well as cords of wood, game-smoking lean-tos, latrines, and food caches.

Their camp's natural defensive position is ideal; many traps, deadfalls, and pits have been prepared on the approaches to it, and it is always under careful guard. Characters may stumble upon this area if they leave the road, but it is more likely that they will track the ambushers back here or force its location from a captive under duress. Planning an invasion of the camp is a difficult affair, and the party is almost certainly outnumbered. Infiltrating the camp by stealth or deception is just as difficult, but all are potentially viable tactics. Defeating the bandits also brings the party into good favor with the government of Dun Eamon.

This particular band of highwaymen is a splinter group of the Ebon Union. Some of them came with the thieves' guild after they were ousted from their previous home city, but most of them joined the group later, during the months that the entire band relied on robbery on the trade road. Most of the men who joined during this time were outdoorsmen and had no desire to dwell in a city, much less below one. Devlin wisely allowed them to stay in the wilderness under the command of his old lieutenant, Hobark. By doing so, he has maintained his influence on the trade caravans while having a ready market for the goods he steals. He provides supplies to the bandits in exchange for marketing their stolen caravan goods — goods that he can sell for a higher price that Hobark could find for them and still turn a profit for the Union. In some cases, he might conspire with Hobark and his men to steal the same item a second time as it leaves the region in the hands of its new owner.

Hobark was one of the first to join the Ebon Union during their wilderness era. He had previously made good money and a bad name for himself as a bounty hunter and freelance killer. Highway robbery suits him well and favors his skills, for he is cruel and sadistic and yet fancies himself noble, and no man in the gang can match him in combat or on horseback.

Pit Trap   **CR 1**
XP 400
Type mechanical; **Perception** DC 20; **Disable Device** DC 20
Trigger location; **Reset** manual
Effect 20-ft.-deep pit (2d6 falling damage); DC 20 Reflex avoids; multiple targets (all targets in a 10-ft.-square area)

Log Deadfall   **CR 5**
XP 1,600
Type mechanical; **Perception** DC 20; **Disable Device** DC 20
Trigger location; **Reset** manual
Effects Rigged to logs in canopies or on ledges, a trip line strung across an area can create a deadly trap. When a creature enters the deadfall's trigger square, the logs drop in a 20-foot line or a 10-foot-square area, affecting four 5-foot squares in all. Each creature in this area takes 4d6 points of damage and is knocked prone. With a successful DC 20 Reflex save, a target takes half the damage and avoids being knocked prone.

Rock Deadfall   **CR 2**
XP 600
Type mechanical; **Perception** DC 20; **Disable Device** DC 25
Trigger touch (tripwire); **Reset** repair
Effect Atk +12 (3d6); multiple targets (all targets in a 5 ft. by 10 ft. area)

Spear Trap   CR 2
XP 600
Type mechanical; **Perception** DC 20; **Disable Device** DC 20
Trigger location; **Reset** repair
Effect Atk +15 melee (spear; 1d6+6)

Hobark   CR 6
XP 2,400
hp 53 (Pathfinder Roleplaying Game GameMastery Guide, "Highwayman")

Description: Hobark is a bounty hunter and mercenary for hire. He was one of Devlin's lieutenants before the Ebon Union divided, and he fell naturally into leadership. His position is based on the most elementary "law of the jungle": he was the strongest, fastest, and most skilled of the highwaymen that remained behind. Devlin's tactics using the crossbows and nets have continued to serve the gang well, and none of Hobark's men find fault with his leadership. Hobark is a tall, black-haired man with a look of intensity on his face and a brace of axes crossed over his chain shirt.

The highwaymen are a diverse bunch of ruffians, but most of them have the same background as the Ebon Union thieves, including the same specialties. Use the stats found in the Ebon Union section of **Appendix C**. In addition, there are two other NPC types in the wilderness gang: Riders and Hunters.

Ebon Union Bolt (10)   CR 3
XP 800
hp 22 (Pathfinder Roleplaying Game GameMastery Guide, "Dealer")

Ebon Union Knife (14)   CR 1/2
XP 200
hp 5 (Pathfinder Roleplaying Game GameMastery Guide, "Pickpocket")

Ebon Union Net (6)   CR 3
XP 800
hp 30 (Pathfinder Roleplaying Game GameMastery Guide, "Slaver")

Ebon Union Shifter (2)   CR 2
XP 600
hp 20 (Pathfinder Campaign Setting: Isles of the Shackles, "Smuggler")

Ebon Union Thug (18)   CR 1
XP 400
hp 16 (Pathfinder Roleplaying Game GameMastery Guide, "Street Thug")

Rider (16)   CR 1/2
XP 200
hp 11 (Pathfinder Roleplaying Game GameMastery Guide, "Bandit")

Hunter (8)   CR 2
XP 600
hp 14 (Pathfinder Roleplaying Game NPC Codex, "Poacher")

Tactics: The Highwaymen fight very aggressively in defense of their camp. Hunters or Bolts guard the perimeter, looking out over the approach to the camp and the network of traps. Make a DC 15 Perception each time a trap is triggered or some other noisy event occurs; success means the camp is alerted to the party's presence. If the perimeter is lost, the Highwaymen gather around their leader (if he still lives) and fight ferociously, but they fall back into the forest and flee if they sustain 50% casualties.

Treasure: The Highwaymen have their personal items, the provisions of their camp, and a stash of gold and silver coins worth 1,200 gp. At any given time, they have plunder equivalent to 2d6 rolls on the Art Objects table in the *Pathfinder Roleplaying Game Core Rulebook*.

WILD BOARS

Wild boars are one of the most dangerous creatures on the forest slopes. While not as organized as the wolves or as powerful as a bear, their sheer ferocity makes them the bane of locals and travelers alike. A campfire or the sounds of a group often draw boars, for they require nothing more than the promise of food to ransack a camp. Normal boars usually attack singly or in pairs, while dire boars are almost always alone. At the DM's discretion, a wereboar could be introduced for further plot development.

1d20	Wild Boar Encounter
1–7	1 boar
8–13	2 boars
14–16	1 dire boar
17–20	Re-roll twice, or **wereboar** if desired

Boar   CR 2
XP 600
hp 18 (Pathfinder Roleplaying Game Bestiary, "Boar, Common")

Dire Boar   CR 4
XP 1,200
hp 42 (Pathfinder Roleplaying Game Bestiary, "Boar, Dire")

Wereboar (Hybrid Form)   CR 2
XP 600
hp 30 (Pathfinder Roleplaying Game Bestiary 2, "Lycanthrope, Wereboar")

SHAW, VALLEY WOODSMAN

The valley woodsmen are wilderness experts in the employ of Lord Angus, although many hunt and trap on the side. They patrol the areas of mountainous forest that are beyond the reach of the outriders — and these areas are vast. The valley woodsmen cover many miles each day, traveling cross-country with only a mentally ingrained map of their beloved wilderness to guide them. They report weekly (give or take a few days) to Bron Angus or to one of his officers at the Mist Watch Garrison (see Area **J** in Chapter Two) before refreshing their supplies and heading back out into the wilds.

Most woodsmen are rangers, but some have levels of barbarian as well. Nearly all are human males, although elves, half-elves, and gnomes have entered into such contracts with Angus, and at least one woman is listed among their ranks. If this encounter is rolled, the party most likely does not notice anything until the woodsman announces himself; the woodsman may track the heroes for miles and may only emerge if they are attacked. Woodsmen assume an aloof, detached demeanor toward adventurers, although they warm to a druid or accomplished ranger in the party. Unless the party is engaged in some forbidden act or misdemeanor, the woodsmen usually inquire about the party's experiences in the wilds, sightings of game, or news from beyond the valley. They recommend that travelers make their way back to the road as soon as possible and are willing to provide an escort if needed. If encountered at night, the woodsman listens at the edge of camp to assess the party's alignment before entering or moving on.

Shaw, Valley Woodsman   **CR 3**
XP 800
hp 30 (Pathfinder Roleplaying Game GameMastery Guide, "Trapper")

NIGHT ENCOUNTERS

Most of the night encounters are simply encounters with the common traffic of the trade road that take place after dark; the others are with nocturnal hunters and foragers. The NPCs have guidelines for night encounters in their descriptive text, above.

1d20	Encounter
1	Bernya the Nymph
2–5	Wolf Pack
6–7	Boar
8	Brown Bear
9	Kamadan
10	Brother Melph
11	Shaw, Valley Woodsman
12	Heavy Fog
13	Rain
14	Downpour
15–20	No Encounter

WOLF PACK

If a wolf pack attacks the party at night, a few members break away to create a distracting howl from a distance. The howling still seems far-off when the pack strikes. Their tactics are the same as for a daylight encounter.

WILD BOAR

When the boars attack at night, no notice is given: they rush into the camp and tear into sleeping characters, though food scraps may distract them.

BROWN BEAR

This large creature is often drawn to a camp by the smell of food being prepared. Sometimes, it waits at the edge of the camp until the party retires before foraging, but whenever it decides to take its meal, it expects the food to be surrendered without contest. It attacks only if the party resists or threatens it.

KAMADAN

This fearsome predator drifts down from the higher slopes to hunt along the road at night. It prefers an individual or a small group of travelers to a large caravan, but it does not get terribly picky, especially if the seasonal traffic has died off. Between the mist, the dark, and the creature's *sleep breath* ability, it can be very difficult to defeat.

Kamadan   **CR 4**
XP 1,200
hp 42 (Pathfinder Roleplaying Game Bestiary 3, "Kamadan")

IDEAS FOR FURTHER DEVELOPMENT

These encounters are simply meant to provide some colorful role-playing and a bit of conflict en route to the Grey Citadel. With some attention, however, they could easily be enhanced into several sessions' worth of gaming. Consider the following hooks:

• Bernya contacts the party with concerns that Hobark and his men have turned to kidnapping. She does not have the resources to go against them herself, but the party may be able to bring in some woodsmen and perhaps an outrider unit to assist. Plotting and coordinating the attack on the camp requires good intelligence, timing, and execution.

• Lord Angus wants the lizardfolk threat neutralized. On reaching their valley, the party realizes that the lizardfolk just want to return to their jungle home. The heroes must avoid the conspiracies of the greedy shaman and escort the lizardfolk out of the region, hopefully finding some way to claim their reward as well.

• Lassilim and his pack find the party one night to report that Gorian's pack and some unknown humanoid agents have captured Bernya and a few woodsmen. Finding Gorian's hidden burrow is just the beginning, because Hobark and his men have negotiated with the would-be wolf king for the enslavement of the nymph and the murder of the woodsmen.